TALES FROM THE
FERMI RESOLUTION

Volume I: Shadow of the Tower

Moe Lane

Flying Koala Press

FLYING KOALA

To my long-suffering wife and family.

CONTENTS

MORGAN BAROD AND THE ELDRITCH TOME

Beyond The Line
New Brunswick, NJ
2110 AD

Morgan Barod ghosted through the ruins of the university. At least, he *hoped* he was ghosting. He'd settle for just being pretty quiet. 'Pretty quiet' should do for the mission at hand.

He hadn't been in the business long, but Morgan thought that Rutgers was pretty firmly in the 'dangerously lovely' abandoned ruin category. There were plenty of decaying buildings that looked promisingly unlooted, and the overgrown clumps of trees were halfway to becoming actual forests. There were birds chirping, various woodland critters doing their thing, and it really was a lovely morning to break into a shuttered library and retrieve an arcane tome.

He didn't trust any of it for a second.

At least he wasn't *stealing* anything. When Morgan had been asked to attend another meeting with Major West, he had wondered whether she was going to try to recruit him for courier duty again. Then, when she offered him a drink of the local bourbon instead, he wondered whether there was another, perhaps interesting, motivation at work here. Freelance scouting and adventuring seemed to be developing a certain cachet these days.

Turned out that she was, in fact, offering him a job. "There's a book in the university ruins," the major said. "My superiors are ready to pay for its salvage."

"Money is nice," agreed Morgan pleasantly. "But why aren't you sending a platoon to go get it?"

Major West shrugged. "I don't have one to spare," she said. "And if I did have one to spare, it'd be already assigned to go do something else. We're just too stretched out. But if I offer a bounty on the book, maybe I can get it without having to make a hole in the patrol schedule."

"Right," said Morgan. "How dangerous is the campus?"

One nice thing about the apocalypse: people didn't mealy-mouth nearly as often anymore. "No reports of people going missing, which doesn't mean much," West said. "If everybody gets eaten, who's left to sound the alarm, right? But there's no *really* big monsters. Probably. If something that ate people in job lots was living so close to the Line fortifications, we'd know. Mostly because it'd end up attacking us eventually."

"How about people?" asked Morgan. "Bandits, farmers?"

"Anybody wanting to farm around here sets up on the *other* side of the Line," replied West. "And there's no bandits operating out of the ruins of New Brunswick, either; it's too close to the Line. We patrol that far out, pretty regular. Anybody or anything that messes with the patrol learns real fast how bad an idea it is."

"So, no major dangers, but it's still not a cake-walk?" Morgan added, "At least, that's the impression I'm getting."

West shrugged. "We're patrolling to keep away bandits, and monsters who can't take a hint. Monsters who lair up in one spot and don't go looking for trouble? We leave those be. If there's something in the ruins there, it's living pretty good on squirrels and deer. So I'd appreciate it if you didn't rile anything up that we'll have to put down later, Mr. Barod."

"Yes, ma'am," Morgan said easily. "I would prefer that, myself. And I understand. But why are you hiring me to go in there, if it's so dangerous?"

"Well," West allowed, "we don't know that it's so dangerous. It just *might* be. Besides, I'm told we could really use that damned book." She shook her head. "It's a miracle that something that old is still in storage there. They couldn't have known how valuable it'd be, now that magic's come back."

#

At least the library wasn't downtown. New Brunswick itself had been fairly savaged by the Demon Cow incident, to the point where entire blocks had been vaporized. Morgan was headed to one of the satellite campuses; supposedly, the damage hadn't been *too* bad, out there. *Then again*, thought Morgan, *that kind of statement begs the question: says who?*

It took longer to get there than he expected. Morgan had never realized just how ubiquitous orienteering micro-drones had been until the first time he tried navigating cross-country without them. The results had been distressingly embarrassing, although Morgan was at least educated enough to recognize a compass, and even be able to use one.

Also, getting across the Raritan was just all *kinds* of fun. The Causeway avoided the university, or possibly the other way around, and the Route 18 bridge had been blown up back when people still thought cars would be a viable military resource. In the end, Morgan used Route 18 anyway, fording the river by wading from one chunk of tumbled roadway bridge to another.

He found it surprisingly easy going; the path looked a lot more formidable from up high than it did on the ground. There were even spots where somebody had come in with a crowbar to make a path through the wreckage. *Smuggler's path?* wondered Morgan. *But what's there to smuggle?* Morgan dismissed the thought and kept going.

Scrambling up on the other side, the highway didn't look too bad, aside from the usual overgrown woods to the side and abandoned cars. Half-burnt, in this case; it looked like a small fire had swept through here a few years back. Or perhaps the cars had been there even longer; there was what appeared to be some kind of military checkpoint. Judging from the various scorches and craters in the ground, the soldiers had been watching out for troublemakers — and found some. *No scattered bones, though,* thought Morgan. *Guess the soldiers won that one.*

#

Morgan stuck to the highway until he was well past the old stadium; there was something about a combined indoor/outdoor facility that seemed to attract pack monsters. Or so he'd been told, but it was one of those things that sounded obvious when pointed out, and there was nothing he needed at the stadium anyway. Morgan had no objection to exploring for the sake of exploring, but he was starting to think exploration these days should only be done with plenty of backup.

Route 18 was an excellent highway in that it was intact and had few cars on his side of it. The backed-up traffic from the abortive roadblock hadn't been too bad, but then again, they probably shouldn't have been on the road in the first place. From all Morgan had heard, there hadn't been any really *safe* places in the first days of the Discovery. Just ones where the madness burned out early.

Then ahead, there was a commotion! In fact, it sounded like a bit of a fight. Morgan Barod found himself moving ahead, sword out and shield ready. It was, he decided, just some sort of training reflex. Maybe there was a monster. Maybe it was bandits. Maybe it was monsters fighting bandits, and he'd have to decide whether to wade in or just watch.

Or maybe, yeah, Morgan just liked to get in on a fight. He had noticed that tendency in himself lately, and sometimes it worried him a little. It didn't really seem all that *safe*, right?

#

It wasn't monsters versus bandits; it was monsters versus a mage. At least, the guy had a staff that trailed tendrils of blue-gray energy as he swung it around. So definitely he wanted people to *think* he was a mage.

The mage didn't seem to be in too much trouble yet, but he wasn't exactly brushing off the critters, either. These particular critters looked like mutated squirrels, puffed up to the size of beagles and tricked out with claws and fangs. *Pack hunters, too*, thought Morgan. *Wonder if they have an alpha?* And indeed, they did; there was one that seemed to be directing the attack. It looked like it was about halfway through the process of becoming a grizzled, wily old nemesis of the forest, the kind that would unerringly prey on the weak and unprepared, its scars bearing mute witness to a lifetime of cunning and savagery.

So Morgan attacked *it* first. He figured that somebody ten years down the line would thank him for that — *no, wait, they'll never know I did 'em the favor*, he thought. *Oh, well.* It was still a good idea to kill the really nasty buggers before they completely grew up.

Half-grown or not, the pack-squirrel alpha was viciously fast, and Morgan was very quickly happy that he was wearing good boots. *And* a cup, because the little bastard also could *leap*. For one horrified moment Morgan was worried that the fangs could actually manage to rip through the chain mail, leather, and stainless steel covering his important bits: but it couldn't, quite.

And it wouldn't let *go*, either. Morgan tried to spin it off, and maybe smack it against the barrier in the middle of the highway, but the pack-squirrel was having none of that. And he couldn't quite get a good stab in. Well, maybe he could get a good stab in, but what if he *missed*? Eventually he settled for trying to use the edge of his shield to pop the damned thing off, or at least smash it in the head enough times.

As he did that, he felt a sudden sharp pain in his left leg. Morgan looked down. Another of the fucking pack-squirrels had latched onto the top of his boot, and was chewing at it while its claws were locked onto his leg. *Right, this is getting out of hand,* he thought. *Even if I win this fight, I can't ever tell this story. Time to end it.*

First things first. Morgan shoved down with his shield and *scraped* off the alpha; as it bounced off the ground, Morgan stepped forward with his squirrel-free boot and stamped down on the tail. That pissed off the alpha, but Morgan didn't care; he aimed his sword blade at the center of the screaming bundle of fur and claws and swept through it with a gratifying shower of blood.

Morgan then dropped his shield, since he'd need his hand for the next bit. The pack-squirrel on his boot was still ripping at the top of it (Morgan was pretty sure that these things were as dumb as stumps, which was nice), and that meant that it was upside down and almost wrapped around his leg. Morgan supposed he could stoop a little, and try to pull it off by the neck, but honestly: there was a much closer target for getting the pack-squirrel's attention. And a more satisfying one.

The horrified squeak that boiled out of the pack-squirrel's throat, as a tender part of it was suddenly *crushed* by a re-inforced gauntlet, might have made Morgan feel bad about what he just did, theoretically. As it was, he simply grinned savagely as the pack-squirrel let go of his boot. *Not as much fun when it's happening to you, hey?* he gibed internally as he turned and threw the pack-squirrel as far as he could towards the edge of the ele-vated highway. And the pack-squirrel went sailing over the side! He hadn't expected that, actually.

Morgan turned, but the mage had killed two more pack-squirrels in the meantime and the rest were finally fleeing. The mage took a knee and aimed his staff like it was a rifle; a red-brown blob of energy shot from it and smacked into one of the fleeing pack-squirrels, to no apparent effect.

The mage levered himself up as Morgan approached. "Thanks, buddy," the mage said. He looked older than Morgan, but that happened a lot when you'd been in cold sleep for most of the apocalypse. "That was getting exciting."

"No problem," said Morgan as he took a moment to see if the pack-squirrel's claws had punctured the skin. They hadn't, but he'd have a hell of a bruise. "Those things were nasty. Shame you missed with that one staff shot."

From behind them, in the treeline, came a sudden boom of magical energy, a good bit of smoke, and multiple yelps of pain. "Ah," said the mage, "but I didn't."

#

It didn't occur to Morgan until much later that possibly the two of them should have gone and decently finished off the pack-squirrels. He mildly regretted not doing so. Very, very mildly. After all, the little bastards had gone right for *his*... well.

At the time, the only thing that either man cared about was distancing themselves from any larger monsters that might be looking for easy protein. As the mage pointed out while they jogged down the abandoned highway, assuming there was a bigger monster around was the smart bet, these days. No sense taking chances.

When the two had retreated about a mile or so, the mage stopped, slightly flushed. Older than Morgan or not, he seemed to be in decent enough shape. He leaned on his staff and said, "Thanks, friend. Name's Ben."

Morgan nodded back (shaking hands had gone out of fashion, a little, at least when it came to mages). "Morgan," he said. "Happy to help out. You need an escort back to your camp?" It was also a bit out of fashion to just come out and ask *So, you out here alone?* These days, people got antsy about answering that sort of question, for some weird reason.

"Nope," said Ben. "I'm out here alone." At Morgan's raised eyebrow, Ben smiled. "Yeah, so maybe that wasn't the smartest idea. But what the hell, I'm alive, right?"

"That's fair," said Morgan. "I'm out here by myself, too." He looked around. "The critters around here are friskier than I expected."

"So maybe we're both dumb," said Ben. "No offense. So, you going to the university, too?"

Morgan shrugged. "I might be, stranger I just met. Why do you ask?" He kept his tone light, though.

"Because if you are, I got a deal for you," Ben said. "I'm tracking down a book I need, and I figure you're looking for something there, too. I help you find yours, you help me find mine, everything's swell."

"Seems reasonable," said Morgan. "Split any incidental loot, too?"

"Sure, although I'd like dibs on magical stuff. Unless there's a flaming sword or something."

"Like *hell* I'd carry something like that around unless I found an off switch," said Morgan. Now he did extend a hand. "But that sounds fine. Oh, wait," he went on as Ben reached out to take it. "What if we're looking for the same thing?"

Ben frowned. "If you've been hired to acquire the *Petit Albert*," he said, "I'd be amazed. And worried like hell."

"Oh, we're good, then," said Morgan. He shook Ben's hand. "I've been hired by the locals to grab some topological maps," he lied. "Really old-time stuff, not even microfilmed. We shouldn't get in each other's way over it."

"Whew!" said Ben. "Had me worried there, for a second. But, yeah, I can help you get your maps."

#

Moving through the campus wasn't all that hard, honestly. The roads were falling apart, sure, and so were the cheap dormitories that Morgan and Ben were skirting. But from what Morgan remembered, they were kind of like that before the Discovery, too. This campus had gotten a hasty expansion during the education bubble in the 2080s, and boy, did it show now.

Ben was looking over the residence halls with the same sort of casual mercenary assessment as Morgan. "You figure there's any good loot in there?" he said, although the obvious doubt in his voice suggested he already knew the answer.

"Sure, Ben," said Morgan. "Remember how much good stuff you had at eighteen? Now imagine a stash like that, only times a couple hundred."

"Damn you, but I had a *curated* collection of bottle caps. Some of 'em were rare." Ben looked over. "What does your map say?"

Morgan looked down at the paper again. It was a tracing of a much older map, but better than nothing. "Well, we're here at Brett Road. We can either go to the left, and take a right at Bartholomew, or we can go to the right, and take a left at Bevier. Or we can cut through. Once we're past the Buell dorm we keep going north and it's just past the BEST center."

"Gee. You sure you got all the Bs?"

"Nah," said Morgan. "There's a Barr dorm I figured we can skip. Unless you wanted to hit it on the way back."

"Maybe if we need to crash overnight." Ben looked at the sky. "Which we might. Damn squirrels screwed up my travel time. Speaking of monsters, those dorms might be full of 'em."

"Yup," said Morgan. "I'm just going to act like all the buildings are full of monsters, though. Because that just seems smart."

"No argument from me," said Ben. "We're being watched, by the way."

Morgan nodded. "I noticed that, too. What location, you think?"

"A quarter-pie to your left and behind. Not too close behind, either."

"Yeah," Morgan said, "that's about right. Good eye, Ben."

"You mean, 'good spell.' And it *is* good. Had to make it myself, to make sure it was." Ben casually looked around. "I think it's a human."

"Yeah," said Morgan. "I think it's a kid."

That surprised Ben. "You think? A kid, out *here*?"

"Sure, why not?" Morgan stretched a little. "He's probably at least half-feral, but if you can hide from the monsters there's stuff to live on. People are clever like that."

"Seems really sad, though. Sometimes the price of magic... well, I'm not really objective about it, am I?" Ben shook his head. "What do we do about him?"

"A damned good question, Ben. I figure that if he's just shadowing us, we can leave him alone. If he tries to make friends, we make friends. And if he tries to eat us?" Morgan shrugged. "We grab him, tie him up, and get on with the missions. I'll take him back with me, hand him off to the Feds. They must have a procedure for this."

"Kind of cold and warm at the same time there, Morgan."

"We're on the job," Morgan said. "I'm not gonna kill a kid, but

I'm also not gonna let him keep trying to stab me or throw rocks at me or whatever. Unless you got a spell for that?"

"Child care? No, I haven't written one yet." At the time, Morgan still didn't really understand just how much of a boast that was. "But I'm not gonna use lethal spells on a kid, either." Ben shrugged. "Yeah, you're right. We should play it by ear. Ha!" At Morgan's quizzical look, Ben went on, "If the two of us can't keep somebody half our size from messing us up, we shouldn't be out here in the first place."

That *was* funny. Morgan laughed, too.

#

In the end, they cut through the residential areas, because the two of them — to quote Morgan himself, much later — were both idiots. In their partial defense, neither man had properly estimated how much time it had taken to get this far (a surprisingly ongoing problem for a world now relearning the concept of 'watches'), and the prospects of being on the abandoned campus after dark wasn't really appealing. Speed seemed smart. Or, as Morgan had realized afterward: he wasn't experienced enough yet to know when to take things slowly.

Close up, the various apartment buildings and dorms didn't look in that great shape. Most of the buildings were missing windows, doors, or both, and a few roofs had collapsed. But that didn't bother Morgan; a lot of buildings looked like that these days. So what *was* bothering him?

When he realized it, Morgan immediately blurted it out: "No birdsong."

Ben listened himself for a moment, and swore. "You're right, there isn't any. No critters, either."

"Yeah," agreed Morgan. "I've been keeping an eye out for scat — sorry, poop," he said, since Ben looked confused about the term,"and I haven't seen any. I don't even think there's deer around."

Ben looked around. "Really? So what's eating the grass? It should be chest high here."

"I don't think anything's eating the grass," said Morgan. He kicked at the ground at his feet. "I think something's been *cutting* it."

Ben joined him to take a look. In the dirt was what looked like rough-cut grass, at every stage of decay from new-mowed to peaty sludge. The grass wasn't exactly cut evenly, either; it had been sliced up with power but not much precision. After a moment, Ben said, "Well. Maybe one of the automowers is still working?"

"Maybe?" said Morgan. "But only if it had gotten enchanted somehow. Anything like that should be long out of juice."

"What kind of enchantment?"

"I don't know. *You're* the wizard, Ben."

"Crap, yeah, I am. Awkward, because I don't have a clue."

"God, that's like the motto of the 22nd Century," said Morgan. "You think it'd be dangerous?"

"They weren't designed to be, so, yeah, a rogue automower would have to be totally dangerous now." Ben said. "On the bright side, look at the trees." The wizard pointed at the foliage. "See how they don't look trimmed? Whatever it is that's cutting the grass, at least it doesn't have much range."

#

Ten minutes later...

"OKAY, FINE!" yelled Ben as the three of them dodged another thick strand of wire and jagged metal bits. "That was a stupid thing to say! Happy, now?"

"All I wanted to hear," replied Morgan as he slashed at the strand the second it caught on something, and went taut. The strand at least cut when you sliced it, which probably wasn't doing his sword any good. But at least the strand wasn't cutting *him*. "How many wires does this fu-" he stopped himself, out of deference to their new friend's age, and instead said, "-*thing* have, anyway?"

He didn't get an answer out of the girl. Morgan wasn't even sure that she spoke English; the kid was maybe six, seven years old, and looked like she had spent all of it living rough. But she did understand enough English to follow directions, like 'run away!' and 'duck!' Mind you, those were real easy ones to learn.

All in all, Morgan didn't mind: good English or not, the kid had saved his *ass*. One of the piles of junk had opened itself up while he and Ben were looking elsewhere. Expanded, it looked like an automower with little stumpy legs — and whirling strands of vicious wire coming out of its arms. If the kid hadn't pegged one of the strands with a slingshot, that strand would have wrapped itself around Morgan's legs. He was wearing armor, but it still wouldn't have been fun.

Ben went back to chanting what sounded like nonsense syllables, although Morgan could barely 'hear' the power behind them. The wizard snapped out a last phrase, and pointed. The air boomed as a ball of pure pressure shot from his hand and slammed into the thing. *Oh, hell, call it a 'whip-golem,'* Morgan thought. The golem went flying, chassis over peripherals, but nothing fell off as it tumbled itself back up to its feet.

"Looks like it's armored!" yelled Ben, as he started building another spell. Morgan noted that the wizard was pretty quick at getting those off. "There a cliff around here anywhere?"

"No!" Morgan grinned, savagely. "But I have a stupid idea. Can you prep a fireball?"

"Dammit, that's a cliché!"

"So you can't?"

"Of course I can, but it's still a cliché! But what's the point? Nothing in that is gonna burn fast."

Morgan nodded. "That's where the stupid idea comes in, Ben. This thing likes to grab, right? So I'm gonna give it something to grab. Long enough for it to start burning slow."

#

Naturally, Morgan Barod cheated. The arm that he waved in the whip-golem's direction was now triple-wrapped in pretty much everything he had, so his arm wasn't ripped up when the barbed whip wrapped around it. And he had picked his spot carefully, half-behind one of the larger trees, where he could wedge himself and keep from being dragged forward. It still felt like his arm was being yanked out of his socket, and if the whip-golem kept pulling for long it very well might be.

Luckily, Morgan had guessed right; when one barbed whip didn't work, the whip-golem threw a second one at him. It tried to go low, this time — but Morgan was looking for that, and ducked just enough to get the second barbed whip on his arm, as well.

And *now* Morgan was starting to feel the strain there, for real. He couldn't hold this for long. But he didn't have to. As soon as the second barbed whip lashed out, Ben popped up and threw off the fireball.

The fireball Ben produced was a *physical* thing, much like Greek fire or burning modeling clay. Not being made of water or paper, the whip-golem might have been able to simply wipe the fireball off before it *adhered*, but both of its arms were currently occupied... and more likely to burn anyway. For five or so seconds, the whip-golem creaked and writhed — and then Morgan gritted his teeth, set his feet, and *yanked*.

The sudden movement popped both arms, now starting to burn, straight off the whip-golem's body. Morgan didn't wait to see what happened next; instead, he rushed forward, pulling out his bat. He smashed at obvious joints, once, twice, three times before the whip-golem shuddered and broke apart.

And then Morgan smashed it a few *more* times, simply because he was there and had the bat out.

#

"So, were you working out some stuff, back there?" said Ben as he wrapped Morgan's arm. Nothing was broken, but the cuts were just short of needing stitches and the antibiotics stung like the Devil. Morgan *definitely* missed analgesic plaskin bandages — but then, so did what was left of the rest of the world.

"Nah," Morgan said evenly, in lieu of wailing like a small child over mere scratches. "I just figure, if you're going to hit something, hit it *really hard*. Saves time later."

"Yeah, but what if you don't want to hit it too hard?" asked Ben.

Morgan shrugged. "Then don't hit it at all, I guess. If I thought it'd listen to us, I would've tried that first."

"How philosophical of you," Ben murmured. He leaned back. "Well, that's as good as I'm going to be able to do. I'd use healing spells, if I knew any."

"You'd think there'd be more of those by now," Morgan said while rotating his arm. He judged that it would do. "It's an obvious line of research."

"Sure," said Ben. "But imagine what a failed spell looks like."

Morgan did, and winced. "Ah, gotcha." Turning to their new friend, he said, "How you doing, kiddo? Want more?" He and Ben had brought some rations with them; the kid ate quickly but carefully, like she had manners if not etiquette. She was really punishing the water they brought along, though, emptying both men's canteens before being satisfied.

That got a word out of the kid! It was just a "No," haltingly uttered, but Morgan figured it was a lot better than nothing. "What's your name?"

Morgan didn't really expect an answer, or at best, a really clumsy few minutes where the kid worked out what names were and why people had them. Instead, the kid smiled and said, right away, "Name is Kiddo."

Ben and Morgan looked at each other. "Ah," said Ben. He pointed at himself. "My name is Ben." Pointing at Morgan, he went on, "His name is Morgan." Now pointing at the girl, he said, "Your name is?"

"My name is Kiddo!" said the girl, smiling again.

Morgan and Ben traded another look; Morgan shrugged. "I guess her name is Kiddo. Hello, Kiddo."

"Hello, Morgan! Hello, Ben!" Kiddo seemed cheerful, but a little restless, as if she'd like to say more but couldn't right now. She waved the canteen at Ben a few times.

Ben frowned. "You want more?"

"No." She shook her head.

Ben frowned, then smiled. "Words. You need words. Canteen? Water?"

"Yes, water! And…" Kiddo trailed off.

"Food?"

"No. Yes, food! And no, food."

"You lost me there, Kiddo," Ben said.

"Maybe she wanted the word 'food' anyway, but there was another word she's looking for?" suggested Morgan.

That got a rueful grimace out of Ben, like he should have thought of that first. "Good point. Thanks, Morgan."

"Yes!" said Kiddo. "Thanks! And good."

Ben was now looking even more curiously at the girl. "You're welcome, Kiddo."

#

As the three of them approached the library annex — Kiddo showed no interest in going away, and she was probably the closest they could find to a local guide anyway — Ben said to Morgan, "I don't know what's going on with Kiddo, but it's weird."

"No argument from me, Ben," replied Morgan as he tried to maintain a watchful calm. It was a lot easier in the books. "But it's not bad weird, so I figure we'll just roll with it. What do you think her deal is, though?"

"If I was guessing? I think she's reading our minds enough to pick up the meaning of words right away. That's why we have to say a word before she knows it."

"That's bloody *brilliant*, Ben. Which means… hey, Kiddo!" When Kiddo turned around, Morgan said, clearly and precisely. "Danger, trouble, weird, enemies, left, right, up, down, ahead, behind, bad, worse, worst, monsters, people, hello, goodbye, please, and help." He then counted up to twenty, and said, "That's all, thanks."

"You're welcome," said Kiddo, and turned back to do her own scouting.

Morgan smiled at Ben's bemused look. "What? We can do more words later."

"No, it's… you don't freak out easily, do you?"

"Ben, I've been freaking out since I woke up." Morgan had

never seen any reason not to tell anybody about the coma. It was worth it for the looks of envious sympathy he got from telling the story. "By now I'm just numb."

"Fair enough," said Ben. "So, yeah, she's reading our minds."

"Telepathy's bullshit, Ben. They proved that before either one of us was born."

"Magic's bullshit too, Morgan. And yet, here we are."

"Well, you got me there, I admit. You don't think she's reading all of our minds?"

"No. If she did, she'd speak English as well as any other seven year old with a full adult's vocabulary. But Kiddo is pretty bright." Ben sighed. "I wonder if she's entirely human."

"Eh, I don't care if she's human," said Morgan. "Just as long as she's people."

Morgan had found that a lot of people were a little twitchy on that topic, these days. The dumb monsters were bad enough; the idea of smart ones kind of alarmed folks. He wondered how Ben would react to the snake story; a lot of people had liked hearing about helpful supernatural critters, and what was the harm? But right then Kiddo's voice ahead called out "Ahead! Trouble! Bad!" and the pair moved forward to see.

#

The two men assessed the scene in front of the library annex. The annex had started out as a one-story building, then had two-story additions attached behind it and to the side, transforming it into an L-shaped structure. Sometime after that, another one-story attachment had been added, this time windowless, as an annex to the annex. Then the space between the one-story parts had been turned into a glass alcove, to connect the pieces of the L-shape and create a main door, but the alcove had lost all of its panes a while back. Bits of weathered, rounded glass nuggets could be found in the overgrowth that Morgan, Ben, and Kiddo were now using for cover.

They figured they needed the cover, because there were *far* too many bones scattered around the parking lot and entrance. Mostly animal bones, but there was at least one human skeleton picked clean. Something had pushed around a plastic car's weathered chassis, too.

Ben said, "So, yeah, that's what we call 'bad,' these days." After a second, he went on, "Okay, we'd have called it 'bad' back before the Discovery, too."

"Or 'fake,' because there's no way there'd be that many bones lying around," agreed Morgan. "So, what is this, you think? A monster lair?"

"Let's hope not," said Ben. "Monster lairs are hard on books. All the blood and ooze and sh- crud around. Hey, Kiddo: what is this? Does a monster live here?"

"Yes, a monster, and no, a monster," said Kiddo.

"She needs more words," muttered Ben. "Okay. Monster, or monsters?"

"Monster."

"Is the monster alive, or dead?"

"Alive, but no alive."

"*Not* alive," corrected Ben.

"Not alive. But alive."

Morgan interrupted "Mechanical?"

"No," said Kiddo. "But..."

"But it is like mechanical?" asked Ben. "Something made?"

"Yes."

"Thank you, Kiddo. OK, so there's a construct of some kind in there," Ben said to Morgan. "Sometimes people make them, but they can pop up on their own where a lot of magic's built up. That mower-golem thing was probably spontaneous."

"Gotcha. Which kind's more dangerous?" asked Morgan.

"Spontaneous ones. Definitely spontaneous ones. Constructs don't think; they just follow rules. The ones people make, you can usually figure out what the rules are. But if whatever in there is spontaneous?" Ben shook his head. "Yeah, the rules could be *anything*. Probably why the golem went after us; it was there to mow the grass, and everything living was grass."

"Got it." Morgan looked again at the front door. "I guess it grabs and eats anything that gets within range, then spits out the bones."

"Probably," said Ben.

"Yes," said Kiddo.

Ben started, then laughed, softly. "I'm sorry, Kiddo. You know about this monster, too?"

"I know this monster. I..."

"You are scared of it? Stay away from it?" offered Morgan.

"I stay away. Not..."

"Close," said Ben. "Close, far, very far. Safe, risky, dangerous. I really need to loot you a dictionary, Kiddo. Do you read?"

"I do not stay close," said Kiddo. "And I do not read."

"Well, that's something to teach you tomorrow," Ben muttered. He didn't sound unhappy about it.

"Is the roof safe, Kiddo?" Morgan pointed at the smallest attached building. "I think we can get up to the top from there. Then we move along the roof, climb down to that addition over there, and get access to the second floor that way."

"I love the optimism found in that 'we,' Morgan," said Ben. He looked at the building. "Okay, I have a spell or two that can help, there. But is it safe for us?"

"It is safe for me. Is it safe for you?" Kiddo looked for a word.

"Maybe," said Morgan. "Heavy, light, quiet, loud, clumsy, quick."

"Maybe," agreed Kiddo. "You two are heavy. And loud."

"So we take it slow," said Ben. "Ah, slow, fast."

"You say fast before." Kiddo sounded a lot like a seven-year-old right then, Morgan noted.

"Sorry." Ben *did* look sorry. "It's hard to remember at this point which words we've been using."

#

Getting up to the roof took a few stages. For the first stage, Morgan simply ran and leapt up, pulling himself to the outbuilding's roof with only a mild twinge from the wounds on his arm. *Forgot about those*, thought Morgan as he let down a rope for Kiddo and Ben to use. *I need to start being more careful. ...And I mean it this time!*

Kiddo went up as quickly as Morgan did. Ben... well, he wasn't in bad shape, but he clearly wasn't a climber; despite his best efforts, he made some noise scrambling onto the first-story roof. The three of them froze at an odd, half-rumbling, half-rustling sound from inside the annex, but after a moment or two it subsided. They still waited another minute, just to be sure: the two men had watched enough movies, after all.

"All right," said Morgan, quietly but not in a whisper. "So, yeah, there's a thing in there. Huzzah! But we knew that already. So we just need to get up the side of that wall quietly." He pulled out the rest of the rope; at the end was a well-made grappling hook. "I can place this well enough to get up there, then set it better for you two. Ben, you got a trick up your sleeve for this?"

Ben was looking up at the roof. "I think so... yeah, that spell would work. One problem, though: it might be a little louder than usual."

His spells hadn't been very loud, so... "Guess we'll risk it," shrugged Morgan. "Unless the thing inside pops outside onto the roof, we should be okay. You want me to wait, or should I go up now?"

"Go up now," said Ben. "It's going to take me a minute to adapt the spell, and the faster we move after that, the better." (Again, Morgan didn't understand the level of skill that implied until much later.)

Morgan's grappling hook was, in some ways, a toy. But it was a *grown-up* toy, designed to assist people who had a very specific, or even esoteric, definition of 'fun.' He had no trouble throwing the line up and over the top of the building, and — miracle! — the hook secured on the first try. Actually climbing up it was a little more difficult, but Morgan was now in the best shape of his life and he knew perfectly well how to climb a rope. Even the arm barely protested. Mostly.

At the top, Morgan gave a quick look at the roof — *yup, it's a roof, right down to the bird crap* — kicked at the grappling hook, and decided it was as secure as it was going to get. He looked over the side and motioned the other two to come up.

As Kiddo scrambled up the rope. Morgan heard the noise that Ben had warned of. It didn't sound too loud, really. No louder than they had been getting up onto the outbuilding below. And whatever it was Ben had cast, it was working pretty good; he was climbing up almost as fast as Kiddo had. And the inside stayed quiet during all of this, which seemed promising.

When Morgan gripped Ben's hand to help him over, he was surprised; Ben got pulled along far too easily. Ben grinned at Morgan's reaction. "I made myself lighter," he said. "I now weigh about eighty pounds. Which makes me real easy to shove around until it wears off, you understand?"

"Sure. Still, nice one," said Morgan. "Can you get rid of the bell tone it makes when it gets cast?"

"Wait, you heard that?" said Ben. "You can do magic?"

"I don't know," said Morgan. "I can see stuff, and I guess hear stuff, too. I haven't learned any spells, though."

"No offense, Morgan, but this is *not* a great time for you to try and learn any."

"None taken, Ben."

#

The roof up here wasn't anything in particular, just bird guano and weathered plastic; even the human skeleton by the access hatch barely registered, at first. That bothered Morgan a little; by all accounts, billions of people had died, all over the planet. Finding their remains should probably trigger more of a reaction than *I hope that collection of bones doesn't reanimate and attack us.* Still, Morgan gingerly pushed around the bones with his sword until he was certain that no spell held them together. Feeling bad about the end of the world was one thing; getting killed because of it was another.

That unpleasant chore done, he and Ben looked at the access hatch. It was fairly new, which was good; old-style steel locks were harder to pick, or bust. This one looked like it could be popped off pretty easily.

"But do we *want* to?" murmured Ben. "You know the layout of this place? I don't have a floor map."

"Neither do I," said Morgan. "I have the call numbers and a physical description, and I was lucky to get that. Hell, I'm taking it on faith that the stuff wasn't loaned out. I'm not loving the thought of going down from the top, Ben."

"Yeah," said Ben. "It'd be faster," he went on, looking up at the sun, "but... yeah. We can try to drop down to the other part of the L. We can get in through a window there, see what the layout is. It'd be nice if we found our stuff right away, and then got out of here."

"No argument from me, Ben, but it's not going to be that easy." Morgan turned to Kiddo. "Anything to add, Kiddo?"

"The monster is inside," said Kiddo. "Inside is the lair."

"It lives there?" asked Ben. At her nod, he went on, "What can you tell us about it?"

"It is..." Kiddo put out her hands helplessly. "Me, it is worse. Us, it is bad."

"Too much for you, but we might be able to kill it as a team?" said Morgan.

"Yes! Maybe."

"But what is it?" asked Ben.

"It is a monster." replied Kiddo. She looked about as frustrated as Ben did. Morgan shook his head and stood up.

"We just don't know what words to teach her, Ben. Look, it's a library, right? There's gotta be a kid's dictionary in there somewhere. Besides," he said as he started climbing down an access ladder to the roof below, "she said we could kill it, the three of us, so let's just play it by ear, all right?"

"She said we *might* be able to kill it," muttered Ben, but he followed Morgan anyway.

#

This part of the L had two roofs: a higher and a lower. The higher one was all right, but the lower roof was in worse shape; it was at least a century old, and probably had been overdue for renovations even before the Discovery made maintenance a literal dead-letter issue. Kiddo and Ben found it easy enough going, but Morgan was hearing an alarming amount of creaking underneath his feet as they edged along the wall from the access ladder to one of the second-floor windows. He figured it wouldn't be a problem if they moved quickly enough.

Then he looked at the window itself, and swore. Ben drifted over, looking absurdly light on his feet. "What's the problem?" he said. "The smart locks frozen in place?"

"Worse," said Morgan. "There aren't any. The locks are all non-powered. Take a look; the damn things use *screws*, for Christ's sake."

Ben looked a little more closely. "It looks like you can't open them from the outside at all. Doesn't that violate about a dozen health ordinances?"

"It did." Morgan shook his head. "But this was a state university; they probably got an exemption. Or maybe nobody bothered to check. Which doesn't do anything to get us in, you know."

"I'm starting to think that maybe we should have brought some specialists with us," Ben said. "Like someone who knows how to pick old-style locks." He stared at the window for a moment, then looked over at Kiddo. "Hey, Kiddo! We could use your help." When Kiddo came over, Ben went on, "Do you know how to get through to the other side?"

Kiddo looked at him, then at Morgan, then gestured for Morgan's pack. After he handed it over, ignoring the creaking underneath him, Kiddo went neatly rummaging until she found a towel and a hammer. She tucked the towel into the top seam of the window, smacked the towel with the hammer a few times, and was rewarded with the muffled sound of breaking glass on the other side. She then shoved the towel over the bottom of the now-broken window, smiled at both of them, and put the hammer back in the pack.

"Well," Ben said. "That's *us* told."

\#

And right about then, Morgan Barod almost died.

It wasn't the old, weakened, and never really sturdy roof giving way underneath him that was the problem. It wouldn't have been the drop, either. The floor was all of eight feet below his suddenly flailing legs as Morgan's hands frantically sought out and found a beam to hold onto. He could have easily survived a drop that small.

No, the problem was how the carpet beneath him rippled and lashed out at the debris that had dropped to the ground. A bit of light now revealed the room below, so Morgan could see what looked like vicious tendrils of dark yarn forcefully stabbing at the plaster and metal. The tendrils quieted down after a moment, but the carpet moved in a way that was distinctly unpleasant to look at for too long.

From above came a soft call. "Morgan?" said Ben. "You all right?"

"Oh *hell* no," he replied. "There's some kind of carpet shoggoth down here."

A pause from above. "A shoggoth? Like from the *Azz and Hastur* cartoon?"

"I really doubt it," said Morgan. "Can I get a levitation spell?"

"If I had one, I'd be using it, sorry. How about a fireball?"

"This is a *library*, Ben. With books made out of old-style *paper*."

"...Oh, right. They'd burn real well, wouldn't they? I really should have thought more about what spells to master before making this trip."

Morgan's hands were getting a little strained. "Focus, Ben, please. Carpet golem, nasty-looking tentacles. What you got? Because I gotta let go soon."

"If fire's out, it's gotta be ice. I can drop the spell down the hole, but I'll need a clear line of fire. How small can you make yourself?"

"How bad will it be if I get it on me?"

"Pretty damn bad."

"Then I'll make me small. Ice it down, Ben. As fast as you can."

"You sure?"

"Yes. Throw down the damn spell, Ben. Pretty please, with

sugar on top."

"All right... In five! Four! Three! Two! One! Dropping now!"

Morgan managed to get a foot hooked onto the beam, and he never quite could figure out how he managed it. Which meant the leg *didn't* intersect the blob of cold. Morgan realized Ben hadn't been kidding: getting that stuff on him would have been seriously contraindicated.

What the blob did to the carpet shoggoth (Morgan decided to call it a 'shaggoth') was deeply satisfying, although far too brief. The blob hit the ground and spread out in a perfect circle — and what it touched instantly froze over, then began to steam. When it was gone, there was an area of cleared space directly beneath Morgan, and the carpet looked extremely distressed.

So Morgan dropped down. Was it the right decision? He wasn't sure, but better to hit the ground *now* then in five minutes, when his arms would be screaming in agony. He took the drop on both feet, frantically pulling the sword from its sheath and readying his shield barely in time to ward off the few tentacles not writhing in what Morgan *hoped* was extreme pain. There *were* human bones in the mix outside, and Morgan Barod was a firm believer in making sure everything understood how *unhealthy* human meat was.

Fortunately, the tentacles were easy enough to sever, and swiftly turned to sludge when cut off. Unfortunately, Morgan could only cut off a few dozen before the shaggoth recovered enough to — retreat? Yup, right under the door, which had the bottom of it worn away enough for the creature to flow under.

Morgan took a rueful breath. *I wonder how many of these things are in here? Kiddo thought only one, but if they all looked the same...* he thought, then called out. "Still here, Ben, Kiddo! How's your floor?"

"Empty," came Ben's reply. I don't think it handles stairs well."

"Well, that's something. I wounded one of these shaggoth things down here. Find a stairwell so we can meet up! And get another one of those ice balls ready; they're pretty handy."

#

Things weren't smelling so good down here. The air was musty, and the stench of shaggoth was pretty strong. *Sort of like rotting acrylics*, Morgan thought. He was pretty sure that kind of thing was impossible, but it was happening anyway, and was probably not going to be great for his lungs in the long term. *So let's just kill the monsters, find the books, and go.*

What little light came into this section of the library annex was from fairly small windows, and apparently shaggoths didn't like them; stuff had been tossed against them, and sometimes smeared, until they were almost dark. Which meant that a light spell might be helpful... *or a flashlight, dammit!* Part of Morgan resented how quickly the trappings of technological society had disappeared; another part of him was bemused at how well he had personally accepted the new way of things. *It's not that I **wanted** to wander through a magical post-apocalyptic landscape*, he told himself. *I'm just not letting it bother me.*

Yeah. That's it.

Morgan internally pondered how to get through the door for about two seconds before he kicked it open. There was no need to keep quiet, there might have been a monster behind the door anyway, and there was no *way* he was going to go through this place without his sword and shield handy. "Hey, Ben! Kiddo!" he shouted, before somebody shot a spell or stone at him. "At the vestibule!"

"Coming down!" yelled Ben from the stairwell. He and Kiddo moved down, Ben holding onto the banister. "Weight's not back to normal," he said to Morgan. "Spell's lasting longer than I expected. Offices above are clear."

"Where I came from was clear, too. I don't suppose your thing's somewhere on this floor, and this side of the door?"

Ben closed his eyes, and thought. "No," he said after a moment. "And before you ask, I can't get a magical feel for these shaggoths. I know they're around, but there's no way to lock on one. How are you going to find your maps, by the way?"

Morgan was already checking the remaining rooms on this

floor, one by one. *Nothing here except offices, dead plants, some poor bastard moldering on the floor...* "They gave me the classification numbers," he said over one shoulder. "Kind of a roll of the dice, but nobody's touched them since the Twentieth Century. They're probably in the same place."

He felt a little bad about keeping the lie going like that. Still: while Ben seemed an all right guy, Morgan *had* only met him today. And he didn't know anything about him except that Ben was a wizard who was at least decent with kids. Better safe than sorry, right?

#

The main doors to the big building in this crazy-quilt of connected buildings were peculiarly pitted and eroded away at their bottoms. Morgan looked at them, squinting. "Acid?" he said. "Maybe teeth?"

Ben squatted down to look. "No, it's erosion. Something's been slipping underneath the door for years, and now there's a groove. I'm going to say it's the shaggoths. Have you been in here, Kiddo?"

Kiddo shook her head. "No. And I said before, this is monster. Not monsters."

It took Morgan a second to work that out. "Urrgh," he said. "I just realized why your spell can't lock onto one shaggoth, Ben. There's only one in there."

"One big monster?" said Ben. "Yeah, that's an urrgh kind of situation. But we saw it off."

"Did we see *it* off?" asked Morgan moodily. "Or did we simply smite one set of uncoiled tendrils from the blasphemous mass before it could seize our shrieking forms and crush out our lives?"

"I don't... know?" replied Ben.

"Well, there's only way to find out," said Morgan, as he readied his sword and shield. "You got a light spell you can use?"

#

Based on everything Morgan had heard, humanity had adapted surprisingly well to the existence of monster-haunted ruins, and the clearing thereof. There had been the inevitable learning curve, but it had been shallower and less blood-soaked than he had expected. A Federal militia sergeant had happily explained to him why over dinner.

We already knew how to do it, right? she had said during dessert (calories were suddenly *important* again). *All those MMOs and VR sims and TIGs out there, and most of them put you in a dark passageway with something on the other side of a door. So we knew about stuff like clearing the door and checking our six. Whatever* **that** *means. One issue, though: lots of people had difficulty getting into their heads that there weren't any respawn points.* The sergeant smiled, not really happily. *But that was a self-correcting problem.*

So Morgan and Ben cleared the doors pretty damned quick. Ben's 'light spell' was more like a flare; it didn't do much to stun enemies, but Morgan figured throwing it in first wouldn't hurt, and probably wouldn't burn anything down, either. The two — no, three; Kiddo had been told to stay behind, but she just couldn't seem to learn that word — ducked through and looked for cover.

Damn! thought Morgan. *There's plenty of it.*

This building had been roughly hollowed out; some of the stacks looked more or less intact, but the rest had been shoved out of the way to make room for the shaggoth. It took up one entire corner of the now-open space, with tendrils of demonic acrylics veining their way up the sides of the walls and digging deep into the floor. But there were still plenty of tendrils free to lunge and strike. Oh, yes, there were. At the moment, the flare seemed to have confused the monster, but that was clearly only temporary.

"Morgan," said Ben almost conversationally from behind a half-fallen bookshelf, "tell me again why I can't throw a fireball at it?"

One of the tendrils lashed out, still reflexively. It landed nowhere near the three of them, but managed to knock over a shelf. Which knocked down another, and another, causing a demented domino effect that ended with a bookshelf slamming and blocking the doors they had just come through.

"Never mind!"

"Already forgotten!" said Morgan as he broke cover, sword out and blurring. "Ice ball on the center of mass!"

"Don't strike with your wrist out of line!" Ben yelled as he threw the ice ball.

"I didn't need to be told that!" Morgan noted with some pleasure that the dark yarn sliced up real nice when cut with a sword. It gave him some hope that they could whittle this thing down to size.

"Neither did I!" Ben yelled, with a grin that matched Morgan's own.

#

They weren't grinning, five minutes later.

Slicing or freezing off bits wasn't the hard part. The problem was that there were a *lot* of bits attached to the damned thing, and it wasn't particularly getting either tired, or weaker. It was also supremely dumb, which came as an unpleasant surprise when Morgan tried a feint that almost got him grabbed because the shaggoth ignored it completely. But it wasn't just an environmental hazard, either; the monster was just 'alive' enough to stay engaged in fighting its opponents, and one of its reflexive moves was to keep prey from escaping.

"Guess we know how this thing hunts," Morgan said during a too-short breather. "It wears its prey down. Patient fu- ah critter," he amended, since Kiddo didn't need to learn *those* words yet.

"This *can't* be a deliberately summoned monster," almost-wheezed Ben. "There's no point to it. But it can't be spontaneous, either."

"Why not?" asked Kiddo.

Ben blinked, whether at the question or who it came from. "Ah. There were monsters like this right after the Discovery, but they didn't last long. A little thing like the automower could stick around, but this needs to eat too much magic to live."

"Every adventuring party should bring a kid along," announced Morgan. "I actually understood your explanation."

"Is that what we're doing?" said Ben. "Then maybe we should start working the problem better, because if we don't figure out something soon, we're going to have to try to get out of here. Based on all those bones, it won't be easy."

Morgan shifted, sliced off another tendril, dodged to avoid the three tendrils that immediately followed, then sliced off those three as well. He frowned; his blade *might* be starting ever-so-slightly to dull, there. "You said this thing needs a lot of magic to live, right?" he called out.

"Yeah." A pause. "Oh, crap, it's got a battery, doesn't it?"

"Probably. But that's good news! We just need to figure out where the battery is."

"Already looking... Found it! Guess where, Morgan?"

"I'm gonna be honest, Ben," Morgan said as he did a quick check of his gear, "I already assumed that it's going to be smack dab in the middle of that abomination. Or am I being too cynical?"

"There's no such thing!" Ben sounded a little more cheerful, though. "I zap it, you stab it..."

"I can help," said Kiddo.

"You can GO!" shouted Morgan and Ben, more or less at the same time. "Sorry," said Morgan, after a moment. "But it's not safe in here, Kiddo!"

"Okay," she said. "Where is it safe?"

"...Fine," said Ben. "Just don't do anything stupid."

"Like this," Morgan agreed, and charged.

#

Morgan by now had noticed that Ben wasn't dumb. Which meant that he'd let Morgan know which bits of the horrible monstrosity in front of him had to be stabbed. And lo! Ahead of him a portion of the foul shaggoth's quivering hide erupted in a flash of lightning and ozone.

I've also noticed that Ben likes to show off, Morgan thought as he cut away two tendrils with the edge of his shield. *At least it wasn't a fireball.* The shaggoth didn't seem very flammable either, although the stink that came out of it after being charred like that made Morgan wonder just what they made carpets out of in the old days. Whatever it was, he didn't like the thought of breathing it in.

It took the shaggoth a remarkably long time to adjust to Morgan's charge; he still wasn't sure what spontaneous spells were running this thing, but it looked like there wasn't any kind of automatic response to prey that wasn't trying to run *away*. He was even starting to dare hope that he could get all the way to the shaggoth's important bits without being attacked when the shaggoth, in fact, attacked.

"Whatever you're going to throw, get it ready!" shouted Morgan as three tendrils grabbed him and lifted him up while a fourth and fifth clumsily plucked his shield out of his right hand. The tendrils then moved to swing Morgan hard against a wall, to stun him, before lowering him inexorably into the monster's opening maw...

Or rather, it would have, except that Morgan Barod *was* left-handed, and thus had a perfectly good sword to hack away three tendrils swinging him around. Not that falling to the ground afterward didn't *hurt* like a bastard, of course. But it was the kind of hurt that he could ignore while ripping this thing a new orifice.

"Move your... Move your... Move your *thing*!" came a yell behind him as Morgan danced for a good position. It came from Kiddo, surprisingly.

"Move where?" Morgan yelled back. "Left, right, jump, duck?"

"*MOVE*!" Kiddo shrieked. *Crap*, thought Morgan. *She sounds serious.* He did a side roll that was almost smooth and only a little over-enthusiastic, and risked a quick look back.

A bunch of tendrils had stealthily come up behind Ben and grabbed him; one had almost managed to wrap around his throat, only to be partially blocked by Ben's hand. Hus other hand was straining under the pull of two more tendrils, but managed to hold steady long enough to gush flame the moment Morgan was out of the line of fire.

Library or not, paper books or not, Morgan decided he didn't really blame him for that. It had a good effect on the shaggoth, too: the tendrils loosened enough for Ben to pour more flame on them. It also gave Morgan enough of a distraction to go in for the kill.

This close to the monster, even Morgan's untrained magical senses could 'feel' where the magic was coming from; a spot to the left and below the shaggoth's maw, and at a bad angle for a sword. Morgan dropped his without hesitation and pulled out twin knives.

The first stab ripped through the shaggoth's hide and, as Morgan expected, the monster reacted immediately with the closest tentacle at hand. *Makes sense,* Morgan thought as he used his second blade to nail the questing tentacle to a handy post. *Monsters that don't react to being wrecked don't last long. Heck, are they even really monsters?*

With his new-found leverage, Morgan pulled his first dagger through the shaggoth's body in an disemboweling stroke until he met resistance. On a hunch, Morgan let go of the second blade to reach deep into the foul hole of writhing fibers and strange, caustic fluids and pull out something hard and subtly *odd* to the touch.

The moment it popped free, the shaggoth convulsed, writhed — and shriveled, its unholy tentacles desiccating and unraveling as Morgan watched. He flicked a look back to see Ben half-collapsing to the floor; Kiddo was already attending to him, pulling out a spare canteen from Ben's pack. The wizard looked like he wasn't about to die on the spot, so Morgan went back to taking apart the odd growth he had extracted from the monster.

Morgan wasn't at all surprised to discover that inside the growth was a reasonably intact copy of *Petit Albert*. He could feel the power inside it, too. *Guess I can figure out why somebody would want it. And I got to it before Ben did...*

Morgan stood up, then turned to the other two. "Hey, Ben!" he said, waving the *Petit Albert* in one hand. "Guess where I found your book?"

\#

The map room was a mess, and that included the topographical maps. They had been like that for a few years, too. Morgan shook his head at that. *Why they didn't take this place back right from the start... oh, well.*

Ben had been a real help in finding what maps *might* still be relevant, even considering that a deal was a deal. He had limited his perusal of the *Petit Albert* to a five-minute scan to make sure that the stuff he wanted really was in there, which Morgan thought was reasonable. Besides: fighting non-sapient carpet monsters *hurt*, dammit. There were cuts to clean and scrapes to ointment and bandage. And the last of the water to drink.

When they had collected the maps, the two of them looked at the slightly pathetic, crumpled pile of papers. Morgan shook his head, sadly. "Well, if that's what's there," he said. "Hrm. I need some actual books."

He went out of the map room for a moment. When Morgan came back, carrying four books with him, Ben frowned. "What are those for?" he said.

"Gonna flatten them," Morgan explained, as he straightened the maps out as much as possible and placed a selection between each book. Once all the maps were placed, he used some salvaged cords to bind the whole stack together. "The old better-than-nothing trick, as we said in my family. This should keep them from getting wrecked worse, at least."

"Sorry this didn't work out better for you, man," Ben said. He sounded sincere about it, too, although obviously things had worked out great for *him*.

"Eh," Morgan said. "I'm still gonna get paid for this. I told 'em going in that this was going to be one of those 'as-is' kind of salvage jobs. I figure that they won't complain."

\#

And they didn't, although for different reasons.

Major West had naturally ignored the maps Morgan had brought back, and was instead poking at one of the books he had used to flatten them. Eventually she shook her head. "Well, it's what we sent you for, Mr. Barod, but I was expecting something else."

Morgan looked at the *Handbook of Mathematical Functions with Formulas, Graphs, and Mathematical Tables* (Abramowitz and Stegun, 1999 edition). "Yeah, Major, log tables aren't really my kind of breakfast reading, either," he said, "but you can see why the engineers wanted one. This all got digitized or put on eterno-paper back in the 2050s, right? And since all of that got wiped by the Discovery..." He shrugged.

"We hire adventurers to go get one of the few real, live paper copies left," agreed Major West. "Why didn't you tell that wizard you met what you were really there for?"

"Because it wasn't any of his business?" said Morgan. "You hired somebody to be discreet, right? I figured the maps were a plausible reason for me to be there, and it worked." He smiled. "If you want to pay me a bonus for those, though, I wouldn't mind."

"I'll see what I can do," West said dryly. "What would you have done if he had come back to civilization with you, though?"

"Probably come clean, right about now." Morgan shook his head. "He wasn't interested in going back past the Line, though. Last I saw of him, he was going back to his own base." With Kiddo in tow; she was more interested in wizardry than wandering mercenary work, apparently. Morgan had not mentioned Kiddo during any of this, and wasn't going to. It was none of *Major West's* business, honestly.

All for the best, really. He'd liked both of them on first meeting, and he'd keep Ben in mind the next time he needed a wizard, but Morgan Barod had things to do. He was still working out what those things were, but they definitely needed doing.

Finishing up payment was simple enough; Morgan had discovered that paperwork got expedited fairly quickly in this post-apocalyptic world. *Must be all the actual paper we have to use.* He had his hand on the doorknob when West said, too-casually, "Oh, Morgan, one thing?"

"Yes?" he said, as he turned to look at her.

Major West looked at him. "'Breakfast reading?' People normally say 'night-time'."

Morgan decided that a small grin would have the best effect, here. "Sure they do, Jenny," he said. "But I try to save my evenings for more interesting things."

THE WOLFMAN OF WESTHAVEN

Ruins of Westhaven, Connecticut
2257 AD

There were five skulkers, but not all of the same sort. While all five walked on their hind legs and could speak surface-human tongues, two had the snouts of hyenas and two more the teeth of sharks. The fifth might have passed for an Old American, save for the grey-light glow of her eyes and the strange sigils inscribed on her flesh. Like the others, she wore a black hood and cape that almost seemed to breathe on its own, and her staff was a tangled mess of carvings and runes that shifted when not looked at directly.

They snuck through abandoned sewers beneath a desolated town, with only a slight shift in the fetid, sea-rank air to mark their passage. Darkness was their companion, for no ray of light would dare venture from the sunlit lands above. And darkness was a welcome companion, too, for each of the five had their own reasons for avoiding the pitiless gaze of the sun.

Even in a world wracked by apocalypse and magic, time marches on; so while the journey seemed endless, the travelers eventually reached their destination. The Old Americans who had built these sewers had included rooms from which to descend from the surface world to these half-Stygian depths. It was to one of these rooms the five had traveled, and now patiently waited for nightfall, and the chance to burst free from the dark and traverse the moon-haunted ruins above.

As the other four made their preparations for the upcoming ascent, the sigil-bearing woman retreated to the center of the room to begin casting scrying and calling spells, all heavy with necromantic energies. One of the shark-toothed humanoids looked at her with unblinking black eyes, then loped over. In the faint light from the spells, she could see the slick, rubbery wetness of his skin as he drew closer.

She raised one finger: he stopped. She closed her eyes, finished muttering her spell, and opened them again as the magic took effect. "What's up, Anton?" she said.

"Not much, Maddie," replied the merman cheerfully. "Just wanted to find out if we can do a fire for our breakfast."

"Well, nobody's died here recently from a gas pocket exploding," said Maddie. "Heck, nobody's died here recently, period. I think the area's really abandoned after all."

"Figured," said Anton. He gestured back at the two hyena-snouted ghulmen — "Jack and Jill didn't smell anything really bad, but you never know with these Old Republic places. This part of the country got mucked up pretty bad during the Fall. There might be something still lurking down here their noses couldn't sniff out."

"Your wife pick up anything new?" asked Maddie.

"Nothing close to here," said Anton. "Susan thinks we're still out of range of all the evil stuff still haunting the ruins up there. So I guess a fire is all right?"

"Sure," agreed Maddie. She stood up. "If the scouts aren't catching anything, the minister isn't catching anything, and *I'm* not catching anything, then either there's nothing here — or there is and we'd never know until it kills us. Either way, I wouldn't mind a cup of coffee."

#

A breakfast cup was all the coffee-drinkers were allowing themselves, anyway; a hundred and fifty years after the apocalypse was barely enough time to get even the most rudimentary trade routes going. Sufficient beans made it north to the Second Republic (which still called itself the 'United States') to make it available for town-crawlers like themselves, but it was still pretty dear. Fortunately, mermen (e.g., Anton or Susan) didn't like coffee much, which meant the other three could stretch the beans out a bit.

Breakfast was pretty simple: salt fish and tea for the mermen Anton and Susan, garum paste and cheeses for the ghulmen Jack and Jill, and Maddie the oldman ate raisins and spinach way-bread. It all traveled well, but even the ghulmen found the fare a little bland (which didn't stop them from eating it). Still, people didn't go on town crawls for the cuisine.

Since it was mostly hand-held foods anyway, Anton reviewed the situation while they all ate. He unrolled the map of the town above them and weighted it down with bits of rubble. One clawed finger (politely and carefully trimmed to bluntness) poked at a point on the map.

"We'll be coming up by the river access, north of the ruins where we think the quarry is probably holed up," Anton said. "The books say it used to be a high school, then got used for a while after the Fall as a medical shelter. After *that*, it became a warlord's den, got fought over a few times, you know the drill. Gonna be a lot of ghosts around there."

"This is Westhaven, Anton," said Susan. She was fiddling with various bits of green-glowing gear. "There's ghosts everywhere."

"Yeah, but these are the unquiet ones. The Magicians' Alliance tried to make a stand here. You know what that means, Maddie."

The necromancer grimaced. "Yes. Human sacrifices and pain magic. Not too bad so far, though."

Susan said, "That's because Congress sent priests here twenty years ago to cleanse the area. I spoke with one from that expedition." She shrugged; the flaming chalice pendant, serving as her holy symbol, flickered in the dim light of the campfire coals. "The worst atrocities were at the old University, but the expedition did a general check. There shouldn't be anything left that's beyond my powers to bless."

Jack snickered. "Shouldn't," he said, with an unmistakable South Boston accent. "Yeah, *that's* gonna fill me with happy thoughts about the mission."

Jill rolled her eyes. "Don't you start, Jack," she said to her twin. "If they had more than us to spare, they'd send more. We got a priest, a *nice* mage," — Maddie smiled — "me to smell the bad things and Anton to make 'em suddenly remember they needed to be somewhere else. What more do you want, a rotten egg in your beer?"

"Heck, I'd settle for just the brew, if it was cold." Jack looked at Jill. "Hold on: you forgot me."

"Nah, bro." She barked laughter. "You're gonna be the bait."

"Speaking of," said Susan, "any scent of our target, Jill?"

Jill waggled one clawed hand. "Yes and no," she said. "Nothing down here, but when I was scouting topside I got a really good whiff. Also some regular trail stuff. Tufts of fur, a couple of cut-up critters. He's definitely going to hide out in New Haven."

"He?" said Maddie. "You finally got that nailed down?"

"Yeah," replied Jill. "He pissed on a tree. He's also walking on two legs at least part of the time, unless he likes to aim high when pissing."

"Yes, thank you," said Susan primly. "Sounds like he has enough self-control to not go full beast. Those poor sheep he ripped apart at the Poughkeepsie settlement looked awful."

"Things there could have gone a lot worse," said Anton. "He didn't go after any of the people, and he had chances to. Both there, and at the caravan he stole from later."

"There was the caravan guard," Maddie pointed out. "Poor kid got clawed in the arm."

"Yeah, but our guy didn't stick around," Anton said. "He ran right past the guard and kept on going. The smartest thing he could do, right? I think there's a brain inside the beast."

"I agree," Jill said. "The carcasses I found were stripped pretty careful. He took the whole skin off the smaller critters, and slabs of hide off the larger ones. I think our target's smart enough to try to make bags."

"And that's pretty damned smart," said Jack. "I ain't as good in the woods as Sis is, but when this guy is near Old American stuff he loots it a little. Mostly whatever metal bits he can break off. But he doesn't know this area at all."

"Of course not," said Maddie. "He's heading for Westhaven, isn't he? Locals know this is a bad place to visit on your own."

"Which is why we're here," Anton said as he finished cleaning out the coffeepot and stowing it away. "And it's time we got going. It'll be full dark soon, and we shouldn't waste any moonlight on this mission."

#

The party would have gotten through the sewer sooner, but they were delayed by giant eels. Which was a bit of a surprise, and also wasn't. This wasn't really the sort of place for giant eels, but there was always going to be *something*.

The first two eels revealed themselves through the time-honored tradition of rearing out of a submerged cistern, grabbing Anton, and dragging him underwater before the other four could react. Maddie snapped out a spell that wreathed her in buzzing, oily bubbles of energy, while Jack and Jill leaped up from the walkway to find any available handholds on the tunnel walls. Susan looked around, curiously. "That's odd," she said as she raised her own blue-grey shields. "Giant eels usually hunt in packs of six or more."

Two more eels leaped from the waters to fall upon Susan — only to bounce off of her shields, and lie twitching halfway on the walkway. "Ah," the minister said. "There they are. Still not enough of them, though."

Maddie strode forward, her hand coming down on one eel's stunned form. The writhing bubbles flowed down her arm and onto the eel; it shuddered and died. "I apologize," she said, then turned her attention to Susan. "Maybe they're lying in wait?"

Jack and Jill leapt down, claws fully extended, striking perfectly at the other eel's vital points. It died as quickly as the other one. "This one smells injured," said Jill as Jack started carving off choice pieces of still-quivering flesh for (much) later. "I think they were in a fight?"

The water around them suddenly swirled dark. Moments later, Anton surfaced, face dripping eel blood and hands full of chunks of flesh. "Saved you some, honey," he said. "But where's the rest of them? Giant eels usually hunt in packs of six or more."

"I was just asking that, dear," said Susan, taking the eel bits from him. "And they usually don't like sewers."

"Well, sure," said Anton. "Humans live in 'em, after all. These must have been desperate."

"Or hiding from something even scarier than humans," said Maddie. "Which is good news for the mission."

"Kinda," said Jack. "Definitely kinda. What if it was the quarry?"

#

If the storm culvert leading to what the map called 'Cove River' had ever had some kind of First Republic smart-tech filtration/security covering, it wasn't working after a hundred and fifty years' worth of post-apocalypse — or maybe it had always been just a plain metal circular grate. Jill sniffed at it a little, then shook her head. "Nothing on it," she said. "Not even electricity."

"What *does* electricity smell like?" asked Anton. "A lightning strike?"

Jill looked at him, confused. "Nah, lightning smells like, what's the word, oxide?"

"Nah, it's 'ozone'," said Jack.

"Yeah, that," said Jill. "Anyway, electricity smells like, you know, *electricity*."

"Never mind," said Anton. "I don't have your nose. Safe to apply the Mark One?"

"Ain't no traps on it I can smell. Dunno why anybody would trap a storm drain, though."

"You never know." Anton set himself, spun, and kicked out with one leg. The grate popped handily over the impact. He straightened. "Mark One Boot, successfully applied."

"Very good, dear," said Susan, peering outward as her hands glowed. "And... there's nothing vile out there ready to eat our faces, either! How *nice*."

"If there had been, it'd have just gotten a face full of steel bars, love."

"Fair point," conceded Susan. She concentrated. "I'm not feeling anything really evil-evil out there," she said. "But I wouldn't put this place on the Resettlement list any time soon. Lots of pockets of lingering badness. You got something, Maddie?"

The necromancer was standing still, staff lifted slightly and pointing to the sky. The light around her staff flared and she relaxed. "Sorry," Susan said. "There were two spirits tangled up in here. Kids, maybe. I think the grate confused them, but I got them to Go On."

"Smells a little clearer in here now," said Jack. "God, let's hope there ain't more of the poor bastards out there."

"If there are, we'll take care of 'em," said Anton. "How about our quarry, Maddie?"

"Right, sorry." Maddie was quiet for a moment. "Still south of us. Hard to tell, but I think he's denning in the high school. I'm guessing there. I can get direction, and a little distance, but not much else."

Jack and Jill were already in front, sniffing the walls and water for stray scents. "Don't worry about it," said Jack. "Once we get a big enough whiff, Sis and I'll be able to, whaddya call it, triangle him."

"Triangulate," said Jill.

"Close enough."

#

It was a dark and stormy night. The wind had picked up a little and was heavy with salt and rotting vegetation; despite the time of year, the river water felt almost ice cold to the touch, offering little frigid stabs every time a drop landed higher on a leg or arm. Around them, the gnarled limbs of overgrown weeds and shrubs surrounded and threatened to choke out the abandoned buildings and works of the Old Americans. And with the moon hidden behind the gathering clouds, the gloom seemed almost alive. Alive, and eager to embrace whatever dared to confront it.

Anton sighed. "Are we *sure* they shouldn't put Westhaven on the resettlement list? I mean, after they clean out the worst pockets of evil?"

"Sorry, dear." Susan said. "I know it looks lovely, but it'll be just too dangerous without a proper mass exorcism."

"Which will take years," added Maddie, with a little regret in her voice, too. "There's a list as long as my arm, and you have to sweet-talk the clerks to even get your site on it. Nice vacation spots are gonna be strictly do-it-yourself for a while yet."

Jill looked around. "I really don't get it," she said. "I mean, sure, it's got ambiance, but it's still on the surface. The sun's gonna come out at some point."

"We don't hate the sun," said Maddie. "Within limits."

"We don't *hate* the sun," said Jack. "It's just too bright and burns our skin."

"There are creams for that," said Anton.

"Yes, I know, your brother sells them for cheap— wait up."

The five stopped. Maddie looked at Jack. "Get something?"

Jack and Jill both nodded. "Faint, but it's there," said Jill. "We're gonna separate and triangulate the scent, but five bucks says it's gonna be coming from the old high school."

"Do I get a cut from your winnings?" asked Maddie. "I told you it was the most likely spot for his lair."

"Yeah," said Jack. "But it's nice to know for sure."

"Only if you *are* sure, Jack." Maddie stopped for a moment. "You two need backup?"

Jill and Jack looked at each other, then Jill shook her head. "Not this time," she said. "We won't need to move too far apart to get distance and direction, I think. The smell's pretty pungent."

"I'll take your word for it," Anton said sardonically as he

checked the cord on his crossbow. "My nose is stuffed up today, for some reason."

"It's not stuffed up, dear," said Susan. "You didn't bring it. It's back in Providence."

"Is it? Damn," said Anton mildly. "I'm always forgetting something."

#

The ruins of the high school were before them; that there was anything left at all was, as usual, a testament to the materials science of the Old Americans. Even to the point of: "Hold on," said Maddie. "Is that a working *light bulb*?"

It in fact was — specifically, an outside light originally meant to illuminate the front doors, and the five of them gathered around it with some bemusement. It was old and fading, but there was definitely still electrical power running through it. Inside the school there were flickers, presumably from more lights within.

"Well, that complicates things," Maddie went on. "Nobody touch any wires. Or pools of water. Or anything sparking."

Anton looked at her. "No kidding," he said. "You usually have to explain that to other oldmen?"

"Sweet Jesus, yes," said Maddie. "You have no idea." She extended her staff, and peered intently at the black-purple tendrils it gave off. "Good on my end to enter; there aren't any magical traps waiting for us."

Jack raised one forepaw. "I'm smelling a regular one." He sniffed. "Metal and rust, and it's got our quarry's scent on it... *here.*" He crouched down, and looked at a patch of wet leaves. "Yeah, there's a tripwire here, and it leads up to here. And, oh, look, there's a deadfall of metal and glass garbage, ready to rain crap down on us. Jill, I need another set of paws on this."

Susan peered at the trap as the two ghulmen worked on it. "There nothing malign bound into it," she said. "No curses, no evil spirits. And the stuff in it isn't heavy enough to kill somebody. So what's the point?"

"Probably an intruder alert," said Anton. "It goes off, gives our quarry a warning. It'd be god-awful loud."

"True," said Susan. "But we're out in the middle of nowhere. What's around there to be scared of?"

"You mean, besides oldmen?" said Jill. "No offense meant, Maddie."

"None taken, Jill." Maddie smiled. "My people's reputation precedes us. And it's such a *helpful* reputation, too," she went on, slightly bitterly. "Especially on nights like this."

"Sorry, Maddie," said Jill. "Now for real. We know none of this is your fault."

"No, but it's the fault of *some* oldman mage." Maddie shook her head. "Those bastards in the west, always making magical messes people like me then have to clean up. And wouldn't I like to repay the favor, some day."

"Yeah," murmured Anton. "But you'll have to get in line."

#

Inside was the usual mess from a hundred and fifty years of neglect and exposure to the elements, but there was a surprising absence of scattered bones. Maddie took center spot, donning a ghostmask that let her see spirits without casting a spell, with Anton ahead and Susan behind to guard against sudden attacks. Jack and Jill promptly disappeared in the shadows, one or the other periodically looping back into view to let the others know they were still alive and scouting. It made for slow going, but none of the party complained. After all, death was forever.

Searching the first floor took about half an hour, and revealed nothing. The five picked an abandoned bathroom to confer in, on the principle that there was only one door to guard and no windows. Plus, if there *was* an attack, Anton and Susan were almost literally built for close-combat fighting.

Jack said, "Our quarry is here for sure, but not on this floor. We found a back window that's been made to look like it's broke." He jerked his snout in that direction. "It must be what he uses to bring in stuff."

"Is he lairing upstairs, or downstairs?" asked Susan.

"Upstairs," said Jill. "I smelled him going down into the basement a few times, but the scent was old. He was probably just making sure there weren't gators or devil-cats down there."

"And thank God there aren't any, hey?" said Anton. "Right, Jill? Jack?"

Jack grinned. "Wouldn't we say, if there were?"

"Depends. How funny would it be for you to forget?"

"Okay, you got me there," said Jack. "But no. Nothing bad in the basement that we could smell. Scout's honor."

"So second floor, then." Maddie had been sketching while they talked. "I'm getting a lot out of the walls," she said, and sighed. "Unfortunately. The warlord who had this place liked to punish people for their insolence. Lots of sudden bursts of pain and awareness for me to read."

"What about ghosts?" said Susan. "I'm not feeling anybody trapped here. How about you?"

"No," Maddie said. She closed her eyes and concentrated. "I'm guessing your exorcists went through this place earlier, got everybody stuck In Between. Although it feels like at least one of them didn't want to go."

"Which one?" asked Anton.

Maddie grinned. "The warlord," she said. "I think. Whatever it was, I can feel the traces where it had to be dislodged and pushed into Going On. Better a ghost in this world than a damned soul in the next."

#

There were more traps on the stairwell, of the noisemaker variety. There was even an actual string of empty cans, suspended from the ceiling. Jack carefully reached out to look at the half-faded label on one. "Huh," he said. "These look modern."

"From the raided supply caravan, you think?" asked Anton.

Jack looked at him. "Okay, Anton," he said. "I'll just use my special ghulman senses to smell if this one can was on that one cart a week ago. You want to know what they were feeding the horse, too?"

"Sure," said Anton agreeably. "If you don't mind."

"Oats."

"That was fast."

"It's always oats." Jack grinned briefly, then went on, "But yeah, it's probably from the caravan. Surprising, ain't it?"

"When you put it like that, no." Anton looked at the arrangement of suspended cans. "Well, I guess this guy has working fingers. Good to know. How do we do this?"

"We could try yelling 'Hello,'" said Maddie. She looked amused at the others' reactions. "What? Either he's peaceable or he's not. If he is, then we can straighten everything out nice and quick and go back to civilization. And if he's not? Well, it's five against one and at least we tried."

"Trying sometimes hurts, Maddie," Jill pointed out. "I don't want to start a fight when we don't have to, but I wanna be ready if we have one anyway."

"Good point," said Maddie. "How about this? Jack disables the traps on the stairwell, but we don't just rush in. If there's going to be a face-off, we're better off *not* scattered up and down the stairs."

Anton squinted at the door at the top of the stairs. "We'd have to go through the door one at a time," he said. "So it's going to be a choke-point."

"That's not so bad," pointed out Jill. "It's a choke-point for him, too. We can push him back easier than he can us. It's not like he's going to have a gun."

The party collectively chuckled. It was *very* unlikely their target had a gun. This deep into the Second Republic, it was generally safe to keep a rifle around for hunting and seeing off non-sapient beasts, but gunpowder had a bad habit of exploding whenever encountering an unfriendly mage. Humanity was back to fighting with crossbows and sharpened bits of metal again, and in fights like those, numbers meant a lot more.

The door at the top of the stairwell appeared neither guarded nor trapped. Unfortunately, the operative word was *appeared.* Opening the door set off a godawful clatter, reverberating across the dark corridors and half-rubble rooms of the second floor. Jack swore as the five of them hurriedly cleared the door. "Bastard propped up a mop and a bucket!" he hissed, pointing back at the offending items as they loped past. "That's cheating."

"Anything else?" Jill said, a slight edge in her voice as she looked at the walls and ceiling.

Susan concentrated, not breaking stride, and shook her head. "Just a noisemaker."

"Yeah?" said Jill. "So why is my fur bristling?"

#

For this floor, the party moved without splitting up. It became clear very quickly that most of the rooms on this level were effectively useless. The roof was starting to collapse in places, filling what used to be classrooms and bathrooms with impassible metal and concrete rubble. Jack looked a couple of times at the ceiling above them, but aside from the odd leak or two, the party moved through the halls unimpeded.

Susan and Maddie both signaled the others to stop at about the same time, about thirty feet from a room with double doors — which did *not* look filled with rubble. "What's up?" Anton said, this time quietly.

"Something arcane on the other side," said Susan, and Maddie nodded. "Don't know what it is, not much of it, but it's real. Kind of old, too."

"Yes," agreed Maddie. "Old magic. The unfamiliar kind. Nobody make any ritual gestures in there."

"What kind of ritual gestures?" asked Jack.

"The kind that randomly summon fireballs or mold golems, Jack," Maddie said. "Just don't point at anything, okay?"

#

They *tried* knocking.

Anton went first; his mace was still at his belt, but he had his shield on his right arm. That saved him from going flippers over fin as the double doors slammed open, but even a merman will bounce away when he gets hit with three hundred pounds of wolfman all at once. Even when the shield takes most of the force.

There were two faint crackles as Maddie and Susan gestured their respective arcane and holy shields into life: the twin glows illuminated their target. He was a chimera half-wolf, half-man blend, about six feet tall, and covered with fur that clearly hadn't been properly washed in a week, if ever. The face looked humanoid enough to allow speech, and the wolfman had clawed hands instead of paws, but the only other sign of sapience was the ripped and tattered shorts he still wore.

That, and the eyes. The eyes assessed the situation quickly, and the great claws reached out towards Anton — and then the wolfman shuddered, changed direction, and jerkily ripped a sagging locker off of the wall to throw at the party. Susan and Maddie didn't duck, but Jack and Jill both scattered as Anton stood, just in time to take the thrown locker right on his shield. It didn't knock him down, but it did stagger him back a step.

The wolfman screamed "GO AWAY!" then scrambled and ran down the corridor to another set of doors. As he fled, Maddie tossed out another spell; a stream of whining, fractal wires of force sprayed from her fingertips, straight at the wolfman's back. But when they hit, they dissipated in a tooth-rattling burst of energy. As the beast-man burst through the doors, his back glowed silver and green, in a chessboard pattern. And then he was gone.

Jack and Jill had instinctively given chase; Jill reached the two doors first, only to be suddenly yanked back by Jack before she could rush through. She turned to snarl at him — then was interrupted by twin crashes as something heavy from above smashed into the space she would have been occupying. "Not gonna say 'sorry' for that, Sis," Jack growled back. "Because I ain't. This guy *ain't* a critter. Bastard planned his escape route ahead of time."

Susan joined them. "We have a problem."

"Yeah, sure," said Jill. "There's a rampaging wolfman out there in the dark."

"That's not the problem," Susan replied. "The problem is,

he's cursed. And whatever is cursing him *stinks* of evil."

"Shit," said Jack. "Ah, sorry, Susan. But are you sure he's only cursed?"

"Yes," said Susan. "It felt imposed, not natural. Besides, he was resisting it. And doing well enough to keep at least a little control. He ran when he could have fought."

"Yeah, but then he threw" — Jill peeked through the doors — "what looks like a metal railing at us. That could have hurt. A lot." Jill peered again. "He popped the other one right out from the floor. This wolfman is *strong*."

"I don't think he's got full control," said Susan. "Maybe Maddie's spotted something more. Maddie, Anton, what are you doing?"

"Finding clues," Anton said from back down the hall. "Come take a look at them, gang."

#

"There's not much here," Jill said dubiously as they all looked down at the things Maddie and Anton had collected. A couple crude bags of hide — one freshly made, one not; a canteen, waterproof tin of matches, and a compass; and the contents of the bags themselves. The older bag was furry, made of badly-cured skin and a strap made from hair, and had held some hunks of dried, moldering meat, a few sharpened stones, and a piece of bark with scratches on it. The newer bag was mostly a sack containing some meat-scraps and eel bones.

"So what is this?" Jill asked, holding up the bark.

Susan peered at it. "It's a map," she said after a moment. "Of the East Coast. See Maine, there?"

"Is that what it is?"

"I didn't say it was a *good* map." Susan shrugged. "He must have scratched it out. Better than nothing."

Jill picked up the canteen and sniffed at it. "I guess this and the other modern stuff all came from the raided caravan?"

Anton shrugged. "It's National Guard standard issue," he said. "So probably. But look at that first bag there. How does it smell, Jack, Jill?"

"Fine," Jack said; Jill nodded. "Why?"

Maddie rolled her eyes. "It stinks like it's half-rotted, and the meat is dried, moldy, and green."

"Yeah," said Jack. "So what? ...Oh, right. You all have sensitive stomachs."

"That's one way of putting it," Maddie said. "The point is, it's *old*. Our wolfman probably brought it with him when he came east."

"East?" asked Susan. "You think you know where he's from?"

"Maybe," said Anton. "Look at the map again. See how it shows all the major rivers between here and the Mississippi? Well, what's beyond the Mississippi?"

"The Alliance," growled Jill. "The fucking Magician's Alliance. Sorry, Susan."

"That's all right," Susan said. "Just use 'damned' next time. It's not profanity if it's literally true." She leaned forward. "You think he's a runaway?"

"Maybe," said Anton. "If he was a commando, he'd have better gear than sharpened rocks. But there was that thing on his back. Maddie?"

"I think he's got some kind of protective charm," said Maddie. "I punched the binding spell; it got him square, and it *should* have put him under on the spot. The way it got shrugged off, it felt like a magic item." She shuddered. "A nasty one. You have to fine-tune protective charms to keep them from making your stomach churn when they activate, but whoever made this one didn't just not care; they designed it to be *extra*-painful. I don't think it's real comfortable to wear, either. We have to assume the wolfman can't just take it off on his own, because if he could have, he would have by now."

"Which is another argument that this guy's running from the Magician's Alliance," Anton said. "Locking somebody up in a protective artifact that hurts to use is exactly the sort of black-hearted thing they'd do. Probably they thought he'd end up going crazy from the pain."

"And in the meantime we can't use magic on him," said Jack.

"Great. Can you turn the artifact off, Maddie?"

"If I can't, Susan probably can," said Maddie. "Can't imagine God's real thrilled about this sort of thing."

Susan looked pained. "You're over-simplifying the theology, and the nomenclature, but... yes, I can ask for an intercession here. If we can find him. The artifact will protect him from search spells, yes?"

"Yes," said Maddie cheerfully. She pointed to the rotting bag. "But not against a straight-up direct invocation of the Law of Contagion. 'Once in contact, always in contact' — and even *I* can tell the hair in this bag-strap never came from a rabbit."

#

Following the wolfman meant taking the stairs up to the roof, and Jill didn't let them rush; she took her time, and kept her snout close to the floor of the stairwell. "If he thinks we can't track him magically, he'll waste time covering his normal trail." Suddenly she recoiled, and started waving a paw in front of her face. "Oh, gross!" she said.

Maddie looked at her. "What kind of smell grosses out a ghul-man?" she asked, with real curiosity.

"Concentrated essence of Bradford pear," Jill replied. "It's just so damned *cloying*. Like drowning in a vat of dessert. And now I won't be able to smell anything else for a while."

"He must have known there'd be ghulmen tracking him," Jack said as they all cleared the door and reached the roof. Up here the school looked considerably more decayed; half the third floor was caved-in from the elements, which at least meant it'd be easy enough to get down. The position of the Big Dipper in the sky above told the party they'd start running out of night sooner than later. "Couldn't have been easy to get the stuff."

"Probably it came from the caravan," Anton said as he pulled out his almost priceless pair of Old American binoculars. "They had a perfume merchant along, and everybody reported a bunch of stuff missing— no, no sign of the wolfman. Maddie?"

"Hold up for a second." Maddie was crouched low, with Susan

looming above her, which handily blocked most of the light coming from Maddie's fingertips. "I just need to find a spirit willing to help. There we go!" The light had congealed into a hazy outline of some small, furry woodland creature. It snuffled at the hair-braid strap Maddie showed it, sniffed the air a few times, then started loping across the broken roof. Maddie immediately followed, with the rest of the party a few steps behind her.

The tracking spirit didn't move ridiculously fast, which meant everybody could talk to each other. "Not a human spirit?" asked Anton, idly. Maddie shook her head.

"Human ghosts here are too dangerous to work with," she said. "Either they don't know what will happen if they Go On, and it scares them — or they *do* know what will happen, and that scares them even more. Animal ghosts are easier to soothe."

"Found us a good way to get down, too," Jack said as the five scrambled down one last pile of rubble to make it to the ground. "How's the nose, Jill?"

"Useless," she replied. "How's yours?"

"Same as always."

"Aww. Too bad. This could have been your moment to shine." The two ghulmen both gibbered laughter before Jill went on, "It's gotta be your spell, Maddie. At least until my nose clears."

"All right." Maddie squared her shoulders. "Keeping it up is going to be a strain, though. So let's move as quickly as we can. We're running out of moonlight as it is."

#

"God *damn* it," said Anton, looking at the map. "He's headed right for another atrocity site."

The five of them were at what looked like the ruins of a church. Susan had murmured for a few moments and declared the ground still consecrated, which meant it was safe enough for them to pause and take a bearing on the wolfman. Maddie's spell showed he had stopped trying to obscure his tracks and was now heading east; if the party could figure out where he was going, they might be able to intercept him there.

Maddie looked at the map, her eyes swirling into twin black voids as she refreshed the cantrip which let her read in the dark. "*Another* atrocity site? How many did they have, besides the university?"

"Seven," Susan said. She had been kneeling on the ground with bowed head and folded hands; her standing up wasn't as smooth as it could have been, and Anton looked worried as he handed her a water bottle. "Thank you, love. If this is the one I'm thinking of," Susan went on as she irrigated her gill slits, "it's pretty bad. The Magician's Alliance took over a nursing school and used it to 'process' the locals for their slave-armies. It got cleaned later, but there are still items in there you don't want to touch. Or look at too closely. And you *definitely* don't want to let your thoughts dwell on them too much; they might hear you."

"Why didn't they get destroyed?" Jack asked.

"The worst ones were. The rest got dumped in concrete. They'll get to the top of the list eventually." Susan looked worried. "Why is he *going* there? What's there for him?"

"Magical stuff?" Jill said. When they looked at her, she shrugged. "His map was to here, right?"

"Kind of," said Anton. "It could have just as easily been to Providence, or Boston."

"Sure," replied Jill. "But those are both cities with people in them. Maybe this guy's looking for a place where there's magic, but no magicians? And Westhaven was one of the places the Magicians' Alliance held onto longest. The Alliance might still remember it."

"Okay. But it's loaded down with evil magic!" pointed out Anton.

"If he's running from the Magician's Alliance," Jack said, "What makes you think he knows there's anything like *good* magic?"

"Point taken," said Maddie. "So what does he want at the nursing school? And why didn't he just lair there?"

"He wants the artifact removed," said Susan. "That's got to be it. You said it: that thing must be agony to wear. So he came east. Halfway across a continent." She shuddered. "I'm amazed he's still sane."

"He might not be," Anton pointed out. "I don't think he'll trust us, either. Certainly not you or Maddie."

"Of course not," said Maddie. "It's the perfect trap, isn't it? The two people who can help him are the exact people he's been taught to hate on sight. And I threw a spell at him, so he knows we've got one of *them* in the party."

"Ayup," said Jack. "So how do we work around the problem?"

"We don't," said Maddie. "We lay a trap."

"Really?" asked Jack. "And what do you think we can use for bait?"

"Lemme put it this way," Maddie said. "You lucked out, Jack. It's going to be me, after all."

#

Maddie got the attention of the wolfman by casting an area-effect general scrying spell which 'happened' to include the spot he was currently in. It was as low-powered as possible, given the likelihood the warding artifact would flare painfully for the wolfman, but she and Susan agreed it was the only way to not give away the fact that Maddie could track their target without using actual spellcrafting.

After the spell went off, it was a matter of waiting — except it wasn't much of a wait. It turned out wolfmen could run very, very quickly. Maddie's first warning was a rustle in the brush around her, then a blur of speed as clawed hands reached out to grab — and miss, as she set off a prepared spell and began to blur with speed on her own.

It was obvious right away she was not *quite* as fast as an angry wolfman, but she had the twin advantages of knowing ahead of time where she was going, and what to do when she got there. By the time the wolfman worked out his own plan, the necromancer was already halfway towards the abandoned nursing school, at top speed. "Perfect," she muttered to herself as she ran. "I'm being chased by an angry wolfman into an abandoned ruin sat-urated with evil death magic. This was a *great* plan, Maddie."

As the twin doors loomed ahead, the sounds of pursuit grew steadily louder. But the wolfman didn't have quite enough time to spring on Maddie before she cleared the doors. She didn't bother trying to slow down: instead, the necromancer dove to the floor, trusting in the spell's ability to dump momentum without hurting her. It worked... well enough.

When the wolfman did enter the foyer behind her, he was promptly blind-sided by Anton. The Second Republic still had football — *and* soccer, which a few stubborn holdouts kept in-sisting was *really* football. In both games, it was universally agreed that mermen made the best tacklers; Anton's charge sent both of them tumbling into the rotted remains of desks and walls, filling the room with dust and black mold as the two punched and kicked in a tangle.

Left to themselves, there might have been a question as to who would have won the fight. Then again, they weren't left to themselves: Jack and Jill were there, and neither had any inclin-ation to fight fair. They were fast enough to grab flailing paws and legs; they weren't strong enough to hold them long, but it was long enough for Anton to wind up and sock the wolfman in the gut two, three times. As the wolfman took a breath to howl, Susan deftly tossed a small bag in his mouth. He reflexively bit down, looked confused for a moment, then fell over.

"Thank you for not punching him in the face, dear," she said.

Anton grinned. "You don't punch people in the face with bare hands," he said. "Even our kind of hands. Besides, what if he lost a tooth or something?"

#

Securing the wolfman for transport was trickier than the party had expected. One good look at the barbed wire mesh half-embedded in the wolfman's back had persuaded the party that trying to get it off in the field, if they could even *find* the necessary tools, might be *extremely* dangerous. The kind of dan-gerous which leaves craters in the ground. Susan and Maddie had decided on a straight unconsciousness charm, which meant they'd have to haul him out on a travois.

Since it was two days' worth of hard travel to the nearest settlement (and hopefully a waiting dedicated disenchantment team), Anton had decided to do the trip in stages; they'd go back to the sewers, wait out the rest of the day there, and move when the sun was down again. It wasn't the best solution in the world, but nobody wanted to hide from the sun in the half-wrecked foyer of an atrocity site. The air felt dead, here; there wasn't even the smell of mold.

Susan was the first to notice the change in atmosphere. They were about to leave when she gasped and suddenly activated the just-in-case protective circle she'd drawn in the foyer; the rest didn't waste any time jumping back inside of it. "What am I preparing for?" Maddie asked as she started bringing forth general protection cantrips and magical energy accumulators. Anton, Jack, and Jill merely pulled out bits of armor from their packs. If there was a ward active, they'd need them.

"This site wasn't as clean as they thought it was!" Susan carefully did not shout. "There's something in the basement, and it's waking up!" She looked at the brightening sky. "We stayed too long, and now the spirits of the day can roam."

"Crap," said Jill. She and Jack were already wearing sunglasses, to ward off the hideous light of the daystar. "Dayghosts are the *worst*."

Maddie concentrated. "Double crap," she said. "It feels like an atrocity ghost. It's what you get when you murder a bunch of people with magic, then stick them in a charnel pit until their spirits all tangle up together. You don't reason with those. You blow holes in them until they untangle on their own."

"What? How did the exorcism squad *miss* that one?" Susan almost yelled.

Maddie shrugged. "Maybe they checked at night? Atrocity ghosts are daywalkers. They're hard to catch when the sun goes down."

Jill frowned. "It's going to come after us, isn't it?" By her tone, she already knew the answer, but Maddie nodded anyway.

"Well, it's insane with pain, and it was formed by evil necromancy, and there's now both an evil artifact and a necromancer here in its hunting range." Maddie gave the stereotypical death's-head grin of her profession. "I'm going to go out on a limb here and say, yeah, it's going to come after us."

"Any good news?" asked Anton.

"Sure," said Maddie. "You can hit them with regular weapons and they say 'ow.' Actually, they scream incoherently until your ears bleed, but smacking them with things helps them untangle."

"Nice to have something to do," muttered Jack. He looked over. "Susan, what's up?"

Susan had pulled out a chalice, a candle, and a white cloth. She was now kneeling on the ground and arranging them before her. "I'm going to remove the artifact," she said. "Once it's removed, we won't have to worry about the atrocity ghost going after *him*."

"Good thinking, love," said Anton. "Plus, you've been wanting to wreck the fucking thing since you first saw it."

"Language, dear," replied Susan. "It is a *damnable* thing, and yes: I want it wrecked. I also don't want it to explode, and take all of us with it." She gestured, and red-yellow flames erupted from both the candle and the chalice. "So keep the ghost off of me until I can finish the job, if you would?"

\#

The atrocity ghost screamed into existence with the sunrise, and it glowed enough with its own pain and rage to make Jack and Jill twitch at the sudden, cruel brightness. The ghost was a hideous thing, full of right angles, crackling razor-sharp segments, and a metallic whine the party felt in their teeth and inner ears. Every line seemed to have its own mouth; and every mouth howled through serrated teeth. The actinic light of its form made horrible shadows as it flowed and crawled over Susan's ward, finally burning through in a half-dozen places before the protection failed completely. The atrocity ghost coalesced into a vaguely scorpion-like form as it smashed a bit more of the foyer into wooden and plastic rubble.

Anton struck first, this time with shield and sharktooth club. His shield bash knocked the atrocity ghost back, and the gutting-stroke following it ripped a handful of the hateful lines free — but the atrocity ghost recovered quickly, slashing a glittering lash of light back at Anton. He fell back enough to avoid being gutted in turn, but there were deep grooves on his breastplate, and the top of his shield had been lopped off.

At their feet, the hacked-off pieces of the atrocity ghost stirred, and began to crawl back to their host. From Jack's fingers flew whirring throwing-bones, to pin them to the ground, quivering. And then it was Jack's turn to be lashed by the atrocity ghost, in a blur of motion ending with Jack sprawled at one end of the room, clutching at splintered and bloody ribs.

Hands writhing in complex patterns, Maddie yelled to Jill. "Get its attention! I need it trying to whip you!"

"That's not gonna be hard!" Jill snarled as she threw a handful of glass spheres at the atrocity ghost. They exploded in gouts of acidic fumes, scoring the spirit's hide. She feinted and rolled as the atrocity ghost lunged, its whip blurring with precise, hateful inevitability.

Maddie's spell snagged the whip just before the tip could wrap itself around Jill's throat. Her magic flowed over and around the pitiless surfaces of the whip, seeking the places where trapped soul was bound to trapped soul. Where it found cracks, the spell bored in, grinding away the unholy bonds and unraveling the very arcane structure of the whip — which was part of the atrocity ghost itself.

Had Maddie enough magical energy to spare, she might've been able to unravel the entire atrocity ghost on the spot. She did not. But the necromancer did have enough power to destroy the whip, and knock the ghost to the ground. Jill looked angry enough to want to foolishly kick at the prone figure, but satisfied herself by throwing knife after knife at anything that looked vulnerable.

The atrocity ghost got up anyway, its forelegs growing claws like shortswords. But Anton had the reach on that kind of weapon, and he waded back in, smashing with his club and battering the ghost with his shield as he drove it back. With every blow, more and more pieces flew off, to be speared by Jill or zapped by Maddie. The oppressive feel of the foyer began to fade —but the atrocity ghost fought on, too locked in its own misery to do anything else. And unlike Anton, it wasn't tiring.

Susan yelled over the tooth-rattling buzz of the fight. "Almost there! Can you pin the ghost? I need it to stay in one place!"

Anton swore something unintelligible and struck down with his sharktooth club. Its vicious edge dug into the atrocity ghost's foot and into the floor below, pinning the spirit — but the ghost reached out with its claws to tear at Anton's armored throat. Roaring with agony and freakishly strong, it lifted the merman off of the floor. It ignored Anton's frantic punches, the knives Jill threw, and even the raw magical energy cast by Maddie.

It could not ignore the machete driven into its unprotected back, and ripped down the length of its spine. As it let Anton go, its legs wobbling, Jack staggered back himself, the terrible wound in his side now leaking slightly as his body fought to heal the new damage. "God *damn*, but that hurt," Jack muttered as he slumped against the wall.

As soon as he was clear, Susan made two precise gestures, reached somehow *into* the artifact binding the wolfman, and pulled out a writhing tangle of energy which moved in ways things should not move. As soon as it was free of the artifact in a shower of sparks and cacophony, she threw it overhand at the atrocity ghost.

It would have missed, except that the atrocity ghost lunged for the tangle, heedless of the damage it did to itself. It grabbed the unmoored enchantment in both clawed hands, then inexorably wrestled the suddenly-frantic tangle into its gaping maw. Susan yelled 'Duck!' as the tangle was swallowed whole; everyone took cover, Jill dragging Jack behind a side-flipped table.

As explosions went, it was very peaceful. Almost serene. It barely even left a crater. The actinic glow of several hundred souls finally going to their reward was honestly the most disconcerting part, and even then the effect was blunted for most of the party.

Susan stood up, and brushed herself off. "Well, *that* worked out nicely," she said brightly. "Hardly even a chore! Now, where's Jack? I saw him get banged up a little."

"Over here," Jack replied, wincing as Jill helped him up from the wreckage of the table. "And it's more than 'a little,' okay?"

"Ignore him. He'll be fine," Jill called out.

"You know it's *all right* for us to get healed, sis?"

Anton looked at the crater while Maddie checked the wolfman, now feebly stirring in the pile of rapidly-tarnishing wires that was all that was left of the artifact. He kicked at the crater's edge a little. "Susan, what did you do here?" he asked.

"I pulled out the evil from the artifact and threw it at the atrocity ghost," Susan said as she healed Jack. "The poor creature just wanted some retribution, after all. So I let it have some by taking apart something vile."

Anton frowned. "But the thing on the wolfman wasn't what killed them in the first place," he pointed out. "Why would that even work?"

Maddie cackled, lightly. "When you've been trapped for a century," she said, "you tend to stop being so picky about where you get your retribution. Besides, it came from the same bastards as the ones who killed those people to begin with, so the flavor was close enough anyway. Oh, our wolfman's waking up."

The other members of the party gathered around, close enough to give assistance if needed, but not quite loom. Absent the artifact's influence, the wolfman... looked much the same, really. More intelligent-looking, perhaps. And generally less bestially vicious.

He opened his eyes, perhaps at the attention. Fortunately, he didn't immediately panic, and when he spoke, it seemed the Magician's Alliance still let their slaves speak English. "Did it work?" the wolfman asked, as he clumsily felt his side with bound hands. His face fell as his fingers twirled in hair. "It didn't work!" he said.

Maddie knelt down to untie his hands, then helped him up enough to let him drink from a canteen. "Hi, stranger. The artifact's gone, and you're free of it. It's just wires right now."

"I can feel it gone," said the wolfman after he drank. "No more pain. But look at me!" he said. "A beast! I thought with it gone, I would be a human!"

Jack was looking much better; better enough to talk and chuckle, at least. "Who says you're not a human, kid?"

"Everyone!" wailed the wolfman. "Look at me!"

"Hey. Look at *me*, kid." Jack moved to give the wolfman a better view. "Look at the rest of us. We're all human, so why can't you be?"

"Because I'm a *monster*," said the wolfman, although in a slightly less panicked tone.

Maddie looked at the other four, then back at the wolfman. "I'm sorry, but we don't know that term," she said with genuine puzzlement. "Is it a Mage's Alliance word?"

THE LAST RAYGUN
IN THE WORLD

Old Louisville
Kentucky Free State
2450 AD

I was sitting at my usual table when the woman walked in. She was dressed for no nonsense, from the tips of her caravan trader boots to the brim of her top hat. Everything in between was sturdy tweed and leather, but not the exciting kind.

Her briefcase was exciting, though: it looked like the kind you keep money in. A lot of money. In my line of work, you need to keep your eyes focused on the essentials.

I knew she was coming to my table the moment she walked into the joint. I drink at Gentlemen Jack's because it's the best dive in the Kentucky Free State, let alone Old Louisville. Jack's is dark and loud, they don't shortchange you, and the green-flaming skull of the last guy to water the drinks is mounted just above the bar. What it's *not* is a place to get work — but then, I don't 'get' work. Work comes to me. And here it was, coming now.

She didn't waste time, I have to say. Came right up to the table, sat in one of the chairs, and flickered a smile in my general direction. I let it go because of the briefcase — and because she wasn't too hard on the eyes, either. She had it under control, though. Like her looks were a holdout weapon, for emergencies.

"Good evening. I am Miss Serenity Mehrotra; I am a duly appointed representative of the Steering Committee for the Hershey Consortium," the woman said. "You are Mildred Deckard. I have a job for you."

I noted that neither of those last two statements came across as questions. "I'm sure you do," I replied. "Question is, do I care?"

"You will find our arguments persuasive, Ms. Deckard. If I may?" This Serenity person waved one gloved hand in the direction of her briefcase; I nodded, and watched with only nine-tenths of an eye as she dipped into its contents. Lazy of me, sure, but there was no particular reason for anybody to try to kill me right now and I was feeling mellow. Besides, what came out of the briefcase was a couple of bank drafts, not a dagger or a fireball wand. Although papers like that have killed more people over the years than any mere weapon ever has.

"Ten thousand dollars, drawn on the Bank of Maysville, simply for hearing our offer," said Serenity. "Or, if you are a speculative woman: fifteen thousand Hershey credits, drawn on the First Bank of Hershey. I would tell you to pick the latter, but naturally I am biased."

I whistled. Either one was a generous way to get my attention. I wasn't surprised at her assumption that Hershey dollars were going to be worth more than money issued by the Free State's own official bank; the people running this new 'Hershey Consortium' were already getting a reputation as being an arrogant bunch. Arrogant, hardnosed, and pragmatic. Then again, when you're brushing up against the Universal Dominion on your western border, maybe you gotta be pragmatic.

Besides, Hershey money already spent real well, so I nodded my head with a smile and grabbed the Hershey Bank draft. "Maybe I *am* feeling persuaded, Ms. Mehrotra. Or at least you have my honest attention."

"Excellent." Serenity paused. "Although, and forgive me for saying this: in my case, it is 'Miss'."

Ah, she was one of *those*. I gave *Miss* Mehrotra points for not being visibly upset by all the drinking going on around her. Or was she upset there wasn't more open depravity? Well, it was

Tuesday. Gentleman Jack's is usually pretty tame during the week.

The indirect reminder of my bar tab brought me back into focus on the matter at hand: my job. My possible job. I have a fairly unique skill set which I don't use for just anybody.

I looked at her. "This kind of money means questions from me," I said. "The first one is: who did you want me to kill? And the second is: why should I, Miss Mehrotra?"

"There is a third question, Ms. Deckard." Her voice was cool, but not in the way people get when they don't like you. I was getting the feeling she didn't much care for getting riled up. "'Why do I need to hire someone with the last working laser pistol in the land?'"

I shrugged and waved the bartender over for more drinks. Tea, this time. In my head I was already on the job. "I figure the answer to the third question's gonna be obvious when I hear the answers to the first two."

#

So it's the end of the world, hey? Only this bit of it has lasted for three and a half centuries. When does the next part start?

I'm not saying this part of the apocalypse isn't interesting. You got your collapse of empires and strange powers arising, complete with monster-haunted ruins and the uncanny happening every darned day. There's even a fairy-tale kingdom filled with unicorns and pixie dust to the east of us — and thank God for that, because there's a nasty evil empire brewing up in the north. Which brings us back nicely to my first and second questions.

"His name is carefully hidden," said *Miss* Mehrotra as she opened folders and spread out papers. "But he deigns to let non-mages call him 'Kragnor the Ambitious.' Technically Kragnor is a citizen of the Kentucky Free State, but he does not recognize your country as being anything except a placeholder until he gets around to conquering it."

There weren't any photographs, even for a job like this. That costs serious money, assuming you can get the chemicals. But somebody with a crystal ball and a set of good colored pencils had made a sketch of the target's head, which was good enough for me. Kragnor didn't look ambitious as much as he looked surly and sneering; and he had the kind of chiseled, regular face you can only get from magic. Sometimes that works, but I could see the ugliness poking through from under, even though it was just a sketch.

"What a swell guy," I said aloud. "But I've never heard of him. Where's he running out of?"

"Right now the mage controls the area around the ruins of Chillicothe. If the name means nothing to you," (it did not) "then let me tell you its location: Chillicothe is an excellent place from which to conquer everywhere from Cincinnati to Columbus to Huntington. And no doubt the Free State and the Consortium as well."

"What, all by himself?" I asked. "Last time I checked, the Free State has armies. Even if this Kragnor *is* a mage." I wasn't really arguing. More like giving the client the chance to explain the why. I actually like to know the why; a lot of assassins don't. Knowing the why lets me know how to still earn my fee when the job goes critical.

"Oh, he is a mage," said *Miss* Mehrotra. "And one most eager to join with the archmages ruling the Universal Dominion. So eager, he is conspiring with them to conquer as much as he can on his own, and only then seek union with the Dominion."

I nodded. The Dominion had made a treaty with the Kingdom of Virginia, a couple hundred years ago: they were to retreat over the Mississippi River and stay there. But there were loopholes, starting with the bit about the Mississippi. And the Dominion was only forbidden to *conquer* to the east. Annexing willing territory was still all right. Still: "Why aren't you attacking?" I said. "Hershey has an army too, right? Hell, you have the Great Wyrm of Philadelphia. *She* doesn't need an excuse to go burn a Dominion mage, even if the Virginians do."

"No doubt she could," said *Miss* Mehrotra. "And no doubt your country could send an army of its own to conquer Chillicothe. But then, the moment either army came into view Kragnor would immediately submit to the Universal Dominion, and then there would be a war. Who wins it?"

"The ravens," quoth I.

"Precisely. So instead of an army, we send a specialist. If you fail, alas. If you succeed, well, your fee is much cheaper than an army's."

"What's the fee?" I was a little curious, but not much. If you don't know how much it costs to hire me, then you aren't prepared enough, and fifteen grand for just the buy-in showed that *Miss* Mehrotra here had done her homework. She didn't even bother to look at her notes before replying.

"One million dollars, or one and a half million credits," she said. She seemed just the slightest bit hesitant in making the offer, and I didn't blame her in the slightest: that was a lot of God-damned money, even for a warlord. "We would normally offer a portion ahead of time as a retainer," she went on, "but I understand you insist on payment only upon completion."

"Yeah," I said. "If I can't do the job, I can't do the job. No harm, no foul." *And no inconvenient, maybe lethal obligations over my head*, I didn't say. She looked smart enough to figure it out.

"This was understood, and is acceptable," she said. "But what happens when somebody does not wish to pay afterward?" From her tone, *Miss* Mehrotra found such a concept to be at the very least highly distasteful. I like hearing that in a client.

I grinned. "I remind them about how I own the last Raygun in the world. Never fails." I let the grin go away. "I'll take the contract," I said, "but now it's time you tell me what the catch is."

I wasn't guessing, there. To call it a guess would imply I could possibly have been wrong, and I knew I wasn't. When it comes to my line of work, there's *always* a wrinkle.

#

The wrinkle's name was Jimmy Wilkinson, and he was not thrilled to be there. Wilkinson had grown up in the area before he went east to try his luck with the Hershey Consortium; he maybe still knew people, and he *probably* remembered the roads. That was fine, but I could tell he visibly resented the assignment, and was annoyed I didn't seem to resent him back. I might have, if a smaller amount of money had been on the table. But one-point-five million bucks can pay for a Hell of a lot of equanimity. I'd have worried more if they *hadn't* sent along an observer, hey?

But it didn't make it any easier how *Miss* Mehrotra made it clear right from the start that he wasn't in charge. The Hershey Consortium apparently wasn't a big fan of sugaring the medicine: "You are there," she told him, point-blank and right in front of me, "to make sure Ms. Deckard accomplishes the mission, Mr. Wilkinson. We are paying her for her judgment; we are paying you for your industry. This mission is her responsibility, not yours."

Wilkinson didn't like that at all. I wasn't sure how I felt about it, either. I don't need to be reminded that what I do for a living can't be contracted out.

#

Several days later, we were halfway from Lexington to the Maysville river crossing, and Wilkinson at least managed to throttle the resentment back a bit by then. I think the stagecoach helped; the retainer meant I could get seats on one of the more comfortable coaches on the old Route 68 run, and I had covered his ticket and meals. He probably had his own expense account, but I'd figured Wilkinson wouldn't mind being able to pocket the per-diem, and I was right.

To be fair, he wasn't abusing it. Wilkinson only drank when he wasn't sure of the water and had a preference for roasted lumps of meat (with the odd root vegetable), and God knows the Free State has plenty of *that* ambling around. I assumed he spent the extra money on barmaids, because there was one coming out of his room in the morning at every inn we stayed at. Not really my style (his tastes didn't match mine, either, not that I'd diddle a barmaid while on the job), but I didn't care as long as it didn't affect me.

Wilkinson had wanted to see the Raygun, but then everybody does. Since I don't go waving it around, he had to be satisfied with just seeing the special holster I wear for jobs. He caught himself staring at it from time to time, but I'm also used to starers.

Stagecoach rides are boring, so I decided to explain. "I know how to fire the Raygun," I said, "and I even know how to fix little things wrong with it. I don't know how to fix it for real. So I don't mess with it."

"What's it like to fire it?" asked Wilkinson. Everybody asks that question, too. I shrugged.

"Like firing a crossbow, but with no kick." Wilkinson looked disappointed, again as usual. I shrugged again. "It's a weapon, Mr. Wilkinson. It's not *magic*. Regular people made it. We just don't know how to make any more."

Wilkinson opened his mouth to say something — and then, almost as if saying the word 'crossbow' summoned one, there was a meaty *thunk* outside and a yell as our driver got shot with a bolt. So Wilkinson yelled "Ambush!" instead and ducked down below the windows. So did I, because I'm no dummy.

We were the only two in the coach, plus the driver. But this was still settled territory, dammit! *Didn't the State Police patrol here?* I thought as I pulled out a spring-bolt pepperbox. Wilkinson raised an eyebrow as he readied a slingshot. "No Raygun?" he said.

I shook my head. "It'd set the damned coach on fire!"

The coach was moving faster now; from the carrying-on from the driver, he was alive, still able to steer, and very unhappy. There were more sounds of crossbows going off, but all the thunks were wooden this time.

Wilkinson grinned. "Guess they want you alive," he said, and watched the left windows as I did the right. Then he spoiled the moment by going on: "At least until they have the Raygun. Then you'll be just as screwed as I am."

I mean, he was probably right, but it wasn't the best way to put it, okay?

As the driver got the team to no-fooling gallop I heard the

whoosh of black powder going off; a few moments later I saw a puff of crackling smoke, up there in the sky. The coach must have had a signal firework, which meant the driver expected there'd be a State Police patrol around here somewhere. Or maybe he just didn't want to go down without trying everything first. Hard to argue with that.

Speaking with things to argue with, here came more horsemen. Riding *forward* to cut us off. "Dammit," I said in Wilkinson's general direction as five riders did their best to swarm us. "They really are here for me."

(In hindsight, I maybe should have said that nicer.) Right now we had five guys trying to grab the stagecoach. I figured I should solve that problem first.

Can a stagecoach outrun men on horses? Not really, no. But a trained driver can make it real hard for the cavalrymen to stop him. Especially these guys.

Now, I'm not saying the ambushers were green, or anything. They weren't at the level of Free State Recon troopers, but as bushwhackers go, they knew their stuff. And I could tell they had a plan. Get one of their guys on top of the coach, shoot the driver, take the reins, and then it was all over. It was one of the reckless plans, but when you live on the frontier, recklessness is sometimes all you got to work with.

The only problem with the plan was, it assumed two things. One, that I wasn't reckless enough to push back. Two, that I gave a damn about their horses.

I swear to God, one of the ambushers actually looked *outraged* as I shot a bolt right into his horse's belly. The horse itself screamed, but more importantly it bucked and kicked and knocked itself into another ambusher's horse, which meant they both went down in what I hoped was a mass of broken bones. But even if I only wrecked one horse, the other one wouldn't be catching up any time soon, so I turned to see the other side.

And... Wilkinson wasn't doing too badly, yeah. He was aiming at the ambushers, not their horses, but that made sense. You can kill a man with a sling-shot easy enough, but you have to work at it with a horse. Right now he had one ambusher swaying in her saddle and looking about ready to fall off, and another clearly unready to push his horse too close to us. And who could blame him? The odds for our attackers weren't nearly as good as they were a minute ago.

But there was still the last damn ambusher to deal with, and he was leaping for the top of the stage even as I tried to line up another shot with the pepperbox. I couldn't get him in time, so I didn't shoot; I heard the thump against the side as he grabbed a handhold somehow and started to climb to the top of the stagecoach. *Crap*, I thought. Aloud, I said, "Keep those bastards from shooting me, okay?"

Then, before Wilkinson could say anything, I kicked open the door on my side of the stagecoach — and then swung up on it, in one smooth motion.

All right, that was a lie. Not me using the door to get on top of the stagecoach, but how smooth it was. I'm sure from outside it looked more like an undignified scramble.

The hinges on the door weren't up to take the extra weight, to start. I'm no axeman but I'm not a beanpole, either. If I'd been letting myself think about it, I'd have said I was counting on the hinges to hold out just long enough. And then I would've gone tumbling onto the road, because I would've been thinking about how stupid this idea was, instead of just jumping up'n grabbing at the baggage rails on the roof. Good thing I had my priorities in order, huh?

Below and behind me I could hear the poor, abused door pop off and bounce its way back down the road; worse, my pepperbox decided to join it a second later. Which was not great, but I was still in the middle of doing something stupid, so I concentrated on that instead. And I needed to. I've got good arm strength, but what I was missing was *purchase*. Trying to get one foot onto something which could take the weight wasn't going too well, and I didn't have much time before I'd have to drop back into the stagecoach.

But Wilkinson, bless him, helped a lot there. By accident, no less. He had come over to my side and shoved his head and shoulders out, I guess to see what damfool thing I was up to, but once I saw him in my peripheral vision, I knew what I had to do. I *think* he was starting to say something inane like "What are you doing?" when I tucked in my legs, rocked on the rails, and stepped on his shoulders, but I'm not sure. I did knock him back into the stagecoach, though. So at least he didn't join the door on the ground.

There were three things on the top of the stagecoach: me, Wilkinson's baggage, and a surprised-looking ambusher. The ambusher had been yelling orders about stopping the frigging stage before the driver got a knife in the back, but he looked back at me pretty damn quick. And didn't look real ready to talk to *me*.

He wasn't quite into knife range, thanks to Wilkinson's ridiculously-sized luggage. I flicked a look down, saw how this stagecoach used quick-release fasteners, and gave the one by my foot a quick kick as I 'tried to get away' from the ambusher who was trying to get close enough to slice. He lunged; I cornered the luggage, just enough to avoid, and kicked free the second fastener in the process.

I figured he'd feint next time, and if he did I'd have to guess in which direction. That meant going to the next step. Well, hopefully two fasteners would be enough.

So I yelled out "HARD LEFT!" and waited to see what happened next.

What happened next was, the stage went hard left. I was prepared for it, and so was the ambusher. What he wasn't prepared for was getting about a hundred pounds worth of luggage smacking into him. Inertia: it's still a thing!

It didn't knock the guy off the stagecoach, mostly because his ankle got stuck under the luggage. It did knock him down, with a deep *thunk* as the back of his head met the wood. I didn't feel like taking chances, so I pulled out a sap and smacked him in the head before he could start thinking about recovering. Then I scrambled forward to the driver.

He had taken a bolt to the leg, and was looking kind of gray by now, but he was still in it to win it. "Repeating crossbow on my left!" he half-shouted, half-hissed. "Six-shooter!" I'd have preferred my pepperbox, but what the Hell. I pulled the crossbow off of its mounting and started looking for targets. The damned thing wouldn't have any range, but if the ambushers stayed out of it we'd get away anyway.

One of the horsemen tried his luck; he was good enough to draw and fire a bow while riding, and young enough to think he was immortal. He took his own shot, close enough so I could see his grin, then did that trick where somebody swings over the side of the horse just in time to avoid the return fire. His horse had barding on it, too: not much, but you don't need much to soak up a repeating crossbow bolt.

Unfortunately for him, I knew he'd try the maneuver. I also knew that for a moment his foot would be visible underneath the horse's belly. Hip-shooting may not be the most accurate thing in the world, but I'm a damned good shot, and I guessed right. And I don't care who you are: two crossbow bolts in the foot will wreck your day. The sudden pain must have wrecked his control, because he went tumbling onto the grass, dragged and battered until the stirrup gave way.

"You still grinning, asshole?" I shouted back at him as I emptied the rest of the crossbow at the suddenly thoughtful ambushers. They scattered, the idiots — even I couldn't hit them at that distance — but making them scatter was the idea. I wanted the time to reload.

#

No need to bother, though; by the time I'd slapped another magazine of bolts into the hopper, the cops had shown up. The surviving ambushers weren't dumb, so they turned tail and ran the minute the cavalry hove into view. Which meant they left behind their dead and wounded, but that's how bandits do.

I went back to retrieve my pepperbox, because it was expensive and I didn't know if I could find a replacement in Maysville.

It took longer than I expected to find it. Why, we must have been going fifteen miles an hour at one point!

Wilkinson was staring at his luggage when I came back. It was hanging off the side of the stagecoach by one strap, and looked pretty battered, but that's what luggage is for, right? I wouldn't really know, because I try to pack light when I'm on the job. Still, it *was* kind of my fault, so as I came to a stop next to him I said "You gonna need help getting it down the rest of the way?"

As if it had been waiting for me to say that, the last strap gave and the luggage dropped to the ground. The hinges didn't quite survive the impact, either. Hell, the whole thing practically smashed itself to splinters.

"Guess not," I said.

#

I didn't really worry about Wilkinson getting pissed at me for the way we got to Maysville, because I knew he'd be even more pissed by the way we were gonna get *out* of Maysville. I was right, too. He was not happy.

"What the Hell you mean, we're not going on the ferry?" he shouted. Which he could do, because when I rented our rooms for the night I decided to shell out a little extra for privacy. And security. I figured we could use the pampering.

I don't think Wilkinson noticed. Or maybe he just didn't like to stop in the middle of a whine-rant. "It's supposed to be real easy! We take the ferry across to Ohio, go up to Ripley, take the trade road to Hillsboro and go east to Chillicothe. That's three days, tops! Instead you want to go upriver? To *Portsmouth*? You know what's in Portsmouth?"

"Sure," I said. "Scum, and villainy. And an ass-ton of elves."

"Yeah," said Wilkinson. "Go figure, huh?"

Oh, hey, he's a human chauvinist, I thought. *Why am I not surprised?* Aloud, I said, "Say what you like about the knife-ears, but elves hate the Dominion too much to take one of their contracts. Which is more than I can say for the human villainous scum in Hillsboro. Or Ripley. Or, Hell, here."

Wilkinson made a face. "Everybody hates the Dominion," he muttered.

"Sure. Elves take it real personal, though. What with the breeding pits, and everything. Besides, this way we can go straight up the road to Chillicothe. They won't expect it."

"Why should they?" asked Wilkinson. "That's the Ghost Road. The Haunted Twenty-Three. Everybody stays the fuck away from there."

"Good," I said. "Which means no traffic. Besides, I hear the ghosts ain't much if you're smart about it."

"Well, I don't know the road at all," said Wilkinson in a huff. "I know how to get there from the west, which is the way you go if you're not *insane*."

"Insane would be going on the road where all the bandits are, Mister Wilkinson." I looked at him, steadily. "Or did you forget what the cops said?"

He flushed a little. The Kentucky Free State Police are all right, for cops. They only take bribes to ignore reasonable crimes, like smuggling booze and smokes; they keep their hands to themselves unless you're into that sort of thing; and when they investigate a robbery, they usually won't walk out with anything the original crooks somehow missed. But if you're a bandit, and they catch you, you're gonna tell them *everything*. Eventually.

And what they told me, after a suitable contribution to their widows-and-orphans fund, was that the ambushers had been absolutely hired to get the Raygun, kill Wilkinson, and capture me, and in pretty much that order. The cops were at least mildly curious as to why, so I asked them whether any of the ambushers had known about Wilkinson being a mage. I then swore them all to secrecy, and backed it up with another contribution to the fund. As I hoped, that piece of misdirection — Wilkinson had no magic whatsoever — and the bribes distracted them from asking any further, potentially awkward questions.

As I left the station, I contemplated how anybody could think that a straight-up bandit raid would work. I also wondered how long it had taken whoever was trying to bushwhack me to find a bunch idiotic enough to try it in the Free State itself. Hell, I was halfway sure the attempt was meant as a loud hint that I should stay on my side of the damned river.

But back to my conversation with my associate. I may have been a little sarcastic with him then. "So since the mage's clearly figured out I'm coming to zap him, *Mister* Wilkinson, I'm gonna assume they're smart enough to read a map, too. Fine. I'll go up to Portsmouth instead, maybe even frolic with the elves a little, and then sneak up north. You wanna jump ship, feel free."

#

Yeah, right. Like Wilkinson had any choice but to come along. I didn't know what contract he had with *Miss* Mehrotra and I didn't really care, either — but whatever it was, I figured it'd only pay off if I got the job done. And since I was still paying the expenses? Where I went, he had to follow.

And it wasn't like I was making him carry my gear, cook my food, or (ha!) share my bedroll. I'm not nasty. I wanted Wilkinson along because he really did still know the area and maybe the people around Chillicothe better than I did, and that'd probably be helpful. Unless it turned out not to be, but even then: so what? I had also brought along bear repellent for the trip, and we never even saw a bear. Should I blame the repellent for not coming in handy?

Well, maybe if the bear repellent pouted about it all the way from Maysville to Portsmouth. Two days by horse — not the best ones, but not the worst ones, either — and it would have been three except I got tired of the silent attitude to push the pace a little. Like it was my fault they didn't have an enchanted paddleboat route between the two towns!

I still wouldn't have bought tickets for one, though. It's harder to corner somebody on land than on water. And if I have to get away in a hurry, I'd rather ride than swim.

#

Portsmouth was great, though. In small doses. Even Wilkinson lightened up after we got there.

Elves are funny. Like, funny-ha-ha and funny-weird and funny-up-to-something, all at the same time. When they started fleeing from the Dominion a century or so ago, the Free State might have ended up encouraging the elves to keep going southeast into the Big Swampy, but it was real nice about it. We gave 'em gear and travel rations and weapons and maps of where all the really big nomad gangs hung out, and wouldn't you know it? Pretty soon all of the pains in the ass on our borders were too busy being dead to raid us anymore. The way I heard it, the Congresswoman who set the whole thing all up stole the idea from the Ancient Romans, or some other country from the Before Times. Whoever it was, those gals weren't dummies, because their trick worked like a charm for us.

But some of the elves stuck around, and they do their sticking in Portsmouth. In the finest tradition of the Free State, they get along by smuggling, playing the angles, and being somewhere convenient to somewhere else, and Portsmouth's a great place to do all three. South, the road leads to the Elf-lands; north, it's the Ghost Road.

You can imagine which way gets more traffic.

#

Wilkinson ended up volunteering to take point in tracking down a good guide for the Ghost Road. Which is to say, he valiantly volunteered to trawl through the dives and bordellos until he found somebody dumb enough to know the road, and smart enough not to try to rob us halfway through. I let him go off to his fun (which did sound like fun, dammit!) and told myself I could always go looking myself, once he failed, and that I was always planning to wait a couple of days anyway.

But damned if Wilkinson didn't find somebody who could do the job. Elf, interestingly. He called himself 'Captain Ilbrin Spring' and he dressed like an explorer from a play, but the gear was well-made and Ilbrin had the right kind of eyes and hands for somebody who liked to run around haunted woods. Which is to say, the hands never moved and the eyes never quite stayed still.

The only problem was that Ilbrin thought himself quite the dish. "The famous Lady Deckard and her equally famous treasure, featured in so many songs," he murmured over my fingers while bowing. "But the bards have betrayed me by not warning me of your dangerous allure." Although I will be fair: he did make the line sound good.

Wilkinson brayed laughter. He had a black eye and clearly hadn't slept much last night, but from the combination of scent of secondhand perfume and his own self-satisfied look I was guessing the guy didn't mind too much. "Barking up the wrong tree there, buddy," he said. "She ain't into grabbing what you're showing." Which was... rude, even for Wilkinson. But it was also true, and getting it out of the way early might be nice for a change.

Ilbrin flickered a dirty look at Wilkinson, but got the hint. He straightened and took the available chair. I gave my standard let's-get-to-work smile. "So," I said, "I understand you know the Ghost Road."

The elf showed a gratifying ability to get to the point. And not waste my time. "Yes, ma'am," he said. "It's a straight run up, about two days by foot. A day by coach, if you could get one up through there. But you can't, because horses don't like the Ghost Road. Critters in general don't care for it."

"Too spooky?" I asked.

Ilbrin shook his head. "Too noisy," he said. "The road, ah, it takes some getting used to. Most people can manage, after a while, but you *will* panic at least once and you *can* get yourself killed doing it. I mean it, ma'am. The first time you really *feel* the Ghost Road, it's gonna bowl you over. There's a reason why nobody takes it north if they don't have to, and with that *casgorn* perched up in Chillicothe, nobody these days thinks they have to." The elf carefully didn't look at my Raygun, and I just as carefully didn't say anything back.

"Wait," said Wilkinson. "You're saying two days now? I thought you could do it in one." There wasn't as much of a whine in his voice as I was expecting, but then both of us could read a map. A two days' walk sounded about right for a trip that long; and since we knew going in about how it was a no-fooling haunted road, it even sounded generous.

"No, Mr. Wilkinson," said Ilbrin. "I said it took two days on *foot*. I have a faster method. One which draws on the lost technology of the Old Americans themselves!" He bowed. "Assuming you can master it."

"Appeals to my self-pride don't work on me," I said, as I stood. Then I smiled, thinly. "But cutting our travel time in half does. Let's go see this mysterious technology of yours."

#

I'm not uneducated. I've seen pictures of Old American vehicles. And I can even tell apart things like 'trains' and 'cars' and 'suborbital hoppers.' But these things? They looked like kids' toys, only blown up to adult size.

Ilbrin clearly loved them, though. "The Old Americans called these 'tricycles'," he said as he polished the metal framework of one. "An *experienced* rider can get up fifteen miles per hour on them, even fully loaded, but we should be able to manage ten miles an hour, at least on the Ghost Road. Not many things like to grow on it."

Wilkinson frowned, but I understood. In my experience, everything the Old Americans ever built did either one of two things: last forever, or fall apart right away. Their roads were absolutely in the 'fall apart' category. But it sounded like the Ghost Road was an exception. "I'm surprised you're being so reasonable about the rental rate," I said. "These artifacts aren't exactly replaceable."

"Yes," said Ilbrin. He looked sad. "But there are not many other places in this fallen world where they can be ridden as they were meant to be. Besides, with two other riders I can bring more items north."

Ah, he's a smuggler, I assumed to myself. I then tacked on another thought: *And it's none of **my** business what **his** business is.* That's a pretty good life rule, right up to the second where it's not.

"All right," I said. "We'll try it." I mean, how hard could it be?

#

I screamed, but only inside my head. I did *not* frantically drive the tricycle into the underbrush by the side of the road, but it was a close thing; instead, I merely pushed the trike to the shoulder of the road and stopped dead. For the third time. Wilkinson had only had to stop twice, but he didn't look very eager to sneer at me. I swear, we had probably both sweated away five pounds apiece by now.

And anyone reading this would have done the exact same thing. Don't believe me? Fine: what do you think of when you hear the words 'Ghost Road?' Ghosts, right? You can see through them; maybe they're moaning, or got glowing eyes and chains; and they're hovering there, being all spooky. Or maybe they're reaching out to chill your bones and feed on your life force, because some ghosts can do that. But the thing is you're imagining human ghosts — or elvish ones, sure. Just how ghosts look, right?

Wrong. Not on the God-damned Ghost Road, they don't. They're giant blurs of light and sound which run roaring through you at, if you believe the few remaining signs on the sides, sixty or seventy miles an hour. It doesn't matter they're intangible, because the monkey part of your brain doesn't believe in ghosts. All it knows is that a monster just showed up — and since the monkey brain *does* believe in monsters, it does the smart thing, and makes you hide.

Hence, the underbrush. I glared at Ilbrin, who had politely paused his own tricycle to wait while we pulled ourselves out of the woods. "How do you *do* this?" I yelled.

"Practice," Ilbrin said dryly. "Here, watch." He stood up from his tricycle, stooped to pick up two stones, then walked onto the cracked but serviceable black stuff the Old Americans used for their roads. He stood there as ghostly blurs sped past him, not even reacting when one ghastly snake-like spectral monstrosity drove straight *through* him with an endless low moan. He threw one rock after it: we watched as it passed through the various apparitions on the road with no effect on either the apparition, or the rock.

"See?" said Ilbrin. "They're not real when they're like this. You probably think you knew that already, because I told you before: but you have to *feel* it, in your gut. Don't worry, there's a trick to it."

"And that is?" said Wilkinson, and this time I heard the hint of a sneer. I didn't mind so much, though, because Ilbrin was maybe being a little smug about how ragged we were acting. But if the elf noticed, he didn't show it. Instead, he just waved us out to the black-topped road.

Gingerly, we followed him. I got run through at least twice, and the worst part was how there wasn't any physical impact. My head and my gut really were having an argument over how bad the situation was, and my head wasn't winning. But we both made it; Wilkinson was, whatever his other faults, not a coward. He saw no reason not to keep jumping at the sudden blasts of light and sound, and neither did I.

"Good," said Ilbrin, once we had joined him. "Now, it's important you don't move around too much for this next part. Trust me on this." He turned until he was facing back the way we came, and threw the rock past the white lines dividing the Ghost Road in two.

A rushing specter smashed into the rock while it was still mid-air. The specter was unaffected; the rock disintegrated, with all the pieces scattering away from us. Ilbrin turned back.

"That's one of the reasons people don't travel the Ghost Road," he said. "They don't know the secret: *stay on the fucking right*. Or they panic and jump left when they should have jumped right, or they don't realize, coming back, it's *your* right you have to fucking stay on. Or they started out by trying to ride it on horseback, which might as well be suicide. But now you two know. Tell your guts: *We'll be fine as long as we stay on the fucking right* and your guts will listen to you. Guts are weird that way." He got back onto his tricycle; after a moment, we followed suit.

And damned if Ilbrin wasn't right; it *was* a lot less scary once I knew what the rules were. The rules didn't make a lot of mundane sense, sure. But you get used to that, with magic.

#

We made Deadman's Crossing by nightfall, screaming or not. And I, for one, wasn't ready to do the run again in a hurry. The living should not walk among the ghosts.

It wasn't the things on the Ghost Road itself. Those were like golems, or a river. They were doing what they were doing, and if you did something dangerous around them they'd just let you die and not care. There was nothing *personal* about them, or what they'd do to you if you didn't mind your step.

The *human* ghosts were the problem. There were a few abandoned towns on one side or the other of the Ghost Road, and those were creepy enough: all that valuable salvage, being left to rot where it stood because nobody had dared go get it. We've picked the bones of the Old Americans pretty clean by now, which just makes the places we won't loot stand out.

But there were two places on the Ghost Road where it went *through* an Old American town, and in both cases Ilbrin insisted we were not to stop, not to stop, and above all: **not to stop**. "There's nobody left in those towns to save," he said. "You hear a voice calling out for help, that's either a lie or they deserve to be there. Either way, just keep on going. And stay on the fucking Ghost Road."

We saw what he meant at the first town (the signs called it Lucasville). At first, the people appearing at the side of the road didn't look all that much like ghosts, although the old-fashioned clothes gave them away. But you could see the sun shine through them, a little, and when they smiled and tried to talk at us no sound came out. Oh, and sure, when they realized we weren't stopping then their faces distorted into living monster masks and their hands became distorted claws. Your standard malevolent ghosts, in other words.

But they couldn't follow us very far. After we got out of range of Lucasville, Ilbrin stopped us for a rest break and some water

— and an explanation. "It's the Road doing it," he said. "It's like an anchor for the towns, keeps the ghosts stuck here who are too heavy to break free."

"How does a ghost get heavy?" asked Wilkinson. I had to admit, I was wondering the same thing. And I guessed I probably wasn't going to like the answer.

And I didn't. "Sin, usually," said Ilbrin. "It's worse there in Lucasville because the Old Americans had a prison east of the town, but it ain't gonna be safe when we go through Waverly up north, either. But just keep moving on the trikes and stay on the fucking road and you'll be fine."

"What happens if they catch us?" I asked.

Ilbrin shrugged. "They'll eat you," he said, matter-of-factly. "Spirits or not, they'll chow you down, no problem. But they can't get on the Ghost Road. Something about the spell. Or curse."

"You could have mentioned all of this before," said Wilkinson. It was a banner day for him to say the things I wanted to! Only I'd have been less snide about it.

But Ilbrin just thought it was funny. "Neighbor, this is the *Ghost Road*," he said. "Spoken of in terror by everybody around it. What were you expecting, a couple of specters in a sheet?"

#

Waverly was almost bad.

Wasn't so much the ghosts. They were smarter than the ones down south, and maybe if we hadn't been warned ahead of time I might have done something stupid when I heard what sounded like a child crying. I kind of almost hope I would have been that stupid; this life of mine isn't for the squeamish but you don't want to be the kind who ignores a kid in trouble, you know?

The trouble was there was a supermarket in the town. A God-damned *supermarket*. Ghost Road or no Ghost Road, hungry spirits or not; somebody should have come in and burned that zombie-attracting sumbitch *down*.

"This, you should have told us about!" I snarled at Ilbrin as we frantically pedaled north. Behind us, the undead from the supermarket followed. They weren't quick, but they'd follow us forever. Or until they ate us.

"They're not always there," said Ilbrin. He sounded disgustingly carefree about it. "Most trips, there aren't enough corpses to form a swarm!"

"*Most* trips?" said Wilkinson, panting. He was the least in shape of the three of us, though he wasn't really flabby. "Where are the new corpses coming from?"

"The ghosts don't actually *eat* people," explained Ilbrin over his shoulder. "What, you thought they did?"

"You said they did!"

"I meant the life force! Ghosts can't eat flesh! That's just *silly*! And eyes on the road!"

"You first!"

"I know where I'm going— oh, crap," Ilbrin said, as he swerved to avoid a fallen, and gnawed, tree branch. I was hoping it was ghosts or zombies doing the gnawing; adding Dire Critters to the mix seemed a bit much. "Besides, there's a plan for this!"

"When are you gonna tell us it?" yelled Wilkinson. "When we're back in Portsmouth?"

"When we're out of town!" said Ilbrin. "Don't worry, we'll be fine."

So, yeah, there's when *I* began to worry.

#

I saw the plan loom up ahead of me, and I was not happy about it. I mean, *really*? This is what we were going with?

The plan looked like a giant L, put on its side, with the long side of the L parallel to the roadway and jammed up against what looked like a godawful tangle of wood and metal, and the short one blocking the right lane. The long side had all sorts of spikes and barbs hammered into it: a broad metal sheet leaned up against the short side, probably for a ramp. Ilbrin headed straight for it without stopping.

Damned if I could see any other options except following. Neither could Wilkinson, and there was almost a nasty little spill as he and tried to drive our trikes up the ramp at the same time. But I decided to let him go first, because you always want the panicky ones in front of you, instead of behind. That way you know when he finally takes a runner.

The ramp was alarmingly off-center as my trike took the ramp, but it held long enough for me to hit the crest — and go flying, because there wasn't a ramp on the other side. Just the fucking hard blacktop beyond, and if I wasn't wearing the bite guard Ilbrin had given us and made us put on I'd have lost a tooth from the impact. As it was, Wilkinson had a bloody nose and a pissed-off look that wasn't directed at me for a change.

Ilbrin didn't bother to apologize, or even visibly care. Instead, he had already dismounted, run over to the barricade, and was now using a long stick to shove the ramp completely off the top. It hit the ground with a loud clang which probably attracted all the zombies who weren't following us already, but Ilbrin didn't seem to mind.

"And now," he said with a typically elvish grin, "we wait."

"For what?" I asked. The first zombies were arriving by then. We all had zombie cures in our first-aid kits, of course, but they could still just eat us.

The grin got wider. "For the Ghost Road to do its magic."

And, okay, it turned out to be a good trick. Shamblers aren't intelligent but they can figure out how to get to the tasty brains, if given options. In this case? Over wasn't going to happen, and to the right there were a lot of pointy sticks which a zombie would get hung up on. But to the left, hey! That was clear. So they started going to the left.

Only the left was over the line in the middle of the road, so most of the zombies got pulped as soon as they shambled into it. Only two or three were able to get around the corner in time, and Ilbrin didn't bother to kill them, or even get off of the trike; he just used the stick to shove them back into ghost-traffic. It was a real interesting operation he had going on there. It was also a gory mess, but then I wasn't going to be the one cleaning it up.

"What do you do when you're going the other way?" Wilkinson asked. He had parked on the shoulder and was now looking at the barricade from the other side, which from this angle mostly looked like two Old American hovertrucks put on their sides and fused together. Two pulleys and chains hinted on how the ramp was going to be put back in position. I've seen worse anti-zombie measures, although using the Ghost Road was cheating a little.

"Mostly I avoid the wet spots," said Ilbrin. "All the big bits will get pushed to the sides by the time I get back. And it'll take the ghosts a while to collect more shamblers anyway."

"Where are they getting more bodies from?" I asked.

"Don't you mean 'us'?" *Wilkinson* asked, more or less at the same time.

"The southbound part of the Ghost Road's been busier since That Guy" — Ilbrin jerked his head in the general direction of Chillicothe — "took over. The ones that get this far usually don't know about the ghosts — and even if they do, a lot of 'em can't really outrun the specters. And since anybody who makes it to Portsmouth isn't ever going back this way..." He looked a little chagrined at my slight look of outrage. "Look, the folks at Deadman's Crossing put up signs," he said. "But sometimes the people fleeing That Guy don't care about signs, or, Hell, can't even read them. All they see is a nice, open road, and once the survivors figure out to stay on the fucking right they think it's a clear run down the line. If I see somebody going the other way, I tell them the problem, but it's a little hard to backtrack once you're on it."

He used the stick to hook the two chains by their handles and fling them in our direction. "Come on," he said. "Let's get the ramp up. This batch of shamblers are all pate by now." Perforce, we used our bikes to pull the ramp back up.

Which turned out to be just annoying enough to distract us from asking further nosy questions. In retrospect, I should have paid more attention to how Ilbrin answered my question about the bodies, and kind of ignored Wilkinson's about what Ilbrin's future plans were. Hindsight, huh?

#

After that, the rest of the trip was no big deal. Ilbrin didn't take us all the way to the end of the Ghost Road; there was a side smuggler's trail which moved us east. It also moved us away from screaming metal and ravenous human ghosts, which was one hell of an improvement.

I've been in Deadman's Crossing a dozen times, even though I'd never been there before, and I don't plan on ever going back. These places are always the same. Whenever a bastard of a warlord has taken over somewhere but still wants to do business with the 'respectable' people, you get a Deadman's Crossing. There's a bunch of inns, a lot of warehouses with big locks and bigger guards, at least two brothels, and one reformer from out of town trying to sweep back the spiritual muck with a rake.

Some people assume places like this would sound like Heaven to me, but they'd be wrong. I prefer that my sin and debauchery *break* the rules. Places where there aren't any rules to break at all aren't real safe unless you have somebody to watch your back. Or, better yet, somebodies.

We started off right away by losing Ilbrin's services. He had been forthright about it, once we were actually in town; now we had gotten to Deadman's Crossing, Wilkinson and me were on our own. And he wouldn't stick around on "retainer" until we needed to go back, either. It turned out that even my retainer could be outbid.

"Nothing personal, Lady Deckard," Ilbrin explained. "But I've got two refugees willing to pay for the privilege of bringing my trikes home for me. In opals."

I didn't get it, but Wilkinson did. "You sure you want to risk helping out-of-favor courtiers?" he asked. "What if somebody comes after you?"

"If they try it on a horse, they won't get far," replied Ilbrin. He touched his hat. "Sir, ma'am. Good luck with whatever it is you plan to be doing." With a nod, he walked out the door of the cheap room we had rented.

Wilkinson looked at me, but when he saw I had already grabbed my go-bag he scowled and got his own. At least he had one by now; he wasn't dumb, really. Just somebody who needed a bit of a prod and a kick to learn things. As he popped open the window, Wilkinson said, "I figure there's only a three-in-ten chance he's gonna sell our location... huh. This window's bars come right off."

"I *hope* so," I said. "I paid enough in advance for a room we could get out of. And, yeah, more likely than not he stays bought. But, hell, better safe than sorry, right?" But Wilkinson was already out the window. I shook my head as I joined him. What if there had been a guy with a crossbow out there?

#

To this day, I don't know if Ilbrin *did* sell us out. We didn't stick around long enough to find out, and there wasn't anything in the luggage *I* left behind worth going back for. And I haven't been back to Portsmouth, either. If I'm going to visit an elven town soaked in danger and debauchery, I'll just go vacation in New Havana again.

The two of us didn't have any trouble getting out of Deadman's Crossing. Sort of. There was the damned fool who tried to mug us, but he somehow managed to no-fooling, for-real shoot himself in the foot. It was so bad I almost took pity on the guy and tipped him a few Hershey credits; in the end I just kept Wilkinson from stabbing the thief while he was down. A surprisingly ruthless bastard, our Mr. Wilkinson. At least, when he had the drop on somebody. A thing to remember about him, to be sure.

But aside from *that* we easily got ourselves hired to help lug stuff into Chillicothe on the morning run. Apparently many of the locals didn't like to take the job. Which should have maybe been a hint.

#

I'd never been to Chillicothe before, but I could tell the damn place was going downhill, fast. I got nothing against mages — I try not to be stupid — and I'm not saying that mage-kings are any worse than any other kind of politician. But mage-*warlords* aren't real nice to be around. People who get off on wearing spikes and skulls to work get even *worse* when they can also set fire to people with their minds. They usually flame out pretty quick, which is great if you take the long view, but not so great when all you can see is the nasty grin and the staff of lightning powering up.

Kragnor didn't seem to be too far along his personal narrative arc, either, more's the pity; he was setting up the area around the ruins of the Old American city on strict 'slave plantation' lines, and about the only thing you could say about his rule was that the man seemed to understand that cholera and ringworm were things. The slaves in the fields were only slightly underweight, but their overseers seemed to make up for it with regular beatings. From where I sat (Wilkinson and I had both gotten driver/guard duty on one of the wagons), the place looked like it would go from 'tense, but controlled' to 'screaming slave revolt' in about two hours. Which gave us a nice rule of thumb of how fast to get out of Chillicothe once I finished the job.

One thing I noticed right away: no other mages. Wilkinson shrugged when I discreetly pointed it out. "I heard this guy doesn't like the competition," he said. "He thinks there's only room for one mage around here, and it's gonna be him. No exceptions, either."

"I'm not surprised," I said. "What does he do with any mages he does nab? Kill 'em?"

"Worse." Wilkinson shook his head in disgust. "He sells 'em to the Dominion."

Which *did* surprise me. And it disgusted me, too. They say the Universal Dominion's a mage empire, but it's really an *Archmage* empire. Any regular mage who gets grabbed by the Dominion gets used up quick unless she can show she's even more of a vicious bastard than her superiors. It works for them, kind of, but there's a reason why everybody hates the Dominion. They're just never quite weak enough for the rest of us to squish safely.

But selling your fellow-mages to the Dominion? "He better hope nobody he sold survived over there," I said almost jovially. "That could make for an interesting reunion. Oh, hey, city wall ahead."

Which meant the 'ruin' wasn't one, anymore: the Old Americans weren't big on putting walls around their towns. This one looked like salvaged brick and stone, which made sense. Not the best construction I've ever seen, but not bad for slave-work. The gate was manned by guards in Kragnor's livery (black, with a black six-spiked circle nestled in red and black concentric hexagons); their gear did *not* look slave-made.

Which we had a perfect opportunity to see, once we went through the gates and to the depot yard. When I dismounted to help lead the horses to the trough, I turned to see six guards pointing crossbows at me — and at Wilkinson, still sitting on the seat. He had his hands up, which on reflection seemed like a good idea, so I did the same thing.

"All right, lads," I said, and I flattered myself I didn't sound too worried. "I've done this dance before. You want me to take it nice and slow, right?" You never know. Sometimes being a good sport about being captured buys you a little, you know?

#

Yeah, and sometimes it doesn't.

Oh, they didn't *really* play. Just a few punches where it wouldn't immediately show and they took my pants. It could have been worse. I mean, you get a certain kind of guy who likes to remind you with his fists just who the boss is, but I worked out quick how they had orders not to go too far. It felt sort of like they wanted to remind me who *their* boss was, and I figure the whole thing was supposed to frighten me.

I almost feel bad for Wilkinson, though; when they tossed my bags and found the Raygun in my luggage, my companion suddenly got the lion's share of the smacking around. Again, not enough for anything permanent, but he had a split lip and a black eye afterward. And he was sending an even blacker glare my way. What, like this was *my* fault?

#

"This is all your fault," said the so-called 'Kragnor the Ambitious' — on second thought: drop the 'so-called.' The epithet was accurate enough and I don't blame a mage for wanting to swap out their birth name for something a little less embarrassing. I mean, I'm walking around with the name 'Mildred' hung around my neck. I absolutely understand the urge for a little reinvention.

In person, Kragnor wasn't as good-looking as he thought he was. Oh, the face was regular and the body was muscular, but I could still tell he wasn't born that way. But I didn't have him pegged as somebody who had been really deformed, or just ugly: transform one of them, and they're just too damned happy at being finally "fixed" to sweat the small stuff. Kragnor had the air of somebody who was never satisfied. Which, I guess, explained the 'Ambitious' part.

But I, as they say, digress. Kragnor also had the look of a monologuer, God bless him: "You technology-worshiping idiots are all the same. You constantly underestimate us. 'Ooh!'" he said, in a high falsetto which was *completely* slanderous towards me, "'He's expecting me to come in from the north, so I'll come from the south, instead! He doesn't have one of those photo-graphs of me, so I can sneak in!'"

Kragnor laughed, in a credibly nasty voice. "Because, of course, a stupid mage like me could never think to make a magical image of you and burn it into all of my guards' brains. They recognized you on sight, Ms. Deckard. If you had come ten years from now, they still would have recognized you. You never had a chance."

I thought of the implications, considered how the victims were all thugs working for a mage-warlord, and decided to wince anyway. Kragnor took my distaste for sentimentality and laughed again. "I should be flattered. The holder of the last Raygun in the world, come to assassinate me! Me!"

The guards had naturally already relieved me of my Raygun;

it had been lying in his lap as he been spouting off. Kragnor lifted the Raygun out of its holster, and looked at it. "I have to admit, though: for all their foolish ways, the Old Americans knew how to make murder pretty enough. This weapon says 'killer' in every smooth line. You look at it, and you know that whoever bears it must be an ang..." he grimaced, as if remembering something, "...a minion of Death."

He looked at it again — and casually tossed it on a pillow. "Such a shame it's a fake, hey?"

Wilkinson and I both had sudden intakes of breath; Kragnor seemed more interested in my companion's reaction. "Oh, you didn't know?" he said, faux-jovially. "Deckard's a complete fraud. When I found out there was a contract put out on me, I naturally investigated who would be sent to do the job. I discovered something most interesting; nobody's actually seen the Raygun in action in years. Decades, really."

"The jobs still got done!" I was trying for a combination of 'badly trying to bluff' and 'defensive' in my tone, there. It must have worked, because Kragnor shrugged, well-pleased with himself.

"A fair point, Ms. Deckard. You did do the jobs — but it always turned out that nobody ever saw the actual attack. All they found afterward was a burned corpse. And if one of your employers suspected you were a fake, so what? The job got done. How you did it was your affair, really."

"Yes, it was." That time I was trying for 'salvaging what was left of my dignity' while viewing the room. There were three guards, but they were all breathing at the same time and they blinked as little as possible. Those were symptoms of a pretty nasty spell which linked the victims' heartbeats to somebody else's. When he died, they died. The Dominion loved that particular magic, which meant they really were working with Kragnor. I didn't need proof to keep on with doing the job, but it's nice to know what's up, hey?

"But you're still a fake and a fraud," said Kragnor. Some people just can't ever let shit go. "Making people believe in that,

that, that *myth* of the old world. The world which men like me destroyed! We have no need for 'science' or 'rationality' or the mewling morals springing from them! We will have power, instead! And the pathetic worms like you, with your conniving and trickery, will be dragged out into the light and burned by our might!"

Full points for ranting, there, but Kragnor looked like the kind of villain who needed a call-and-response for his best work. I obliged, with a slight hesitation: "Tri... trickery?" And I flicked my eyes at Wilkinson, *almost* subtly.

"Oh, yes, trickery." Kragnor sneered at me. "My minions found no sign of the lightning wand or whatever *real* weapon you must normally use in your assassinations, so you must have had a different plan in mind. Let me guess: you *wanted* to get captured, didn't you?"

He took my silence for assent. "It's a gambit for stupid stories, you know," Kragnor said. "Use a decoy to penetrate the hero's defenses, confront him in his lair, keep him focused on the decoy while the true threat prepares a treacherous spell. Only I'm smarter than the usual hero, and I'm certainly smarter than you. You can't use magic to kill me, now — and you could never use technology."

This would be the really risky part. "Magic?" I quavered, and screwed up my head like I was trying to somehow look inside it. "Get out of my head!" I half-yelled. What I did next would depend on his response...

Fortunately, Kragnor was the kind of guy who couldn't resist showing contempt to a helpless captive. "Please," he almost spat. "Like I would waste an anti-magic charm on you." He jerked his head towards Wilkinson. "It's on *him*. And it'll stay on your mage until the Dominion comes to collect my goodwill gift to them."

Perfect, I thought — and then decided, *Oh, why the Hell not?* So I said "Perfect" aloud, and before he could quite react I said a certain word and the room erupted in crackles and ozone.

I had my eyes closed for it all. When I opened them, Kragnor and his guards were all on the floor. The guards were untouched; Kragnor... wasn't. It wasn't pretty, but then it never is.

I spat out another syllable and the locks on my chains snapped. And if you think it's easy to cast spells without gestures: well, it's not. It's almost as hard as keeping every trace of your magical powers hidden from other mages. But not freaking out on the damned Ghost Road was even harder than either of those, and you don't carry the Raygun unless you have complete control of yourself. Always.

I grabbed the Raygun and its holster, first thing. Then I went to Wilkinson. "Hold still," I muttered as I popped off his own chains with precise jolts of sorcery; I looked at the anti-magic charm on his ankle, but decided a blast of lightning would do neither him or his ankle any good. We'd get it off later.

"We need to go," I said. A sudden breeze made me scowl. "Just as soon as I find my damned pants."

#

I found pants. They weren't *my* pants, but they were clean and fit — so what the Hell, right? I was just grateful Kragnor apparently collected boots, because mine were in his private sanctum, just waiting to be mounted to the wall along with all the others. Strike that: I was grateful and *appalled.*

Why were we in the sanctum? For the paperwork. Always grab important-looking paperwork on your way out of the impromptu overthrowing of a warlord's regime — oh, yeah, the good people of Chillicothe figured out right away what happened when half the guards fell over dead. At least, that's why I assumed all the nicer-looking buildings in the city were burning as we ducked out of Kragnor's 'palace' and headed west.

I figured the two of us could get away easily enough in the chaos, and I was right. There was one bravo who thought we looked like mage-loving bastards, but I didn't even slow down for him. Most people have to work themselves up to fight, you know what I mean? I don't, which is why he ended up whimpering around the knife in his thigh as we left.

Wilkinson seemed still a little peeved at how I had used him as a decoy, which would be fine as long as he got over it eventually. He still sneered, "What, no Raygun?"

"I had a knife." In fact, I had three knives, a sword, and a shield which felt lighter than it should have been.

"You also have magic." Wilkinson seemed *very* upset. I didn't figure him for a mage-hater, but a lot of people are. Or maybe he just didn't like how *I* had it, which was too bad for him.

"I'm not going to cast a spell in this *town*, Wilkinson. Not today. Not the next time I visit, either, assuming I'm stupid enough to ever come back here. Hold up, there are guards at the gate."

Wilkinson laughed. "*These* oafs? I got this." I was surprised to hear it, but I let him have his head.

And, you know? It wasn't a bad technique, actually. Wilkinson walked up, bold as brass, with another looted sword in one hand and a coin bag in the other. He tossed the bag on the ground, lifted the sword, and looked at the guards.

They weren't real guards, obviously. Hell, I don't know why they were on the gate. Somebody told 'em to watch it, probably. But they were smart enough to figure out the difference between a bribe and fighting two people with swords and blood on their clothes (even if the blood was mostly ours). They got out of our way.

I wonder if it would have made any difference if I had told Wilkinson how slick a trick it was? Ehh, probably not. But I still should have, maybe.

Oh, well.

#

I blame myself for what happened to Wilkinson. Oh, I don't feel *guilty*, really; he brought it all down on his own head. But I'm not the easiest person to work for, especially when you don't think you should be working for me in the first place. And that's probably what it came down to. He had to work for me, and I guess the money the Hershey Consortium was paying him just wasn't worth enough.

Wilkinson got me pretty slick, too. I had forgotten about

the ankle bracelet until we camped for the night and I came back from grabbing firewood to see him on the ground. He was working on the lock with a set of picks he either had and kept, or found somewhere. The picks slipped, he swore mildly, and then looked up at me. "I need two hands for this," Wilkinson said. "Can you hold the lock stable for me?" His request seemed reasonable, so I squatted down to help him.

...Only to have him pop open the lock in a flash, slap the bracelet around my wrist, and lock it shut again. Then he skittered away, trying to get out of range before I could react. Not that it mattered: ever have your magical abilities get suddenly taken away? It's distracting, for just long enough.

And when I did realize what happened, he was already out of immediate range, and holding a club. "Don't be stupid, Deckard," he said. "This doesn't have to end with you dead."

I had instinctively put my hand near to the holster holding the Raygun (which was still there, thank God). But I didn't draw it, because I'm *not* stupid. Even if it was for different reasons than Wilkinson thought. But the situation could still be salvaged: "What's the deal here, Wilkinson?" I asked. "Trying to get all the reward money for yourself?"

"Ha!" he said. "No, I won't get a dime of your reward money if you die. They made sure to tell me. Hell, I get a bonus if you come back alive." *Well, **shit**, I thought. They might have mentioned that to me.* "But I want the damned Raygun."

"What for?" I asked him. "You heard Kragnor say it doesn't work, remember?"

"Yeah, I heard him. Still worth a hell of a lot of money though, in the right hands. Maybe the rich snot from the Consortium, maybe an elf sea-baron down south, maybe even the King of New California. People just eat this Old American shit up, don't they, Deckard?"

I assume he took my silence as consent. "Yeah, they do. Kragnor was right about one thing: you've been scamming people with your 'Raygun' for years. Pretending to be something you're not for higher fees. Making everybody think how the old stuff

was still out there and working, just waiting for us to figure out how to use it again. Well, Deckard, it's not.

"So here's what we're gonna do, Deckard. You're gonna take off the Raygun, drop it on the ground there, and I'm gonna grab it and leave. By the time you get the charm off, I'll be out of here — I know how to keep a mage from following me, don't you worry — and we'll never see each other again."

What I could see of Wilkinson's face didn't reassure me. Neither did what he said next: "The other option, I come over there, beat you fucking unconscious, and I take it anyway. I kinda want to do that, Deckard. The longer you take to make the decision, the harder it's gonna be to keep me from stopping, hey?"

Would you believe I actually considered it? But I decided at the end that I just didn't trust him not to kill me. So I pulled out the Raygun and said, "Different deal, Wilkinson. You get the hell out of here, get your fee from *Miss* Mehrotra on a different day than I do, and we go with the 'never see each other again' bit. Otherwise" — and here I pointed the Raygun right at his face — "go to Hell."

Wilkinson laughed. "I was hoping you'd say that. Nice bluff, Deckard, but you don't got any magic, and your gun doesn't work." He took a step forward.

So I shot him in the head.

#

If you were expecting me to say something quip-like, sorry to disappoint you. At the time I was too busy for the next five minutes trying to keep the God-damned plasma regulator on the Raygun from exploding. Or whatever it was called; the person who passed the Raygun along to me didn't really know too much about it, either. Just that it made this weird whine and got stupid-ass hot and how this one doohickey started flashing red whenever you fired it, so just do these things to the handle and hope nothing goes boom, okay?

And eventually the whine died away and things cooled down and the flashing stopped. It came real close, though. Close to what, I didn't know, and didn't want to know. All I knew was, I didn't want to be there when it finally went bad forever.

By then it seemed mean to be rude to Wilkinson's burnt-skull corpse. I did say, "You weren't *completely* wrong about the fraud part," but quietly. I figured it would do for a funeral eulogy.

Afterward? I popped the lock off of the charm, pocketed it — those things are worth money — and broke camp. There was a trading post at Hillsboro, east of here, and from there a coach to Maysville and civilization. I had a bounty to get.

Wilkinson? I left him where he lay. For all I know, he's still there. It's a shame, but he made his choice.

#

And so it ended as it began: with me in an Old Louisville bar, looking over the papers *Miss* Mehrotra had given me. This was a much more festive sort of paperwork, though. I liked the sight of all those zeroes.

I had told *Miss* Mehrotra about what happened, on the principle it didn't matter anyway. Also, if my zapping Wilkinson in self-defense was going to cause trouble with the Consortium, it was best I find out now. Turns out I needn't have worried: *Miss* Mehrotra took his would-be bushwhacking almost personally.

"He was fortunate he did not live to try to sell your weapon to the Consortium," she sniffed. I fancied I almost saw a whiff of steam come out of her nose, she was so quietly angry. "You would have gotten your property back, with our apologies. We do not tolerate thievery in our ranks."

I picked up my drink. Surprisingly, *Miss* Mehrotra drank whiskey, neat. "Fortunate? I ended up blowing his damfool head off."

"I stand by my statement. And he should have known better." *Miss* Mehrotra went so far as to smile. "I believe this settles our business here. Do enjoy your fee... I am sorry, Ms. Deckard: was there something else?"

"Yes," I said as I put down my drink. "I have something more for you." I shoved a package across the table.

"More papers?" She sounded slightly surprised; I had handed over the ones we had found in Kragnor's study, and taken only a minor, almost token bonus for my share. The rest of the reward money could go to Wilkinson's heirs, if he had any. I didn't know, I didn't really care, but you never knew. They might have been alright people.

When she opened the package, she almost blinked when she saw the Raygun inside. "Interesting," she finally managed. "What is the offering price?"

Instead of answering directly, I said, "Confirm something for me, *Miss* Mehrotra: the Great Wyrm of Philadelphia resides in territory now claimed by the Hershey Consortium, right?"

She flickered a look at me before responding. "Yes, she does."

"And you folks are on good terms with her, right?"

"That would," said *Miss* Mehrotra, "be a reasonable but incomplete way of putting it."

"So would 'Well, she's *actually* the Chairman of the Board, so yes.' No, don't answer," I went on. "Hell, I'd put the dragon in charge, too. I hear she's real smart and doesn't eat people, so why not? I also hear she likes unique things. Well, the Raygun there is as unique as it gets."

"True. And alas," said *Miss* Mehrota. "But it is still in use."

"Maybe it shouldn't be. Definitely I shouldn't be using it." I leaned forward. "I don't mind killing bad people, but I've been doing it too long to think I'm immortal. It's time to get out of the business, now that I'm rich. And anybody I gave it to would probably burn her hands off the second, third time they fired it. So... let the Great Wyrm have it as a gift. It'll be safe there, and so will everybody else."

"I will not say 'no' to your offer," *Miss* Mehrota said very quickly, and slid the package to her side. She looked at me. "And despite your intentions, you will not find the Consortium unappreciative of this gift. But there is more, isn't there?"

I considered it. "Only that Wilkinson and Kragnor both *did* have a point, damn them both. It's from the old days. It probably *is* the last Raygun in the world. Maybe it's time we let go what we can't bring back."

"In that spirit, I agree," said Miss Mehrotra. Her hand was now resting on the Raygun, in a way which was possessive and protective at once. "But perhaps it would be better to say, 'what we cannot bring back, *yet*'."

"Good luck having that happen as long as those bastards in the Dominion are around," I said as I downed my drink. In my head, I was already planning my trip to New Havana. I half-debated suggesting she join me, but I can tell when somebody's just not interested. Besides, *Miss* Mehotra was too busy narrowing her eyes at the mention of the Dominion. Hell, in the darkness of Gentleman Jack's they almost *glittered*.

"I have come to the same conclusion," she hissed.

A BARGAIN WITH YIG

Occupied Deseret
2456 AD

Mark Smith would never forget the sound his last surviving bodyguard made as the patrol-monster's stinger plunged into the man's gut. It wasn't even a painful noise, mostly; more like one of surprise and despair. It was the kind of sound you made when you finally admitted to yourself how all was lost, and hope was dead.

Mark had made that sound himself a few days ago, after he had watched the last regiment of his father's Presidential Guard — well, by then he supposed they had the dubious honor of being *his* Presidential Guard — get ripped apart by five times their number of Universal Dominion slave-soldiers. The regiment had died well, savaging the enemy to a standstill until the last Deseret trooper was dead at the top of a pile of Dominion corpses. All so Mark Smith, hereditary President of Deseret, could run away. Which meant they had died for absolutely nothing.

Well, his surviving guards might have disagreed; but then, what did they know? The last one had just been gut-stabbed by a Dominion patrol-monster, which looked like a horrible, pointless way to die. As Mark assumed he was about to personally find out.

Mark had a very good sword on his belt, as befitted the heir of what used to be Deseret, industrious realm of the Mountain West. He even managed to get it out and readied as the patrol-monster finished yanking its stinger out of the guard's guts. Mark did not have the worst combat stance in the world, as even a half-spoiled and frivolous prince can learn much from the kind of swords-masters his father could afford — but truthfully, neither the sword nor the man was up to the task of facing off a Dominion battle-monster. If Mark had been asked what he was thinking right then, he would have replied he was too much of a coward to *not* die as well as he could.

The thing about to kill him looked like a scorpion large enough to ride, with a disturbingly prehensile stinger and an even more disturbing purpose in its movements. The first swing of the patrol-monster's stinger almost indulgently batted Mark's sword out of his hand and into the underbrush. It then scuttled towards him, rocking from side to side, but holding off on striking again. Mark could see his own reflections in its faceted eyes, and whether by magic or imagination he thought those reflections were grinning back at him with pure anticipatory malice. The patrol-monster clearly was ready to *play* with its food a little.

The thought of *that* fate might have paralyzed Mark; instead, the sudden spurt of anger cut through the miasma of fear. "Come on, then!" he snarled, his too-pampered hands stiffening into as close to claws as he could manage. "Or I'll come to you!"

Mark was never sure how much Trade English a Dominion monster could understand, but he always thought the tone at least broke through where the words did not. The patrol-monster focused on him, and suddenly somehow appeared even more dangerous than before. Its stinger raised itself up, clearly ready to strike long before Mark could close the distance and rip those mocking reflections out of the monster's eyes with his bare hands. Mark charged anyway...

...only to see his guard, his gut an abomination of red and yellow, leap onto the back of the patrol-monster in joint-cracking desperation. One hand carried a knife, which the guard used to strike at the scales on the monster's back; the other ripped off one loosened scale as it screamed far too like a human. The stinger instinctively struck, but missed — and then the guard grabbed the stinger-tip, and slammed it into the monster's now-exposed flesh.

It seemed patrol-monsters were not immune to their own venom. The monster threw the guard off to one side as it rolled and writhed and convulsed; Mark rushed to pull his rescuer away before he was trampled. There was a cave nearby; the one he had been trying to reach before being ambushed, in fact. Perhaps there was still something Mark could do for his last companion there.

#

Mark Smith tried to close the eyes of the dead bodyguard, only to give up after a minute of futility. *Just like everything else lately*, thought Mark. And, equally bitterly: *And I am tired of watching better men and women than me die, just to keep me alive.* Although his ongoing humiliation was probably almost over. To say things looked bad was to stretch the definition of understatement until it snapped like a rotten longbow.

Mark looked around. At least the cave he was now hiding in appeared unoccupied; a fissure in the back possibly led to another chamber, but it would take a lot to make Mark consider fleeing down it. There were enough kinks in the passage leading to this chamber to let Mark risk starting a small fire, over the last feeble protests of his now-dead companion. The bodyguard had been right, as usual; even a tiny campfire might attract notice. But Mark had been past caring. Offering a little warmth and light in the dark seemed a far too small reward for the man's loyalty.

Twenty men and women had been in the guard detail that pulled Mark Smith out of a burning Salt Lake City as Dominion mages ravaged it. The detail's staring corpses marked the path of their futile flight into the mountains; so it seemed almost petulant for Mark to dwell on how his entire family was likely also dead (or, worse, *wishing* they were). Eradicating the ruling dynasty of Deseret had been a goal of the Dominion for hundreds of years, and now they were apparently all the way down to just one scion left.

He couldn't stay in the cave for long. The bodyguard's corpse would attract scavengers, and putting him outside the cave would attract notice. As far as Mark could work out, he was still in Dominion-occupied territory, so getting far enough west (*assuming they stop before the Pacific*, he thought) had to be the next step before, well. What, really? Mark didn't know. He did know he would be probably literally damned before he would spend less effort trying to avoid the inevitable than the people who had traded their lives for him. It would have to be enough. It wouldn't be, but it would have to be.

In the meantime, the fire no longer served any purpose; he wasn't going to freeze, and the man it was trying to comfort was dead. Mark carefully smothered it. He also appropriated back the blankets the bodyguard no longer needed. He deserved the warmth no more than he did the firelight, but it was his job now to survive for as long as possible. Mark would have enough to answer for — for the disaster which had befallen him, his family, and the realm and faith they once ruled over. Better not to add ingratitude to his list of sins.

Sleep came easily enough, surprisingly. Mark contemplated offering prayers, but *now* seemed like an obscenely hypocritical time to start. He settled for a heartfelt *I'm sorry* to the heavens, because it was all he had left.

#

Mark awoke (but carefully did not open his eyes) to the smell of snake. Snakes. Rattlers. The musky scent was familiar to anyone who spent any time outdoors, and Mark Smith had always preferred a morning's ramble to a sacrament meeting, including the ones he was supposed to oversee as a bishop. The musk was stronger than any he had ever smelled, which clearly meant Mark Smith had managed to take shelter in a rattlesnake den. Getting out of it alive might not be a realistic goal.

Under the circumstances, this was almost a relief. Death by rattlesnake would be a horrible and fairly pointless way to die, to be sure, but in no sense could his trying to escape be seen as an attempt at suicide. Mark was likely dead either way, so there was no harm in trying.

So he opened his eyes — and then blinked them, several times. There were a *lot* of rattlers in this cave. And they were not acting normally for the weather; each rattler was alert, moving smoothly through the cave in an almost purposeful way. Most seemed to be watching the opening to the cave, but one of the larger ones looked over at Mark's movement. It gracefully slithered over to consider the human, its unblinking eyes steady.

Mark opened his mouth to say something. What, he was never sure of, even later. A cry for help? A muttered swear? A senseless attempt to communicate with a wild serpent? Whatever it was, his abortive attempt at speech was interrupted by the feel of a rattlesnake's tail being carefully but firmly placed over his mouth. He turned his head to look up. Looking back and down at him was the tail's owner, who was another enormous rattlesnake. Mark turned back to look at the one in front of him — who, slowly but unmistakably, shook its head in an obvious 'no.'

Well, thought Mark, *we'll just take that as a hint*. He put himself in a sitting position against the wall, gingerly raised his hands briefly (the rattlers seemed to take no offense at either of those things), and smiled just as gingerly. The tail from above retreated, and the contemplative rattler gave Mark an equally slow and unmistakable nod 'yes.' Then it went back to look at the cave front.

Whatever was going on, Mark hoped it would work itself out before a chamberpot was required. A bit later, he was cursing his naive optimism. The lack of a chamberpot was proving to be the least of his worries.

#

It would be a cliché to say Mark had been obsessively thinking about the last few weeks — but clichés exist because they're usually accurate, at the core. He was trapped in a cave full of passive yet disturbingly intelligent rattlesnakes. Morbidly remembering the past had its points.

What was so confusing was how *quickly* disaster had struck. A month ago, Mark was the heir to a reasonably prosperous desert and mountain realm. Nothing was really wrong, was it? Oh, certainly to the west there were the California barbie petty-kingdoms, but their kens never came east except as mercenaries or bodyguards. The lands to the south and north were quiet neighbors, uninterested in bothering Deseret, and it pleased Deseret to return the courtesy.

And, sure, to the east there was always talk about how the Universal Dominion was moving in Deseret's direction, but those stories never seemed very important. Or not as important as the latest coffee-house or bordello or wizard's spectacle. The few times Mark had thought to ask his father about the situation, he had been given a reassuring pat on the shoulder and a mostly-genial reminder to not worry about the cares of State until he was the one sitting behind the President's Desk.

I should have made you ready for this, Mark fancied he heard his father say. More likely it was a thought in his head. *But I remembered my own youth too much*, the voice went on.

Now Mark was *certain* he was making up his father's voice: the court had long ago learned it was unwise to remind Oliver Smith how his older brother Wallace was originally the heir. It was usually conceded Oliver was the better choice to succeed old President Eliza when she abdicated; he was certainly the one with more ken mercenaries at that moment. And soldiers often mattered more than other factors, in a succession crisis.

But his father never seemed willing to let anyone else really *do* anything themselves. Particularly Mark. Although Mark never tried, once he understood how low the expectations actually were for him. 'Don't throw up in public' and 'No means no' seemed mostly sufficient.

I was afraid you would do to me what I did to my own mother. Mark shuddered. Hallucination or not, impossibly frank or not; his imagination was doing an amazingly good job of reproducing his father's voice. *I feared you would set me aside, before I was finished with my work*, the voice inside his head went on. *And now others have set me aside, and the work shall remain undone forever.*

And wasn't *that* a cheerful thought to have, in a cave full of venomous snakes.

#

When things finally changed, it was heralded with the sounds of rattles. Every snake in the cave had started up rattling, from the ones nearest the cave mouth to the ones in the fissure behind him. The sudden cacophony nearly made Mark not need a chamberpot after all — but it was damnably peculiar. The snakes weren't reacting to him. All the ones he could see were aligned to face the cave mouth, and ignoring Mark completely.

Mark Smith was not a coward, although he had been thinking of himself as one for the last, horrible week. But he could taste his own fear on his lips, and right then he hated himself for it almost enough to do something suicidally reckless. What saved his life was the cold fact he was too tired and heart-sore to react properly to any kind of new situation. A state of shock can take many forms.

As the rattling intensified, Mark began to feel queasy, as if he wanted to vomit but couldn't quite remember how. He could also feel a pressure approaching; it was a wind which pushed only the mind, bringing with it a hungry-sound hum. He knew both the wind, and the hum. Both had the horrible feel of Dominion sorcery. Which meant the bastards had found him, after all, or were about to.

When the ball of painful, tooth-jarring light of a Dominion scrying probe finally drifted into the cave, the rattling from the snakes grew louder than anything Mark had ever heard before. The rattling was relentless, and just this short of frantic, and as the probe moved over the snakes Mark could see the waves of sound from the rattling make it bob and shimmy in the air. But the probe kept pulsing waves of horrid colors all over the cave, missing not an inch. It *would* see him. It probably already had — but Mark sat resolutely still as the colors from the probe crawled over him. He saw no reason to die tired. Or more tired.

The wave of colors passed over him, and it was all Mark could do not to vomit at the crawling chaos flowing over and through him. The greasy outrage left him feeling uncleaner than he had ever felt. And then the probe seemingly ignored him completely, and kept scanning the cave.

At first he didn't believe he had really escaped the notice of the Dominion probe. It wasn't until the foul thing left, and the rattling slowed, softened, then stopped completely that Mark accepted he was *not* about to be caught and tortured to death. Or, at least, not right away. He felt no relief; merely a certain amount of detached confusion and curiosity. He was too worn-out for anything else.

So when the snakes began to flow around him and guide him to the dark fissure in the back of the cave, Mark went with them — not willingly, but not reluctantly, either. Why not? Well and truly, why not?

#

The fissure was deep and long, but Mark reflexively followed it down and into the dark for a goodly while. By the time he had recovered enough to get a good panic going, it didn't matter anyway. He couldn't see a damned thing, and there was no chance he'd be able to find his way back. But it still felt rawly tense to stumble through the absolute blackness.

If only it had been as quiet as it was dark!

Mark could hear things in this state he would never hear, otherwise. Not just his breath and heartbeat and the slight rustle of his own clothing, either. He could hear the dead. That day Mark Smith learned how the dead *can* still sometimes speak, if only the living would bother to listen.

Here, down in the dark, Mark had no choice but to listen as the dead souls flopped and squirmed in the thirsty, dry dirt. *Your family failed us*, he could hear them say. *What have you done?*

At first Mark assumed that, like before, this was merely his own guilt lashing out in his mind, but as he was led downward through gentle serpentine pushes on arm and leg, the voices grew more forceful, and the snakes seemed almost eager to move him along past them. *You were false shepherds,* Mark heard.

False priests. The voices were bitter with accusation. But the voices also seemed to be fading as he and the snakes moved, which was a comfort, surely?

False rulers. The scorn was heavy, if harder to hear. *You run from us, as you ran from our killers.*

That made him stop. It even made him angry. "What do you want me to do?" Mark shouted at the darkness, as the snakes all around him started to rattle what he assumed now were their protective spells.

And then *something* seemed to coalesce out of nothing, or perhaps it concentrated the Stygian blackness into an even deeper blackness, a dark that could eat light itself. Later Mark considered it might have also eaten *him,* but at the time he was simply too tired to be afraid.

The more-than-darkness spoke. *What could you **possibly** want to do?* That came out with an almost tangible bitterness, but also disappointment. Mark blinked back sudden hotness in his eyes.

"I want to stop being taken places for my own good," he said, quietly at first but building up quickly. "I want to do something. I want" — and this, Mark almost yelled — "I want to hit *back!*"

The darkness paused. It almost seemed provoked to pause, as if that was an answer it had not expected, but felt obligated to respect. And then, over the now-frantic rattling, Mark heard a soft response. *Then do so.*

"I don't know how!"

Learn.

#

In the moments of frantic travel which followed — the snakes were eager to leave behind that greater darkness, which seemed disinclined to follow — Mark felt empty and lost. Perhaps the snakes tasted the despair on his skin, for after a few minutes the movement around him died down again; as Mark stopped, he felt a snake slither up his body and onto his arm. He did not cry out, because at some point in this endless darkness he left his fear of snakes behind, but it was still startling to feel the serpent's head press something into Mark's hand. Something which glowed at his touch.

Mark looked at the artifact; it was one of the glowsticks of the Old Americans, still working somehow after three and a half centuries. The light wasn't much, even after it brightened at his touch, but it was enough to let him now see ceilings and walls and sudden fissures in the ground. More importantly, it was a comfort. "Thank you," said Mark to the snake coiled around his arm. It tightened itself slightly in apparent response before it gracefully half-flowed, half dropped off of his body.

He still felt like he was in the grips of a fever dream. But now that Mark was calmer, he was now certain of one thing; the snakes were not his enemies. They had protected him from danger now twice. And even if he was just being preserved for some later horrible use, the snakes were likely to be less cruel about it than the Dominion would happily be. Besides, the snakes seemed to know what they were doing, and they clearly had some sort of plan. Which put them two up on Mark Smith, and he knew it.

#

Either they were not going far, or the darkness had distorted Mark's perception of time and distance, but fairly soon Mark and the snakes arrived at a larger cave entrance. Surprisingly, the cave inside smelled of water and green and there even appeared to be some kind of natural light from above. They had gone down ledges, and gone up them, too, so this meant — well, this meant Mark Smith was seriously lost at this point. But he knew that already.

At one edge of the cave was a patch of what proved to be actual *sunlight* from above; in it sat a cloaked and hooded figure, on a roughly-hewn stone throne. Around the figure were a few creatures, half-sitting, half-sprawled on the cavern floor. Mark looked upon both figure and creatures, and knew immediately he was the only human being in the cave.

But it wasn't really too bad, honestly. The figure was so obviously a pile of snakes in a robe it was almost comical; and while the creatures were humanoid in shape, at least from the waist up, they were definitely not close enough to human to be upsetting — and they all gave off a distinct aura of 'childlike.' Well-behaved children, valiantly trying to stay still like they were told, but still being fidgety about it. They had big eyes, too, which they used to look curiously at Mark until something else distracted them; like a surreptitious poke by one at another's side which made the whole bunch hiss and click at each other until the figure made its own multi-tongued hiss.

"Enough, children. Well done! But go off and play." Again, it could have been worse. The figure's voice wasn't *awful*, once you accepted how it was made up of a hundred snakes trying to duplicate Old American through the use of clever harmonics. The figure had about as good a mastery of the slightly archaic tongue as Mark did, in fact. "They see few men," half-explained, half-apologized the figure. "I promised them they could come forth and greet you, President Smith."

Mark had forbidden his guards to call him by his father's title, out of shame, but he could not command — well, who, or *what*, was this? Mark collected the tangled remains of his manners and managed to get out, "They seem very, ah, civil. Please forgive me, but I do not know your name?"

"Indeed you do not, for I have neglected to give it to you." If the figure had any trouble with using the formalities and cadences of Old American, it was not obvious. "My name is itself a tale. Would you care to hear it? And, please, make yourself comfortable." The figure indicated a table to one side, complete with what looked like a pitcher of water and some fruits and — praise the Lord! — cheese. There was even a real chair to sit on.

Mark Smith had enough self-restraint to eat like a proper Deseret gentleman, but it was hard not to tear up at the simple courtesies of clean food and the chance to eat properly. If the figure noticed any random tears which did form, it courteously ignored them. Instead, it waited until Mark had drunk deep from the deliciously cold spring water before speaking again.

"When I was first created," the creature continued, "the sorcerers who brought me forth sought to yoke me with a name of dark binding, the better to suit their foul vision. For a long time after breaking free of their chains, I rejected the name they gave me. I had no wish to give them any satisfaction at all." If a hundred serpents could hiss a sigh, the figure sighed. "But with age comes learning, and hopefully wisdom. I have thought long on my origins, and I have learned the legends of the Old Americans, and so now I take for my own the name which my makers thought to force upon me.

"My name is Yig, Father of Serpents. I greet you, O exiled Lord of Deseret. And rest assured: 'We be of one blood, ye and I.' For we share a bitter enemy."

#

Domain of Yig
2457 AD

The twin swords in his opponent's hands did their level best to mesmerize Mark. It was almost hypnotic, the way they swayed easily, first here, then there, then high, then low — and suddenly they snapped out of their pattern to slash. He might have stopped them, even then, except for the vicious stamp-kick his foe somehow managed to painfully administer to Mark's leg. The twin swords slammed into Mark's gut, smashing him to the floor.

He was wearing leather armor there, naturally. And on his legs. And the 'swords' were padded wood, because this was a training bout, not a death-match. But *Goddammit* if it still didn't hurt like the Devil.

Settling into Yig's Domain had been surprisingly easy. He had plenty to eat, clothes to wear, and even a bed to sleep in. Everything was far cruder than he had been used to as the heir to Deseret, but Mark ruthlessly forced down even any hint of petulance or disdain which tried to bubble up. Self-pity was a decadent luxury, these days.

So was boredom, so when Yig had suggested a training program, Mark had happily gone along. He had assumed it mostly would be about keeping his edge, for hadn't he been given proper training? He soon learned the depths of self-delusion in that slightly arrogant assumption.

For example: fighting a collection of snakes in full plate armor (steel, and slightly dusty) was something which sounded easy enough to Mark, right up to the moment where he realized how the snakes were more or less enchanted to use the armor effectively. Also, they didn't fight fair. And they had reflexes like, well, a snake's.

Mark picked himself up off the cave that served as a gym. In front of him, the ambulatory plate mail waited just enough for Mark to be vertical, then started swinging both of those damnable padded swords at him again. This time Mark dodged properly when one steel foot suddenly tried to slam into his shin. He even almost managed to use his shield to block both sword shots. Almost.

As Mark clattered down again, he consoled himself about how he was living longer in these bouts, at least. And that there would be archery next. Archery, he had always been good at. But then, hunting was far closer to war than honor-duels in the old days were.

#

Being attacked in the dark is hard. It's harder when you don't allow yourself to fight back. It's hardest when your opponents know this, so they take their time beating you. And never mind how none of the blows were physical; there's more than one way to drive a man to his knees in pain.

We hid out for nine months, the latest voice told him. *My youngest girl died — her name was Eliza, after your grandmother — but the rest of us stayed alive. Then we went looking for somewhere to farm. We didn't care what it was, as long as the family could stay together.*

But my wife was so thin by then, and she got the coughing sickness, and we had to bury her under a pile of stones because of the coyotes. Then we lost little Hannah to bad water, and my boy Joe fell into the ravine and Jack just never came back from hunting one night, and then my eldest Billy got wild about getting a lick in against the invaders and ran off to join the Danite resistance. When they sent me word how his band got wiped out in an ambush, well, I didn't have anything left, did I?

There was one of the invaders in Myton, living it up like he was some kind of bishop. He figured he could do what he wanted because he'd fireball the town if anybody looked at him cross-eyed. And they were real scared of him, too. So I didn't tell nobody nothing about what I was gonna do until I got close enough.

The look on his face when my knife went into his gut! He was all wriggling and howling and burning me with fire and I was howling too when my eyeballs burst. His soldiers were hacking at me, too, but it wasn't nothing much, so I held on with the knife and kept shoving it back and forth until he stopped moving and then I could hear the screaming outside. I guess he had spells set up for if he died. I died hearing the whole village scream.

The worst part was, this last voice wasn't even as angry as some of the others had been. When it said, *You want to hear them scream too, boy?* — it didn't seem like a rhetorical question. At first, the voices made him listen to it all whether he wanted to or not. But the more he came here the more — well, they didn't become more *forgiving*. They still thought Mark owed them a debt. But perhaps they were beginning to believe how maybe Mark acknowledged the debt, and would try to pay it off.

So... "Yeah," mumbled Mark through lips sore from where he had bitten them. "Give me all of it. *All* of it." **Somebody** living needs to hear it, he thought. And it looked like Mark Smith was going to have to be somebody.

#

Domain of Yig
2458 AD

"Why am I reading this?" Mark asked, not quite peevishly. "Why do you care if I do?"

Yig looked over at Mark. Which is to say, the hood which contained the snakes he was using to see with today shifted direction to have him 'face' Mark. After a couple of years, Mark had finally gotten used to it, to the point where the hood pretty much was just 'the head' by now.

"It is one of your Holy Books," Yig observed. They were speaking regular American; Yig's command of the modern tongue had improved, once he had started getting more practice. "A bishop of your faith should try to read it at least once."

"How sharper than a serpent's tooth," Mark murmured.

"I'm flattered you see me as a father figure," responded Yig. "And the verse is from your *other* Holy Book. But full credit for remembering something from it which wasn't nasty about snakes."

"Fine," said Mark. "But why do you care? I mean, shouldn't you be trying to seduce me away from my faith?"

"Really?" Yig sounded honestly confused. "Why?"

"Well," Mark said. "You're some kind of god, right?"

"That is a complex question which is best answered vaguely," said Yig. "In other words: it depends."

"Well, the snakes worship you. And your Children do, too." At the word 'Children' one of the snake-kids looked up, briefly. Mark was struck by how much more intelligence there was in the kids' eyes, these days. But they were still good-natured.

"I admit, this is more or less true," Yig said. "But I give the snakes protection, and I am uplifting the Children. They have perfectly good reasons to worship me. But, Mark... how do I put this nicely? You're not a snake. Besides, you already have a god. I'm really not interested in pissing him off."

Yig jerked his head. "And that's why I want you to read your own scriptures again. Or for the first time. Because I don't think you want to piss him off, either."

"Like my family did?" Mark said, just a little bitterly.

"You're sounding a bit too prideful," said Yig, "in an upside-down kind of way. I don't know why we've been cursed with the Universal Dominion like this, but I don't think it was because of anything any one person did. I mean, I'm stuck with them too, and I haven't really done anything to deserve it."

Mark was quiet for a moment. "How bad is it, up there? I hear the whispering horrors when I'm in the dark, but none of them know the whole tale."

"It's very bad," said Yig. "The Dominion didn't conquer all of Deseret. But it did take a third, and made another third lawless. Something about bands of desert raiders and slavers appeals to the bastards. Or maybe they just like to watch your country-men scramble to keep everything they've built and sweated over from being wiped out."

"I should be up there."

"And doing what, besides dying? Oh, you're doing better with the fighting, now that somebody's making you practice every day. But if you want to *rule* your people again, you should know more about them. Which starts with actually reading the holy books for the religion you're the high priest-king of."

Mark grimaced. "But do they want me to rule them?" he asked. "The dynasty didn't end well."

Yig sighed. "There's a book in here somewhere — where is it? Oh, thank you," he said to one of the Children, who had brought an Old American tome up. This was one of the things about the Children of Yig, Mark had noticed: they still weren't exactly smart, but they were really very good at being helpful.

Yig peered over the book, somehow giving the impression of wearing spectacles despite the fact he was still a collection of snakes in a robe, and started to read. "The dwarf says — You should understand, these two aren't *exactly* a dwarf and an elf talking," explained Yig. "It's kind of complicated. Anyway, the dwarf says, *It is ever so with the things that Men begin. There is a frost in Spring, or a blight in Summer, and they fail of their promise.*

"And then the elf replies, *Yet seldom do they fail of their seed. And that will lie in the dust and rot to spring up again in times and places unlooked-for.*" Yig looked over. "You're down here in the dust for a reason, Mark. And it's not for any reason of mine, al-though I'm happy to host you. I don't think your god is quite done with your dynasty yet."

Mark sighed. Yig was right. He couldn't even complain that his own parents had never prepared him for this, because, despite what Yig said, Mark was fairly sure his dynasty becoming such irreligious religious leaders probably hadn't helped matters much with God. And since Mark did want to rule his people — even if only it would make it so much easier to Smite the Dominion properly — he would just have to buckle down to work.

#

Mark was up to three-versus-one bouts by now in the combat drills, which well and truly sucked. And archery wasn't as much fun, thanks to all the enthusiastic snakes trying to mess up Mark's aim. Well, that last part was a lie. It only wasn't as much fun when the distractions worked. Which was happening less often.

Right then, one of his sparring partners took advantage of Mark's flicker of self-congratulation to fling itself — well, themselves — at his legs, accepting the reflexive hit to let its two companions strike high and low. They were all using steel weapons and armor by now; the blades were dull, which was the only concession made for training.

And, to add insult to not-quite injury, Mark fell over the prone set of armor. Being on the ground there meant he could hear the good-natured derisive rattling from the snakes inside. "Yeah, yeah," Mark said. "Rub it in."

When Mark stood, he extended a helping hand to the prone snakes-in-armor. They could move around pretty well in full plate mail, somehow, but once they fell down, regaining their 'feet' could be a problem. Mark had long since stopped noticing how it was odd to spar this way, or that he was interacting daily with a host of highly venomous reptiles. He did vaguely remember being afraid of snakes, but it all seemed rather silly now.

Mark got back into the center of the circle, snapped down his visor, and took his stance. "Best two falls out of three?" he asked. "Let's see if you can fool me twice."

#

My name is Godfrey Carter, the voice said. Mark knew this whispered accusation in the dark would someday come, and he thought he had prepared for it. But that was silly; of course he hadn't.

Me and my buddies, we figured it wouldn't be hard to be Guards for the snotnose. Carter's whisper wasn't even too scornful, which felt bizarrely insulting, somehow. *And it wasn't. He didn't care about us, and we didn't care about him. I didn't hate him, either. What would be the point? And it was real soft duty.*

And then it got hard. The Old Man, he told us himself to get the snotnose out of the City, 'just in case.' Like there was a chance the Dominion wasn't coming over the wall! But we saluted and got the snotnose out of there. And we ran. We ran, and every time one of us died keeping the snotnose alive, the rest of us looked at each other and wondered who the next person was gonna be. And then it was just me, and the snotnose.

I'll give him this, though. When he had no fucking choice left, the snotnose at least tried to go down swinging. It would have been better if Carter's whisper had sounded anything except surprised. *Still had to save his ass, but that's the job, hey-hey? And he lit a fire for me, before I died. Put me in a blanket and everything. That was something.*

But you never knew my name, did you?

Mark was silent, but not for long. He wasn't going to permit himself the luxury of self-pity. "No, I didn't," he said aloud. "No excuse for it, Guardsman Carter."

No apology, either?

"You already know I'm sorry, and I can't make restitution," said Mark. "What entitles me to get off the hook for this?"

Fair enough. That surprised Mark; the whispering dead were usually understandably unwilling to bend even that much when it came to criticizing him. *But you are **sure** you can't make restitution for this, Smith?* Carter's voice felt silent, and never returned that day, or ever. But Mark thought about his words for a long time afterward.

#

Domain of Yig
2459 AD

"What *do* you want from all of this?" asked Mark, one day. The question seemed to come out of nowhere, even to him. But the way Yig looked at him suggested his host had been waiting for this question for a while now.

"Right now?" Yig shrugged. "When you leave, I want you to be as prepared as you can. Not that I'm throwing you out, Mark."

"I know," Mark said. "But we both know I'm not going to be staying here forever."

"Yes. And it's going to be rough for you up there," said Yig. "Won't lie, Mark: you may end up getting yourself killed."

Yig spread his hands. "But!" he said. "If you end up winning up there, then yes, I would like something from you. Something you won't mind granting, either."

"I'm going to assume it's not gold," Mark said dryly. One thing he had discovered early was that Yig didn't lack for treasure. Yig's vault had coins from Deseret and Sonora, New California, Old America, and even a few legendary *reales* from the equally legendary (and ancient) *conquistadors*. As Yig had said, once: humans were good at burying valuables, but not always as good at remembering where.

"You're right, it's not," said Yig. "I want something more valuable: peace." He waved a hand at his Children. "They're not quite ready to slither and think and live their own lives. But when they do, I want there to be somewhere where they won't be afraid to slither under the open sky. And I'm pretty sure the Dominion will never be that kind of place."

"Yeah, I'm pretty sure I agree with you," said Mark. "What about the regular snakes, though?"

"Even easier," said Yig. "They'll be happy with simple coexistence. Just don't attack them, and they won't attack you. Even if one of your people accidentally steps on one of mine." Yig paused. "'Course, this means a lot of them might move into your basements. Which should fix your mice problems, anyway."

Mark nodded, judiciously. "I think I can live with the bargain," he said as he rose. "And if I can ever get anybody up there to do what I say, so will they." He extended his hand. "Shake on it?"

Yig snorted and lifted his sleeve, which was of course filled with snakes. Mark shook his head. "Yeah, I know, but still. Shake on it?"

Shaking hands with a humanoid-shaped pile of snakes is an experience most people never get to have. Mark wasn't ever sure if he was blessed or cursed with the memory, but he never regretted the handshake itself. It ended up meaning too much.

#

Domain of Yig
2460 AD

Yig could have let him leave by a more convenient way, but Mark thought it best to exit the Domain by the same path he had taken to enter it. Well, up to a point; he wanted to be well south of what was once the capital when he walked again under the open sky.

By now the way was easy. Years underground had taught Mark how to feel the clear paths from changes in the air or the way sounds reverberated off of the walls. The torch didn't hurt, either; after all, Mark needed to get used to daylight again. But when he found a certain spot, he doused the light. He suspected it would be easier to hear the voices from before that way.

And they did come. They came with five more years of weariness and pain, but they came. *Are you done running?* they asked.

"I didn't run," Mark said. "I *learned*." He bared his teeth in what wasn't even remotely a smile. "As you asked."

As you were told, one voice from the throng seemed to chide. Mark shivered; it sounded far too much like his grandmother's. But he shook his head.

"No," said Mark. "You do not command a king. You entreat him."

So you call yourself a king, then?

"I call myself nothing," Mark said. "I am who I am. Mark, of the Smith Dynasty. Styled President of Deseret; but the gentiles would call me a king, so I recognize their term. Would you contest my decision?"

And what if I do? That familiar whisper had a deeper tone, somehow, and the darkness congealed around the whisper seemed more solid than Mark expected.

But Mark's voice was steady. "Then we would have a dispute," he said. "And let me ask you; when our dispute was settled, would you be any closer to seeing the Universal Dominion receive retribution for their crimes? Whether you win, or lose?"

The deeper darkness seemed to consider this, and retreated without further comment. At least this time. Mark suspected he would eventually hear something further on this, somehow. Hopefully, he'd find out whether the objection was to the authority Mark was now claiming, or whether it was to Mark being the one claiming it.

But the other whispers were no longer silent. *And what will you be king of?* came from a dozen places at once. It was, Mark conceded, a fair question.

And this time, someone could fairly call Mark's expression a smile. "Watch, and see."

REX FANG-BLADE
AND THE RAID ON
THE SLAVER CAMP

Western Wastes
Former Deseret
2463 AD

Tabetha Frei stumbled in the coffle, despite the hats that had been given to her and the other captives. The hats (and the regular drinks of water) weren't offered as kindnesses; they were a grudging admission that you can't sell dead slaves to anybody, except the traders even the new bandit gangs found a bit too foul. Well. Most of the bandit gangs. In what used to be the north of Deseret, you could always find somebody who wasn't *too* finicky to make a sale.

The captive just behind Tabetha managed to keep her upright long enough for nobody else to fall down, but even the half-fall was enough to get that poor bastard Dallin Hatch running over. "You gotta keep up!" he hissed, trying for vicious and instead sounding worried. "We're almost at the stopping place. Just, just do it, alright?"

"There a problem, Dally?" came a lazy-cruel voice from the front of the slave caravan. Rude Jimmy didn't sound real pissed, just amused. Tabetha hadn't been a captive long (it was for damned sure she wasn't ready just yet to be a slave), but she'd already seen that 'amused' wasn't any less dangerous.

Dallin flushed, his own fading marks from the collar and chains briefly visible on his skin. Tabetha guessed the boy hadn't been 'promoted' to bandit long. For one thing, he was still a 'poor bastard' in Tabetha's reckoning, instead of just a 'bastard.' For another: his hands didn't wander.

"No, sir!" yelled Dallin. "Just making sure they all keep walking! We'll make 'em get there on time, sir!" As he turned back, Dallin pulled out his canteen and gave Tabetha a quick drink from it. "You just gotta get through this," he said. "We all do."

Right, thought Tabetha. *Because this is as bad as it's going to get.* She looked at Dallin's back as they kept walking. *I don't care to think about what made you decide being a bandit was better than the alternative.* Tabetha even dared take a glare at the slave caravan leader. *You, on the other hand... I bet you were doing this even before the Scourging. Or you took to this life like a chupacabra takes to blood.*

#

As dusk fell, the caravan made camp along one hill, where they could light a fire and not attract attention. This section of the ancient Route 80 road was mostly deserted since the Scourging, but there was still the odd scouting party from what was left of Deseret, down in the south. The slavers were much more worried about patrols from Wendover, though. Those townie sons of bitches didn't always remember that they were being paid off regular.

Six men (and Dallin, who was clearly there on probation), to guard twenty captives. No oldsters, of course. No kids, either; the slavers knew they'd just have to throw them away halfway to the breaking-camp at Oasis. Besides, the kids could grow up, have more kids, *then* get captured later. None of the slave-taking gangs that had popped up after the Universal Dominion's conquest of eastern Deseret were particularly sophisticated in their thinking, but they had grasped the principle that you can't over-raid your source of human flesh.

So they just killed the people caught with weapons, left the oldsters to raise the youngsters, and filled up their slave chains with the rest. It was a good business, especially in a world where guns had been banished by cruel magicians.

But sometimes running a business requires a mentoring session, to quote the old Americans. "Dally!" yelled Left-Ear. Tabetha had already worked out that Left-Ear wasn't the worst one of the bunch. But that was only because he just did whatever Rude Jimmy told him to do, and while the caravan leader *was* the worst one of the bunch, he also had other things to do besides tell Left-Ear how to be nasty. Rude Jimmy was sitting on a rock by the fire, and smiling, so whatever Left-Ear was about to do would be all right with him. That meant it was going to be bad.

Dallin ran over on the double, of course. He didn't cower enough, to Tabetha's increasingly-educated eye, and Left-Ear didn't like that. The rest of the slavers found it kind of funny, in a mean way, and that made Left-Ear even unhappier. "You get your ass over here, Dally!"

The newly-made bandit was young, and made the mistake of bravado. "Yeah, Left-Ear? Whaddya want?" That earned him a backhand out of nowhere that knocked him to the ground.

"I want you to fucking forget your old place, boy," said Left-Ear. His voice was surprisingly calm. "You got out of the cages, but part of your head's still back there. So we gotta yank that foolishness out of you. Here and now, where the walking meat can see."

Tabetha snuck a glance at the other slavers; a few of them had quietly got some sacks of sand together. The captives had already discovered the slavers liked to hit people with those, since there were fewer chances for value-destroying marks and bruises that way. Tabetha supposed they'd work just as well for adjusting the attitude of a new bandit, too.

"You ain't one of the walking meat no more," said Left-Ear. "You don't get to go back to them, either. You're either one of us, or you're just *dead* meat. What's it going to be?"

Dallin stood up. For a second Tabetha thought he was gonna

cave, but that had apparently been one casual cuff too many. Instead, Dallin dabbed at a cut at the corner of his mouth, looked around, and said, "You know what? Fuck this, and fuck you."

That, weirdly, was apparently the right thing to say — or maybe just what Left-Ear had expected to hear. He laughed as the other slavers stood, their sacks of sand beginning to whirr. "Wrong answer, jackass. You think you're the first punk I've beaten the dumb out of? We'll ask again in a little bit; I betcha I'll like your answer a little better then."

Thanks to the campfire, Tabetha was close enough to easily see the vicious grin on Left-Ear's face, which meant she could also see the arrow come out of the night, go through the left ear that Left-Ear actually did not have, and the tip pop through the right ear that he *did*. It took a good fifteen seconds before the corpse finally overbalanced enough to fall down, which was enough time for another arrow to find the eye of a second slaver, and two to hit the arm of a third as he scrambled for his shield.

A hooded man came into the firelight, his bow already slung over a cloaked shoulder and bright steel in his hands. He roughly bowled over Dallin a second time, sending him flying, and within seconds had hamstrung and sliced open two more slavers.

"Sorry to interrupt," said the cloaked man, "but you weren't listening to the lad."

A decent leader might have challenged the man that had just killed most of his followers in under a minute, but Rude Jimmy didn't bother with nonsense like loyalty or duty. He just grabbed the nearest slave and put a knife to his throat. The head slaver actually moved faster than he needed to, because the stranger was still staring down Dallin instead of killing him.

"Now, what's a good Deseret lad doing in a place like this?" Tabetha heard the man say (although she was already focused on going after Left-Ear's damned bundle of key-rings). It surprised her, how polite that question was. Almost as if Dallin had been found in a pre-Scourging coffee house on a Saturday night, drinking an illicit cappuccino.

And for some reason, that simple question hit Dallin hard. Even harder than Rude Jimmy ever did. "I'm sorry," mumbled Dallin.

(This was all very dramatic, to be sure — but Tabetha was too busy getting her neck collar off with Left-Ear's keys. Neck collar, foot chain, and hey! There was even a knife. The night was definitely looking up.)

The man looked at him. "*Are* you?" he said, staring Dallin down until the kid nodded. "Then start earning it. First by helping that lady get those damn collars off of those folks." Tabetha blinked at that; whoever this man was, he was *real* good at keeping track of things. "I got this last bandit to sort out," the man went on.

"You talking to me, asshole?" said Rude Jimmy.

"No, I'm talking *about* you." The man looked at Rude Jimmy for the first time, and now that Tabetha was paying attention to something besides the key-rings, she could tell the slaver did not like the gaze the man was bestowing. The man went on, "But since you want to join the conversation? Fine. Do yourself a favor. Drop the knife, and run like all the demons in Hell were behind you. I won't kill you if you do."

"I got a better idea," Rude Jimmy said. "You surrender, and I won't kill my hostage— HEY!" The slaver directed that at Dallin, who'd grabbed one of Left-Ear's key-rings and now sidled past Rude Jimmy, well out of lunging range. "You fucking don't do what he says! You do what *I* say!" Reflexively, Rude Jimmy moved the knife from the hostage's throat to point. Just for a moment.

The second the knife-edge was clear, serpents sprang from the shadows to strike Rude Jimmy. Three went for his knife-hand; the rest struck at ankle, arm, neck, anywhere flesh could be pierced by fang. The rattle of their attacks was inter-cut with the screams of the untouched hostage as the newcomer leapt forward to drag him out from the fray.

To the side, Dallin stood, transfixed, until Tabetha tapped him on the shoulder, pretty hard. That snapped the boy out of it, and he went back to his job. And so did Tabetha. No snakes were near *her* — and if there were, they clearly were here on other business.

#

A man bitten by a dozen rattlesnakes will likely die hard, but not quickly; Rude Jimmy was still writhing on the ground when the man walked up to him and gave the mercy-stroke. By then Dallin and Tabetha had gotten the rest of the captives freed. When it was done, the man said, "Leave the damn chains to rust. Where were they going to take everyone — Dallin, was it?"

Visibly relieved that it was 'they' and not 'you,' Dallin replied, "There's a breaking-camp about a day from here. It's called Oasis. It's one of the ones where they sort out captives, see who can fight."

"So," mused the man, "There's going to be folks with a grudge there. Perfect. How many guards?"

"Twenty," said Dallin promptly. "They keep sentries, though. And dogs." He absently rubbed a still-livid scar. "Mean ones. They sic 'em on people trying to escape."

The man shook his head. "They won't be keeping sentries for long."

"Sir," said Dallin, "you're going to need more than a dozen snakes for that."

The man chuckled. "Look past the firelight. On the ground," the man said; the rest of the group did, and saw with a slight thrill of horror that it seemed to be moving. "You see, I already worked that out for myself."

#

"All right, folks," said the man as they all sat around the campfire. The dead slavers had been stripped of anything useful and tossed down a ravine; the former captives were enthusiastic about equipping themselves with armor and weapons. "First off, you can call me 'Rex.' Or 'sir,' or 'Mister,' or even 'hey, you.' I'm not fussy about that."

Tabetha's family had been armorers and weaponsmiths before the Scourge (something she had planned to *never* tell the slavers); she was now working on the worst gear. It wasn't bad, and it wasn't even badly maintained, but she knew what she was doing and the former owners hadn't. She looked up at, all right, 'Rex.' "So what *are* you fussy about?" Tabetha said. "There's gonna be something that sets you off, Rex. Sir. Mister. Hey-You."

Rex earned a few more points with Tabetha by having a nice laugh. "Right to the point," he said. "You in charge, then?"

"Nah, I know this one, Hey-You," said Tabetha. "I say 'Yeah,' you say 'Wrong,' and then things get real exciting for me until we all get the point. So, nah, you're in charge." She managed a smile. "I'm not even fussed about it." Which she was not. Much. The collars were off, weren't they?

Tabetha couldn't quite see why saying something so obvious would bother Rex, but it... did? He got a look on his face that would've made her nervous if it had been directed at her, but instead he was glaring off at where they had tossed the corpses out for the coyotes and chupacabras.

"God, damn all slavers to Hell," Rex muttered. The sentiment didn't alarm Tabetha, particularly. What *did* alarm her just a little was how the sentiment, in Rex's mouth, sounded like a helpful reminder to the Almighty.

"Fine," said Rex as he turned back. "You're right. I'm the biggest hard case you can see, so I'm the one in charge. Since that's the way things are up here now, then that's how it is. So what orders should I be giving, Miss Tabetha?"

Tabetha blinked. "Excuse me?" She hastily added, "Sorry. Excuse me, *Hey-You?*"

"You were sitting there with a calm face for a half hour," Rex said. "A woman does that, she's either not thinking about anything at all, or she's thinking *really hard* about one thing in particular. From the way the others are looking at you, I'm guessing you don't have a reputation for woolgathering. So what's your plan? Or were you still chewing on it?"

Tabetha scowled at him, but the bastard (*the tall, strong, good-looking bastard*, a treacherous voice in her head said) had her pegged; she *was* prideful of her wits, dammit, and she had been brooding about the place where the slavers had been dragging them. But since the man had asked...

"Well," she said, "I was working out in my head the best ways to burn Oasis to the ground, nice and good. I can't do it the way I was planning, seeing as I'm not captured any more — and thank you kindly for that, Hey-You — so now I got to figure out how to do it all from the outside. You got any thoughts about how I should get on with that?"

"Sure, Miss Tabetha," Rex said. "You start off by asking for help from the man planning to burn it down himself. *After* we get the slaves out," he added. "Just in case that was a question."

"I do admit, emptying the slave pens was easier in my old plan," Tabetha conceded. "Since I'd be in them anyway. But what's your quarrel with Oasis, besides the obvious?"

"The obvious will do," said Rex. "And if it won't: well, I'm looking for motivated people. I think I'll find them in a liberated slave camp."

Dallin spoke up. "You got to be careful about that, sir." His tone was respectful, the whine and the bluster already fading from his voice. "The slavers see anybody with spirit, they pull him out of his pen and raise him up just enough to make him scared of having to go back into it. Guess they got it all worked out how to do it, by now."

"Yeah," said Rex. "But that doesn't make them strong. It makes 'em weak, because it means every man Jack of them chose their road because they were afraid. You fight a man who's scared, you're halfway to beating him right from the start." Rex poked the fire, idly. "All you have to do then is make sure that he ends up getting scared of *you*."

"You do know that hitting Oasis is going to set off the rest of the slavers something fierce though, right, Hey-You?" asked Tabetha. "I didn't take that into consideration, because I was gonna just keep burning things until I couldn't, but if you're planning to get away afterward, you should think about who'll be chasing you."

"Sure," said Rex. "If the Dominion's a cancer on this land, then the 'city' of Wells is the gangrene. When we cauterize Oasis, all those gangs in Wells will come out running." He poked the fire again. "Better that way. It's easier to kill a man when he isn't behind a wall."

"You're not thinking small," Tabetha said, with a little (and unwelcome) twinge of admiration at the audacity. "Guess the snakes help there, though."

Maybe it was the mention of the snakes that finally set off one of the other former captives. Tabetha didn't know all of them — they'd come from a half dozen settlements, and the slavers had grabbed her when she was well away from hers, thank God — and they had mostly been quiet since the chains and collars had come off. A few had looked hard at Dallin, but nobody seemed inclined to get personal about it. For the most part, they just sat there, eating decent for the first time in days and sticking together out of habit.

But one fellow looked like he'd been a loudmouth before the slavers had smacked that habit out of him, and now that the bad men were dead and unburied maybe he was ready to indulge in the luxury of bluster. "Now see here, drifter—" he began, only to be interrupted by Rex.

"I gave you a bunch of names at the start to use, mister. Pick one. Except for 'Hey-You'." Rex pointed at Tabetha. "That one's just for her."

Tabetha thought it was right informative just how quickly a calm tone and *almost* easy manner could shut up the loudmouth; but Rex wasn't done quite yet. (*Maybe he was waiting for somebody to spout off*, that voice in her head said.) He stood up. "Let me guess: now that it's over, most of you want to go home," Rex said.

There was a murmur at that, which got a half-nod out of Rex. "Can't say I blame you," he replied, then turned and waved one arm at the road, and the desert, and the night. "So go ahead! Feel free. Take your share of the water and the food and head on out. I'm no slaver.

"But I'm no slave, either," Rex went on. "If I got no hold on you, you got no hold on me. I'm going west to Oasis, to yank out what's rooted there. Anybody who wants to come along is welcome; anybody who doesn't, well, that's fine too."

A thought struck Tabetha, and she looked around. Yeah, every other person who'd ended up with an actual weapon was listening pretty hard to what Rex was saying, and they all looked interested. Tabetha sure was, which is why she had grabbed a shortsword. Rex had seen, but hadn't said anything.

Come to think of it, Rex had been watching pretty careful over who got what weapon. He had even stepped in a couple of times to stop disputes — and he *had* stopped them, too. Nobody wanted to argue with a man who had rattlers for friends.

#

They got going pretty soon afterward.

When it was all over and done with, Tabetha allowed herself to be impressed by how fast the group could move that night. Maybe it was the example of Rex. Maybe it was the first decent amounts of food and water in days. And maybe it was all those damned snakes taking up the rear.

The snakes definitely took getting used to. Tabetha wasn't scared of individual snakes, aside from the sensible fear that any person might feel about a reptile that could kill her with a single bite. But rattlers were supposed to have a sensible fear of human beings, too. These didn't: they'd come right up to Tabetha, completely bold as brass. When the group stopped for a quick breather, one snake even went so far as to crawl up the pack Tabetha had put down and wrap itself around the top. It took a lot of self-control for her to put that pack back on.

But she did. And, wouldn't you know it? Five minutes later Tabetha had half-forgotten there was a rattler in her pack. Even scary things stop getting really scary when nothing bad happens, and the snakes didn't even rattle at the humans. They just stayed out of the way of people's feet, and kept on going.

It was at the next stop that Tabetha realized the snakes were actually moving a little more slowly than they should have been. It took her a minute to figure out why, and she swore when she did. Then she started rounding up people to begin picking up the damned snakes.

She had to get the other people going by first doing it herself, which got Rex's attention. "They can keep up, Miss Tabetha," he said. "It's cold for them, but we don't have far."

"And what good are they gonna be when we get there, Hey-You?" she responded, maybe a little grumpily. "You were gonna use the snakes for something, right? Because twenty people with seven weapons is pretty long odds against a whole breaking-camp's worth of bandits."

She then noticed that Rex was carrying a few snakes of his own; not many, but a decent number. "Yes, the body heat will help them," Rex said. "But we decided not to ask."

"Then I guess it's a good thing that you didn't have to, Hey You. We're not idjits, you know. We gotta take care of these" — Tabetha almost said 'critters,' but something stopped her — "little fellas, so they'll take care of us."

She looked around, just to make sure the other people weren't doing anything stupid. And for a wonder, they weren't. Even the loudmouth was wearing snakes, now. Hell, he even looked like he was enjoying it.

As she turned back, Rex gave her a nod. "I take your point, Miss Tabetha. My apologies. Oh, and the snakes? They can't say thank you, but if they could, they would." And on that weird note, Rex took point again.

As Tabetha followed, a certain tentative movement made her scowl. "Oh no, you *don't*," she said to her reptilian riders. "Arms are fine. Neck's fine. You can even stuff my pockets, if you can fit. But stay out of my blouse. It ain't seemly."

#

Even before the Scourging, the name 'Oasis' was almost a lie. It perched right off the Old Eighty road, which meandered its way west until it came out in the Californian barbie lands. Trade caravans used it and the wells there, back when there were caravans. Or trade.

Now it was where slave-catchers brought their catches for the first wave of slave-breaking, and even at night Tabetha thought Oasis looked just as shabby-evil as expected. The slave shacks huddled on one side of the road, surrounded by rusty fences and a couple of towers. A few lights here and there warned where the guards were; they didn't move around much.

From the sound Rex was making, he didn't seem too impressed by that. "Stupid," he muttered as he looked through a pair of remarkably high-quality binoculars. "Don't they care about the guards getting lazy?"

"Why should they care, Hey-You?" said Tabetha. "What are they worried about? Slaves breaking out and hiding in the high desert?"

Dallin had come with the other two to help point out details. He hung his head, a little. "Depending on how high the sun is up," he said, "they don't even bother sending out a chase party. They just wait a day and go looking for the buzzards."

"I'll keep that in mind," Rex almost snarled; Dallin half-flinched at the tone, although Tabetha figured it wasn't aimed at him. *Hey-You takes Oasis real personal*, she thought. Tabetha was taking it personal, too, but that was because a bunch of raiders had put her in a collar and dragged her off. With Rex, it was... *It was like this place was a judgment on him, or something.*

But at least whatever was going on in Rex's head wasn't making him soft, or stupid-mad. The way he'd taken out the careless sentry, now tumbled on the ground behind them, had been almost pretty, in its way: a quick punch from the dark in the man's gut, then a ruthless throat-slit as the man struggled to get enough breath to shout. It was all so *fast*; Rex moved like, well, a snake. And the only mercy he showed in a fight was the sharpness of his blade.

Rex grunted once, and began the tricky task of putting away his binoculars while still stretched out on the ground. "How are his weapons, Miss Tabetha?" he asked, calmly.

Tabetha was sitting at the fire, pretending to be the silhouette of the sentry against the small, stupidly allowed campfire.

In her lap she was checking the dead sentry's blades and hilts for rust or rot. "Not bad," she said. "For no-account raider trash. It'll last at least the next fight. Armor's not worth stripping off, though. Who the hell puts spikes on shoulder pads?"

"They're to scare people," Rex said.

"They just piss me off, Hey-You."

Dallin spoke up. Like Rex, he was lying prone to keep his profile low, although from the look of things none of them needed to bother. "They won't let anybody wear them, right away," he said. "You gotta earn them by doing things."

Rex snorted. "Guess it was a good thing you were a slow learner, Dallin."

"...Yes, sir. I guess it was."

#

Tabetha discovered something that night: she didn't much care for killing men. Even when they were filthy slaver trash with bad teeth and hard eyes like the one she was killing now. When her sword was in his gut and her other hand was squeezing his throat shut, those eyes got real wide and pleading, fast. Like if she'd only stop right there and pull out the sword, maybe everything could get fixed because it was all just a big misunderstanding, right? The fellow got that, now. She didn't have to keep going.

But Tabetha kept going until those eyes got glassy and fixed. And when she pulled out the sword she made sure to slit the dead man's throat anyway. She didn't like killing, sure. But she'd already had to do a lot of unhappy things in her life, and they didn't get any easier to do if you flinched.

Dallin had an easier time of it, maybe because in some ways this was more personal for him. He knew these men. Hell, if Rex hadn't come by, Dallin would have *ended up* one of these men. That made him a little more enthusiastic about the job of sentry removal. At least, the outer line of sentries. The ones on the wall were still there. Hopefully, they were just as dumb as these had been.

Rex had brought three of them for the job: Rex, Tabetha, Dallin, and — ha! — the loudmouth, who now wanted people to call him "Desert Joe." That probably wasn't his real name, but didn't sound as weird as she had thought it might. Maybe it was all the snakes draped on him. They sure seemed to like him a lot, at least.

Desert Joe was even claiming the snakes were hissing things to him now. "They say the scouts on the northside fence tower were all asleep, Mister Rex," he said. "Drunk on rotgut and dead to the world." The funny part was, Rex took that at face value. He even seemed happy that Desert Joe was talking to the snakes, like it was a necessary job and now it wouldn't be just him doing it.

"Good," said Rex. "Half of us will go whittle down the slavers a little, and the others will break through the wires there. Dallin, Desert Joe, that's going to be your job. Get the captives ready to break out when you hear everything bust loose."

"Yessir," said Dallin. "I know just the people to wake up first, too."

"That's why I'm sending you," Rex said as they cut wires in the fence. "Desert Joe, you get these weapons back to the others and keep track of things. Including me and Miss Tabetha. If it looks like we're getting into too much trouble, grab everybody with weapons, and come on for a *big* fight. But if we do this right, there won't be one." Rex grinned. "No slaver ever born fights fair, so neither should we."

As the two of them started sneaking towards the first shack, containing more hopefully dead-drunk slavers, Tabetha asked, real low, "So, Hey-You? Why me? Dallin knows how to fight all right."

"You heard him," Rex said. "He knows who the trouble-makers are already. Makes sense to send him inside the fence. Besides, he'd burn too hot at this." He crouched at the door of the shack, careful to open it quiet. "This needs to be a night when cold winds blow."

#

Well, it almost worked. That's what Tabetha told herself,

later. Still later than *that* she realized that Rex hadn't planned on things staying as quiet as they did for as long as they did. But these were some *really* overconfident slavers and bandits.

There were about thirty, forty inside the breaking-camp and another twenty or so patrolling or standing guard outside, but Rex didn't seem too concerned about them. Neither was Tabetha, after she saw what passed for keeping watch among 'em. But the first two shacks of sleeping bandits weren't real hard to, ah, *secure*. Sneak in through the door, visit each bed in turn, do what you had to do.

Rex didn't stumble once and neither did she. It wasn't fun or scary or horrible or anything else like that. It was just something she had to do, and though they deserved worse it wasn't her job to do worse to them. Tabetha was just there to clean out the shacks.

So it was a shame about the girl in the third one.

She wasn't even in one of the beds; the bastards had made her sleep on the floor, Tabetha guessed. But she was on the floor and in the dark, and Tabetha had the bad luck to step on the kid's hand as she crept to the second bed. The girl yelled, the two bandits woke up, and then things got messy.

It wasn't so much those two that were the problem; they woke up fast, but not quite fast enough. The problem was that they'd been yelling, too, so she and Rex weren't going to be able to do for the rest of them quietly. And when they got out the door, lights were already showing from the other shacks as more of the enemy awoke.

Rex actually chuckled; Tabetha gave him a look which he probably missed, but he explained anyway. "If they'd left the lights off, they'd be able to see. Instead, they're all half-blind."

Tabetha allowed to herself that, yeah, this was maybe worth a chuckle. When it's two against twenty or thirty, you need all the laughs you can get.

#

You can't make weapons and armor without knowing something about how they're used, and before the Scourging, Tabetha's family had been fairly prosperous. She knew how to use her shortsword, and if any of the salvaged armor had fit her — spikes or not — she'd have worn some of it. Instead, she had the first dead sentry's leather vest over her shirt, toted a small shield, and hoped for the best.

And it actually wasn't too bad, at first. If the slavers had thought to rush 'em from the start, it would have gotten nasty, fast, but they ran up in spurts and drabs, and they died the same way. Hell, at least four, five guys got sliced by their own side, because apparently that was how these things went. In the first confused minutes, Tabetha figured she and Rex took care of another ten or so. Either dead, or not really going anywhere; at the moment, it didn't matter which.

So, she thought, four in each shack. *That's twelve, add the ones we did for, the ones they did for themselves, that leaves... hell. Too many, and now they're getting lined up.*

#

"We're doing good, but we're not there yet," Rex said, his breath just a little labored. Tabetha was almost happy about that; if the bastard had been as fresh as a daisy, she'd start thinking he wasn't quite natural. Well, the snake thing *was* unnatural, but it wasn't scary to her anymore so that didn't count. "The others are coming, but we have to whittle down a few more slavers."

They were fighting and running by now, and it was getting harder to take bandits by surprise. The bad guys had stopped using torches, too, which was letting their eyes adjust. Tabetha still managed to kidney-stab one who had run around the corner while looking over his shoulder. As the bandit fell to the ground, she said, "What about your friends? Why aren't they in the stew here?"

"They wanted to be!" said Rex, as he mercifully stamp-broke the neck of the mortally wounded bandit while lunging at the bandit's buddy. "I told them to go after the scouts and the dogs. Too many men with swords and armor here!"

"Oh, you *noticed* that, Hey-You?" Tabetha said as she smacked the reeling second bandit in the face with her shield. It made an unpleasantly wet sound. "I was starting to wonder!"

...And then she swore as — well, Tabetha Frei was never what you'd call a poet. To her, it felt exactly like somebody had just grazed her arm with a crossbow bolt. She looked down, and hey! Somebody had.

Then she was suddenly yanked out of sight around the corner, just before another four bolts followed the first. "Right," said Rex, and if Tabetha thought that his voice was controlled before, well, now she knew what he really did sound like under stress. "I'm charging them. Coming?" He didn't wait to hear her answer; instead, he bolted around the corner, likely to his death.

Tabetha always told herself that she would've followed him anyway, sure: it wasn't the twang of a couple more crossbow bolts that made her forget the wound and the fatigue and the fear. But the twangs didn't hurt, either. Besides, since he was dead or dying, then what the hell else was she supposed to do? Run *away*?

So... she charged.

#

And, oh, Rex wasn't dead. It didn't even look like he had gotten hit.

There were a half-dozen guys with crossbows, maybe more — but it takes time to reload most crossbows, and they had used up their backups shooting at Rex and missing. But there were at least three who still had their hands full cocking their weapons while Rex fought the other two (one was already on the ground, dead). *Another unfair fight*, that voice in her head thought. The voice sounded happy about it as Tabetha headed for the crossbowmen.

Her first bandit just died from a slashed throat; the second got two broken hands for his trouble when Tabetha's shield smashed into his crossbow, and that put him out of the fight for a while. But the third was smart enough to drop the bow entirely and close on her, and he was bigger and stronger than she was. He knew it, he knew she knew it, and he was clearly looking forward to proving it. It was all Tabetha could do to get the shield between him and her, and the man grinned nastily as he grabbed the shield with both hands and wrenched it away.

Only he used too much effort, because Tabetha didn't even try to hold onto the shield; she let it fly out of her grasp and dropped to a crouch, her sword blurring in an arc that ripped into the bandit's exposed legs. Nobody wears greaves to bed, not even a hardened desert slaver. And when you can't walk and the blood spurts, strength and size mean nothing.

Tabetha told herself that she didn't end that bandit's life right away because she had to finish helping Rex first. Sure. That was the reason. And real soon now she'd start believing it, too.

#

The rest of the fight wasn't much of a thing. Dallin and Desert Joe brought up the rest of the slaves to Rex and Tabetha; the captives were in rags and only a couple of 'em had weapons, but they were screaming, and they were *there*. Some of the slavers got torn limb from limb; the others ran... right into the rest of the folks from the slave caravan. Even then it could have been a fight, but by then the eight bandits left just gave up. They threw their weapons on the ground and surrendered.

They were the first and only ones in the entire fight to do that, in fact. Tabetha was inclined to hang 'em all, on general principles, but when she saw Dallin coming up with Rex to look over the captives, she muttered angrily at herself. Dallin had taken a wound or two, but looked better: more sure of himself than Tabetha had ever seen him, although on admittedly short acquaintance. *Maybe we can salvage some of these slavers, too*, she thought.

And Dallin did pick out two as being worth saving. The others? Rex made them strip down to their drawers, then pointed west, away from the rising sun. "I've heard you got another camp down that way," he said. "Better get going. It's a long walk on a hot day."

One of the raiders started raising a fuss over that; Rex gave him a minute to get up to speed, then reached out with one hand. Desert Joe — who had somehow found a hat, a tall stick to lean on, and a long coat filled with pockets full of snakes — promptly handed Rex a crossbow; Rex swung it into position, and fired from the hip without a word.

The bandit fell to the ground, still twitching from the bolt in his brain. Rex pointed west, *again*, with the crossbow. "Don't worry," he said. "Your friends will find you. Even if it's just by looking for the buzzards."

The remaining bandits decided not to hang around while Rex reloaded.

#

Rex waited about three minutes before instantly taking command of what was, honestly, a mob. "All *right*," he said. "You know who you listened to, inside that fence. If you still listen to them, and if *they'll* listen to *me*, we're going to be fine. We're not staying here, and even if you don't want to throw in with us, you shouldn't stay here either."

He turned to Desert Joe. "Desert Joe, you and Dallin take those two new recruits here and get everything we need to go take our own walk. Shoes, water, food, clothes, weapons, armor, in that order. No alcohol, nothing too heavy to carry in the desert."

"And what am I doing, Hey-You?" asked Tabetha.

Rex looked at her with honest surprise. "We're going to shake these people into order." He drew closer, to talk a little quieter. "And then we're going to get out of here *before* those people in Wells figure out we wrecked their breaking-camp, and come after us."

Tabetha narrowed her eyes. "You don't strike me as a runner," she said.

Rex smiled. "We're not running," he said. "We're making them chase us. I have *plans* for Wells, Miss Tabetha. And those plans start by making them afraid of what's out here in the desert. Having a scouting party never come back should send a message."

"For a start," said Tabetha. She looked around and asked, "We leaving the bodies where they lie?"

"Yes," Rex said after a moment. To Tabetha's surprise, Rex sounded a little uncomfortable about that. She decided this was a good thing; it was probably for the best that Rex not get too much enjoyment out of his work. She patted his shoulder in what she hoped was a determinedly friendly way.

"Don't worry about it, Rex," she said. "That sends a message, too."

THE CASE OF THE VANISHING VISITOR

A Tom Vargas mystery

Rick's
Cin City
(Formerly San Felipe, Baja)
Kingdom of New California
2529 AD

I didn't know that the dame was trouble when she pushed her way through the bead curtains at Rick's. Hell, I didn't even know she was a dame. High nobles here in Cin City like to dress down when they're slumming around with the common people. Sometimes a big shot likes to drink or get indelicately proposed in peace, you know what I mean?

Me, I wasn't worrying about that. I wasn't worrying about anything; my latest Case had Cleared, and so had the check. I had enough simoleons for a small carouse of my own, so picking up more work could wait until Monday. Besides, work was coming to me. And she was moving just as straight as a ley line, right my way.

The dame sat down like she owned the table. And from the look I was getting of her earrings, she might have. It never fails: a noble might dress up in jerkins and jeans to have some rough fun, but they'll be damned before they wear costume jewelry. It's a rookie mistake. Sometimes it's the last one they ever make, too, depending on how rough the fun was.

This one didn't look that clueless, though. She didn't seem scatterbrained at all as she took out a cigarette and waited for me to light it. As I did, she said, "I'm being followed, Shamus."

I shook my head as I snapped a smoke out of my own pack and flicked the lighter again. "You youngsters. Always rushing the story."

"Flattery is nice, Shamus Vargas." my new companion said, "but we both know you're not that much older than me."

"Ah," I said. "You're a high noble, then."

"Why?" The noblewoman sounded actually curious that I had pegged her so fast.

"You have to be pretty high up to not give a damn how old people think you are. How many, how soon?"

The sudden subject change didn't faze her. "Three, at least." She thought about it. "Maybe five minutes. They're definitely going to come, though."

"What, they got a trace on you? And where are your body-guards, anyway?" This town isn't as rough as some, but it never hurts to have some muscle to glare away the drunks.

The noblewoman shook her head. "There's no time." I'm not going to lie; when you're a Shamus, you get an almost dirty thrill down your spine when you hear a sentence like that. What happens next is usually gonna be painful, eventually, but at least it ain't gonna be dull.

"All right," I said, and took a quick drag at the smoke before stubbing it out. "You can call me Tom."

"So you're taking the Case, then?" she asked, one eyebrow raised. "Just like that, without even my own name?"

"Sure." I waited a beat. "So, what's your name?"

That got a smile and an outstretched hand. I noted with interest the callouses on it. "Sofia. Sofia Huston Redgrave, if that might change your mind."

"Nah," I said as somebody at the entrance of Rick's started to shout. I stood up. "But with fancy monikers like those, you ain't gonna get the hard-luck discount."

#

There were three of the galoots pushing through the crowd now, and two of 'em looked like Central Casting *sicarios*, all machismo and no brains. I could tell the third was the one in charge, and not just because he had better shoes. There was the doohickey he was peering at, for one thing. It looked like a kid's compass, only the arrow pointed right at us.

I decided to skip any jokes about personal magnetism (okay, okay: I didn't think of a good one until a couple of days later) and instead ducked left and around a table as the three moved closer. The three of 'em didn't waver on their path, so I figured they weren't here for me. Which made sense. Why would they be?

The two *sicarios* were smart enough to recognize the suit and the tie, though. As I moved closer, I could tell they were getting ready to slap back if they thought I was about to get frisky with them. They weren't subtle about it, either. After all, they had two to my one, and they knew it.

That's better math in an alley. In a waterfront dive with plenty of rotgut, 'outnumbered' is more of an opinion. And I didn't need to work myself up to a fight; it had already started. I just needed to let them know it.

I started the inning by snatching a handy mug from one drinker's hand and throwing it in the face of the *sicario* to the left. Right away, I ducked low and slammed into his buddy, hard enough to send him sprawling. Then I whirled around again and got three, four punches into the first guy, just as he was blinking away the cheap booze.

Now, they grow *sicarios* tough in Cin City, and nothing I had just done was going to put these guys down for the count. But this was Rick's. When somebody starts punching around like this, everybody else figures it's time for the bar fight. After the first ten seconds, it doesn't even matter who's on which side. It'll all get sorted out when the coppers show up.

In the meantime there was plenty of confusion and delay, to quote the Lore. I took advantage of it to get up to the doohickey guy. Up close he looked foreign, northern foreign. Not barbie foreign, though. He looked like he was maybe from the badlands up by what used to be Deseret; he had the cold eyes for it, and the gait that comes when you wear leathers all day instead of an off-the-rack Cin City suit.

I smacked the doohickey out of his hands, on general principles. "The hell you thinking, pal?" I shouted in his face. "You know what the cops do if you're caught with a magic item in this town?" I figured, being a foreigner, he wouldn't know the answer was 'not a damned thing, unless they had to.' Although using one to stalk a noblewoman wasn't real smart—

And that's when the son of a bitch stabbed me.

#

It *hurts*, that's what getting stabbed feels like. Getting a knife stuck in you *hurts*. I've had it happen before, and it never gets any more fun. All of that stuff about 'a cold spike of fire went through me' or 'a wave of pain ripped through my side'? That's how people who *don't* get stabbed talk about it. When it happens to you, there's only two things you think about. One is: *Dammit, that **hurt***.

The second thing is: *I'm gonna get that **cabron** who just stabbed me.* That's the problem with using knives, you see. It takes longer to kill a guy with one than the Lore would have you think. And for damned sure I wasn't gonna let him wind up and have another go at it.

I think he wasn't expecting that, or that I can move my battered hide pretty quick when I got the right motivation. He really didn't expect me to make a game try at breaking his knife arm with both arms and a knee; and didn't *that* just make the hole in my gut a bit bigger, with pain on the side? But even if I didn't break the arm, I made him let go of the knife.

Which was still in my side. I might have pulled it out and freaked him out even more — I got a glance at him through slightly dizzied eyes; he had the look of somebody whose day had just gotten weird — but I'm not a dumbass. The knife was fine where it was, plugging the hole. Mostly plugging the hole. That was going to be a problem.

But that could wait until after the damn fight, so I took a pretty good swing at the now-knifeless guy's own gut. I was hoping that he wasn't wearing a kidney belt, and surprise! He wasn't. Didn't quite fold like a cheap suit (whatever *that* means; it's just something Shamuses say), but he went sprawling.

Only, as he staggered away, the bastard threw down some kind of weird ball. When it hit the ground... ugh. The sight was worse than the sound, and the smell was worse than both. I might have been able to bull through it, only the damned knife chose that moment to plop out of my gut. Oh, who am I kidding? I was gonna take a nap pretty soon anyway. And so I did.

At least the knife wasn't still in me when I fell down. That would have sucked.

#

I woke up, which is always nice to have happen after a fight. And I itched like a *bastardo*, too. Come to think of it, that was probably what woke me up.

When I opened my eyes, I was lying on a table at Rick's. From the clock on the wall, maybe ten, fifteen minutes had passed. That kind of pissed me off; just once I'd like to wake up after being knocked out to find out it's two weeks later and the guy who put me under had already been caught by hard-working Cin City street cops. But no, I was going to have to run this guy down myself. As usual.

I swung to a sitting position, and winced. *Maybe I won't* **run**, I thought. Hobbling seemed more my speed right now. I peered down at my side, and winced again. It looked like I'd need to buy my next Shamus suit a few months early. On the other hand, I had gotten better than the usual rough bandaging. And I felt... better than I should have. "Must have been a flesh wound," I muttered.

"Only if you count a kidney as 'flesh'," came a voice behind me. I gingerly turned my head to see... Sofia, was it?... gamely smiling at me. She was wiping her hands dry with a napkin as the hubbub of a police investigation went around us. We were in a bubble of nobody bothering us, though, which confused me until I remembered her *last* names. 'Huston Redgrave' was about as noble as it gets before the King starts keeping a spare eye on you.

I tried a chuckle. I could live with how much it hurt. "Didn't you hear? Shamuses don't have organs. We're like potatoes, inside."

"You mean, all eyes and starch?" Sofia was quick with the comebacks, which was nice.

"And loud ties. Where's mine?"

"I took it off before it strangled you. Why the hell do you people wear those, anyway? Nobody else has for centuries."

"Exactly," I agreed, and levered myself off the table. I had the predictable weak knees halfway through; I expected Sofia to rush over to help, but not how quick she'd be getting there. She was stronger than she looked, too. No, *tougher*. Our nobles try to stay in shape, sometimes with a little magical assistance, but she wasn't sporting any kind of gym job. It was more like she *worked*, instead of worked out.

"Careful," she said as my legs decided that they were going to let me stand up after all. "Those stitches will hold until I can get a real doctor to you, but don't push it."

I gingerly touched the bandage. Didn't feel too bad, really, although you can't suture away a sliced kidney. "Nice work," I said. "Yours?"

Sofia shrugged. "I've picked up a few things," she said, as if field surgery (and probably a little officially-illegal healing magic) was the most normal thing for a New Californian aristocrat to know. "Seemed the least I could do, since I got you stabbed for nothing."

"Nah," I said. "You never get stabbed for *nothing*. That's how you know you're getting somewhere in the Case." Which is true, but I do prefer getting punched. Or kicked. Or just threatened. Threatening is nice, because I won't need a new suit afterward. A thought struck me. "Wait. What's the Case?"

"My friend's been kidnapped," said Sofia. "And if I don't find her soon, I never will. But it doesn't matter, because you're going to the hospital."

"Now, Sofie," I said as I found my hat and tie, "you're from around here, so you know how it goes. If that guy didn't want me on the Case, he shouldn't have stabbed me without even saying 'hi' first."

#

"Her name's Irene," Sofie told me as we went into the night. "She's in way over her head, and I can't go to the police. Do I need to say why?"

We weren't attracting too much attention as we moved away from the bar. Rick had found me a spare shirt out of the grab box. It fit all right; he runs the kind of joint whose regulars sometimes find it handy to exit dressed different than when they came in. I didn't even have to leave a deposit. Getting stabbed on the premises apparently got you points there.

"Gonna guess she's in the wrong line of work?" I said. "And you're not going to tell me her full name, either?" Which worried me, a little. Usually the only time you were cagy about names like that was if there was magic involved somehow. Not that we have any mages in New California. Just ask anybody; they'll tell you.

"I know the one she gave me," Sofie said carefully. "I don't know if it was her real one. She's from Deseret."

I barely managed not to swear. "She a regular refugee, or on the run?" It's not like the old days, when it seemed like half of Deseret fled south after the Universal Dominion beat them in their war, but we still get a trickle of refugees. And usually they're bringing trouble with them, the poor bastards.

"On the run," said Sofie. "I think. But I never asked her why. Should I have?"

"Probably," I said as I looked around, in the vain hope that the guy who stabbed me was waiting patiently outside for me to notice. You never know, right? "But I guess it doesn't matter, right this second. You have a plan? Because the trail's cold." Shamuses can get these hunches about where somebody's gone but only if we're actually chasing somebody. It's all part of our damned luck.

"I don't have a plan," said Sofie, "but I do have this." 'This' was the doohickey I had manhandled before. It looked pretty bent, not to say broken, but Sofie didn't seem to care as she ducked into an alleyway. She found a convenient barrel to use as a table, and started working on the thing without a care.

I followed her, more than a little bemused. For a member of the nobility, Sofie here had a real interesting knack of getting herself into bad places. Didn't she know that mashers and bashers and the odd thug hung out in alleys? And they didn't always like having people drop by unannounced.

#

No mashers in the alley; I guess they were on their coffee break. Or they just didn't want to watch a New Californian noblewoman field-strip a broken magic item. Come to think of it, I didn't want to watch that, either. Or at least, not this close.

Sofie knew what she was doing, though. Nothing blew up, and the miniature toolkit she pulled out looked like the ones that pros use. In fact... "I hear the Adventurer's Guild has been busy lately," I said casually.

She flicked me a look and a smile. "Yes, I hear that too," she said as she cleaned out some kind of crystal vial in the center of the doohickey, then refilled it with a hair she had wrapped up. "Lots of recruiters around, trying to get people for some digs going on, up in the Cold-Lands. It seems like they'll take *any-body*, too." Sofie straightened up. "Well, it's not pretty, but it'll work for a while."

"Great!" I said, and paused. "What did you do?" Although I could guess.

And I was right; Sofie rolled her eyes and said, "I turned the thing tracking me into something that will track Irene. It won't last forever, though, so we need to go." She lifted the item, and it indeed hummed with magical energy now. Although I didn't like the faint whine coming from it. That was going to get old, quick.

"Lead the way, Benefactress Sofia," I said with a bow better suited to a Castle royal reception. Sofie gave me a mock-dirty look at my use of her title.

"Sofie's fine, thanks," she muttered as we left the alley. I had guessed *that* would be the case, too. Some nobles like not having to work for a living. Some don't. I had Sofie pegged as one of the latter.

#

The trail took us south, towards the docks. It was early enough in the evening that people were still working at having a great night instead of living with the aftermath of one.

We moved through the crowds pretty clean, but I wondered why Sofie didn't have a Brute Squad along for the walk. She could afford it. She could also afford to bribe the cops out of officially noticing a fugitive Deseret mage. Hell, *I* can afford that level of bribery. Nobody wants to hand over mages to the Universal Dominion.

I wasn't too worried about it; *every* Case a Shamus takes is complicated. If it was easy enough for the cops to handle, my clients would never darken my door. Or interrupt my dinner.

But since I was on the Case, I was doing my job: which, right now, meant looking out for the two of us. Sofie seemed to need both hands and most of her attention keeping the doohickey running, and I didn't have her pegged as somebody who could spot a tail anyway. But I could — and after three blocks, I did.

Never hiss or stage-whisper when you're telling somebody on the down-low. People notice that. Instead, I casually said, "We're being followed. One block back, other side of the street. Guy, northern coat and hat. Friend of yours?"

"If I had somebody helping me, he'd be walking next to us," Sofie said. She didn't sneak a look back, which surprised me. It's hard not to peek. "What do we do? And you should know that I'm no good with a blade."

"Gotcha. How are you with your fists?" I asked as I used shop windows to keep an eye on our tail.

"I'd be better off using the blade."

I sighed. Guess 'duelist' wasn't on Sofie's secret skill list, too.

"Well, maybe you can dump a garbage can over him if this doesn't work."

"If what doesn't work, Shamus?"

"Nothing too bad, Sofie." I turned around and walked back. "I'm just gonna go break a rule, that's all."

#

Yeah, yeah, the Lore says you're supposed to shake a tail. The Lore isn't on a schedule like I am, though. This guy would run, talk, or fight. Any of those would tell me something. Sure, maybe it would be something I already knew, like how nasty the pavement tastes, but you don't get much time to waste when somebody's been snatched. I was willing to donate a split lip to the cause; it wouldn't be the first time, either.

Up close, our northern friend looked even more out of place than he had when I spotted him. Which was the only reason why I spotted him; on his home turf he was probably a ghost. He was of medium height, sported a short beard, and had grey-blue eyes that didn't keep moving because they were already seeing everything at once. If the heat was bothering him in his leather coat and trail jeans, he didn't show it.

He didn't run or posture, either. What he was, was *careful,* as I approached, and I made damn sure I was, too. I nodded at him. "Evening, mister."

He looked at me, calmly enough. "Evening. But I thought it was 'Señor' down here." He spoke Court English with an almost Deseret rasp. I don't know why that didn't surprise me.

I gave him a smile. "We try to be friendly to visitors," I said. Which is true: visitors have money, and we have so many things for them to spend it on. "But can I ask why you're tailing us?" He blinked at that, so I shrugged. "I know, it feels dirty to just come out and say that, somehow. But the lady and me, we're kind of in a hurry."

"Huh," he said. "So am I." His hand came up; I tensed, but he was only pointing. "Those friends of yours?"

Like a damned idiot, I looked where he pointed — and saw three guys pushing their way towards Sofie. Again.

"Dammit," I said, largely to myself. "I already used that line."

None of the three were locals, this time. These didn't look Sonoran, either. Maybe farther south; you hear there's some orc tribes down there causing trouble, pushing folks north. I don't worry about that stuff, because I figure some bright folks in Sonora and the Castle are busy worrying about it for me. Whoever these guys were, they were dumb enough to think they could just snatch a New Californian noblewoman off of the street.

And since nobody ever tries it, these winners got away with it, too. One made a distraction by suddenly gesticulating and ranting in the middle of the street, while the other two crowded her quick and started hustling her to the nearest alley. Sofie wasn't saying anything, either, which could mean anything from some alchemical goop to a knife pressed against her side. Dammit, dammit, dammit. I'd need to move fast, but the crowd was big enough that I'd need a distraction of my own to push my way through. In front of me, the guy doing the ranting saw me glaring at him. He stopped, touched his fingers to his hat, and grinned as he turned to go — only right then a knife blossomed in his shoulder, and the grin turned into a scream.

Which, as distractions go, wasn't too bad. A little loud for a Cin City street, though; the street erupted in shouting and running, the kind of both that attracts the cops. I knew Sofie didn't want them sticking their noses into this, so I figured I'd just have to go rescue her myself.

#

Ever try to run with stitches in you?

And no, it's not a real scream. Only people who've never gotten a knife in the side think that joke's a knee-slapper.

So, yeah, it hurt; worse, it felt like a strain. But I didn't need to go far, and when I got there, I decided not to stop. Which is a nice way of saying that I barreled into one of the guys leading Sofie away, and bounced him off of a wall. I didn't hit the wall myself, so I totally meant to do that, yeah. I also totally meant to hit the other guy in the face without putting on my brass knuckles, too. Luckily I hit him in a softish spot, so I didn't totally wreck my hand.

But it didn't knock him down, either. He gave me a nasty smile and flicked out a knife. "You hit like a..." well. I don't know what the word was, since his Spanglish was really Spanish, and from deep in the sticks at that. But I'm guessing it wasn't polite.

"Yeah, this is where I came in," I muttered as I did a spin kick and knocked the knife out of his hand. And that *really* hurt, because I had forgotten the damned stitches again! But they were real eager to remind that they were there. And unhappy as hell, too. But they didn't quite pop out, so I told myself to behave better and stop pissing 'em off.

After this fight. The guy still on his feet was circling me, clearly trying to get some grappling and gouging in. That turned out to be pretty dumb, because Sofie pulled a bat out of her purse in one of those old gags, straight from the Lore. The nobles get all the fun toys, don't they? And she was... pretty bad with a bat, yeah. But when you're hitting somebody in the back of the head with your magically summoned one, just how good do you have to be?

You kind of expect little blue birds or something, again just like in the Lore. Instead, the guy went wobbly-kneed, staggered a few paces, fell down... and then Sofie smacked him with the bat again, only this time in a place where getting hit spoils the rest of your night, or maybe week. I know I'm supposed to wince in sympathy when that kind of thing happens, but I didn't feel like it.

Instead, I slipped on my brass knuckles and did a little circling of my own around the first guy, who was just now pulling himself out of a trash pile. One arm was bloody and didn't look quite right, which explained why he hadn't already started dancing; but he had that look. The kind that said he wasn't done just quite yet.

Now, I'm not the kind of guy who likes giving beatdowns, and it looked like I already had given him one anyway, so I tried to make nice. "Look, *amigo*," I said, in as slow a Spanglish I could manage, "Whatever they're paying you, it's not worth it, see?

You give up, tell us who sent you, and you can go get that arm seen to. Hell, I'll even throw in an orson for the sawbones." Well, why not? It'd go right to Sofie's bill, under expenses. I'll rescue somebody for free but the nobility pays for what they get. "I think I'm being real reasonable here, neighbor."

Instead of replying, the guy *pulled* his arm straight with the other; the cracking of bone wasn't fun to hear. Neither was the sudden smell of ozone and corruption coming from him as he started to chant, hard enough to raise a wind. Guess the *hechicero* didn't think the negotiations would go the way he'd want.

#

Well, at least he wasn't summoning demons. If it had been one of those, it wouldn't have mattered what Sofie wanted; I'd go right to the cops with that, or probably the Flatfoots up at the Castle. They take diabolism real seriously in this town. New California doesn't have any mages, see? So when a bad one shows up, the mages we don't have gotta be careful about taking them down. They get too public, there's a bastard ambassador from the evil mage-empire in the middle of the continent who'll notice, and start looking for them. And we'd all be supposed to give them up. Which we would... if we had any mages in New California, which we don't.

But it wasn't that bad, as I said. But it *was* still bad, because what he did call up looked like it was made up of spite and meanness, with needles for teeth *and* eyes, with both all over its head. The stench was even worse, a mix of rotting breath and alchemical stink. I'd never seen anything like it before, and I was guessing it was supposed to be hot stuff, seeing as how proud the *hechicero* looked about bringing it to my attention.

Fine. To quote the Lore: shit just got real. I pulled out my pistol.

My buddy finally proved that he was wasn't from around here, because he laughed at the sight of me pulling a gun. His spirit didn't bother; instead, it leaped at me — and bounced. It was now blackened everywhere its skin touched my body; if I'd thought I'd get all my fingers back, I'd have grabbed it with my other hand and held on until the vicious thing burst into flames. But at least it was more thoughtful, now. And in a lot of pain.

I was a little surprised. Most local spirits know better than to take a swing at a Shamus. In fact: "Didn't you see the hat, *tarado*?" I snarled at the two of them. My gun was pointed right at the *hechicero*, because I figured I could risk a bluff. "The hat means you picked the wrong fight in the wrong town with the wrong Shamus. Get on the damn ground with your hands on your head."

For a second I thought he'd even do that, but then he decided to run. Faster than I could catch him, too. I swore at that — it wasn't that I could shoot him for real. The gun doesn't do that.

But then the *hechicero's* spirit tried to run for it, too. It got ten feet before I shot it in the back. It rolled a few more feet, then feebly tried to put back in all the bits of it that I had just blasted off. I doubted it'd work, but I limped over anyway and ground its face in like it was a really annoying cigarette butt. I really, really hoped that this was one of the spirits whose master felt what it felt.

...What? Oh, yeah, about what I said earlier: the gun doesn't usually work on *people*. On spirits it still does the business. But it's not magic. Ask anyone.

"At least we still have two to talk to," I said as I joined Sofie, still eagerly waiting to see if her guy was going to do something stupid, like move or breathe too much. If she wasn't already a member of the Adventurer's Guild, there was something seriously wrong with their recruiters. Sofie had all the right instincts for the life.

A cough got my attention. "Sorry, but that's the only one left." It was our tail from outside the alley. He was cleaning a knife that I'd last seen in a guy's shoulder. "That guy back there didn't know when to take a hint," he went on, sounding slightly apologetic.

Sofie looked at him steadily, not quite brandishing the bat. "Can you?" she said.

That got her a respectful, short nod. "Yes, ma'am," he said.

"Name's Jed. Jed Smith. I may or may not be wanting any trouble."

The name didn't really mean much to me, but it clearly did to Sofie. "You're a diehard, then?" she said. "That's a dangerous brag, even here. Next you'll be telling me you're a Danite."

Smith smiled. "If I *was* a Danite, ma'am, believe me: I would lie about it in a heartbeat."

Sofie raised an eyebrow. "Your people stole that line from the Jesuits," she said.

"Oh, I'm sure they still had it afterward." Smith looked over at the last remaining thug on the ground. "I need to know something he knows," he said.

"Same here," I finally interjected. "We're looking for a girl named Irene. You, too?"

That got me a look from both of them; Sofie's startled, Smith's was steady. I shrugged. "Why waste time? Your friend's from Deseret, this guy sounds like he's from there, that *cabron* who stuck me was a northerner, too. I don't need to be hit more than three, four times before I can take a hint."

"Fair enough," said Smith. "Yeah, I'm trying to track down Irene. She tell you her last name?" Sofie shook her head. "Good. Then I can maybe get her out of this town in one piece."

"What makes you think she wants to leave?" asked Sofie.

Smith snorted. "What makes you think she wants to stay? A lot of things had to go bad to make her run this far south. I'll believe she won't be coming back when I hear it from her own lips."

"Fine," said Sofie. "I'll hold you to that, *Mister* Smith."

"Thank you, ma'am." Smith gave another of those spare nods; I was starting to wonder if he had noticed doing it annoyed Sofie, just a little. Hell, I wonder if *she* had noticed. "I take it I can come along on this rescue mission of yours?"

"Yes," I said before Sofie did. She gave me a mild glare, and I shrugged. "He's looking for her too, right? It's easier if we're all sharing a cab." I also wouldn't mind having somebody else along to take a few of the punches my poor, abused gut would likely be getting otherwise — but I didn't think I needed to bring that up. It might have been considered impolite.

Did I really trust him? Nah. And yeah. I figured there was something he wasn't telling me. There always is. I mean, I knew there was something that *Sofie* wasn't telling me. You get used to it, when you're a Shamus. The best you can hope for is to get people to spill the beans before they end up in the campfire — yeah, that's a lousy metaphor, but it's the best one I got. I'm a city boy at heart.

#

Interviewing the last mook wasn't really hard; part of it was the way Smith kept fiddling with his knife. But mostly it was because the mook didn't want to talk to the cops any more than either Sofie or Smith did. And let me tell you: it's weird when I'm the guy in the Case who's most willing to aid the police with their inquiries. It feels almost dirty, and I didn't even have the excuse of having a few drinks first.

The problem was, this guy didn't know that much. His name was Odis, he was from across the Gulf, and this was just a job, all right? Didn't help that his Spanglish was really just Spanish, but Sofia apparently knew all the dialects. Smith didn't know any, but he spoke Evil Grin good enough to get through the language barrier.

Me, I just went through the stuff in the guy's pockets and listened for the police. They were getting to the scene a little *too* slow; I didn't like it. Cin City cops ain't sprinters but there was a dead body in the street, see? Made me wonder what was going on.

I turned back to the impromptu interrogation scene. We had gotten to the 'justification for bad choices stage' from Odis — I couldn't follow his lingo without concentrating really hard, but everybody whines in the same body language — so I interrupted. "Whatever you got, you got," I said. "Clock's ticking."

"Fine," said Sofie. She didn't look too unhappy, which was good. "He's repeating himself anyway." She flicked a look at Odis, then back at me. "Ah. What do we do with him?"

"Well, *I'm* not going to off him," I said.

"Same," said Smith. He paused for a moment, as if waiting for us to say something. When we didn't, he nodded. "Nice of you folks," he said — and then proceeded to punch Odis twice, once in the gut and the second in the back of the head. Odis didn't even have time to throw up before he was knocked out.

"...But we can't have him warning people." Smith looked around. "Any reason not to sling him in a dumpster some-where?"

"Nah," I said. "Garbage day ain't until Saturday. He'll wake up before that. You grab his arms, I'll get his legs."

#

We couldn't find a cab. Which is weird, because normally they're so many of 'em it's a nuisance, but the street was getting restless, like something was riling it up. People didn't seem real happy to be out and about, but they didn't know why yet.

Smith picked up on it, too. Guess those desert instincts were kicking in, or something. "The place always this jangly?" he asked, as we followed Sofie's tracker. She had fiddled with it a bit more, hopefully to keep still more people from finding us as we found them. So far, so good.

Then again, one of the things Odis had told us was that he hadn't been running with a big crew. But it wasn't a nice one. If I had gotten the full briefing beforehand, I would have left him tied up, and somewhere more convenient to the cops. Odie was part of a snatch gang.

If you haven't heard of snatch gangs before, good. They're nasty. It's a real bad world out there these days, and some people like the idea of having other people doing all the work, whether they want to or not. They'll pay a lot of money for fresh work-ers, too. And there's always a bunch of idiots out there who think that New California's a great hunting ground.

Well, it's not. But we have to work at keeping it that way. The problem is, some of the gangs sell to the Universal Dominion — the mages have a standing bounty on any magic-user handed over to them, and it's one bill they always pay promptly — so we have to get rid of them on the quiet. But since we do get rid of them on the quiet, we keep getting new idiots showing up.

This bunch was the latest batch. Punks and mooks from all over, running from the fighting down south or the badlands up north. Their boss — the one who stabbed me — was from up there. 'Posh Fred,' they called him, and Smith had been just a little too quick to give a blank look when he heard the name for the first time. I figured it was probably some kind of Mormon diehard thing.

No, I wasn't assuming. Me and Sofie had a couple of minutes at one point to ourselves (Smith was checking our backs for yet another tail), and I took the time to ask a few questions. "So," I said, "I figured out what 'diehard' means. But what's a Danite?"

"Fanatics," Sofie said. "You know how the Mormons lost their king, right?"

"Sure," I replied. "The Dominion killed everybody in the dynasty they could find when they took Salt Lake City." And a whole bunch of other people, too, but that never makes it into any of the sagas. "But they missed one or two."

"Probably," Sofie replied. "Well, definitely, depending on how far out you go. But there's been rumors for a long time that some people from the main branch of the Smith dynasty have survived and are still out there. True Kings, and so forth."

I looked at Smith. He didn't look very kingly. He didn't look scruffy enough to be a True King, either. "So Smith there is royal?"

Sofie shook her head. "The exact opposite. He's taken the 'Smith' last name in case the Dominion ever tries to seriously track down the bloodline. The idea is, the magic will detect him, instead of whoever the spell was supposed to be looking for."

"That's..." I stopped, at a loss for words. Sofie shook her head.

"That's who the Danites are, Shamus. If they were real. But they don't exist, hey? Just like the true king of Deseret."

#

"So, tell me about Irene," I said when we finally found a cab.

"What's her deal, Sofie? Or *you* could tell me, Mr. Smith."

I didn't expect a straight answer from him, and I didn't get one. He just shook his head and said, "Don't know enough about this place or what she's doing here, sorry. I'll tell you this, though: Miss Irene won't take kindly to being captured. She sees a chance to ruin somebody's day over it, she'll take it and worry about it later."

"Yes, that sounds like her," said Sofie. She turned to me. "I met her about six months ago. She's been a very good friend ever since."

"Of you, your husband, both, or neither?" I asked. Smith's eyes bugged out slightly, and he started to cough. Sofie and I looked at him, confused. "What?" I said. "It's a reasonable question."

"Yes. And the answer's neither," said Sofie. "Irene didn't pursue any affairs. She only even flirted when she was worried about not fitting in."

"Not interested?" I said.

"No. I asked her about it once, and she said that as a foreigner any liaison could be dangerous." I chuckled at the joke; Smith looked a little confused. "We met because of— well, remember that dig I was telling you about, earlier? It's to the north, and in some pretty sketchy territory. Fought-over territory, if you get my drift. Not everybody wants to do salvage archeology in debatable lands.

"But that's where the work is, right? If you can get it." Sofie looked at her newly-roughened hands. "They'd take my money and even make sure I got a good return on investment, but the Guild wouldn't even think about letting me go along at all unless I could pull my weight. So I needed tutoring, and Irene had the right skill set."

"That sounds like the— Irene," said Smith. He shrugged. "I'm sure it's no surprise I know her. And she's not running from *me*."

"She didn't mention her friends much," said Sofie.

"I didn't say I was her *friend*, ma'am. I would never presume to claim that privilege."

Sofie nodded. "I had several people teaching me useful life skills; after a few days I paid them off and just worked with Irene. We got along well, and I didn't have to spend half the session convincing her that I wanted to learn the messy things, too. She's a good teacher; if she didn't have other plans, I'd have sponsored her for the University.

"But she wanted in on the dig itself, so I offered to grubstake her. Goodness knows I could afford it, and I bet that making her and me a package deal couldn't hurt with the Guild. And it worked! Yesterday they let us know that we had been accepted. The two of us were waylaid on our way out for a celebratory drink. Well, a drink for me. Irene takes her religion seriously."

"Where was your entourage?" I asked, reasonably. High nobles like Sofie usually don't go anywhere without at least somebody to keep the drunks away. Even if it's just for the look of the thing.

"I didn't bring them along, Shamus," she replied. Flatly. Too flatly.

I sighed and shook my head. "You know how this works, Sofie. You're gonna tell me eventually, and it's never gonna get any easier to tell. So why not just come clean now, before you *have* to blurt it out and maybe start crying afterward?"

"Does anybody ever do that, Tom?" she asked.

"No," I admitted. "But it'd be nice if somebody would. Just so I'd know what it's like."

"Well," said Sofie, "there's still a chance that I can get her out of this without betraying a confidence — or getting the Castle involved." She continued talking over my groan. "Yes, Tom, sorry, it's *political*. Wasn't it obvious?"

"It is. Now. It's been a long night, Sofie. I haven't even had time to drink dinner yet."

"Not to interrupt, friends," said Smith, "but this cab is being followed."

"That tears it, Sofie," I said. "Somebody's got a tracker on you." I turned to look at the cab behind us, and winced. Speaking of tearing: damn stitches were acting up again. They might even be getting worse.

"Improbable: I checked twice," replied Sofie.

"Improbable?" asked Smith.

"I'm not perfect. But I'm checking again... no."

"What about that gizmo?"

"That's the first thing I checked, Shamus. I cleaned it out before redoing it. They're not tracing us through it."

"Tell you what," said Smith. "I'll just go ask. Excuse me, friend?" he said to the cabbie. I knew him, a bit: Memo was reliable, didn't gouge you on the fare, and kept his damned mouth shut about what he heard.

Only problem was, Memo spooked easily. He already looked a little nervous as he peered back at us. "Yes, *señor*?" he said, apprehensively. He might not talk about what went on in the back of his carriage, but Memo could hear it just fine, and cabbies hate it when a Shamus shows up while on a Case. Things can get exciting.

Smith smiled, almost reassuringly. "Nothing to worry about..." he peered at the guy's license, "...Guillermo. I just need you to make a quick turn to the left at an intersection. Quick enough so I can pop out on the other side. That's all, friend."

"Leave a cab while it is in motion? That is illegal, *señor*!" It is, too. But Memo was being a little theatrical, there, and Smith picked up on it like he had been born here.

"You'll have to forgive me, friend," Smith said as he pulled out a billfold. "This isn't my birth speech, so for a moment I thought you said 'illegal.' But you said 'expensive,' right?"

Smith pulled a few grants out of his fold, and flicked a look at me; I quietly rubbed my fingers together. He pulled out a few more grants, and when *Memo* looked at me, I shook my head slightly and gave him a look that told him not to try to fleece the nice foreigner. I *do* like to be helpful.

#

I still don't know if it went down the way Smith intended, but I gotta admit: it was pretty exciting while it lasted. Memo did what he was told and made a hard left turn at the next intersection. The second the cab was out of sight of the guys tailing us, Smith popped out the other side and dived into the crowd on the sidewalk. I've seen Cin City dippers with maps of the city tattooed on their eyelids do it worse.

"You trust him?" Sofie asked me.

"Sure," I replied as I kept an eye out. Memo had slowed the carriage because of — surprise, surprise! — traffic, and the tail was just now clearing the intersection. "Time to go, though. Keep the change, Memo. And sorry!" I popped open my own door and half-yanked Sofie out with me. I say 'half-yanked' because she was right behind me; she obviously didn't know where I was going, but since I was clearing the cab, that was enough for her.

I think that's when I really *believed* Sofie was gonna end up in the Adventurer's Guild. She just had too many of the right instincts. Although she did ask, "Why are we getting out of the cab? And why did you say 'Sorry'?"

"I got the same answer for both, dollface," I intoned — every little bit helps — and pointed. "I know that *hechicero* standing up in front." And from the way he was throwing down — in damn public! — he recognized me, too.

Memo screamed, and I winced. Mostly because it was my fault, but also because he had one of those screams that you re-member for a long, long time afterward. At least it wasn't the scream somebody makes when they get skewered by a night-mare monstrosity of evil and spite. Nah, it was the scream somebody makes when a nightmare monstrosity of evil and spite suddenly manifests right *next* to him.

Lucky for Memo (and my conscience), the spirit wasn't inter-ested in him; it wanted *my* liver, and from the screeching it made when it leaped off the cab, it figured now was a great time for a snack. And, unlike the other one, a protective haze around it hinted it wouldn't burst into flames if I touched it. I hate it when the bad guys pay attention.

Still, at the time, I was so flabbergasted I almost didn't dodge out of the way. A summoning. In the damned *street*. Was this guy out of his *mind*? The alley was bad enough!

But yeah, I dodged out of the way. This time when I moved I could feel something bad going on inside those stitches, but it felt more like a stab than a tear. It was starting to get rough, and if I didn't do something quick I figured I'd end up eating the pavement. Or even if I *didn't* do something quick, but I'd rather have the choice about what lays me out, see?

So I figured it was time to do *something* quick about the *hechicero*. That meant being a little dumb, but that's all right. Dumb and me, we have an understanding; I let it hang out and... that was it. Crap, if my patter was that bad I was even closer to the edge then I thought.

#

You know how spirit summoning works? What am I saying? Of course you don't know. We don't have mages in New California. Everybody knows that.

But if we *did* have mages, and if some of them *were* good at summoning spirits, then the way it'd work would be like this. First, you'd get a spirit that'll do what you tell it. How you do that is up to you. How you do it doesn't have to be nice, either. Once you get that spirit, then it's all about making it manifest the way you want it to. Which, again, doesn't have to be nice.

Based on how this spirit was moving around, the *hechicero* summoning it *really* wasn't big on being nice. The spirit wore its body like a cheap tunic, always fighting itself to make everything fit right. The teeth were the best part of the spirit's body, which should give you an idea of the sorcerer's priorities.

So the spirit didn't have much left over to concentrate on the *mechanics* of taking a bite out of me, and I didn't make it any easier. But I wasn't going to be able to dodge for long, thanks to my side; strike that. I didn't dodge at all. Instead, I tripped over myself, and the damned thing jumped on me.

I almost lost a few fingers grabbing and squeezing shut the spirit's muzzle before it could rip out my throat, and I wasn't going to hold on for more than a second. I was pretty much out of options at this point... except for one, of course. So I leaned forward, and whispered a few words in the beast's misshapen ears, just as hard as I could.

Look, I'm not a mage, all right? I don't do magic. I don't cast spells, or anything like that. I just know some stuff, like how things... *ought* to go. And I know a hell of a lot of the Lore. Everything's in there, somewhere. Including what a living whirlwind of death and destruction *should* look like. Because what the sorcerer had come up with? Total amateur work.

Again, I didn't cast any spells: I just told the spirit what it *could* look like, and it did the rest. Okay, maybe I said it *really, really strongly*, and we were close enough to Mt. Jeannie out there in the Gulf that my words had some of Her oomph behind 'em, but it didn't have to heed me. But why wouldn't it? The Lore's idea of a good form for it was *so* much better than the sorcerer's.

It wasn't even a contest, although the sorcerer tried to make it one. The spirit broke free from me and staggered backward as it broke the sorcerer's hold on its current form and redefined itself. Although there weren't many changes. It kept the legs and arms, and the mouth was just as big and just as full of teeth as before. But now it had fur, and a proper face, and a tongue big enough for the mouth that now made up half its body.

And it was no longer interested in me. Instead, it faced its former master and started to growl. When the sorcerer sensibly started running, it gave chase, somehow *spinning* its lower body in place to build up speed. I could hear it howl "¡COMO CONEJITOS!" as the two left the scene.

I opened my mouth to quip... and fell flat on my ass. Which was a shame; I don't remember what I was going to say, but I'm pretty sure it would have been good.

#

You ever wake up because some guy's poking your gut with a knife? Really? Must be nice. This wasn't even the worst time it's ever happened to me.

The funny part was, mostly it didn't even hurt; there was something shoved between my teeth, but I could breathe, and I got a whiff of eucalyptus and menthol and... roses? They were using some kind of alchemical gunk on me, then. I tried to get up to look better, but somebody was holding onto my shoulders.

"Crap! He woke up!" Sofie's voice. If it was anyone else, I'd have gone librarian, whatever *that* means. Not all of the Lore still has its original labeling, if you know what I mean.

"Just another second, ma'am... there! Got it." That was Smith. I wondered what he had gotten, and whether it was nice.

I felt something faintly tapping on my side while Sofie cursed again, this time using a word I won't write down. "How did I miss that?" she went on. I tried to spit out the thing in my mouth; I had the horrible suspicion it was my tie.

"It was made that way," Smith said. "A slaver blade always leaves bits behind; they wriggle together later. If you don't know what to look for, you'll just think the wound's a little sore."

"This Dominion work?"

"They say no, ma'am. Funny, though: slave-takers in the badlands always seem to have a slaver blade handy. Okay, let me tie this off. I'm done. You can let up."

I felt the weight move off my shoulders, and lo! I could see. The rose scent faded, too. *Must have been Sofie,* I thought groggily as I removed, indeed, my tie from my mouth. The first hints of pain from my side where the stitches had been suggested why they had given me a medical gag.

Still, I felt a *Hell* of a lot better as I levered myself up. Guess the stitches hadn't been the only problem. "I got some of that," I said. "Evil knife?"

"Evil knife," said Smith. "They were using it to track you. You want to see the piece?"

"Only if it's under glass."

"Damn straight it is." Smith showed me the piece, now in a glass vial. It looked bigger than it should have, and it almost *dripped* evil. He shook his head. "This should have had you rolling on the ground a half-hour ago. You're tougher than you look, friend."

"Thanks. I think. Was it going to kill me?" I put my tie back on. The bite marks would fade. They usually do.

"It's not that nice," Smith said. "It's supposed to mess you up, make you easy to track by anybody with the knife it came from. That's why they call it a slaver blade."

So *that's* how they'd been tracking Sofie: they were tracking me. And why they weren't much in a hurry. "Now you *really* have to tell me why I can't go to the cops, Sofie." I said, standing up. Yeah, it didn't hurt nearly as much. "Because an illegal magical weapon like this? I should be calling in *everybody*."

"All right," said Sofie. She didn't sound happy about it, but why would she? It's never fun to admit things to the Shamus. "If I have to. It's Irene. She's not just a mage from Deseret. She's a diehard."

"No kidding," I said. Smith raised an eyebrow at either my response, or else the way Sofie didn't gasp in surprise at it. "I got the first part right away," I explained to him, "and the second part right after you joined up and Sofie didn't pitch a fit. There's only one reason you'd be down here," I unhesitatingly lied in self-defense, "and that's to bail out a mage who got in over her head and needs help. But does the *snatch-gang* know she's a die-hard?"

"If Posh Fred is here, he's at least figured it out," Smith said with a growl. "Mage-catching's one of the thing he's known for, up north. Spells don't bite on him too well. Nobody knows why, but they don't. Probably he followed Miss Irene down. He wouldn't have told anyone else in the gang, though."

"Why?" asked Sofie? "Is the other thing he's known for being a backstabbing weasel?"

"...Yes," said Smith. "Though it's not what I meant. The other thing he does is ransoming. He'll grab somebody and make it known that for the right price he'll think about letting 'em go. Goes through with it just often enough, people will keep paying up. The badlands are getting too hot for even him, though."

"Got it," I said. "That's why he wants to grab you too, Sofie. He figures you're either a mage, or you harbored one, so somebody will pay to get you back, and pay more to keep him quiet."

"He doesn't know New California very well, then," said Sofie. I'm gonna confess something: if Smith hadn't been there, either me or her might have made a comment about 'dumb hicks.' Which, to a Cin Citier, can mean anybody living more than forty feet past the city limits.

Still, it applied. I explained to Smith, "Nobody grabs people off the street here. Nobody. You try to kidnap somebody for ransom, that's instant High Justice, and the king means it literally. Kidnappers are taken to the highest building around and checked to see if they can fly."

I almost turned to Sofie at that point, because she should damn well know that, too, but just then I figured out the *real* reason why she didn't want the Castle involved. So instead I said, "You can still track Irene, right?"

"Yes," she replied. "Barely: I think they had some kind of spell-blocker artifact on her. But if this Posh Fred is really a null — sorry, somebody who can interfere with magic — then he's going to make it even harder than I thought to track her down precisely."

"But you can still get an idea of where she is generally, ma'am?" said Smith.

"Sure. Within a block or two before Posh Fred messes it up. It's technical. The spells get kind of tangled up."

"I'll take your word it, ma'am." Smith held up the vial with the evil hell-knife piece in it. "All we need is to get this close enough to *her*."

And then the two of them gave me a *look*.

#

When Posh Fred's gang found me a bit later, I was even worse than before. Split lip, black eye, and the bandages around my side had a certain *smell* to them which you usually don't get for a few days when a wound goes bad. I didn't give 'em much of a fight when they shoved me into their carriage, either. Things were kind of hot and painful.

I saw that one of the guys was local, though. Even in the state I was in I was pissed. We expect Cin Citiers to be *better* than that.

I mean, we ain't perfect but we don't run snatch teams. But this *tonto* didn't even seem to be ashamed about it.

The carriage ride was three flavors of awful, but I could tell they were taking me north, to the docks up at Cant. Made sense: the Elhai docks had too many cops and crooks and Adventurers snooping around. And all of 'em would treat breaking up a slaver gang as an act of civic virtue, not to mention a fun thing to do on a Friday night. Cant's a rougher part of town these days.

They weren't any nicer about getting me out of the carriage then they were putting me in it, let me tell you. They didn't like hauling me around, and Local Boy wouldn't even touch me at first. But they must have had orders not to let me up and die on them, because I mostly got to be carried and not dragged. I liked it, almost. It was nice to rest.

Posh Fred's hideout was in the obligatory warehouse, and in deference to their boss's name they had tried to deck it out like it was something classy, with fancy rugs and lampshades and stuff. I have a confession to make: they managed it. Usually that sort of thing comes across as tacky and pathetic, but not this time. From what I could see, this was not a bad lair.

At least Posh Fred made up for it. I had only gotten a quick glance at the guy the first time before he stabbed me; when I got a closer look, I decided that he had one of those ironic titles, because the man looked like they'd shaved a bear, given it a toupee, and made it wear a trail coat. And not a big bear, either. The sight wasn't as funny as it sounds, though. Posh Fred here just looked scary-messed up.

He had that authentic badlands rasp, too. "Damn," Posh Fred said as he looked me over, "you came down with a bad case of fucked-up fast, even for a spellboy. And if you wanna ever feel better, you better do what I say, you hear me?"

#

You know how they catch chupacabras? That's right: they stake out a goat. So guess who was baaing away? ...Look, I don't *know* what a goat sounds like. I'm a city boy. But that's not the important bit. The important bit was, I needed to be here.

And since this guy didn't know a damned thing about how we did things here: "I hear you," I made sure to wheeze out. Then I rolled my eyes back in my head, because I knew the Lore...

"Master," Posh Fred said. "You call me 'Mast'- hey! HEY!" He slapped me in the face a couple of times, but I was expecting that. These *bastardos* can't just have the whip handy; they want to see the other guy cringe at it.

So I played half-dead, eyes pretty much closed, and I wasn't real happy about how easy I was faking it. It had been a night, you know? And it might be a longer one, if Posh Fred decided that he wanted me present for a bit more fun before it was time to throw me in a cage or whatever.

Local Boy was just smart enough to know he needed to explain stuff to Posh Fred, and dumb enough to try. "Bossman," he said, the weird foreign word clumsy on his lips, "you gotta get rid of the Shamus! It ain't safe!"

"Why? The meat's a spellboy, ain't it?" said Posh Fred. His voice sounded like he was about to get nasty. "They pay good for those."

"He ain't like a mage. We don't got those," Local Boy said, reflexively. "What he's got, it's... different."

"Well, they pay even better for those." Then I heard a smack — sounded like a hand to the face — and a cry from Local Boy. "And you damn well have tons of mages here. We're gonna make a fortune, once we send the latest batch of meat north.

"But tell you what, I'll prep the meat now." I felt him lift up my hand and snap something around my wrist. "There. The meat's neutralized. We know how to fuck over spellboys, up north. Even 'different' ones. Now toss the meat in with the other one."

I almost sighed with relief. *Finally.*

#

Typical Shamus luck: instead of a cage, I got a room with a door and a lock. With not a sprig of hay to break my fall as Local Boy and some other guy tossed me in. I almost broke my nose on the floor; well, it wouldn't have been the first time.

I wasn't sure how long I'd need to wait before I should come to, but I had that problem solved for me; there was somebody else in the room. After a minute had passed without anyone coming back, she moved forward to check my pulse. When she found the whatever-it-was on my wrist, she muttered something under her breath. It didn't sound polite.

Then she moved away for a moment, then came back with what felt like a wet rag. When she started to wipe some of the crap off of my face I was *really* tempted to just let her do it for a while. Did I mention that it had been a long night?

But the job never ends. I sat up, startling her more than a little. As she retreated, I nodded politely. "Irene of Deseret, I presume?" I said.

"I may have been called that," Irene said. There was enough light to see her; she was dressed in a fairly shapeless dress, had hair that been recently shorn, and had a bracelet that — I looked down — yup, it matched mine. She also looked seriously unhappy. The kind of unhappy that slops over onto other people.

"We're getting out of here," we both said, at pretty much the same moment.

I admit it; I laughed. "All right. You first. What's your plan, Irene? I'm Tom Vargas, by the way. A Shamus?" I said helpfully.

The title didn't have any real impact on her, though. Eh, foreigners don't always catch the nuances. "I can get the door open," she said. "They got a padlock on the door, but the hinges are on this side. *And* the windowsill had a metal piece on the underside, so now I can lever up the bolts on the hinges."

"Smart," I said. "So why are you still here?" I waved the bracelet. "This thing?"

"Nah, that's just turning off our magic," Irene said. "No, the thing is, there's too many of them. I wanted to see first if anybody else would get grabbed. I figured with two people, we had a chance."

"And if I hadn't shown up?"

"Either I leave this place alive or they do, Tom Vargas," she said flatly. "It ain't gonna be both. I have sist... never mind."

"Huh. How committed are you to that?" I asked. "A blood oath, or anything? We might need somebody to throw to the Flatfoots."

"You're a sure one," said Irene. "Even now we only got a chance, mind you. We don't have any magic, you know?" She rattled her bracelet. "Don't think you can power through, either. It just reflects it back to you."

"Really? Lemme check that." I closed my eyes, and felt around the spell that was holding this unholy artifact and abomination together. After that, all I had to do was get the Mountain's attention, and She did the rest.

I opened my eyes. "Yeah," I said. "That would *mess up* any mage that cast a spell."

There was a click as the bracelet opened up and fell to the ground. "Good thing we don't have any mages in New California, hey?" I said with a grin. "Your turn."

"How did you... never mind," she said, as her own bracelet popped off. "Won't argue. Hope you're not expecting some kind of super-wizard, though."

"Nah," I said. "But every little bit helps. Gimme yours, in fact." With a look, she handed it over; I wrapped both the bracelets around my hands. "That'll do. ...What? I got sensitive mitts." Posh Fred's boys had taken my shoes, tie, and belt. They had also grabbed my cigarette case, which really steamed me (mostly because I'd brought it along, like an idiot).

"All right," Irene said as she yanked out the bolts to both hinges with two, quick upward shoves. She'd been busy in here. "You the only one coming?"

I shook my head. "Nah. Sofie and Smith are gonna drop by in a bit."

"Dagnabbit," she said. "Sofie should have gone to your police... hold on. *Which* Smith?"

"He says his name is Jed."

That stopped her cold. "Oh, come *on!*" Irene said, not really to me. "I wasn't in *that* much trouble."

"We're sneaking through a slaver den without real weapons,

lady. Or shoes. If that ain't trouble, you lead an interesting life."

\#

The good thing about slaver dens is that they don't have too many big pointy things. Your average slaver likes clubs, because it ain't as easy to kill somebody with one by accident. I prefer clubs for the same reason. Shamuses can kill, but we don't like to. Usually it's for the law to decide if somebody's gotta take the long dive into the dark.

Irene wasn't as fussy about it, though. The first guy we found got that piece of iron right in the— look, she killed him quick, okay? I didn't say anything, because I was too busy keeping him from yelling, but I didn't say anything afterward, either. I didn't ask her what it was like, being locked in here for a couple of days — and she didn't give any details, either. Probably better that way.

Besides, the guy had a club, and a real dagger. And some keys, which was real nice to see. It was gonna be easier to get out of this warehouse with 'em.

\#

I swear, just sneaking out was my plan. Sneak out, reunite Irene and Smith, then Sofie gets the cops and we let *them* knock around the bad guys. Ain't that why I pay taxes, am I right?

But maybe Irene wasn't really on board for that because we managed to run across three more slavers before I twigged. All by themselves, and the third one was looking real nervous when we took him down.

"You know," I said as I tied that one up (Irene wasn't doing the old 'hold person/slit throat' thing, though she *had* gutted one guy who hadn't gotten knocked out quick enough), "we *do* have doors to the outside in Cin City."

"And if enough of 'em start running for one, I'll go through it, too," replied Irene. "In the meantime, I have a dispute with these people. And I want to make sure they know it."

"You could send one back, let him know that way," I said.

"Nope. Don't have to." Irene carefully spat. "Posh Fred is getting the message just fine."

So I followed her. Well, what was I gonna do, throw Irene over one shoulder and leave? Assuming I even could: I still had the damn stitches in my side, though they were much better now that the evil hell-knife piece was out of me.

But we were definitely not sneaking at this point. Nothing loud, no band or anything, but we weren't gonna surprise Posh Fred any. When I mentioned that, Irene laughed, real rough. "There's more than one kind of surprise, Mr. Vargas."

#

We ran into two more guys, this time at once. That one, I had to sweat a little, and Irene a little bit more. "Darn it," she said as we went through their stuff afterward, "don't these people have any *food*?"

"What, in their pockets?" I said. "This is a warehouse, though. There's got to be something in here to eat."

"Everything that stays too long in this place ends up stinking of slavery," she said. "I couldn't eat the victuals here. I'm trying real hard not to burn the whole place down until we're out of here."

Yeah, I noticed that last bit, too. But I wasn't gonna eat anything in here, either. And for the same reasons; I was kind of relieved somebody had taken my matches, too. Better an itch you can't scratch than one you just *shouldn't*.

#

Posh Fred had eight or so guys left with him when we came through the doors to the central... whatever they call it in warehouses. It was big and it had lofts or something. Including two goons with crossbows, up there; they seemed a little confused when I saw them and waved. Figure they were more used to people cringing, were they?

When we burst in, Posh Fred had been remonstrating with Local Boy, complete with grabbing the *idiota's* lapels and screaming in his face. I could tell Posh Fred was the kind of guy who needed a second to switch treads, and I had some vague hope maybe of getting this done without more of a rhubarb, so I helpfully filled the silence: "You should listen to him, Posh Fred.

It's the smart play."

And hey, it worked! Posh Fred started paying attention to me. So did Irene, but I figured she had just been casing the joint for the best way to tear out everybody else's throats or something. I'd worry about her in a minute.

"What the fuck do you know about it, meat?" Posh Fred grated out, about a second too late to be effective. I shook my head sadly.

"Don't need to know a damn thing about it, *señor*. Whatever Local Boy told you is gonna be better than what you came up with on your own. He told you how this city works, right?"

"Actually my name is..." started Local Boy, only to stutter to a stop under my glare.

"Zip it, punk," I growled. I didn't have a cigarette to draw on, but that just made me more pissed, and Local Boy could tell. When I saw him visibly wilt, I switched back to Posh Fred.

"Yeah, starting with that, buddy. He tell you about Shamuses? The Mountain? The Castle? The King's Left Eye? And, here's the big one: *how we don't have any mages in New California?* Because you don't act like you heard that last one. It ain't real healthy for a foreigner to have ears that bad. No offense, ma'am," I said to Irene.

"None taken," she said, her eyes still keeping track of everybody else. And maybe the slight extra movements of dust, up there in the loft. I'm not gonna lie: I only saw them myself because I was looking.

Oh, right, back to Posh Fred. Who was snarling, "I don't know what the hell you're talking about, meat. There's tons of your kind in this city. I'm gonna enjoy sending 'em north, too. Starting with you. Now get those bracelets back on!"

I looked at him, puzzled. "Or what?"

Posh Fred sneered. "Not afraid of death, yourself? Guess what, meat: everybody's got a family. You know what the penalty is for harboring illegal mages..." and I couldn't help it at that point; I laughed. Which shut him up. *Again.* Geez, the north must be a weird place.

"No, I don't. Didn't you hear me the first time? *We don't have mages in New California.* Ask anybody. The artisans, the cleaning ladies, the cops, the Flatfoots, the nobles, the king... and, hey, you can even ask the Dominion ambassador. But I wouldn't; I hear he's a brooder. Whaddya think he'll do when you show up on his doorstep and tell him you found some mages when he ain't never even seen one?"

Okay, I was bluffing a little, but not much. The Universal Dominion may claim all the mages, but we're so far away they can't exactly check. Their latest ambassador was an absolute stick-in-the-mud, and that was working out for everybody. Besides, if Posh Fred had brought him a mage like Irene, the ambassador would probably have incinerated Posh Fred on the spot and pretended *he* had found her instead. Keeping the status quo all around.

Speaking of status quo, it was shifting. Slaver gangs ain't what you call smart, but they were maybe hearing now how things here were different from their usual stomping grounds. And they weren't liking the news. There were a bunch more shifting eyes and twitchy hands.

I guess Posh Fred picked up on it, because he shook himself a little and started ordering. "Enough! Kill the asshole, bring me the girl." When they paused, he yelled, "Do it!" and they started to move forward.

"Enough talk," Irene muttered, and threw a knife I didn't realize she'd had — right into the throat of Local Boy. Well, nobody told him to take this job.

#

So, it was eight against two. No, right, seven against two. Nope, still a bad count: Posh Fred jumped as his two crossbow guys suddenly took screaming swan dives to the floor below. I didn't, because I figured that Sofie and Smith had been doing *something.* A shame they didn't drop the crossbow-men on some other guys, but five against four would be fine. Assuming the two of us above got below in one piece.

Ever fight mooks who got armor when you don't? It ain't fun, but at least they weren't wearing plate. Hell, one of 'em wasn't even wearing a helmet, which he probably regretted for a second or two after I bounced my club off his head. I ain't no home run hitter but I know how to swing for the fences; he dropped and lay there like he meant to do it all along.

I flicked a look to my left; Irene was fighting two at once, but before I could move to help, one of the goons was rolling on the floor trying to stick his hamstring back together and the other one was suddenly backing up from a flashing sword, bared-teeth grin, and glittering, pitiless eyes.

The last henchman? He ran... right up to the point where Smith decided to use him to break his fall. Smith got up; the other one didn't. I thought it was a little bit of a showoff, but it worked, right?

Posh Fred didn't run. I'll give him that. Instead, he gave us all a nasty grin and held up two things: a knife that didn't look quite right, and an odd contraption that looked a lot like the thing Sofie had taken off of a goon, one million years and a few hours ago. "Stop, or they die!" he shouted.

"You really think this will work?" drawled Sofie, who had sensibly taken the stairs down. As she entered the light, she continued, "If you kill them, there's no reason for us not to get *creative*. Millstone and the Gulf of California."

"There's always anthills and molasses," offered Smith.

"Ah, the classics. But there's not much sugarcane around here, Mr. Smith. Perhaps stuffing him in a barrel of icemold for a week?"

"Nasty, ma'am, but it's real slow. How about tying him down in front of a stampeding herd of bison?"

"We could improvise with cows, but I hate the thought of cruelty to animals..."

"STOP IT!" screamed Posh Fred. "Screw you both — and screw you, spellboy," he said to me. I had been looking for my damn cigarette case, and had found it in Local Boy's coat pocket.

I looked at him. "What did *I* do?" I said, in the most annoying way possible as I lit up. I had a good idea of what he was gonna try, and I wanted him focused on me as much as possible. I had a slight hunch, and shifted position just a little to make him shift positions, as well.

People say I'm real good at pissing people off. Don't see it, myself, but you can't argue with results. Like now: Posh Fred said, "I don't know how you broke my bracelet, but you really should have done something about that knife wound of yours, meat. *That which is mine, come back to me!*" he shouted, brandishing the hell-knife.

What was probably supposed to happen next was: the piece of dagger still in me would rip out of my gut, all swollen with stolen energy and iron and killing me in the process. It'd slap into the knife, giving it and the wielder a boost of power or whatever, and demonstrating once and for all that Posh Fred was a vicious bastard who shouldn't be crossed. It would have been all very dramatic.

And yeah, it was dramatic. Only thing was, we had stuck that piece of the knife in my tie (well, I wasn't gonna stick it back in my body!), which Posh Jack had duly confiscated, and tossed in a pile. Directly behind him.

That rogue piece was still straining to pop itself out of his ribcage when Irene stepped up with a liberated broadsword and sliced off first Posh Fred's head, and then his hand. At that point, it stopped straining, and instead flat-out caught on fire. The kind of fire with authority.

We stood not on the order of our coming but left at once. As we ran, I saw my shoes and belt, and grabbed them in some haste (my pants were fine, but I don't walk Cin City in my socks and neither should you). We got out in good enough time before the entire damn warehouse caught on fire.

As the four of us looked at the destruction, I started to swear. Sofie looked up from her quick disassembly of whatever it was that Posh Fred thought would keep Irene under control. "What's the matter, Tom?"

I pointed to the flames in sadness and horror. My only solace was, there was something about this in the Lore (there always is).

"My hat was in that place," I more or less quoted.

#

Of *course* Sofie bought me a new hat. New tie, too. The old one was wrecked, not to mentioned steeped in evil hell-magic. She also finally bought me a dinner to make up for the one I hadn't drunk earlier. Would that all my Cases had such a good return on investment.

And she wanted to talk, too. "Tom? I have a confession to make," she said.

I chuckled. "I'm the wrong guy for that. Talk to Father Mike; his church's the one cranking out the penances." Mike's an old buddy and one of the local Catholic priests; the Castle currently had him off-the-books cleaning up where the warehouse had been. They wouldn't stiff him on it, either; when you hire an orc priest, you pay him on time and with a smile.

"Be serious, Tom. I lied to you." She looked unhappy about it, too, which is always nice.

"So what, Sofie? Everybody lies to a Shamus. We're used to it." I drank some more beer. "Besides, I already know Irene wasn't a mage."

That didn't seem to surprise Sofie, which meant she was paying attention. "The fact she never cast any spells?"

I nodded. "Yup. That and how you never went to the Palace for help. Posh Fred didn't think that was weird, because he always got to do his dirty deeds in the open, but this is New California. Of *course* the king would hide a mage on the run from slave-catchers. Which Local Boy should have told Fred, but some people don't listen real good."

"You know, I did some digging and his name was..."

I interrupted her. "It doesn't matter, Sofie." Then I grimaced. "Sorry."

"No, you're right." Sofie looked at me. "You figure out the rest?"

"Kind of. Was she the True Queen of Deseret, or just the heir?"

"I think... both? Like, she's going to be the True Queen as soon as she and Smith sneak back north?" Sofie gave a little shrug. "She never really told me, but I kind of guessed — and when Smith showed up, it seemed obvious. I wonder if Posh Fred knew."

"He had to," I said. "Good thing Fred there realized he'd have to keep it a secret, even from his own gang. A rogue mage from Deseret ain't worth shiving your boss over to get the full reward. The True Queen? *Absolutely* worth putting the knife in. That should keep them safe enough until they get back to wherever home is."

"Makes sense," said Sofie. "I noticed that you didn't let either of them know you figured everything out."

"Just like you, Benefactress Huston Redgrave. Just like you." Irene and Smith: they weren't bad people, but they were pretty damn *hard* people. I didn't know whether they'd have decided to clear up some loose ends of their own if we had shown off how clever we were, but since we hadn't, they probably were just as relieved as we were that the question hadn't come up. All for the best, really. They had their own story, and neither Sofie nor I really wanted to be in it.

I looked at Sofie. She had enjoyed everything, I decided: there was the glint in her eye you only see in a dedicated Adventurer. She was gonna do great on that dig. It was still a little weird, the way the nobles were trying to be useful all of a sudden — but, hey, it's a free kingdom.

"A toast," I said. Sofie raised first an eyebrow, and then her wine glass, as I raised my own mug high. "To a beautiful friendsh — wait, what the *hell*?"

Outside the window there was a sudden breeze; no, wait, it was a no-fooling *wind,* which was blowing papers and junk every which way. I could also faintly hear a whine that got louder and louder... to reveal a huge-mouthed, beetle-browed spirit that was racing down the street, its bottom half spinning so quickly it looked like a miniature cyclone.

It didn't seem to be attacking anybody, despite a couple

of chances — but it was also out there, in the middle of the damn *street*. And yeah, I recognized it. The last time I saw it, it was chasing down a rogue sorcerer. I guess it finally caught up to him.

I sighed as I rose. This was something I'd have to sort out, and never mind dessert. Just my luck. So I tipped my hat to Sofie and gave her a grin, because at least I didn't have to worry about *her* not getting a reference from the Lore.

"That's all, folks."

IN HOC SIGNO VINCES

Contested Lands
(Just outside Lubbock, Texas)
2835 AD

Another Christian missionary had been sniffed out in the legionary camp.

It was only by sheerest accident Liza saw the *Carnivores* carry him off. They had been smooth about it, as you'd expect from the Emperor's secret police: a quick distraction one camp row over, then a quiet snatching of one particular human slave while everybody else was looking in another direction. And if someone saw, who would care? Or who would be stupid enough to even visibly notice?

Well. Liza cared. She had been watching this particular slave for a few days, picking up on certain subtle signs, and trying to decide when would be the best time to approach him. But it seemed the *Carnivores* had picked up on the signs, too. And were faster at moving on their suspicions than she was.

None of this showed on her face as Liza kept carefully sharpening her sword, cool and collected despite a West Texas sun in July. To all appearances, Liza Skullcrusher Lupator (*primus pilus*, Third Imperial Legion) was the perfect centurion. Her gear was perfectly maintained, and her posture was stiff even in repose. Her mien was stern, even callous. Utterly Imperial, utterly orcish, utterly reliable. Certainly not even worth the trouble to investigate. Such dissimulation was necessary, in this year of Our Lord 2835. The human slaves might mutter how orcs liked to keep hearts on sleeves, and sometimes they were even their own hearts, but being a secret Christian in an army which officially and brutally despised all gods did wonders to teach discretion.

Once the sword was sharpened, Liza went over the rest of her gear. Some might have let slaves maintain their weapons and armor, but fools didn't stay in the Third long. One way, or another. Besides, the familiar actions allowed the centurion to at least *try* to think things through. Liza knew she needed to take every chance she could to not rush into things, every time she could. Especially when it was something this important.

Her involvement could easily end before it even started. The days where a Christian would be publicly crucified or thrown to monsters in the arena were long past, for far too many Christians had died far too well for the Empire's taste. The humans were the worst, in some ways. The arena crowds expected orcs to die bravely, but a religion which could inspire *humans* to do the same? It not only flat-out contradicted Imperial propaganda, it suggested this God the humans had might have something valuable to offer the orcs.

Permitting thoughts like those was completely against Imperial policy. Worse, it was also against the policy of the distant mages who made the Emperor himself their puppet. So these days, when missionaries were found, the *Carnivores* simply and quietly disappeared them whenever possible. This offered no spectacle, but it also offered no chance for public awkwardness or contradictions. That sort of thing was bad enough at home; for an army on the march, in what was becoming a frustratingly confused war, awkwardness could be lethal.

Liza thought for a few moments more, and decided she was in the mood for awkwardness.

#

After Liza finished inspecting her battle line armor, she hung it carefully on its stand. She expected, forethought or not, she was going to go do something stupid this evening. Which meant there was an excellent chance she was never going to wear this particular set of armor again. It would be a shame if the next person to don it were to think Liza was slovenly or lazy as well as an insane religious fanatic. *Christians are allowed self-respect,* she told herself, safely inside her head. *It's not Pride.* Liza wasn't quite sure if she believed herself, though. It seemed the sort of rationalization a Proud person might use.

Liza's next move was to do something she would have done anyway: go to the mess tent. There she would find food. And getting herself fed *would* be important. But Liza would also find a few humans to discreetly talk to, in ways which might not immediately arouse suspicion. That would be perhaps even more useful.

It would have surprised most outside observers (not to mention the Ancient Romans) to discover human slaves and orcish legionaries ate the same food, and at the same tables in the mess tents. And how there was little if any friction between the two groups. Officially this was for perfectly pragmatic reasons. Humans were better cooks than orcs, and the legions knew it. The legions also insisted that making everyone eat the same food simply cut down on poisoning attempts.

Liza privately thought these excuses were bullcrap, and from a cow with diarrhea, to boot. The legions' slaves had always been treated far better than the poor bastards owned by either the nobility, or worse, the Imperial dynasty; that had only gotten more obvious as the war in the north against the Grand Alliance heated up. Which was one reason why Liza was appalled the *Carnivores* had actually snatched a missionary from the slaves; the secret police's legendary brutality usually got directed towards the nobility, not the army. This change in focus would increase resentment even among the non-Christian slaves, which would hurt the legions in the long run.

Liza found the very idea intolerable. The Third Legion was home and country in a way the Imperium was not, despite the Emperor's pretensions. Having him and his court personally along on this campaign had merely confirmed to Liza the decadence of the former, and the odiousness of the latter. It would be better for the Legion if the missionary escaped, or at least got a decent chance to escape. Clearly.

Which meant, someone would need to do something. And since nobody else was volunteering, it seemed she would have to be 'someone' this evening.

#

Liza picked her seat carefully: a half empty table, with the human she wanted to talk to sitting at one corner. As she sat down, Liza murmured "*Piscis*" and noted happily how the human didn't react strongly. The human instead looked significantly at the other two humans at the table until they finished up, and left her and Liza alone.

The slave's name was officially Calpurnia of Mendacium, and officially she was no different than any other slave. Unofficially, Callie was who you talked to when you needed something from the humans, and who told you what it would cost. The arrangement had gotten a little frayed during this campaign, since the Emperor and his toadies had come along personally to 'help' the army kick the Grand Alliance out of Lubbock, but less than Liza and the other officers had feared.

Well, the other *useful* officers. The Legatus and the Tribune were both newly foisted on the Third by the court, and both of them would have been appalled to hear that the legions cared about human opinions. Assuming any legionnaire would have even tried to tell them.

Callie gave Liza a publicly fawning smile, over narrowed eyes. "What can I do for you, most fearsome Centurion?" she said. This kind of kiss-arsery happened all the time now, thanks to the presence of the Imperial Court, and it made Liza's tusks ache. From the centurion's point of view, the biggest difference between the legion and the humans was that Callie's people wore *visible* slave collars.

"They took a human for questioning today," Liza said normally, if a little quietly. Not quietly enough for people to notice, she hoped. "Do you know whether they took him anywhere special?"

Callie flickered her eyes, in lieu of an actual eye-roll. "I am but a mere worm," she said, "most fearsome Centurion. I do not dare interfere in the business of my betters."

Fine, thought Liza. *If that's the way you want to play this.* Aloud, she suddenly shouted, "How dare you spill soup on me, human?!" Liza stood, pulling Callie up with her with one hand, not *quite* dragging her off the stool. "I think you need to be taught some manners!"

The humans seeing this were horrified, and offended, and a few of the burlier ones moved their hands towards certain bulky parts of their tunics until a short head-shake from Callie made them relax. Some of the orcs looked disgusted too, though. Rather more than Liza expected, in fact. It was a bit of a comforting thought as she propelled the human out into the night and around a convenient corner.

In every camp, there's always a place around which can give people a chance to have a quiet word or two. In this case, there were a couple of wagons parked close enough to make for a little privacy. Liza took a quick glance around as they entered the impromptu corner. Nobody looking on: good.

"Jesus Christ, Centurion," Callie said, low but not too angry. "You people are as subtle as a hurricane."

"Don't swear," said Liza. "It bothers me."

Callie grinned. "Yeah, I had already figured you for a Christian. Smart of you to get us out of the tent, you know. There was at least one informer in there; he's a sneak, but real dumb. The best kind. So, are you beating me up right now, or kissing me?"

"Ugh," said Liza. "I don't want to do either."

"Kissing, then. Easier to fake." Callie paused. "So, what do you know about the preacher?"

"So he *is* a priest?" Liza asked.

Callie nodded.

"Just my luck," Liza said. "I have to get him away. Or at least try."

"Why, Centurion?" asked Callie. "I mean, sure, he's gonna die if you don't, and I don't want it, but the *Carnivores* got him. You know what that means. Shoot, so does he."

"Why? Because I want to," said Liza. She didn't say anything else, and Callie shrugged after a minute.

"Fine," she said. "Those *Carnivores* bastards are up to something, for sure: this is the fourth or fifth preacher they've grabbed in the last two weeks. Maybe more. Nobody's heard anything else about them, either. Whatever it is the *Carnivores* are doing, it's gotta be bad. You think you can get this one out?"

"Maybe?" said Liza. "They're watching you humans, I bet. But they won't expect someone from the legion to be ready to go in and try to grab him, spirit him away. I've got a better chance than any of you have."

"It's still a crappy chance," Callie said, then shrugged. "But it's your martyrdom. What do you want?"

"Just an idea where he is."

"What makes you think I know?" asked Callie.

"What, the *Carnivores* clean their own tents now?" replied Liza.

"This bunch does," said Callie. She grinned at Liza's look of surprise. "The guy they got running this bunch is a real hard-ass about security. But the people they do let in say it doesn't look like the new guy's changed the way they lay out their camp, so I can tell you where to go. You won't like it, though. I guarantee it."

"Of course I won't," said Liza. "But it's got to be done anyway."

"All right," said Callie. "Hold on a second." She bent down, rubbed some dirt on her tunic and trousers, and disarrayed her hair. Then Callie slapped her own mouth two, three times, almost hard enough to bruise. Certainly hard enough to leave red marks.

Callie smiled at Liza's confusion. "What, don't you know? You orcs kiss *very* hard." And then Callie outright smirked at Liza's sudden blush. "Huh. I guess you *didn't* know."

\#

Infiltrating a *Carnivorus* camp by herself was on Liza's list of things to never do on a campaign. Or, well, ever. But it seemed the Lord apparently did work in mysterious ways, because here she was. And it was a good thing Liza had faith, because there was damn-all else she could count on right now.

For starters, she had to do it alone, because the only other Christian Liza knew of for certain was the priest she was trying to save. If Liza had to *guess*, she would have said maybe one in five legionnaires in her cohort were also likely to be either secret Christians, or at least leaning that way. But she didn't know who any of them were, and the same discipline which would have ensured her cohort would follow her into a martyrdom attack on the secret police also kept Liza from betraying their implicit trust in her.

There was also the minor detail about how the *Carnivorus* tents were on the edge between what she thought of as the *real* legion camp and the decadent mess of the Imperial field 'court.' It had been made clear to all of the fighting orcs that they were only to cross the invisible line when summoned for information, punishment, or amusement. Fortunately, Liza was just a little too high-ranked to have to worry about the last category, but not every legionnaire was that lucky. There was at least one case she knew of where a 'deserter' was probably anything but.

Oddly, the *Carnivores* never bothered to investigate *that* sort of thing. In some ways, this infuriated Liza even more than the likely original outrages. Better an openly vile miscreant than hypocrites pretending to virtue and duty.

Hypocrites or not, they were still orcs, which meant simply bowling down *Carnivorus* sentries wouldn't get her very far. *Best to make a single strike*, Liza thought. Or as few strikes as possible. She would have to talk her way in as far as possible, and hopefully back out, too. And if it didn't work, she could always cut down the guards around the priest, and hold the rest off long enough for the captive to escape. It wouldn't be survivable, but since when had good orcs worried much about mere survival?

In retrospect, getting into the *Carnivores'* small encampment among the legions should have seemed too easy. The first checkpoint, she barely had to slow down. Liza just said, "Here to get a prisoner," and the two sentries waved her right through. One even pointed her to the right tent to go to next.

There, she actually had to spin her tale. Liza did not consider herself a fool, although trying to bluff her way into a secret policeman's camp might argue otherwise. She had settled on a simple story, which might pass muster, if only out of laziness on the guards' part. She was just there to pick up the prisoner. *The Imperial Court wants him for something. No, I didn't ask why; would you? Exactly. Hey, want to take him over yourself? No? Okay, where do I make my mark to sign for him? Thanks. Let's **go**, human prisoner.*

With the right standard-issue, walking-around armor and a cloak, Liza figured it *should* work. Or at least it wasn't *suicide*. She wasn't *trying* to die; she just knew the stakes were death and the dice were loaded the other way. But choosing not to do anything was also a choice, and Liza had enough bad choices on her conscience to make her willing to endure another one.

And her plan seemed to be working, at least so far. There was a bad spot where the clerk in the tent asked, "Your name and rank, Legionary?" and she blinked, because Liza had completely forgotten to come up with a false one. But she recovered and barked out, "It's Decanus. Decanus Barb Eyegnawer Spumator" quickly enough to cover for the pause.

Doing that might end up being bad luck for an actual Eyegnawer, but Liza was reasonably sure nobody from the *gens* she had picked was in the part of the army Liza cared about. And if one was? Well. 'Skullcrusher' may have been an easier *nomen* than usual to honorably live with — but many Eyegnawers didn't even *try*.

It wasn't until Liza had spent five minutes waiting alone in the *second* tent before she realized they had simply stashed her somewhere out of the way — and that was only because the tent flaps on both sides opened up simultaneously to admit three *Carnivores* apiece. Those were bad odds. Those were *such* bad odds.

One of the *Carnivores* spoke, surprisingly without much if any in the way of contempt. "Settle a bet for me, Centurion," she said to Liza. "Did you really think this would have worked?"

Liza scowled, but answered honestly. "No." She flicked her eyes to either side. "So, are you going to come in all at once, or are we going to have a proper fight of it?" ...and then Liza felt the sting of a spell go off. Her limbs suddenly froze before she could even ready her sword, and her sight began to dim. It was all she could do to remain conscious, and Liza could feel the spell trying its best to overcome *that*, too.

"Impressive," murmured the *Carnivora*. Liza thought the secret policewoman might even actually mean it. "Zap her again."

"What, really?" said a voice behind Liza — and outside the tent, from the sound of it.

"She's a strong one," said the *Carnivora*. She looked at Liza again, and shrugged. "Which is why we're not going to go with either of your options, sorry."

Again, there was no real contempt in the *Carnivora's* voice. Liza might have pondered the oddity more, except that right then whoever was casting the spells (and since when did orcs have their own mages?) hit her again with another oblivion spell. And this one absolutely kicked like an onager, all the way down to unconsciousness.

#

When Liza finally regained her senses, she was mildly unhappy to actually be awake. Legionary rumor said that the *Carnivores* knew far too much about how to make an orc's last day memorable; best to not really 'be' there when the knives came out. This batch of them apparently liked to work very quietly, too, which was doing nothing to reassure the centurion about how she was faring.

Still, things currently could be worse. Liza was only handcuffed to a chair (a shifting and stifled grunt suggested they were either genuine Old American relics, or something just as strong), instead of strapped to a gurney, or the rack; there seemed to be no bits of her currently missing; and she could see just one guard. And there was an actual officer-type *Carnivorus* present, which confirmed that things were bad, after all. He was clearly one of those jovial ones, too, which made it worse.

"Ah, Centurion. You have come back to us. Let it be noted for the record how I took this moment to leer at our lovely witness." That last part, Liza noted, was not actually accompanied by a leer, but behind her a pencil dutifully scratched on paper anyway.

Since the *Carnivorus* interrogator was looking at *her*, Liza saw no particular reason not to look back. Why not? You didn't handcuff the Third's *primus pilus* to a chair unless you were sure you could get away with it, and the *Carnivores* would burn the defiance out of you whether you showed them any or not. You might as well give yourself the momentary pleasure.

And admittedly this interrogator wasn't actually awful on the eyes. Quite attractive, really, in a very careful manner which probably required a certain amount of work to keep it that way. Hair a bit longer than the regulations strictly allowed, but on him it looked urbane, not decadent. He also had a quite respectable scar on his neck that looked like it had come tantalizingly close to ripping out his jugular, but his face was otherwise unmarked. 'Dashing' wasn't in Liza's vocabulary, but 'dangerous' was — and this *Carnivorus* looked both. But he also didn't move like one of the Emperor's noble lackeys, which hopefully meant the torture would be professionally done. Or at least end with a mercy-dagger.

If the interrogator was bothered by her lack of cringing, Liza couldn't tell. When he spoke, his voice was smooth, and almost tusk-grindingly self-assured. "My name is immaterial," he said, "but my rank is high enough to permit a 'Sir.' Are you ready to assist the Empire in its inquiries?"

There were two answers; but Liza gave the one anybody not a damned (*Lord, have mercy!* ran through her mind) fool or a barbarian orcish 'auxiliary' would. "Of course, sir."

"Excellent, Centurion. There's one small question I need cleared up, and then you'll be free to go." The interrogator pulled over a folding chair and sat down so that his intent eyes were on the same level as hers. "Why were you trying to 'sneak' in? It was pathetic in its ineptness. Much like me trying to order a counter-march on the field of battle or some other tactical maneuver, really."

Two years ago, Liza wouldn't have cared if all the Christians in the world perished. Six months ago, Liza would have struggled with the idea of *dying* to save one. Three months ago, she would have resisted the temptation to try for her martyr's crown. But now, she was done. The interrogator knew of her faith, so why lie?

So she laughed in the interrogator's well, not *face*, but certainly in his general direction. "I came here to rescue the prisoner you took today, sir. The Christian prisoner, sir. The *other* Christian, sir. I assumed you would not just let me *do* that, sir."

The interrogator looked at Liza. No: he looked *behind* Liza, and actually chuckled. "Told you, Jan," he said.

A female voice spoke. Liza couldn't see, but it sounded like the *Carnivora* from before. "You *guessed* she'd do that," the *Carnivora* said.

"You know I didn't," said the interrogator. "But you can keep telling yourself that. You're off the hook for tonight, by the way. She's more suitable for our — ah, write down 'my' — purposes."

What does he mean by 'purposes?' Liza could think of a few things, and wished she couldn't. As much to stop thinking about that as anything else, Liza took a deep breath, and went on: "Before you ask the next question, I do not know of" — and then she stopped, for there was now (her eyes narrowed to see) a finger pressed to her lips. The *Carnivora* behind her whispered, "Only answer what you've been asked." The whisper and finger retreated before Liza could quite react.

The interrogator looked behind Liza again and jerked his head. The Centurion stared straight ahead, already working through the appropriate prayers in her mind — only to blink as the cuffs came off. And then the arrogant bastard had the sheer effrontery to *smile* at her.

"Next time: *ask* first, Centurion. The result would have been the same if the answer had been 'no,' and we could have all saved some valuable time." The interrogator stood at the same time as Liza, albeit he did so a good deal less confusedly. "Here. Your sword and shield. Your prisoners' passes. And safe-conducts through our lines for the lot of you."

That last bit caught her up short. "I am no deserter!"

The interrogator snorted. "Then," he said, "feel free to come back here after you drop them off and face me *again*, Centurion. In fact... yes, I think I will *order* that you go. And once you are done with your little task, you will either come back in a reasonable amount of time, or else *truly* desert the Legion. There. That should satisfy your honor.

"In the meantime, the lives of these priests of yours are in your hands. Not because we'll kill them if you don't take them back to the Grand Alliance, but because I suspect none of them could even make it out of the camp by themselves without tripping over their own feet, or possibly mine. But the armies on the other side probably won't attack you, if only for the sheer shock of seeing your arrival."

At this point, the interrogators' incessant use of plurals finally caught up with Liza. She blinked. "You captured more missionaries? Yes, you must have. And now you're letting them all go at once."

"Not *bad*, Centurion," said the interrogator in what sounded like another one of those confusingly approving tones. "And why not? If we're getting rid of the one you cared about, I might as well include all the others."

Liza flushed. "I didn't *know* about the others," she said. In her head, she amended that as *Well, I didn't think they were still alive, anyway.* "You *Carnivores* are good at not making scenes. I was lucky to see this one."

"That's one way of putting it," murmured the *Carnivora* behind her.

The interrogator tsk-tsked. "Behave, Jan. It's not like you actually *took* that bet."

"Yes, sir."

The interrogator turned back to Liza. "Someone will take you to the prisoner tent, and those safe-conducts will get you out of the camp. You will have no trouble there. After that, well, I'm sure you can wrangle five holy people across no-man's-land towards a suspicious enemy ready to kill our kind on sight. Think of it as an adventure! I hear those are entertaining."

That was clearly a dismissal, and Liza's *gens* raised no fools. But they did permit curiosity as a character trait, and Liza had more than her share. She was halfway to the tent flap when she stopped for a moment. "This is pointless to ask, yes, I know, but: *why*, sir?"

The *Carnivorus* looked like he was about to, well, *smile*? Surely not. "Finally, she *asks*. Know that I am a prophet, Centurion. I foresee the leaders of the armies, there on the other side of tomorrow's chosen battlefield, will likely ask you the same question. I tell you what I would tell them: look to the east, and there they will see a Sign."

Ah, thought Liza. *He's a madman*. But he was a madman providing her with a way to get five Christian priests away from the camp, so she decided not to stay and argue further.

#

And wasn't getting her charges safely away just so much *fun*, too?

The *Carnivorus* interrogator was correct about getting out of the camp itself. Finding a way through the orcish lines was easy enough, between the safe-conducts and the way the sentries all shuffled and looked uneasy. Liza started upwardly revising her assessment of the number of secret Christians in the legions: clearly, some of the legionaries recognized some of the humans. There were a lot of hesitant legionary glances at the part of the camp which housed the Emperor, his toadies, and the wizards from the north who truly ruled the Empire; Liza recognized their worry, but did not indulge in it. She was not betraying the Legion, and in her opinion she was not even turning traitor against the Empire itself. But the puppet who sat on the throne, and his shadowy puppet masters? Yes, Liza was *their* enemy.

And it felt good to strike a blow against those enemies, even though they'd likely kill her when she came back. She didn't mind, much. If it would suit God's purpose for Liza to don the martyr's crown, she would do so, and joyfully.

Assuming she didn't kill these idiots in her charge first.

Dear God in Heaven, Liza thought, *but how have any of these priests* **survived***?* The three men and two women weren't in bad shape, exactly. The *Carnivores* hadn't tortured or starved them, although baths had apparently been rationed. And the priests weren't even complainers.

But none of them knew how to *move*. The plain which was likely to be the next day's battlefield wasn't empty: there were probably scouts and raiders from both sides skulking about, and Liza was not confident her safe-passages would work out there in the dark. Strike that: she knew they wouldn't.

So Liza had to make sure, somehow, that she and her five human companions got all the way across the field without being pursued, or hopefully not even seen. And Liza had certainly *thought* she had gotten this idea across to the others, right up to the time one of them had started to climb a small hill 'to see better.'

In a way, the priest was lucky: the limb she put too close to a trapdoor gator nest was an arm, not a leg. The problem was that trapgator bites were *nasty*, even when they didn't break the skin. By the time Liza got there, the human's arm looked broken and the priest herself looked like she was in too much agony to scream. Liza's sword stabbed out and skewered the trapgator precisely in the right place along the neck to make it let go. And die, writhing, in the dirt.

Liza ignored it as she grabbed the priest by her good arm and brought her back to the others. Fortunately, there were no loose rocks, so Liza was able to drag her back down the hill without making even more noise. "Stay as low as possible," she muttered, barely managing not to add the words 'you idiot' afterward. "There's moonlight. *Somebody* would see you, and take the free shot."

To be fair, they all managed to get *that* specific message, and none of them complained once, the entire time. But even after the near-miss, Liza still felt she was shepherding a herd of suicidal sheep. Until she decided she was slandering suicidal sheep.

#

She took the time to explain the problem to the priest — no, minister — the others had decided to more or less be their spokesman. 'Minister' was a weird word; it turned out there were apparently three (or more!) different versions of Christianity, which surprised Liza a bit. And worried her, too: how was she supposed to know which church she needed to join? Anyway, this minister seemed sensible, considering. Maybe he'd understand the problem.

"Look, Father," Liza said, ignoring the slight wince on the other man's face, "we're *not* safe. We're just not being hunted by the Legion right now. There are other things on the field here tonight besides my side's patrols, and yours."

"Do you mean beasts, my chi... Centurion?" replied the minister. "I would have thought the larger animals would have been frightened away by our armies. And the smaller ones would be no threat to us."

"You mean, like the trapgators?" Liza replied. "But yes, regular beasts are going to stay away from us, as long as we don't climb any hills. But the mages release some very nasty creatures sometimes, just in case somebody's trying to desert. Maybe one is out there tonight. Maybe one isn't. And we can't just run for it and hope for the best. If there is something bad out there, it's going to smell that blood from the trapgator, and it'll be looking for an easy meal."

"I understand," said the minister. "How do your mages control these beasts? What stops them from attacking your patrols?"

"Nothing," said Liza, bleakly. "And they're not *my* mages. They think we belong to *them*."

"Oh, that is *foul*," hissed the minister. "Every time I think the Universal Dominion has hit rock bottom, they manage to sink a few feet deeper."

"Is that what you call them?" asked Liza, curious.

"It is what they call themselves. What do *you* call them?"

"We're only allowed 'Master' or 'Mistress'," said Liza; her nostrils flared as an unwelcome scent wafted past, and she drew her sword. Luck was apparently not with them tonight. "And it's good to have their true name. If we're about to die at the claws and teeth of one of the Dominion's monsters, at least I'll die knowing who to curse."

#

The good news was, the monster hadn't been sent to find them.

And that was *it* in the good news column. The monster was a mutated centipede, about as long as Liza was tall, had incredibly nasty-looking teeth oozing something which would probably dissolve whatever bits of her it touched, and could probably go through Liza's charges in roughly the same time it would take all of them to scream. A regular Imperial patrol would probably be able to hold it off without losing more than one or two soldiers, but one-on-one... *Would just have to do*, Liza thought grimly as she bore down on the filthy creature.

At least this kind of monster didn't make noises when it fought. All right, that made *two* items in the good news column. Which was *so* much better.

The centipede struck first, with an alarming burst of speed which didn't surprise Liza but alarmed her quite a bit; she took the strike on her shield, then instinctively dropped it before the centipede's venom burned its way through the tough layered wood and metal. The Centurion swung her sword hard into the centipede's side as it briefly tangled up in the new hole in her shield, and was rewarded with a spray of foul-smelling blood. A splatter landed on her cheek, and it stung like the very Devil.

"If I fall," Liza called almost conversationally to the five priests just now scrambling out of the way of the fight, "scatter and run west." And then she stopped worrying about them. There was an enemy in front of her, after all.

The next minute was nasty. She was forced to dig into the centipede's neck with one hand and stab with the other, and the sword was barely useful for that task; Liza would have much preferred an ax, or possibly one of the fabled demon-killing chain-saws of the Old Americans. The centipede kept taking blows, and kept wriggling underneath her feet and hands, trying to twist around and take chunks out of her flesh instead of the scratches and lacerations she had suffered so far. There wasn't a handy rock to dash the literally damned thing against, either.

It was a stalemate, but time wasn't on her side, either. If another centipede had been summoned and released tonight, it'd probably find them soon — and all of this would have been pointless.

There was a way to win this fight, but it would probably leave her badly injured at best, and dead at worst. *Fine*, she thought. "Run!" Liza shouted urgently. "Just get to your camp! I'm going to end this thing!" And with a mighty heave, she lifted the centipede with her free hand and threw it as far as she could.

This would finally give the monster a chance to strike — but it would give her the same chance, and Liza was confident in her ability to *kill* this monster before succumbing to her wounds. Taking things with them down into death was what orcs were for, right? Mages with flaming whips had told her ancestors that for long enough. They could hardly complain if Liza demonstrated now how well she had soaked in the lesson.

The centipede was half-maddened, which was perfect; angry creatures don't fight subtly. It sprang for her, but Liza ignored the whirring, ichor-spitting teeth and concentrated on a spot just under the chin where the tip of her blade would go. It was going to be a beautiful thrust, she thought. It was a real pity how nobody with training would see it, including quite possibly her. Those teeth looked like they were going right for her face.

A human might have closed her eyes, but orcs don't have that reflex. So she *was* able to see the sudden flicker of distortion in the air in front of her, just before the centipede inexplicably bounced off of absolutely nothing and crashed to the ground. That was *different*. So was the way her blade had suddenly taken on a gold tinge in the moonlight.

But Liza was an orc *and* an Imperial centurion, which meant she was trained in two brutally pragmatic martial traditions. Beneficial mysteries didn't require explanations until *after* she split this disgusting filth's unnatural monstrous head with a downward thrust. Which she promptly did.

Well, not as promptly as she should have, from her point of view. She suspected none of the human priests had noticed her instant of surprise. *Wait... why didn't they run?* Liza thought confusedly as her adrenalin ebbed. Well, one of them *was* running— to Liza, with what looked like bandages ripped from his tunic. The others were getting up off their knees and making odd gestures with their hands.

Liza shook her head as the priest with the bandages started fussing over her. "I told you to run," Liza said, more strongly than she expected. In fact, the pain was starting to recede, but she didn't feel light-headed or about to go into shock. This... didn't usually happen with bandaging.

The priest she had dragged down from the hill earlier shook her head, and smiled. "We weren't going to abandon you, when we could help," she said. "Although we should probably go now."

Liza stood up, marveling at how easy it was. And though her armor and shield had seen better days, her sword... "It glowed," she said. "And now it doesn't. Was that you?"

"No," said the minister. "That was God. I just asked Him to aid you."

Liza stopped, and stared. "Wait. Priests can *do* that?"

"When the need is strong enough, yes," said the minister. He frowned. "We had to be very careful while on our missionary work, but I thought — surely, you have seen the power of the Lord before? From your own priests?"

"We don't have our own priests," said Liza. She spat. "The *Carnivores* are expert at sniffing them out. Before today I've met one, maybe two in my life. And they performed no miracles where I could see."

The minister looked at her. "And yet you converted." His tone was respectfully surprised. "That is an impressive display of faith, Centurion."

Liza hefted her shield, despite the hole. It was still better than nothing. "Not really, Father," she said as she started to march west again. "The priest told me Jesus traded His life for mine, because He thought I was worth it." She smiled, wistfully. "It sounded nice to be wanted like that."

#

After *that*, getting some damned (*Lord, **still** have mercy!*) fool of a sentry on the other side to not kill them after all wasn't too hard. Although the way the Alliance soldiers at first thought the priests had *captured* Liza annoyed her for a little while, until she decided to offer it up as a penance for Pride. Or maybe try to see it as funny.

But the priests straightened it all out. Pretty soon she was being escorted to a few hastily-wakened Alliance leaders. This batch were mostly humans from Deseret and Kentucky, with someone from the Second Republic in charge. Strictly speaking, the head general was ugly, with bulging eyes, webbed feet and hands, slick skin, and a generally frog-like appearance; but he had been more relieved to see the priests brought back safely than anyone else at the table, so perhaps looks could be deceiving.

He was also as confused as everybody else about what was going on, including Liza. "So, he just gave them to you and told you to deliver them, Centurion?" the general said. "No conditions, no explanation?"

"Just how you should look to the east, and you would be shown a Sign, General," Liza said. She wasn't sure if she was technically a prisoner. They hadn't handcuffed her, which was nice. But they showed no sign of sending her back to the Legion, either. This would be a problem, because orders were orders. "I have nothing further to add, General."

The general looked smart enough to recognize that Liza's answer wasn't the same as *I don't know anything more*, but he let it go. "Thank you for bringing back the priests," he said as he gestured at a pair of competent-looking guards. "I think I can safely offer you parole."

Liza frowned. "What's that?" she asked. "Some sort of food?"

The extremely large eyes of the general were uniquely suited for a slow blink. "It means we offer a trade," he said after a moment. "You promise not to escape or spy on us, and we don't put you in chains or lock you up."

"Oh," said Liza. "I'm very sorry, but I can't, then. I was told to return to the Legion after this." She thought. "But he did say 'in a reasonable amount of time.' I think the order will stretch to until after the battle tomorrow."

Part of her didn't want to concede that much. But she was tired, and a larger part of her didn't want to fight these people all the way back to her lines, then fight them *again* (on no sleep!) several hours from now. Assuming she wouldn't just be killed on sight, which was probably really going to happen now because of the centipede.

The general didn't order Liza chained, but he did have her placed under guard and sent away. Infuriatingly, the prison tent she was sent to was better than hers. It even had a cot that could support her frame! No bedrolls *here*, apparently. She gratefully stretched herself out and closed her eyes. *I can figure out how to escape after the battle*, she thought. *After all, we're probably going to win it anyway.* The promise of victory did not make her happy, but then it had been years since it had.

Several hours later, Liza rolled out of bed before she quite woke up, grabbing for a sword that wasn't there. There was an earthquake of some kind — no, the encampment was echoing from the sound of an angry explosion in the distance. Whatever it had been, it was fairly big.

Liza was at the tent flap looking out; the two guards still on duty didn't even think to forbid her. From their vantage point, they could all see the firecloud coming up from the Legion camp. It actually looked rather pretty, what with the way it reflected the colors of the dawn.

A nervous, watery cough interrupted her shock. "Pardon me, Centurion?" Liza turned to see the head general from last night had come up, and was now looking at her almost apologetically. The general sprayed his neck with some sort of water bottle and continued, "Our spies tell us the explosion..."

"...is where the Emperor, his court, and the mages were encamped, yes."

The general craned what neck he had, blinked repeatedly, and — remarkably — chuckled. Its dryness was the only thing about him which was, really.

"Ay up. That's what I'd call a Sign, then."

#

There were now crosses *everywhere.*

Liza found it a little uncomfortable, as she was escorted through the Legion camp. Crosses were on the Forbidden List. And they were *particularly* forbidden, to the point where you had to be careful in what graffiti you scribbled on the walls. But now they were on poles, hung above tent flaps, there was one being erected on the flat bed of a wagon where a priest was now preaching... *everywhere.*

And this was another thing. Where did all the priests come from? They were all orcs, too. Some of them looked fairly battered. But they all sounded sincere, and so did their congregations. Well, many of them did. Some looked a little calculating, but apparently there were even more secret Christians in the legions than Liza had dared hope.

And there wasn't going to be a battle today, after all. The orcs had put up truce flags immediately after the explosions; *so* immediately after that it was brutally clear those explosions had been planned. A delegation had been sent from the legion lines, formally offering a truce and offer of peace "from the Emperor, Senate, and People of the *Imperium Orci.*"

Oh, and a polite enquiry into whether "Our trusty and honorable Praefectus Liza Skullcrusher Lupator" had turned up.

Under the circumstances, the Alliance general had decided to just let Liza go. He had suddenly more important things to deal with, like ensuring the sudden end of fighting in the entire southern theater of the Great War. What was one Centurion — or Praefectus — weighed against *that*?

Liza was still thinking of herself as a Centurion. She had decided she'd believe in the promotion when she actually got paid.

#

They were still setting up new tents and so forth in the Imperial Court, which reeked of gunpowder and burned bodies. Or *burning* bodies; there were funeral pyres placed downwind of the encampment, and a lot of busy humans (and orcs!) throwing stripped corpses on them. The orcish (and human!) 'honor guard' escorting Liza proved happy to talk about it.

"Yeah, ma'am," said one of the humans, who looked just the slightest bit too small for his armor. But he had the hands and arms of a spearman and the attitude to match. "Those fuckers, begging your pardon, ma'am, they was in the court when they all got blown to kingdom come." He spat. "Or maybe somewhere else, mind."

"So all the nobles died in the blast?" asked Liza.

One of the orcish guards spoke. "Yeah," she said. "Eventually."

Liza looked around. "And the mages?"

Everybody in the honor guard chuckled. "Ain't gonna say," said the human. "Himself likes to tell the story, and you ain't heard it yet."

Liza stopped, with a sudden, horrible realization. "Wait, who's Himself?" she asked, and hoped she wouldn't be given the answer she dreaded.

#

It was just as bad as Liza thought. 'Himself' was the *Carnivorus* interrogator, now lounging on a freshly-carved Imperial throne as if he had been born to it. But then, really: who else could it have been?

Admittedly, he looked the part. The new emperor wore a light but functional breastplate and mail, with an artfully simple laurel circlet in place of a crown and a crucifix around his neck. His hangers-on included the *Carnivora* named Jan from last night — and Callie, now dressed in the *palla* and *stola* normally forbidden to humans. Clearly things had gotten *different* around here.

The Emperor brightened as Liza approached. "Excellent!" he said. "Our trusty emissary has returned! Well done, Praefectus. Well done, indeed."

Liza had had time to think about it, on the trip over, and her *gens* really did raise no fools. She stopped at what she hoped was a reasonably respectful distance, and bowed. "As you commanded," she said, "I have returned, your Imperial Majesty." Liza did *not* do the full *proskynesis* previous Emperors and nobles had required; partially to see what would happen — but mostly because she was, frankly, tired of that shit.

From the quick grin on the Emperor's face, she wasn't the only one. "I *told* you, Senator," he said. "I wish you had taken my bet."

Callie shrugged. She was apparently a 'Senator' now, and Liza wondered for a moment what the title meant. She wasn't obviously old. "I would have, your Majesty," Callie said, "if you hadn't offered it."

"An interesting paradox," noted the Emperor. "And a clever compliment. I look forward to your thwarting my will in the Senate."

"By your command," murmured Callie; her tone made the old masters' — no, 'Universal Dominion's' — usual inferior-to-superior affirmation sound remarkably unservile.

The Emperor chuckled. "But of course. Now, back to you, Praefectus. You will find your duties will be a bit heavier than your rank: the Legatus proved a little too inflexible for the new Imperial Way. We'll either find you somebody suitable for the job, or adjust your rank. I fancy it will be the latter, but it's up to you."

"Thank you, your Imperial Majesty," said Liza. "But how was the old Legatus inflexible?" The old Legatus was a worthless crony of the court, but she would have expected him to turn his coat on a *denaro*.

"Oh, he proved ready enough to take up the cross," said the Emperor. "He was *most* impressed by seeing the Emperor and mages get blown into the sky. Those gunpowder barrels the *Carnivores* buried underneath the Imperial court's encampment when we first laid out the camp worked perfectly." The Emperor grinned again at Liza's start of surprise. "What? I'm hardly going to *lie* about it. The old court was so busy conniving against their mage masters — and the mages were so determined to make sure their orcish slaves stayed under control — that both sides were eager to let us do their skulduggery for them. They assumed we had our own agenda, of course. But they never realized we didn't have the same *kind* of agenda. Or that the *Carnivores* might be happy to *recruit* Christians and humans instead of suppressing them.

"This has all been planned," continued the Emperor, "for a good, long time, and I am happy to make sure our enemies and soon-to-be-allies both understand that while the *Imperium Orci* will be ruled by a— what's the term you used, Jan?"

"I believe the phrase is 'sneaky-ass bastard,' your Imperial Majesty."

"Yes, that was it. But I am a sneaky-ass bastard who still keeps his promises, and the Legatus did not care to hear about the one I had made to the humans. The idea of them becoming equal citizens of the Imperium appalled him." The Emperor shrugged. "I expected nothing else from the Legatus, but he was wearing a legionary uniform. I gave him one chance to live up to it."

Liza nodded; that was fair enough. "Very good, your Imperial Majesty. So what am I to do with your new legion?"

"Prepare it," the Emperor said. "We will be at peace with the Grand Alliance very soon, and likely joining it. Which means we will be fighting the Universal Dominion for the rest of our lives"

— every orc in the room smiled at the thought — "and for that I need the legions ready. All of them. We'll be using this one to secure the region. I expect the Grand Alliance will be much more comfortable at the thought of Old Texas being wooed into the Imperium, instead of conquered. Particularly once we recruit enough human cavalry legions."

Liza forbore to wince at the way the Emperor mangled the military terms, but she would have been willing for him to mangle it still more if she got reliable cavalry out of the deal. "I expect they will, your Imperial Majesty. But our former masters aren't going to like it," she said. "Neither will the nobles who aren't here."

Jan smiled, and looked at the Emperor. At his wave, Jan said, "Fear not, Praefectus. We have such problems well in hand."

"Indeed," said the Emperor. "They are being seen to even as we speak. I expect the Empire's loyal legionaries will find hanging the lot to be a remarkably pleasant diversion."

"Then I suppose I must see to the Third Legion, your Imperial Majesty." Liza bowed again. "Do you have any other instructions for me?"

"Not at this time, Praefectus," said the Emperor. "Please consult with the Tribune here" — he waved to Jan — "if you require anything. She is most keen to assist the military arm in our grand fight against the Dominion."

That sounded like a dismissal, and normally Liza would be happy to get herself gone, but unfortunately there was one last issue to get on the record. Or as on the record as these things were going to go. "One last question, your Imperial Majesty. Are we a Christian empire, now?"

"The *Imperium Orci* will not interfere in the right of its citizens to worship how they please," said the Emperor; his voice was not angry, and lacked its usual mocking tone. "And not by pretending to overlook what choices its citizens have made, either. Especially when those choices will reassure our new citizens and allies." He smiled.

"Or is your question instead as to whether I truly share your faith?" said the new Emperor, "Well, Praefectus, as long as there is no persecution, then that is *my* business. But either way, I would *still* think Texas is worth a Mass."

ANSTEORRA RANGERS

Bossyton, Imperium Orci
(Ruins of Shreveport, Louisiana)
2892 AD

You expected the Imperial province of Abiete to be hot, wet, and gooey. At least, you did if you weren't a damfool and didn't skip the Ranger briefings. But this weather was ridiculous. The rain was almost going *up*, and that was just plain unnatural. These days, when you got this close to the New Muddy, the difference between the sky and the ground became a matter of opinion.

Join the cavalry and see the world, gibed Captain Michael Abilene Salvator (Fox Company, Second Legion, Ansteorra Rangers) to himself. *Then sink into it up to your armpits, and God help your horse.*

And he wasn't even the most miserable one in the cavalry troop. "Having fun yet, Sergeant?" Mike asked, resolutely suppressing a grin.

To the left and the back came the stolid response. "Of course, Captain Salvator, sir! Every day in the Ansteorra Rangers is a miracle of glory and adventure, sir! I feel privileged to be in this mud, sir! I shall keep some as a souvenir, sir!"

Mike turned back to look at Juanita Sharpfangs Fectum. "Now look what you did there, Nita. You done used up all your sirs for the day. Gotta ration them out."

The orc flashed a quick fanged smile. "But I don't feel like more bullshit, Cap'n."

Mike looked around at the muddy, unstable mess which one month ago had been a bustling farming area. "You're in the wrong place, then." His face grew just a little bit harder. "We all are."

#

Mike was happy to see the refugees from the Red River settlements weren't in the worst of shape, at least. Half of them were sneezing and all of them were muddy, but there was enough food and clean water to last the caravan to the Imperial base at Marshall. The refugees were even lively enough to complain, although from what Mike heard, elves just plain liked to talk all the time.

Still, after herding them to Marshall they'd be some Imperial bureaucrat's problem, not Mike's; he'd be off to run escort duty on some other half-drowned refugee caravan. Only this time, he'd have enough dry socks to last the whole trip... even if it meant blackmailing the quartermaster.

Mike was mostly worried about the horses. This current batch was pretty knackered out, and Nita's were the worst of all. It wasn't the easiest thing in the world to find a horse that could tolerate an orc and vice versa, and Nita was only short and slender by orcish standards. She changed remounts three times to Mike's two, which was an improvement over when she'd started out in the troop.

Oh, Nita pulled her weight. Three more months and she'd be running her squad; give it a year, and it'd be a platoon and probably a commission. She was fitting in fine. But Mike still wondered why the hell Nita wanted to join the human cavalry. That 'Sharpfangs' *nomen* she sported could open a lot of doors for her.

On the other hand, one of the privileges of being an Ansteorra Ranger was that you didn't get asked too many awkward questions. You didn't want to talk about the past? Fine, within limits. Mike figured it'd be pretty hypocritical to expect Nita to trot out her life story when he wasn't going around telling *his*.

#

"The rain, it is getting shitty, Captain." From anybody else, that'd be griping. From Mike's second in command, it was more of a warning.

Mike looked up from 'dinner.' He liked a joke as well as the next guy, but this one the cooks kept making was older than dirt and half as tasty. It was also technically cold, but he couldn't remember offhand the last time where the meals had been actually hot. "We talking regular shitty, Jimmy," asked Mike, "or for-real shitty?"

"For-real, Captain. You can see the traces of mud in it, and it gives off a stink like from the bottom of the river."

Mike looked over at his lieutenant. Jimmy Monterrey Nemo looked like a southern *bandito* come north because of one too many local feuds, which was pretty much exactly right. But he liked to fight, knew how to lead, and while Jimmy happily fought dirty, he never fought filthy. The Imperium was always ready to find a combat slot for someone like that. Plus, Jimmy didn't like to bother him with unimportant things.

They got along pretty well, in fact. Jimmy was second-in-command when Mike got rotated in, he'd likely be the S-I-C when Mike rotated out, and that seemed just fine with the man. Mike wondered who was getting the better part of the deal; Lord knew Jimmy got first crack at leading actual cavalry patrols, which was usually more fun than writing reports.

River dirt in the rain was bad news, though. These days, it meant a mudnado was coming through, and had already taken a big bite out of the Old Muddy riverbed. It was time to find some damned cover.

#

The Universal Dominion. The God-damned Universal Dominion. You'd think the bastards would know when they were up Shit Creek and their paddle was on fire, but no. They'd been fighting all of their neighbors at one go, for longer than most people had been alive, and what had it cost them? Just most of their lands south of the Arkansas River, and everything they had hacked off of Deseret.

They still had themselves a damned huge hunk of the continent to rule over, and none of it was really 'theirs' to begin with. Any reasonable country would have thought about the possibility of suing for peace, maybe. Just to see what it was like, perhaps. But, no: the Dominion instead decided to use the Mississippi as a giant flail.

Mike could see the thinking; he didn't think it was smart, but he could see it. Divert the river by sorcery and make it crack like a whip, down by the Gulf of Mexico. That'd wipe out all the river communities (including the ones still controlled by the Dominion, but they weren't mages so fuck 'em), keep the *Imperium Orci* busy on one side, and keep the Elf-lands scared and neutral on the other. And it was something their battle-mages could *do*. They couldn't win a lot of battles and they couldn't keep half-pacified territory, but Dominion magic was just barely up to the task of wrecking everybody's day.

Only it turned out moving the Mississippi just got the elves pissed off, not scared. Which any orc could have told them, assuming said orc wasn't too busy screaming "FOR GOD AND SAINT MIGUEL!" while lopping off wizardly heads with a *gladius*. The Imperium's rumor mills were saying the spell probably killed at least a thousand Dominion mages outright, and permanently maimed another four or five thousand. Even the Dominion couldn't soak up those kind of losses without noticing, and it had cost them in battles on the eastern *and* western fronts. All in all, not a bad outcome for the Grand Alliance.

Assuming you weren't one of those half-drowning in the mud. Or assigned to the detail whose job it was to pull people out of it.

#

Mike and his Rangers needed four hours to get twenty wagons and a hundred-twenty, hundred-thirty people somewhere safely out of the way. They got three. Mike figured they were all lucky it wasn't two.

Nobody could get this far from the Old Muddy by being

dumb about the weather, so most of the wagons didn't need to be told twice why the rain suddenly stopped, and there was a breeze to the east. They knew damned well what it meant: a mudnado was in the area, and they'd be smart to not stick around for it to come by and take a slap at them. It'd happened before, to other refugee caravans, and the survivors all had agreed the results weren't pretty.

That meant it only took a *little* too long for the wagons to be creaking their way up the paths, looking for ground broken enough to keep them from getting washed away. Mike sent half the troop forward to scout out likely sheltering spots; the others he stayed with and kept close, in case they'd need to load up their mounts and remounts with refugees and move right quickly. Mudnados were mean, but they were slow, and often couldn't steer themselves worth a damn.

Nita was one of the scouts; when she rode up, she looked even greener than usual. It took Mike a second to remember that meant she was agitated, not about to throw up. "Captain!" she called over the strengthening wind. "The lieutenant's compliments, and he says the main trail is fucked to hell-and-gone because a God-damned pine tree slid off the bank above it and shoved its ass right up the road's."

Mike shook his head. "Was that the clean version, Sergeant?"

"Yes, sir. I left out the parts about the road's mother."

"Good job, Sergeant," Mike said. "I like a little couth in my officers." *And for damned sure Jimmy hadn't got much to spare*, he thought. "No way to get through it?"

"Not with the wagons. There's a trail to the west which goes the same kind of way, but it's longer and could wash out." Nita paused. "The tree isn't moving, sir. And it's a real monster of a tree, too. Not the kind that moves and eats people, I mean. It's just huge."

#

Afterward, they never really figured out when the caravan ran out of day. The sky went brown-yellow fast, with lightning sparking up the sky and only rarely deigning to come down to the ground. And the rain *bounced*, getting muddy droplets into everything, making the whole excursion more miserable. Since it wasn't exactly a steeplechase to begin with, Mike found himself so muddy and sore that it started to feel like armor.

Rain of frogs? he mused fuzzily as a scattering of half-frozen ones washed across the caravan. *Sure, why not? I wonder if they're the good-tasting ones.* Although the crunching sounds as the wagons rode over them kind of put Mike off the idea. Besides, the idea of a campfire was at this point just a fond memory.

His lieutenant rode up. If Mike looked as beat as Jimmy did right now, it was time to find something, anything, that looked like shelter. But Jimmy was smiling. "Captain, you will not believe our luck!"

Mike squinted at Jimmy. "You're right," he said. "I won't. What have you got?"

"We found an Old American ruin."

"What? Here? What the hell is it?"

"It looks like something they put things in, Captain. Big things; there are ramps to use, wide and tall enough for the wagons. No walls, but the hills have grown around it. Three sides are enclosed, and the fourth is covered with vines. I looked, and saw there are two floors we can get at."

Mike frowned. "The rest?"

"Collapsed," said Jimmy. "The floors left look sound, though. No cracks, no shifting. I think they were the top of the building, so not yet filled in by the dirt. There will be enough room for us, and only one entrance. If this was a war, we could defend ourselves for quite a bit there, until of course our water ran out."

"Great. What were the monsters?"

"Ah, Captain, that is the problem," said Jimmy. "We saw no sign of any. No beast-sign, either."

"How was the *vibe*?" By this Mike meant the innate magical feel of a place. Most humans could pick up on at least the really bad locations, and Jimmy was better at it than most people who weren't mages.

Jimmy shrugged. "Nothing vile or overpowering, Captain,

but I did feel the signs of a presence in the ruin. I think it might object to our being there, but we are two hundred and there is only one of them. So perhaps it might abide us, if we can placate it?"

"Well, that'd be a nice change," observed Mike. He hawked out muddy spit like it was tobacco juice. "Right, it's better than getting stuck in the open when the mudnado finally finds us, and we outnumber whatever-it-is in there anyway. Get the caravan steered in the right direction and keep extra watch for stragglers or drop-offs. Once we get there, I don't want to keep having to come back out in this crap."

#

Of course, there was a straggler.

They were lucky, in a way: the wagon had managed to fall pretty far behind, by the time they counted wagons and came up one short. Which meant the remaining wagons still had a chance to get under cover, if somebody made some hard calls about what could or couldn't be saved. And if somebody *else* was a real son-of-a-bitch about ramrodding the caravan on its way.

That's what Mike told himself when he assigned Jimmy to getting the rest away while he and a few Rangers went back to find the lost wagon. Besides, 'lead from the front' was what an Imperial Ranger captain *did*. There was no shame in enjoying your work, hey? Even if your lieutenant *might* have preferred to be the one riding pell-mell down half-wild trails as the winds rose.

You can have the next one, Jimmy, thought Mike as he and his team rode.

#

In a bit of *bad* luck, when the Rangers finally found the wagon, there wasn't anything actually wrong with it, except the teamster was bad with horses. Mike had been hoping for a lost wheel and maybe even a strategic sprain or two among the refugees. Anything which would convince a bunch of stubborn elves to stop trying to save the family gimcracks and just *git*.

But they weren't getting. "It's all we got," shouted the teamster over the rising rain. He called himself Malma Jefferson, and he probably looked a lot smarter when he wasn't soaked to the skin. "If we lose it, where are we?"

"Alive," said Mike sharply. "This ain't an argument, Citizen. It ain't even a discussion. We got room on our horses for y'all" — husband, wife, three kids — "and we're putting you on them and getting the Hell out of here."

Malma still looked mulish, and muttered in a way that reminded Mike that all elves supposedly knew a little magic. But he wasn't looking directly at the Rangers when he did, which was smart of the guy. This wasn't a great situation, and it was getting worse every minute.

Thing calmed down, though. The wife (she was called Gertrude, which at least was more normal) seemed more on the ball on how messed up things were getting; she was already busy packing thankfully small bundles for the family. Which was why Mike wasn't pushing it still harder. Yet. And, damn, he could see the guy's point. *He* knew the Imperium was going to be openhanded when it came to resettling the elves, out of both simple Christian charity and naked self-interest. Malma Jefferson didn't, not really.

His wife did, though. "Get on the *yarush* horse, Malma," Gertrude snapped. She and the children were all clutching their bundles; Malma's was pointedly at her feet. "We don't have much time left."

In the distance Mike could hear a very nasty whine in the wind. No, actually, the wind *itself* was whining. He bit back a curse.

"Wrong, ma'am," said Mike. He jumped onto the wagon and grabbed the reins. "We don't have any time at all." He looked at his sergeant. "I'll get the wagon away. Take the refugees back, use my horse. I'll use this one to catch up with you."

The sergeant grimaced, but saluted. Mike grinned as he concentrated on getting the wagon moving. Unlike Citizen Jefferson, *he* knew how to make a wagon go.

He'd need to.

#

There was a trick to getting away from a mudnado. First, you had to be crazy. Mike figured he had that one down, already. He'd joined up with the Rangers, hadn't he? Why, if he had listened to his dad, Mike'd be right now running herd over the finest cattle to be found north of Sancte Antoni.

But since he *was* already crazy, Mike figured he should get down to being good. The big advantage he had was that the mudnado was just as dumb as it was clumsy. This one could move a fair clip, once it noticed Mike. That nearly got him killed right away at the start of the chase, but the mudnado got (ha!) winded fast.

And the mudnado kept trying to lunge at the wagon when it wasn't *quite* able to reach it. Oh, sure, the wagon end lifted up a few times, only to come back down in a jarring slam, but as long as the wheels held out Mike would be fine. Or the horse held out. Or, hell, Mike's kidneys from all the bouncing around.

Right, he wasn't actually fine. But Mike had a plan. That was the third thing you needed: a plan. A crazy plan that'd only work if you were good. And as soon as he found a convenient steep slope to drive the wagon off of, he'd put his plan in motion.

#

And lo! there was a steep slope now. To Mike's eyes it didn't look *all* that big, but beggars can't be choosers, right? It'd just have to do.

Mike stood up on the wagon as it rolled to the edge, the mudnado behind him and maybe gaining a little because it was a straightaway. He had the reins in one hand and his knife in the other, because you never (*never*) carry a knife in your teeth. If Mike were the sort to gibber in fear, he'd have done it now. As it was, he just felt a mild sort of concern. This next part would be tricky.

A desperate leap propelled Mike from the wagon and onto the back of the frenzied horse pulling it. He pulled the reins with one hand while the other lashed out with his knife, to slice the leather ties binding the horse to the wagon. If this didn't work on the first try, he and the horse would go over the cliff tangled up with the wagon...

But it did work! Which meant Mike and the horse and the wagon still went over the cliff edge, but at least they weren't attached to the wagon. This was good. Well, better.

The next fifteen, thirty seconds to Mike were a collection of impacts which would later turn into spectacular bruises: the damned horse managed to find every tree branch on its pell-mell descent down the gully, and Mike was convinced to his dying day the horse did it because it hated people. But the horse didn't actually roll over, and it managed not to break a leg—and once the two hit solid ground the horse was ready to bolt and Mike was cheering the would-be murderer on.

And, as Mike had hoped, the mudnado went after the wagon first. Why not? It was larger. And by the time it realized there weren't any broken people or horses around the wagon anymore, Mike was long gone.

The truce between man and steed lasted until Mike rejoined the caravan. Then the horse tried to bite Mike. But even then it was just a perfunctory attempt, as if the horse was doing it out of some sort of half-understood obligation.

#

Resolving the status of possibly-haunted Old American ruins was a worked-out process by the end of the 29th Century AD. There were two ways to do it; the first was to send in somebody to look for spirits, all nice and civilized and steady, and then start talking to any that they found. If the spirits could be talked or worked around, all right. And if they couldn't? Well, at least you tried.

Once he came back, Mike's team did it the other way.

Magic might not be as common in the Imperium as it was in the Elf-lands or Virginia, but Imperial mages were common *enough* to make sure every cavalry troop had a ghostshouter. It was about the size of a satchel and heavy by human standards, so Mike had Nita hold it while he lit the fuse. It caught, even in the driving rain, thanks to chemistry, alchemy, and thaumaturgy. Imperial mages cared a lot about results, and not much about style.

Subtlety wasn't even considered as an option. The ghostshouter exploded about twenty seconds after Nita lobbed it into the ruins, and the sound and flash came damned close to spooking all the horses, even exhausted as they were. But it didn't matter for this, because Mike and about half the troop were already rushing in on foot.

They had more gear that was good against the supernatural: torches with strange herbs woven in, stones which glowed in the presence of ghosts, various blessed weapons. But the important thing was that the Rangers were looking for spirits, and expecting them to show up. So many people ready to *believe* makes it easier for the incorporeal to become corporeal.

Certainly this one wasn't shy to appear: seven feet tall, clawed, and ready to spit fire. "Assholes!" it screamed as it popped into existence on the lower level. "Get out of my place!" it screamed again.

Mike really *looked* at it, which made the spirit start shrinking on the spot. Which was the idea, really. Manifestation via living people's belief was a double-edged sword here, because when they did, it would be in a form more favorable to the Rangers. Most inimical ones would prefer to solidify on their own terms; which was why the Rangers had fired off a ghostshouter. Until the spook got over the effects, it couldn't really stand up to the opinions of a bunch of mortals.

And probably it kind of knew it, because all the spirit was doing was screaming. Mike let the haunt get it out of its system for a minute, because why the hell not? Then Mike pulled a bottle out from his rucksack. Just the sight of it shut the spirit right up.

Mike grinned. *Stick, then carrot,* he thought as he carefully cracked the seal on the tequila and poured it into a bowl on the floor. "This is yours," he said cheerfully as he poured. "We're paying for our shelter. You want it all now, or later?"

The spirit looked at the tequila, looked at Mike, looked at

the Rangers already dragging wagons into the ruins, and looked back at the tequila. It got a little smaller still, and lost the claws. "Some now, rest later," said the spirit. "You got tobacco?"

"Of course," said Mike, rummaging through the rucksack again for a spare pouch. He lobbed it at the spirit, who caught it easily. "What's booze without smokes? You need a light?"

The haunt looked at him, a pinch of tobacco in its fingers. The tobacco ignited, and the spirit calmly put it in its mouth and started to chew, its eyes never leaving Mike's.

Mike put his hands up, all nice and friendly. "Guess not," he said. "No problem, Mister Spirit. We'll leave some more of both when we leave."

"And chocolate," said Mister Spirit.

"And chocolate," echoed Mike agreeably. "See, here it is. We good?"

The spirit looked like it kind of wanted it not to be, but booze, tobacco, *and* chocolate wasn't something to risk. It nodded. "We good," it said finally. "I swear."

"Same here," said Mike. "I swear, no more attacks — hey, Sergeant! Put out that damned ghostshouter!"

#

As the spirit drifted over to the pile of bribes, its form shrinking down until it hit about five and half feet or so, Nita came over to Mike, still holding the ghostshouter. "It's got about a third of a charge left, sir," she said. "Keep or toss?"

It was a fair question: magic items cost a lot, but some of the stuff in them didn't always mix well with people. "Keep," Mike said after thinking it over. "There ain't nothing in one of those that's bad for us, even half-burnt. The ignition spell's probably dead, though, so if we want to use it again, we're gonna need to dunk it in something that burns first. Bag it up tight and stow it on one of the wagons."

"Yessir," said Nita. As she did, she added, "Some good ghost-wrangling you did there, sir. I've never seen it done for real, before."

"Doubt you would have, Nita. You had the legionary training, right?" Nita nodded, no doubt thinking she had hid her wince. Mike went on. "Yeah. The training's good for letting you know what a ghost looks and smells like when it's in your face, which is what it's supposed to do. But when you're in the classroom, you always know the spirit's not about to try to *eat* your face, right? And it's gonna wait around for you to get the exorcism just right. Not out here. Here, you gotta be fast and smart. It's all about knowing which corners you can cut."

Mike stood up, started catching the eyes of various sergeants. "Time we got this goat rodeo organized. We're guests here, and I don't want our host to get second thoughts about letting us in."

#

"What the devil is that thing searching for?" asked Jimmy, one eye screwed shut while the other looked through a spyglass. His tone was more resigned than confused; he'd probably had already guessed what the answer was.

Mike gave it to him anyway. "Us," he said while using his own binoculars. The two of them were on the second level of the half-buried ruin, carefully spying through the canopy of vines camouflaging their resting spot.

This gave them an excellent view of the mudnado. It had poured in about twenty minutes after the last wagon had been secured; Mike was pretty sure it was tracking them, in the same way a feral chupacabra might track a sheep herd. Right now the mudnado was only about fifteen feet tall and lazily spiraling, but Mike knew damned well from earlier it could hit twenty-five feet's worth of dervish-spinning death at the first sign of trouble. And it wasn't showing any signs of leaving, either.

Jimmy had clearly reached the same conclusion. "If it was a beast," he sighed as he collapsed the spyglass, "we could expect it to wander off for different prey. But water spirits do not hunger, and it will find plenty of water here. It will not 'starve' any time soon."

"Yup. And it's not hunting us for food anyway," agreed Mike. "It's hunting us because it's mean." He lowered his binoculars.

"Suggestions, Jimmy?"

"Besides blowing it up, Miguel?" asked Jimmy.

"Jimmy, if I had enough kisses to do that, the sergeants would be detailing a throwing party right now." Hand-grenades were a newish thing, imported down from Greater Hershey now that the Dominion's ban on magical gunpowder was no longer quite so unyielding. Mike had no idea why they were called 'kisses,' and wouldn't have cared about the mystery even if it had been pointed out to him.

#

Five minutes later, Nita was blinking at the two humans. "Shouldn't you be asking one of the more senior sergeants what they think, sirs?" she pointed out to them. "I'm the most junior of the bunch."

Mike looked at Jimmy. "We got any other sergeants sporting a moniker like 'Sharpfangs,' Lieutenant?"

"No, Captain," replied Jimmy. "Although you never know, with Sergeant Laredo. He might be in disguise."

Nita bit her lip to hide a smile: Sergeant Edward Laredo Abactor was five foot six and was about the *weight* of a preteen orc, too. The sergeant could also brawl up to four men at once before he started getting tired, so Nita just said, "I'm here to do my duty, sirs. I don't make a fuss about the *nomen*."

"Didn't say you had, Nita," Mike said amiably. "But we're figuring out what we have to work with, here, and one of the things we have is a Sharpfang. You got any thoughts about the mudnado?"

"Just to ask the refugees," Nita replied. "Maybe they have a better idea of what that thing is than we do."

Jimmy shook his head. "The refugees are elvish farmers and boatmen," he pointed out. "They say the mudnadoes started happening after the Dominion attack, and so they assume it is all just a Dominion curse. It is hard to argue."

"But is it, sir?" said Nita. "If the mudnadoes come from the Dominion, why didn't they use them before? Those assholes aren't shy about throwing curses around."

"Hrm," Mike said. "A good question, Sergeant. What's the next one?" He noted Nita blinked a little at that. Her response was a bit more careful, and despite her best efforts, tentative.

"So we would, well, ask the refugees again, only this time we check if there was anything which could have been made *into* the mudnadoes." Nita paused, and went on. "We should also see if any of these boatmen were smugglers. You hear stories about Elf-lands smugglers and marsh-witches. Maybe they heard a story or two."

"Which they wouldn't tell us about because we're soldiers," said Mike. "Very good, Sergeant. We have the other sergeants asking *those* questions now."

"Oh," said Nita. "Was that a test then, Captain?"

"A little one, Sergeant," said Jimmy after looking at Mike for permission to answer. "But we also wanted a good look at your wits. A Ranger lives or dies by them."

#

It turned out Mike's new friend Malma Jefferson *did* know more than his share of marsh-witches. He could hardly avoid it, seeing as he was one himself. Indeed, Malma seemed surprised the Rangers were surprised. "It's not a secret," he said to them. "I thought you knew, Captain. Especially since you took my horse and wagon. Figured you knew they'd be spelled against danger."

"They didn't really brief us much, Mr. Jefferson," Mike said dryly. "What with the river staggering around like a snake with a broken back, and such. We're lucky we got told y'all were elves."

"Okay," said Malma. "I guess that makes sense." Malma looked a little disappointed, but then he smiled. "So *that's* why you didn't ask me about the Hellfair!" he said. "Okay, yeah, I feel better now."

Mike had told Jimmy and Nita they could ask questions without permission, just as long as nobody was talking over anybody else. So it wasn't really a breach of what the Rangers called 'military decorum' when Nita leaned forward and said to Malma, "Ask you about the what-now, Citizen? That the name of your horse?"

"No, the name of the monster, ah, ma'am?" replied Malma, visibly trying to read Nita's military insignia, and just as visibly failing. "Or the name of what it *was*: a Hellfair." He saw their blank looks, and said, "Sorry. A *halfaer*, a river-fish spirit? I think it was maybe one of the real old ones, from the dawn of the First Age."

Nita whistled, then explained to the two humans, "He means about AD 2100 or so. Collapse of the old world, birth of magic, all the rest." Turning back to Malma, she went on, "So what do you know about this kind of spirit, Mr. Jefferson?"

"That's most of it, ma'am. I never saw the big Hellfairs up close, 'cuz they're real mean-tempered. Bite you as soon as look at you, and they got lots of teeth to bite with. You get 'em in the parts of the rivers people don't use much. A few of 'em. They don't get on with folks."

"How clever are they?" asked Jimmy.

"Oh, they're real dumb," said Malma. "Makes the regular kind tolerable enough, although give me a gator-spirit any time. You can make a deal with gator-spirits; Hellfairs you just drive off. Or you could." Malma shook his head. "Too much screaming and blood in the water right now. Gave 'em all a taste for both."

"You said you could drive them off, before all this happened," said Mike. "What were their weaknesses, back then?"

Malma scratched his head. "Well, fire, of course."

"Doesn't water beat fire?" asked Mike.

"And fire boils water," said Malma. "Works both ways. Or, you could lead 'em around some with blood or piss — oh, and salt. They loved salt, couldn't get enough of it. I knew some fellas who used to use salt licks to keep the Hellfairs under control. Doesn't work now, mind you. They're too big."

"But still just as dumb?" asked Mike.

"But still just as dumb," agreed Malma. He looked at Mike. "You have an idea, Captain? I can't do too much, since my things are scattered from here to the old Muddy, but I can still manage a few things."

"Yeah," said Mike. "Gotta work out some of the details first, though. I'll let you get back to what you were doing."

"Sure, Captain. Happy to help out with whatever needs doing," Malma said as he went back to looking for whatever he was looking for.

"Famous last words," Mike muttered.

#

"A'ight," said Mike after thinking things over for about twenty minutes, "I have a plan. We'll go with blowing the damned thing up. Sergeant, I want you to go around to the men and collect whatever holdout blow-em-ups they might be carrying around for a rainy day. Every little bit helps."

"Yes sir," said Nita. "Get their firewater, too?"

Jimmy laughed. "You would need a whole squad..." He stopped, and looked at Nita for a moment. "Well," he said, "perhaps *you* would only need *half* a squad."

"Pry at least an extra bottle or two out of the sergeants, Sergeant," said Mike. "But only the stuff that burns. And tell Sgt. Laredo we're going to need the honey buckets secured. If these things track piss, we gotta keep extra clean."

"Yes, sir," repeated Nita. She saluted in proper Ranger style (small gestures; nothing which would stand out to a sniper with a crossbow) and went off.

Jimmy looked at Mike. "I do not think we have enough explosives to harm this Hellfair from the outside, Captain," he said. "Even with what the sergeants can glean from the men. Were you thinking of offering it bait?"

"It's the best thing I can think of," said Mike. "I don't know much about this stuff, but I know it goes boom harder if it's enclosed in something. So, if we can get the Hellfair to *eat* the bomb, set it off from the inside? Well, I can't imagine the monster would enjoy that."

"It would not." Jimmy thought it over. "But it will *take* work to *make* it work. How do we even get it all to explode? Gunpowder and spirits are easily doused by water."

"Sure," said Mike. He stood. "Good thing we have a marsh-witch along, hey?"

"Yes. But is he *enough* of a marsh-witch?"

#

"Sure, I can make your bomb waterproof," Malma said, once Mike caught up to him. "Even got the things to do it. Can't blow it up for you, though."

"Can't you cast, you know, a spell for it?" asked Mike.

Malma snorted. "Oh, *Hell* no. Here, watch this." He extended a finger and stared at it; a moment later, a bit of flame appeared and danced above the tip. "Behold!" he said. "My 'fireball spell.' Great when your pipe goes out in the rain, but it doesn't have a damn bit of range. I'd have to get right up to the bomb for the spell to work. And I ain't doing that, sorry. Sounds just a bit too much like suicide."

"Right," said Mike after a moment looking at one corner of the ruin. There had been a little flicker of flame there, too. Mike went on, "Maybe some kind of slow match?"

Malma hiked a thumb back towards the outside. "Check my wagon, Captain," he said with maybe the smallest, littlest bit of ill-will. "It'd be where I was keeping mine. I went scrounging for more, but turns out nobody else thought to bring along mage supplies. Go figure."

Mike shook his head ruefully. "Fair enough, Mr. Jefferson, fair enough. You just make sure the bomb stays nice and dry. I'll worry about getting it blown up."

Mike ambled over to the corner where he had seen the flicker of light. Nobody there; at least, nobody visible. Mike grinned, tightly. "Hey, Mister Spirit," he said. "You wanted to talk?"

#

The way Mister Spirit materialized, Mike was never really sure where it — he? — was the exact moment it appeared. But it was definitely there: if nothing else Mike could smell, fine, 'him.' Mister Spirit was now exuding sort of a combination of burning lamp oil and nicotine. It actually smelled pleasant enough, although that might change if the cavalry troop was cooped in here for too long.

The spirit was still chewing his smoldering plug of tobacco, too. Slowly, just like somebody trying to savor a treat. "Yeah," Mister Spirit said. "We gotta talk."

"Sure thing," Mike said, and found a reasonably flat bit of rubble to sit on. He briefly wished for a smoke, but the spirit was currently chewing most of his tobacco. "What can I do you for?"

"You ain't gonna get close enough to the devil-fish water thing," said Mister Spirit. "You ain't strong enough. Not even the big green gal. It'll suck you in, pull you up, and then it's chomp-chomp!" The spirit snapped its mouth open and shut a few times. It hadn't bothered with teeth, but those jaws looked pretty strong. "I don't mean nothing by it," continued the spirit. "Just sayin', that's all. You get me?"

"I get you," replied Mike. "But one of us has got to try anyway. I got all these people to look out for, and getting chomped's part of the job. But I think you have an idea?"

"Yeah," said Mister Spirit. "I ain't afraid of no devil-fish, no Hellfair. Water tries to put me out, I float on it and keep burning. Fish tries to bite me, there's gonna be a big fry-up. I can light your big bomb, Captain Ranger."

"Now, that's real generous of you," said Mike. "Worth all the tobacco, booze, and chocolate we have." He wrestled with his conscience a little, lost, and went on. "But we don't have much more to give."

"Nah," said the spirit. "Not that. I want something else."

"Okay," replied Mike. "What?"

"I want out," said the spirit. "I help you kill this Hellfair, then when you leave, you take me with you. You take me someplace where there's plenty tobacco and booze and chocolate and other good stuff. This is a good deal. You should take it."

"I figure you'd know if you could leave," Mike said after a moment. "But isn't this your home?"

The spirit laughed. "This place? Nah. It's a hole. Nothing but rocks and dirt and a few lizards. I like to *go*, me. I dunno what you got that ain't this, but it ain't gonna *be* this, and that's good. Don't worry about me going with you. I show you something you can dig up and carry, and I can ride along."

"You know something, Mister Spirit?" said Mike. "It's a deal." He stood up and extended a hand. The spirit took it: the grip felt harder and far colder than Mike expected, but it wasn't awful. "Hell, I'd do it for you even if you *didn't* want to help out."

"Really?" said the spirit. "Why?"

Mike shrugged. "I'm a Ranger," he said. "We solve problems."

#

"Yeah, but do we have to solve them up close and personal?" said Mike aloud a couple of hours later, from behind the rubble they'd chosen as a watching-post. The land around here was flat enough for horses, if you were careful; the trees grew in solid, gnarled clumps, as if there was something stopping them from growing anywhere they pleased. If Mike was going to hazard a guess, he'd figure there had been a city here once. More recently, there'd been a mudnado, but it wasn't immediately around.

Beside him, Nita frowned. "You say something, Cap'n?" Her eyes never left off watching Jimmy ride his horse as scout/bait, fast enough to move but slow enough to be safe, more or less. Neither did Mike's.

"Don't worry about it, Sergeant," he said. "Just talking to myself." *And wishing I hadn't promised that Jimmy could have the next one.* Being a Ranger Captain was a lot more fun when you *had* to lead from the front.

But it made sense. Jimmy was the best rider, and he'd need to be, if he wanted to get away in time. Nita was there because she was the strongest one in the troop: if they had to drag Jimmy back, she might even be able to bring along the horse. And Mike was the one ordering people to go do this damfool plan. You could usually get away with doing the damfool plans yourself in the Ansteorra Rangers, but sometimes you couldn't — and this was 'sometimes.'

But of course, now that they had a damfool plan, there was no sign of the damned monster it was supposed to be destroying. Mike couldn't even hear it. He assumed Nita couldn't, either: orcs were better at smell than hearing.

"A question, Cap'n?" asked Nita.

"Go ahead, Sergeant."

"What are we going to do if it doesn't show up, Cap'n?"

"That's an easy one, Sergeant." Mike used his binoculars to scan the area. "We wait a day, then just leave. The elf said this thing isn't smart, or patient. If it's left, it's not real likely to come back. Even with these wagons, we're only a day or two from the base, and— never mind. There's our bastard." The damned thing had been oozing its way through what were either very small hills or very overgrown rubble, and while it wasn't knocking over trees, it had been shaking them pretty hard. It was far enough away not to see Jimmy yet, but it was going to, pretty soon.

Nita had her own binoculars, which actually looked better than Mike's own, and his were top-notch Virginian opticals. Mike wondered why the Sharpfangs were being so extravagant. Oh, sure, he expected orcish nobles to kit out their scions properly, but the Imperium didn't stint on military equipment, either. "I see it. So has the lieutenant." She frowned. "Is it wrong of me to wish it *had* gone away, Cap'n?"

"Not when the job's herding civilians, Sergeant." Mike studied the mudnado, which, while visible, didn't seem very active. "If we were sent out to kill it, well, you wear the star for a reason. But this is just a damned nuisance that won't stop getting in our way."

"Yes, sir. But I am an orc, sir." Nita grinned. "We are *very* good at killing monsters, sir."

"And that's why there's an Imperium," agreed Mike. "I wonder if it's sick."

"Sir?"

"The Hellfair," said Mike. "Sick, or injured, or just tuckered out from chasing things all over the mud. It's not moving the way it did earlier." It always looked like something was moving under the 'skin,' but right now that movement was slow and sluggish, like a muddy river after a flood. It also splattered more bits of it as it moved, now.

"I'm just going to assume that's bad, Cap'n."

"Yeah, smart of you." Mike looked at the mudnado through the binoculars again. "Injured critters are dangerous. Injured monsters are just plain *scary*."

#

It was just bad luck. Damnably bad luck; Malma's horse must have used up all of the local supply. Jimmy's trotting steed found a gopher hole, just as the lieutenant was starting to look for the best way to provoke the monster into giving chase. And a little too far away for the other two to offer immediate help.

Mike couldn't hear the crack of the horse's leg breaking, but his mind filled in the sounds of agony and disaster as Jimmy went flying from the saddle and the explosives stayed behind. For a moment he thought the Hellfair had heard it, too, which might not be too bad — but it didn't seem to care much about the screams of the horse. The Hellfair certainly wasn't going out of its way to investigate, although it did draw closer.

Jimmy rose with one arm broken, and a bloody leg. *That*, the Hellfair noticed. *The scent of blood*, Mike realized, and cursed himself for an idiot. *We could have baited a trap with some!*

Well, no use crying in your beer, Mike thought as he vaulted other the rubble, leaving his own mount behind. Another gopher hole, and there'd be *two* Rangers needing rescue. *Ranger down, and we need to get Jimmy's horse butchered before the Hellfair can really get moving.* He saw Nita hadn't hesitated to run along with him, which he was starting to suspect might be really awkward to explain to his superiors later. Unless Mike got killed right now, in which case he wouldn't care.

If it had been two days before, the Hellfair would have stripped Jimmy down to the bone before Mike and Nita got to him. But the monster *was* slower, and as Nita ran to Jimmy, Mike dodged left and started yelling. "Hey! Remember me? You still hungry, you muddy bastard?"

Which worked: the thing maybe did remember chasing him, because it started swaying in his direction, while Nita managed to yank the lieutenant off the ground with what must have been one incredibly painful effort for both of them. She was almost at the closest tangled clump of trees before the mudnado noticed; Mike was waving his shortsword to keep the monster distracted, but he wasn't bleeding and Jimmy was.

It didn't attack Nita and Jimmy directly, though; it just tried to try to pull them into the air, and right towards its maw. Nita didn't hesitate as the winds rose around her. One hand locked around Jimmy's good arm, Nita dived into the dirt, grabbing a tree root with her free hand. As the winds rose, so did the two Rangers... but for the moment they weren't going anywhere.

But that wouldn't last for long, unless the mudnado could be distracted again with still more blood. Mike dashed to Jimmy's stricken steed. *Sorry, old hoss,* Mike thought mournfully as he ripped through the horse's neck with one quick slice. *If it's any comfort, this ain't making me safer right now.* The whole thing reminded him far too much of the old stories about the Witch Queen of Tulsa: *she* was fond of sacrificing a horse whenever she sent a courier to Hell, just to get the message there faster.

There's a lot more blood in a horse than a man, and a spurting neck-wound bleeds out pretty quick. Mike could feel the Hellfair's attention snap toward him, and it wanted that blood. Wanted to chew on Mike's flesh, too, and Mike reckoned that he was now just a little too close to run away, dammit.

Only, as he raised the shortsword in a likely futile gesture, Mister Spirit popped into existence beside him. "Better run, you're-a-Ranger!" the spirit howled over the wind. "I give you ten breaths before I bring the fire."

"The mouth's not open enough!" screamed Mike as he scrambled on top of the sprawled horse, cutting free the bundle of explosives.

"You saying I can't jump in that?" Mike was no expert in spirit psychology, but it did sound like Mister Spirit had his own doubts on the matter.

"Hold on! I'll make it bigger!" Mike threw his shortsword so hard it wrenched something in his arm, but the important thing was that the sword went spinning right above the mudnado's mouth. He wasn't sure what he'd hit, but it apparently was painful; the Hellfair somehow managed to open its mouth even louder. Hot, acidic mud splattered across Mike's face.

The last thing he saw before everything went loud and bright was Mister Spirit diving into that windy maw, dragging the bundle with it.

#

The next day, Mike led the caravan west. Or rather, he lay in a wagon with Jimmy and a box carrying Mister Spirit's focus (or whatever you called it), while a couple of competent sergeants led the caravan west. Concussions were no joke, and the same stuff keeping him from losing his lunch was also stopping Mike from riding a horse.

Hell, even Nita was on the wagon, although she was well enough to be the teamster. Strained tendons were one of those things orcs bounced back from pretty quick, and there weren't likely to be many problems, now that the Hellfair was dead. It had been an ugly thing, when Mike had finally seen the pieces: all teeth and dead eyes and skin which would cut you if you touched it the wrong way. If he hadn't known damn well it was freshwater and probably demonic, Mike might have mistaken it for a shark. But it was dead, and that was fine with Mike.

"How long to the fort, sir?" asked Nita.

"A day, maybe two, Sergeant," said Mike, and winced. "Why?"

"The Lieutenant, sir. He hasn't really woken up yet." Nita worried. "We got battered pretty bad by the mudnado and the blast."

"Which is why he's probably still sleeping it off, Sergeant." Mike put as much calm assurance in his voice as he could. "He's a tough old bastard, Nita. The doctors will get him squared away." *And hopefully he'll still have his arm afterward*, Mike thought but didn't say.

"Yessir." Nita paused. "Ask you a question, sir?"

"If you like, Sergeant."

"Is it always this exciting, on the frontier?"

Mike thought about it. "Only if you're lucky," he said after a moment. "Sometimes it just plain *sucks*."

SWAMP PATROL

Halfling Protectorate
(Former Northern New Jersey)
2950 AD

The Slappy Rat screamed and leapt.

Captain Tim Salvager could see this one was an old bull rat, with a bunch of scars and a stink straight from the swamps, and it had a maw full of half-broken teeth aimed right at Nora's throat. *It probably can't believe its luck,* the Alliance Scout Ranger thought. *It must think she's a kid.* Slappy Rats could get nasty that way.

But Nora wasn't a kid, and she could get nasty, too. The biting mouth closed on a studded wrist bracer instead of a vulnerable throat, and Nora's other hand had unsnapped her balisong with typical halfling quickness. She shook a little from the impact of something half her weight, but it didn't stop the knife from ripping through the Slappy Rat's guts with brutal speed.

Tim casually stepped out of the way of the blood spray, but watched intently as Nora flicked the balisong closed in one smooth motion, then smashed the Slappy Rat against a swamp tree hard enough to break its neck. Luckily, this particular Dire Critter didn't lock its jaw, even in death; it slid off Nora's bracer and into the swamp.

Nora looked down at the limp creature, half-submerged in the muck. Tim could see she was visibly resisting the urge to kick the damned thing, which was smart of her. After a second, she said, "There any good eating on this thing?"

Tim didn't laugh. Halflings could get touchy about humans commenting on their fondness for food. He gathered that when you belonged to an ex-slave species who had fled halfway across the continent, it took a few generations before you stopped being *very* concerned about where your next meal was coming form.

Instead, he said, "Naw. See the grey on the pelt? They get that way after ten, twelve years old. By then they're pretty tough. Although Slappy Rats ain't what you'd call tasty, even at the best of times." He bent down with his own, orcish-made Gizzardsbane 'knife' — most people would have called it a 'sword' — and hacked off the scarred, callused tail. "There's a bounty on them, though. Here you go; it'll be worth twenty Second Republic dollars, back in town. Make sure to tip your waitress."

Nora Alfafor, Alliance Scout Ranger Trainee, took the tail easily enough. But she looked at Tim quizzically. "We can claim a bounty on these, Ranger-Man?" she asked. "I thought it was our job to keep the swamps clear."

"Oh, it is," said Tim cheerfully. "But we *really* hate Slappy Rats. Don't worry: you will, too! Bastards get into everything, if you let them." He looked up at the sky, then at his wristwatch. It looked like both the swamp's and the real time of day were matching up, which was always nice. "All right, Recruit Alfafor. Time we hightailed it back to camp."

And then Tim waited patiently while Nora realized it was now her job to figure out where they were, where camp was, and the best way to go back. It didn't take her long and she didn't get too flustered, both of which Tim approved of. If you didn't like just getting on with the job regardless of the situation, then the Scout Rangers probably weren't for you.

#

Tim had to admit, this part of Cursed Jersey — *Whoops!* he thought. *I mean, the 'Halfling Protectorate'* — was pretty enough. Nothing like Kentucky, mind you. In fact, around here it was more or less the opposite of the Free State: swamp instead of mountains, and the air had a salt tang even this far inland. The

Dire Critters were worse, too, which you just had to expect. For centuries, the Universal Dominion had used what was now the Protectorate as a proving ground for their curse spells. These days, the Dominion might be too busy losing a war for its life to keep on doing that, thank God, but the damage wasn't going to get fixed in a day.

Tim took point and had Nora navigate. You learned by doing in the Scout Rangers, and the halfling needed the practice in telling somebody how to get from Point A to Point B without getting them both lost. This far into the training, Nora was handling it a lot better than she thought she was, which Tim would have to work on. It could be just as bad to underestimate your skills as overestimate them.

Tim stopped, suddenly. Behind him, Nora took a step or two more as her own nose warned her of an unpleasant scent. Rank, vaguely chemical, and just a little unsettling; "You smell that? Tyrant Bee," Tim said over his shoulder. He talked normally, but carefully. "Not fresh, though."

"It's long gone, then?" asked Nora, her sling already out and held in one ready, steady hand. "Or is that bad?" She talked normally, too.

"Not too bad," said Tim. "If it was hunting for a new hive anywhere near us, we'd have heard the ruckus. It's probably hunkered down somewhere, waiting for when it's time for it to swarm-crawl again. We should be all right if we don't throw a rock at it."

"Says you, Ranger-Man. I've read the manual; Tyrant Bees ain't no joke for somebody normal-sized." Nora smiled. "Well, somebody normal-sized and dumb. We're gonna track it, right?"

"Hellfire, yeah." Tim started looking for signs of the Tyrant Bee's passage. "Hunkered down or not, those things are a menace. Even to us giants. We'll find where it is, then bring the rest of the squad over to clean it out proper."

"Ain't that cheating?"

"Yup," agreed Tim. "But it's the *good* kind of cheating."

\#

The two followed the spoor of the Tyrant Bee through the swamp, both by scent and the occasional floating bee husk left behind by the Dire Critter. They were common enough that Tim figured the Tyrant Bee was about to go into molt. Which wasn't exactly the best news.

"Though it ain't the worst news either," he said to Nora. "Before it molts it's gonna go hibernate for a while, digest the rest of the bees it's got tethered, then go track down another hive to eat. As long as we don't stumble over it, it won't wake up easy."

"So what's the bad news?" asked Nora. "It wakes up grumpy?"

"Grumpier. Tyrant Bees are mean."

Nora laughed. "You call everything you've shown me in this swamp 'mean,' Ranger-Man. When do I start seeing the *nice* critters?"

"Well, most of the trees are all right," mused Tim after a minute. As usual, he cheerfully ignored Nora's grousing; Scout Rangers weren't much on sir-yes-sir and halflings had taken to mouthing off with a convert's zeal. "Just don't eat from any of the ones with blue fruit."

"Poison?"

"Nah, they just taste like crap. For real." Tim shook his head. "The ecology of the swamp's real strange, Recruit. You ain't ever gonna really know how it all works, either. Best you're gonna manage is getting used to it."

#

The Tyrant Bee *was* hibernating, sure. Nora half-gagged at the sight of it, and Tim didn't blame her one bit. It looked like a snarled, crusty pile of goo about four feet long, which somebody had decorated with short spikes, then impaled a bunch of bees on *those*. Some of the bees were still feebly moving, which meant their queen bee was probably not completely digested to death yet, deep in the Tyrant Bee's gut. It was the kind of thing which made the more excitable anti-magic types yell "ABOMINATION!" at the top of their voices — and, really, with this one, they had a point.

Nora didn't lose her second breakfast, though. She even managed to get a little *sangfroid* back, as the Quebecois might say. "Is this Dominion work?" she asked, in as close to a whisper as she dared.

"Kinda," said Tim, conversationally. Nora started at the sound. "The damned things can't hear well, Recruit. Anyway, the books say these things started showing up in the 2600s. The Dominion was trying to make shoggoths again, and when it didn't work, they catapulted the leftovers into the swamp here, same as always."

"And they started eating the bees?" asked Nora. She idly gave the area a once over, then suddenly focused on one patch of ground. "Wait. That's weird."

"Well, not really. Like you were saying before, everything here is weird…"

"No," said Nora. "I mean the big hole in the ground all the way over there. It's glowing. *That's* weird. Or is it normal around here when things are glowing in daylight, Ranger-Man?"

Tim looked where she was pointing, and shook his head. His voice was a lot more serious now. "No, Recruit Alfafor, it is not."

#

As it was getting towards dark, Tim brought Nora back the next morning to take a better look at the hole in the ground. In fact, he took a few more from the larger group of halflings he was evaluating. One-on-one scout forays in only marginally dangerous territory were one thing, but when something was serious, you wanted to make sure you had a group with you. 'Glowing hole in the ground' always qualified as serious.

He wasn't sure how worried he should be about the situation. In Tim Salvager's expert opinion, halflings would do just fine as Scout Rangers, even when you took into account their eating seven times a day. The ones with him right now on this evaluation patrol were in ridiculously good shape, moved like whispers through the woods even before the training regimen Tim had set up, and they never quite relaxed while out in wilderness — which was most of their Protectorate, from the Atlantic to the Delaware River. And those extra four meals were just five-minute food and water breaks (halflings were absolute fiends for drinking water, or at least these were).

The problem for Tim was that his training regimen wasn't really designed around investigating glowing holes in the ground. Come right down to it, his training regimen really needed more than one trainer, but thanks to the War he was doing the job of three people and the halflings were lucky they weren't learning all of this out of books. If his old trainers could see Tim now, they'd have apoplexy over the corners he was cutting — but then, if his old trainers were within grabbing range, he'd have ruthlessly grabbed them to do this job.

Still, so far things had been mostly a milk run. Tim had picked this particular site because it was swampy, hot as Hell, a haven for Dire Critters, close to Ghostly Manhattan, *and* a thoroughly picked-over ruin. Nobody had wanted to permanently live this close to a site so famously and specifically cursed by the Universal Dominion, and there weren't supposed to be any natural cavern complexes that could breed dangerous giant animals. Death Skeeters and Slappy Rats were good enough practice for Scout Ranger recruits, and that's what this place had. Even the Human-built basements and sewers had filled up with flood silt centuries ago.

Tim thought about killing the Tyrant Bee before anything else, but decided against it. It was far enough away from the hole and not likely to wake up on its own in the next few days, and it wasn't as important as the glowing hole. He'd rather deal with the maybe bigger, *definitely* unknown problem first.

So: here was the hole, still raw-edged, and big enough for two or three people to descend at a time. Better and better, it was now making Tim's thaumameter give off unpleasant sounds. One of the halflings — Marcus Gamatoo, who could actually read Old American a little better than Tim could and showed real promise at camouflage — asked, "So, Ranger-Man. What does the sound say?"

"It says something down there is eating magic," Tim said calmly. "Hear how the sound is going up and down the scale?

Means whatever's down there eating it ain't eating it regular."

"Is that bad?" asked Nora. "It sounds bad."

"Eh, if you're made of magic, it's bad," said Tim. "And it might be bad anyway. But we're okay for right now."

It was damned odd, though, and *that* made a quick scout at least a good idea. Tim couldn't shut down an unstable magic anomaly himself, but he knew how to do the preliminaries. There was a mage in a Protectorate settlement only a half-day's journey away, so he had time to go down and get a careful look-see, at least.

Tim thought about sending the halflings back, but going into a cave alone was stupid. Besides, checking out things like this was part of what a Ranger did. A thousand years of magic had left a lot of scary problems lying around, and Cursed Jersey had gotten more than her fair share; if they were really going to be watching over their Protectorate, these folks would have to do this sort of thing on their own soon enough.

Hell, it's better than make-work, Tim thought. Which was another reason to go down. You didn't *join* the Scout Rangers unless you enjoyed these little outings.

#

Getting in was alarmingly easy. A little digging revealed the hole to be originally man-made; it looked like a grate of some kind, and the hinges popped right off. There was even a rusty ladder of obvious pre-Collapse make leading down into the depths, although Tim didn't intend to use it. The Old Americans might have been canny builders, but Tim had only one neck and he didn't feel like trusting the work of an engineer whose bones were dust by now. The halflings, being lighter than Tim, seemed more inclined to take the risk, but Nora (who was somehow not their leader, just the one whose orders were obeyed by the others with only token grumbling) quelled them with a look and a jerk of the head towards the rope Tim was securing.

Tim went down first, because Rangers break trail; then came the others, one by one. Tim made a note to cycle through the rest of the evaluation group and let them get a feel for the site, but not all at once. Even four halflings and one human was probably stretching it a little. Any more and it'd be a mob down here, not a teaching moment.

It wasn't completely unfamiliar territory. The Old Americans were fiends for standardization, in ways that made a Grand Hersheyian look like a disorganized poet, and Tim had done some of his own Scout Ranger training in the half-flooded sewers of Boston. He had also been raised on cheerful tales of the Universal Dominion's ill-fated assaults against the Philadelphia Wyrm, and why it's a bad idea to attack a dragon underground. He had an idea of what to watch out for, all in all.

But Tim was a little surprised the tunnel at the bottom turned out to be for moving people, and not sewage. He was more surprised at the way this complex seemed to have once been part of an actual underground rail line. And the biggest surprise (the nastiest one, too) was how the site showed less wear and age as the group got closer to whatever was causing the thaumameter to go off. There was a bit of Ancient wisdom Rangers lived by: *If you don't understand it, it's dangerous.* That likely applied here.

#

But as tunnels go, it wasn't so bad. There was even some light to see, which puzzled Nora. "What's causing it, Ranger-Man?" she asked. "It should be pitch black down here."

"That?" said Tim cheerfully. "Oh, that's just light getting shat out from whatever's eating all the magic. As long as it's not glowing greenish yellow-purple we'll be fine. Or making the walls bleed. Bleeding walls are always bad, Recruits."

He looked around. "Now, what are we doing wrong?"

It took his students a second to figure it out; as usual, Gordon Mutoo figured it out first, being a little older than the others. "Crap," he said, shaking out a slingshot. "Nobody's keeping guard!"

"You're right!" Tim said, smoothly pulling his Louisville Slugger from the sheath on his back as the whine of fiercely beating wings broke the silence. "Remember, Recruits: critters live in caves. And they get attached to them."

#

Death Skeeters weren't much of a muchness, really, although Tim wouldn't ever tell a recruit otherwise. Better for everybody if they figured it out on their own. You can tell a Scout Ranger recruit over and over how Dire Critters will go down when you hit 'em often enough, but there's no amount of telling that's as good as doing.

So five, six of the damned things swarming wasn't so bad. *Make that five for sure*, Tim thought as his bat smashed one of the Skeeters into the wall. *Let's see how this bunch fights as a group.*

They... weren't bad, actually. Nora and Leya Betawon had their butterfly knives, Gordon had the slingshot, and Marcus was relying on his boots; even after the last few weeks, it still impressed Tim how *fast* halflings all moved. They kept track of each other, too, each one lashing out at the Death Skeeters as the monsters buzzed around, looking for a chance for blood.

It would have all looked very elegant, except that two Death Skeeters could kill a halfling, and five a human. *Guess I was right not to come down here by myself,* thought Tim as his bat stunned another Skeeter long enough for Nora to stab it in the thorax. They were working through it with nothing more than moderate scrapes, which was good. You didn't want people skewered or anything, but getting them smacked around a bit always helped.

And then one of the damned Skeeters skewered *him*. Oh, the leather kept the stinger away from his flesh, sure. Instead of penetrating, the tip broke off, and the proboscis ended up trapped between Tim's chest and armor. But the impact still *hurt* and then it started to burn as the venom spurted out.

The Ranger winced and gritted his teeth, grappling the Skeeter as it tried to withdraw and sting again. Unfortunately for the Dire Critter, Tim was far stronger. Better still, he had leverage.

Tim Salvager might not have been the biggest man the Kentucky Free State ever produced, but he hadn't been the weakest, either. All four of the halflings blinked as the human pulled the Death Skeeter apart with his bare hands. The squish as the corpse hit the wall and slowly dripped down seemed extra loud in the suddenly-quiet cave.

Tim began to gingerly remove his leather breastplate. "Somebody get me some talcum from my pack," he said. "It'll stop the stinging. Grab me a towel, too. This stuff clumps when it dries, and the smell's only gonna get worse. And before you ask: no good eating on these, even if the poison sacs don't pop."

#

Once everyone had cleaned up and Tim had put his breastplate back on, the group kept moving down the tunnel until Tim heard the *special* warning chimes from the thaumameter that he'd been anticipating. They came all at once, too: three long chimes, which were about two chimes too many for true comfort. But it wasn't really a drastic problem, yet.

Tim stopped, said, "Stop. Retreat the way we came, steady but with no rush," and led his group back until the thaumameter stopped making the long chimes. He then started unbuckling the straps to his pack. Slightly hesitantly, the halflings started doing the same.

Tim grinned in the gloom. "Okay. Good job! Now, the meter started yelling just around the corner, so we're gonna leave here anything using magic. Weapons, armor, gear, underwear — I don't care what it is, if it's magic it stays here. Both because we could set something off, and because I don't want to hear y'all complain when your favorite toy gets broke. Got it?"

Marcus raised a hand. "I gotta spell put on me for my ribs while they heal, Ranger-Man."

"I know, Markie. That's why you're staying here to watch the packs. And our backs. The rest of us will check things out. Remember: nobody draws until I do. If I run, y'all run. Again: if I run, *all* y'all run. This ain't the place to stop to see whose feet are biggest. Besides, mine are." The others chuckled, although Tim chose not to think about how much of it was at the human being a prude. Even after over a century away from Dominion slavery,

Protectorate halflings were still pretty casual about certain things.

For right now, Tim had to concentrate on checking out the tunnel. Obviously, Tim couldn't use the thaumameter to look for the source of the magical drain, given how the gadget was itself magical.

#

Lucky thing standard Ranger field kits had dipsticks, then: wooden dowels that had been magically painted and maintained. As the magic in the dipstick's spell was sucked dry, the paint foamed away. It was a good rough-and-ready way to suss out where a mana drain was, although the items were limited by only being single-use. The fizz also faintly glowed, which made following easier.

In any event, the source of the drain was fairly close, which argued that source was also pretty strong. Tim stopped as he looked at the artificial cavern holding the magical anomaly. Yup, it was just what he expected, and frankly sort of feared.

The cavern was clearly once one of the Ancient Americans' "subway stations" — apparently they were some combination of coach houses and inns — and all but a small part of it had been ripped up a thousand years ago. The schoolbooks had said the world had not handled the sudden emergence of magic very well, and from this? The books weren't exaggerating. The marble and plastic and metal were charred in some places, melted together in others, and all mixed together in still others.

There were also a remarkable number of undisturbed skeletons; either scavengers had never gotten down here, or else they instinctively stayed away. Likewise, there was almost no smell of mildew or mold. That screamed 'magic' all by itself.

And in the center was the obligatory glowing globe of pure magical energy. It seemed to be centered on one blurry figure inside it, frozen in a crouch with his hands over his head; there appeared to be several other people — old-style humans, Tim guessed — also caught inside the globe. There were what looked like poles and chairs and some kind of wall, too.

Tim blinked. Then, very calmly and very carefully, he motioned for his team to go back the way they came. "No sudden running," he told the halflings. "It's a magic spell, yes, but it won't eat you up. We're too far away. We will walk back to the packs, pick them up, and go back up the rope line.

"So, what are we doing, Leya?" The halfling blinked at her name being spoken, then focused properly. Which was the idea; Leya Betawon was the hardest to rattle of the four, and hopefully was going to be the easiest to recover from the fear and shock of seeing uncontrolled magic up close. Tim had forgotten halflings had a problem with that sort of thing. *But they'll have to learn to get over it*, he admitted to himself. Cursed Jersey was *full* of not-quite-safe magic.

"We're walking, Ranger-Man," said Leya. "We go to the packs, get Markie, then we climb up the rope. No running scared, no freaking out."

"Exactly. This thing ain't going nowhere, and when we get back up top we'll all go back to town and report in. It'll be their problem then. We did our job, and they can do theirs."

Tim almost believed it, too. Although he had an expectation he'd end up being the one who brought the mages back here. But that was fine. He'd have a full Ranger squad coming along, and maybe even some actual soldiers down from the base at Hart's Ford. Second Republic troops, sure, but at least they wouldn't complain about being stuck in the swamps and caves. Thanks to the Dominion, they were literally born for that kind of work.

#

In bad adventure books, it's always just one person who realizes something's wrong, and has to hastily warn the others. Sometimes he's in time, sometimes he's not. It all depends on how much the author needs his characters to be dumb. But in real life? In real life Tim Salvager spent most of his working days in dangerous, magic-slapped territories, and the four halflings with him were raised on parents' and grandparents' stories about being hunted by mages with fiery whips. They all knew something bad was going on, the moment they got topside.

Nora spoke first. "Not just me who smells something?" Tim noted approvingly she didn't stop at the edge of the pit to talk, staying aware while not getting jumpy. Nora wasn't really noticing how the still-hibernating Tyrant Bee was twitching a little fitfully now, but that was fine. She just didn't have enough experience yet.

"Nope," said Tim. "Though for me it's a sound. A nasty whine which doesn't go away. The swamp doesn't like it, either."

By now the four halflings were all aboveground, and quietly prepping their loads for a quick run. Tim gave a tight grin. *They really are good at this*, he thought as he motioned them close.

"Okay," Tim said. "The air feels wrong, and it ain't anything from the swamp. Whatever it is, we don't worry about it right now. We just head on back to the camp, get the others, and suss out what to do next. Maybe we fight, maybe we run, maybe we have to lead something away from the settled places. But first we make sure we're not running scared. Got it, Recruits?" Tim looked over the four trainees, liked what he saw, and nodded.

"Good. Let's break some trail."

#

Tim might have thought halflings moved silently before, but when the reek of bad magic was in the air, you could almost track one from where the sound wasn't. And they were fast. Maybe even a little faster than Tim was.

But they were keeping pace with him, which was the important thing. It meant when he heard the unmistakable accent of a Universal Dominion mage — which was absolutely *impossible*, this far east — the Ranger was able to get and keep their attention with no fuss. And get them to stop.

"Remember what I said about running scared?" Tim said, his voice low enough to not carry. "There's more than one kind of scared. Hate ain't smart, and it'll get you killed. So y'all start thinking of yourself as a rescue squad, because we're probably gonna have to be one when we see what's up in camp."

The halflings took the hint, and when they started moving forward again it was in good order, with no delays or confusion.

Good order would be important. "Nora," said Tim as he and she moved silently through the brush, "You running hot, or cold?" A quick look sideways told him the answer, but everything was training. Everything, including this.

"I'm running hot, Ranger-Man," admitted Nora as they paused for a precious minute to catch their breaths. "I know I want to run cold, but it's a fucking Dominion mage. They make it hard."

"I hear ya, Nora. But you know you. You fight better hot, or cold?"

"Depends on the day I'm having, Ranger-Man." Nora looked at the rest of the recruits. "We won't lose our shit, if that's what you're asking."

"It's not, Recruits. I'm asking if y'all are where you need to be. Bring the ice, bring the fire, just as long as you bring something."

"Don't worry, Ranger-Man," said Marcus. He sounded like one of the ones who liked to run cold. "When it's the Dominion, we bring everything we can carry."

#

Tim was glad to see the halflings back at the camp hadn't been ambushed. But from the various scorch marks on the ground they had been forced to retreat, fairly quickly, up into the trees. Currently they were glaring down at a Dominion mage and about six of his thralls.

Tim and the four halflings had found some decent cover; close enough to survey and even intervene, but far enough away a thrall wouldn't trip over them. From what Tim could see, the mage was not quite *painfully* young, but was still at the stage of using far too many spells to alter his appearance; this one had bear arms and snakes for hair. The thralls were well-armed, but duller-eyed than Tim had ever seen a Dominion soldier be. Evidently it took a lot of loyalty magic to make even thralls operate so far behind enemy lines.

As usual, the mage liked to hear himself talk. "Ha, ha!" he called up. "'Fifteen birds in five fir trees!'" From the way Tim saw Nora slightly stiffen, that was apparently a quote of some kind

—and not a nice one, either. "And no Real Person to keep you out of trouble. Where's your Longshanks, hobbits?"

Nora's voice was low and even calm, as long as Tim ignored a definite undertone of her wondering how the mage's liver would taste raw — and it didn't actually carry past their hiding spot: "None of your business, *nerd*." And now the Ranger had an idea how insulting the word 'hobbit' was; you did *not* call a Dominion mage a 'nerd,' although Tim had no idea why. Even among themselves, Dominion mages only used the term 'geek.' Which was *also* a killing insult, in the mouths of others.

"What's a Longshanks?" asked Tim as his eyes surveyed the area for other thralls, mages, monsters. Nothing unusual, but then, what was usual around here? To his surprise, the question made Nora flush a bit.

"It means humans," she said after a moment. "Kind of. My grandparents said the mages used to call the overseers that. Some kind of filthy Dominion joke."

#

Unscrewing this pooch was going to be tricky. The trouble with fighting mages is that the first spell any mage learns is the one that explodes gunpowder, and the second spell is the one to make missiles, well, miss. You didn't become a Dominion field mage without showing how you could cast both of those spells instantly, and perfectly; which is why Tim and the halflings had left their coach guns and revolvers safely away from the fight. However, there's a difference between teaching a mage how to be bulletproof, and how to be panic proof, and Tim had a plan.

Tim's party had been equipped with a gunpowder firepot, because the swamps around Drowned Manhattan didn't just have alligators; they practically had water dragons. Tim also had a one-shot flare pistol. So Tim started the proceedings by having Leya simply lob the firepot (with the pin still in) into the middle of the thrall soldiers; a half second later, Tim gave a Kentuckian war scream and fired the flare directly at the mage.

The mage startled, of course. More importantly, he reflexively set off both spells, which caused the flare to miss, then explode in his face. None of the pieces hit him. Nor did any of the pieces of the firepot, which had also obediently blown up at the feet of the Dominion soldiers. But the spell did nothing about the overpowering sound and light of the exploded flare — and then Tim was out of the underbrush, his Gizzardsbane in a killing grip.

As fights go, it didn't last long. The mage hadn't bothered to cast any melee spells before attacking a bunch of halflings, so his reflexively raised arm didn't do a damned thing against Imperium-tempered steel. Tim might have felt bad about it, if the little sonuvabitch hadn't been taunting his recruits not half a minute earlier. Tim's expression didn't change too much as his blade shaved off a hefty chunk of the mage's furry arm, then turned the slice into a vicious snap-thrust which buried itself in his pop-eyed opponent's gut. His other hand grabbed the mage's throat and *squeezed* while Tim ripped the knife out again. If the mage had a death-curse picked out, he didn't get it out in time.

The mage might not have died nicely, but he did die quickly: even the snake-hair didn't have time for more than a half-hearted strike. Rangers don't like to fight, and this scrap was already loud enough as it was. The halflings in the trees were commendably smart about jumping down, given they were as surprised at the sudden turn as anybody else, and then all that was left just quick, brutal butchery of the thralls. It sickened Tim how the poor bastards had to keep swinging until their hearts were stopped, but that was the Universal Dominion for you.

#

Tim quickly cleaned the last of the thralls' blood off of his blade — using the mage's robe for a cloth, since he had nothing against the dead *thralls*. "Nora!" he said, low but firm. "Break camp!"

He might needn't have bothered; when Tim looked up, he saw Nora had already half-shoved the other halflings into dropping everything absolutely unnecessary for a run back to the settlement. Tim took a second to grin, then squatted down to loot the dead mage's gear. He figured he could find a bunch of stuff there they'd need.

Nora half-skidded up to him. In a low voice she said, "You know he's got a master, right?"

"Yup," said Tim. "The kid was way too green to be out here by himself. And whoever he was serving..."

"...is coming here right now, hopping mad and shitting fireballs. You know how they feel about somebody killing their own, Ranger-Man."

"Then they shouldn't have messed with mine, Ranger Nora," Tim snarled — but still low, so it wouldn't carry. "This ain't their land, you ain't their property, and they ain't the boss of me."

Nora narrowed her eyes, although it might have been because of the sudden field promotion. Tim figured that even if everybody here died tonight, the halflings all deserved the title. "We're not just running, are we?" she asked.

"Christ, no. First rule of the Ranger: don't shit your own bed. We lead him back to the settlement, they won't thank us for it." Tim held up a few random magic items looted from the mage's corpse. "Besides, I have a plan."

"Sir—" (*Well, that was new*, Tim thought.) "—why is it I'm suddenly a little scared?"

"Because you're in the Rangers now! Getting scared of the dumbass ideas your boss comes up with is all part of it. It's why you joined." Tim was steadily fiddling with the items, scratching lines in some places, defacing phrases and symbols in others. "Like what I'm doing now. Don't ever do this to magical items. It makes them blow up real good! So don't ever, *ever* do any of this. But don't worry! If we get back alive you'll be shown exactly how to never do things like this all nice and proper, and by experts."

"Can't wait, sir. Rangers! One minute, then we're gone." Nora lowered her voice a little. "Going down the hole, sir?"

"Going down the hole, Ranger. How did you figure it out?"

"I asked myself, where would be the place around here I most don't want to go?"

"Exactly."

#

Getting a Dominion mage to follow you without having him rely too much on magic was tricky. Fortunately the halflings had already been taught how to rig their ammo pouches into a few improvised firepot traps; the extra gunpowder they simply dropped. Half of the firepots were left behind at the first distant sound of explosions as the mage found the loose gunpowder, and the other half as soon as the squad heard the second, considerably closer booms of the first batch of improvised firepots going off. The idea was to mimic a fleeing team which was sensibly dumping their gunpowder because they were being chased by a mage, while making it look like they weren't sensible enough to realize they were giving the mage a trail to follow, if he was ready to travel at top speed.

The idea seemed to be working. In point of fact, Tim had sent off three of his fastest Rangers in different directions, on the principle that one of them would probably manage to warn a settlement. But for *that* tactic to work, the mage had to be kept distracted.

Tim had three distractions, all made from the dead mage's magic items, and he threw the first one a bit before his squad reached the hole with the rope. Tim was no mage himself, but even he could feel the greasy thunderclap of power as the sabotaged magic item shattered itself against a tree. Actual magic users would find the sensation unpleasant, disquieting, and most importantly, *loud*. Easily loud enough to distract. And damned if there wasn't a rather awful responding rustle in the trees behind him, just a little too close for comfort.

Time for step two, then. The Halflings were obnoxiously good at sliding down rope, probably because they weighed so little and had hands almost immune to rope burn. Tim went last, which meant he was in the clearing and carefully throwing the second decoy at a precise spot when the mage came crashing through the underbrush.

The mage had shapeshifted into a beast. Tim hoped it was

some kind of custom spell, because the idea that there could be some kind of weird hybrid monster out there incorporating a gorilla and an octopus was alarming. Then again, baroque spell-craft was how the Dominion did things.

The second item detonated in its turn — and this time Tim was close enough to feel the effects. It was a testament to his training (in bars, from Old Louisville to Toronto, City of Necromancers) that he kept his stomach under control, but getting a face-full of arcane backwash still wasn't fun. Certainly the mage didn't find it great, either. In fact, it enraged the mage-beast chasing them. Hell, Tim was counting on that, although when the mage locked three red-yellow eyes on him, the Ranger wondered if maybe he *had* overdone it a little.

But as the mage-beast charged, it did *not* see the enraged Tyrant Bee that Tim had aimed the second magical artifact at. Tyrant Bees weren't very smart, but they made up for it by being *reflexively* nasty when woken from their torpor. This one ripped into the side of the mage-beast with no regard for its personal safety.

Even so, the fight wouldn't last long, but Tim didn't really want it to anyway. Carefully ignoring the alarmed gibbering inside of him, because not losing your head when things were bad was how the Rangers did things, Tim stooped quickly to make one quick hack at the rope. He then straightened, smiled, tossed off a one-fingered salute at the fighting Tyrant Bee and mage-beast, and slid down the rope.

He was rewarded for his efforts by having it snap when he was only three feet from the ground below. That wasn't so bad, although his knees would hate him later. It was a small price to pay for keeping away whichever leftover thralls might still be managing to stay in pursuit.

#

Tim got to his feet, waving the other Rangers to move as far down the tunnel as they could manage and not fall down. Nora stuck with him, though. "Sir!" she shouted. "What about..."

Behind them, there was a sudden scream of collapsing metal

and an unfortunately-meaty impact.

Nora winced. "...yeah, never mind the ladder. Guess these thralls were keeping up, even if they can't climb worth a damn. But maybe they could jump?"

"You'd break bones and I'd die, Ranger, so no."

"Every little bit helps," muttered Nora. "What now, sir?" she asked, as they ran.

"We get 'em past the ball of energy. Past, you hear? Marcus'll just gonna have to gut out the ribs. When you see me running, the fucker up there's gonna be right behind me. Feel free to hit him where it hurts."

"Got it," said Nora. "Is he here for the ball of energy, you think?"

Tim shrugged. "I hope so, because if he ain't, we're gonna have to figure out from the corpses why the Dominion sent a party here, and rooting through their stuff is gonna suck. Now haul ass, Ranger! I want the team ready to sting this bastard in the snout as soon as they see him." *Because they're maybe gonna freak if I give them any time to take a good look*, Tim thought.

As Nora ran down the passageway, Tim listened to the fading sounds of battle above. It sounded like the Tyrant Bee was getting shredded, and wasn't *that* a damned shame? But the next part was gonna be tricky. Tim wanted the mage-beast to focus on nothing besides than how he'd apparently caught the Rangers trying to cover up their tracks — and then the mage made it easy for him. The cocky asshole actually decided to shove his head/beak/maw through the hole and roar. He *roared*. At a man carrying an unstable, throwable magic item.

The mouth was an irresistible target.

The roar turned into a howl, then a series of half-comprehensible ranting and threats. *Did I do some real hurt on the bastard? Probably not more than the Tyrant Bee did*, thought Tim with some regret. But it had gotten the mage-beast's notice, so now he wasn't thinking about anything else but the Ranger who had just run around the corner. Even hurt, once he got up to speed, the mage-monster was going to be faster than Tim was in any footrace. But the Ranger only had a short way to go.

#

Somewhat to his surprise, Tim made it to what he devoutly hoped was a safe spot with a little time to spare.

"Sir! Here!" said Nora. She waved him to a hiding place on the other side of the ball, behind a bench a chunk of column had landed on, long ago (Tim could feel various pops on his gear as the ball ate his enchantments). She looked at him. "Problem?" Nora said.

"Could be," said Tim. "We need him pissed. So pissed he can't think straight." The ranting in the distance was dying down a little. If the mage had started paying attention after all, then, well, this was going to be messy.

And then Nora, bless her, started laughing. "Is that all? Watch and learn, Ranger-Man."

She stood up on the low bit of rubble acting as cover and laughed louder. This wasn't cheerful or happy laughter. No. This was mocking laughter, clearly coming out of a halfling's mouth — and it was aimed at a mage of the Universal Dominion, one of the lords of the Midwest, self-declared highest of humans and a master of all he surveyed. And it was the unforced laughter of contempt, not the cringing chuckle of servility. In the sudden, complete silence following it, Nora cupped her mouth with her hands and bellowed:

"You know why the Universal Dominion made halflings, Ranger-Man? It was because they got tired of people looking down and saying 'Is it *supposed* to be that small?'!" She paused for a precise, merciless second. "And it *still* didn't work!"

She jumped back into cover. Tim blinked. "Christ, Nora, do you kiss your mother with that mouth?"

"Who do you think taught me the joke, Ranger-Man?"

Right then was when the mage came screaming around the corner, down the passageway — and right into the magic-draining orb.

One of the things you learn quickly in the Ranger business is when *not* to look at something. Such as, say, a power-hungry spell sucking all of the magic out of a shape-changed mage, and taking all the mage's life force with it. Tim assumed most of his Rangers would realize that keeping their eyes almost closed and their ears carefully *not* focused on the screams was a smart strategy. The ones who didn't, well, it wouldn't kill them and they'd know better next time.

He did keep an eye on Nora, though. Fortunately, whatever glee she might have taken at the sight of a Dominion mage slowly sublimating had quickly fled. Which was good; you couldn't take things *too* personally, when you were a Ranger.

The mage was strong, definitely. Which only meant he finally stopped twitching about the same time the ancient spell he had inadvertently fueled finally completed itself, and winked out. There was a half-minute of almost-panic until enough people got their lanterns lit to push back the sudden darkness. Tim, Nora, and Marcus (wincing a little, now) approached the place where the orb had been, while the rest started moving to make sure of the area. Without being told, either.

To Tim's absolute lack of surprise, there were now four unconscious people lying there, clearly released by the bubble. Two men, two women, all dressed in the bizarre styles of the Old Americans. Tim sighed.

"Well, *that's* going to make getting back to camp a real son-of-a-bitch."

\#

Tim was going to miss halfling cooking, once this assignment was over. They put some thought into their suppers, and when a bunch of halflings had the resources of even the small Ranger station here, back in town, they could really shine. Decent-sized portions, too.

Having finished dinner and put the dishes away, the halfling Rangers had promptly gone through the daily process of converting their walking sticks and spare gear into barbells and weights. Lifting weights was apparently the favorite hobby of every halfling in the Protectorate, given how they all instinctively paired off and urged each other on with low mutters of

"Get that last rep in, Brother" and "Push through the burn, Sister" and whatnot. It was interesting to watch, as long as you didn't feel obligated to participate. And Tim did not.

But Nora had asked him to be a 'spotter' — Tim understood what the word meant, from context, but not why the others had suddenly looked a little blank-faced and elaborately disinterested about it. As she puffed and lifted, she asked, "What's gonna happen to the Great Old Ones, Ranger-Man?"

Tim needed a second to figure out what Nora meant; it sounded like a Dominion phrase. "Oh. You mean the Old Americans? Above our pay grades, Nora." If she wanted to be less formal again, it suited Tim. "I hear they're awake, and somebody's gonna be coming east from Greater Hershey to let 'em know nice and easy just what happened. I figure if they don't go crazy, they'll probably end up back there."

"What if they do go crazy?"

"They'll all go to Virginia, instead." After Nora stopped chuckling, Tim went on, "It's not great, but those poor people were trapped for hundreds of years. They're only alive because one of 'em was a natural mage and managed to toss off a spell in panic when whatever happened down there happened. Let 'em spend some time getting used to the modern era."

Nora nodded, and set back her improvised weights. "And what about us?"

Tim raised his voice to carry. "You mean, you Rangers? Yeah, you're all Rangers. I've signed the papers. They still need to suss out your assignments, but y'all can do the work, so you get the title. We'll do a ceremony in a couple of days. Try not to be hungover for it." Tim and the halflings matched smiles. "It's gonna be tough, because traditionally the first cask is on me, and I don't drink weak shit."

Tim looked down at Nora. "As for you, Ranger: you should be thinking about how you're gonna say 'Yes' when they tell you to volunteer for officer training. You've got the right instincts for it."

Nora squinted at him. "You offering to do the training, personally? Groom me for greater things?"

"Absolutely not," said Tim, in an even tone of voice. "As of an hour ago, I signed myself right out of your chain of command. And I ain't never gonna be in it, ever again." Nora squinted, then relaxed as she took Tim's meaning.

"Good. Because I would have said 'Hell, no' if you wanted to play that game." Nora looked up, sighed, and pulled down Tim's shoulder to draw him just a little closer. "Just make sure you save a few drinks from the cask. For *after* the ceremony."

JOB ALONG THE
BORDERLANDS

Peoria Sefirot
Universal Dominion (occupied)
Near Oquawka, Illinois)
3054 AD

Jimmy Waterblossom could always tell when he was inside territory the Universal Dominion had held for a while. It wasn't just everything was shabby and run-down; as a member of the Adventurer's Guild, he'd been in plenty of places where the locals were poor. No, what made the Dominion so different was how *efficiently* shabby things were. The mages who used to rule these lands hadn't wasted a single resource they didn't need for maintaining either their rule or their bloated egos — and sweet Jesus, but how it showed.

This 'road' he and his crew (Reasonable Solutions Adventurers, fully bonded and incorporated in the Kentucky Free State, competitive rates, and references on request) was a case in point. It went straight as a line from point A (what used to be a Dominion mages' tower) to point B (another former mages' tower), ignoring any and all obstacles in its way, and it was precisely wide enough for two of the self-rolling carts the Dominion used to transport goods not worth more difficult magics to move. The local ex-slaves said the Dominion didn't even bother to forbid their subjects to use it; they simply seeded the road with death spells, and assumed people would figure it out.

Speaking of: "You getting anything, Leo?" Jimmy called ahead. The guy on horseback he was half-shouting to looked back, started to shake his head, then held up one finger. It was easy enough for Jimmy to urge his own horse forward while motioning the rest of the RSA crew to stay in place. He figured it was safe; if bad crap was about to come down where Leo was, then the Virginian would have been moving by now. People from that kingdom might be *crazy*, but nobody ever said they were *dumb*.

"I sense magic, milord," Leoncino di Lubsang said as Jimmy came within regular talking range. Jimmy ignored the 'milord' with barely a repressed wince at this point; Leo called everybody male that, including ex-slaves. Jimmy had given up trying to get Leo to call him anything else during working business hours. "It was just a for a moment, but I think there is a pocket of normal magic around here."

By which Jimmy knew Leo meant 'normal' by *Virginian* standards. Virginia was so magic-heavy, everybody knew a cantrip or three; unlike Jimmy, Leo wasn't a strong enough mage to cast spells outside of his birth country, but he was pretty sensitive to changes in the local magical 'temperature.' Hell, he was even more sensitive to it than elves like Jimmy were. One reason why Leo regularly took point.

Jimmy took a quick look about, but there weren't any obvious magical curses or occult blasphemies wandering around. "It moving around, Leo?" Jimmy asked. "Or are we just getting in range?"

"Just getting in range, milord," said Leo. "It is either stationary, or it has not noticed us yet. Before you ask: I am not sure which."

"Joy," Jimmy said. He waved a certain way, and the rest of the RSA crew went from relaxed-but-aware to alert-but-loose mode. "Not your fault, Leo. But, dammit, that gal from the Alliance swore up and down the army had cleaned out this route."

"Maybe they had," said Leo. "This could be something which cropped up after they went through. Or maybe sabotage?" He shrugged. "I suppose we'll figure it out when we get closer."

Jimmy had to smile. *Say what you like about Virginians*, he thought, *but the ones who go abroad take to the Adventurer life like ducks to water.* Damn straight they were going to check it out. Aside from everything else, this was too good a road to just give up on without even trying to stay on it.

#

Besides, till now, things had been pretty quiet. Which was how Adventurers were supposed to like it. Officially, Jimmy did like it that way, but inside he was a little bored. And if *he* was a little bored, his crew was probably ready to go find some excitement if some excitement didn't come calling on its own.

It didn't help how the job was so simple. The official client was a private citizen from Greater Hershey; she had supposedly discovered the final location of a shipment of First Age textbook grimoires that had been lost during the Universal Dominion's hasty evacuation of Peoria, and wanted them 'acquired.' Jimmy naturally assumed that meant the client was really just the front woman for one of Greater Hershey's government agencies, which was fine by him. Greater Hershey and Kentucky were both part of the Grand Alliance; more importantly, Greater Hershey's checks never bounced.

Jimmy had decided upon taking a team into the Occupied Territories to track down the ten crates, convincing whoever currently had the crates to give them up for a reasonable price, and bringing the crates back to the 'client' without attracting too much attention. It wasn't an 'easy' job, but it was really, really *simple*. Especially since Jimmy always took the position that a sensible elf was a lazy one, and that the best way to be lazy was to be as prepared and efficient as possible. And doubly especially since the client had coughed up valid travel papers for the Occupied Territories, which *absolutely* meant she wasn't a private citizen in any possible way.

Again, Jimmy didn't really care. But sweet *Jesus*, this run was dull! Even the various Alliance garrisons they'd passed were bored on occupation detail; they were downright eager to help anyone with legitimate travel papers, to the point where Jimmy barely had to bribe anybody over the case-of-booze level. And even then it was more for networking than anything else. You never knew when an Alliance sergeant or captain might be ready to muster out and get into professional Adventuring, after all. Never hurt to headhunt early.

But none of that was really interesting. A possible magical threat, though? Definitely interesting. Hopefully it'd turn out to be nothing at all. Sure. Absolutely.

#

Leo escorted Jimmy to the Weird Thing in the road, but he didn't really have to. Elves have a certain affinity with magic, so at this range Jimmy could feel the Weird Thing's presence, in ways Leo couldn't manage himself, higher local magical energy or not. It was the difference between expertise and instinct.

Jimmy's reaction was almost as instinctive. He made the hand gestures for 'spread out' and 'pick a shelter point' as soon as he got a good 'whiff' of the Weird Thing, and the RSA crew obligingly scattered in an intelligent and disciplined manner. Leo stuck by Jimmy, though, and shrugged when Jimmy gave him a raised eyebrow.

"I'm not going to shout, milord," he said. "If one of us approaches it, then I will keep more of a distance. But the artifact doesn't feel very dangerous."

To Jimmy, it looked like a set of sticks and spheres, all attached together in a roughly cubical fashion. "I don't know what it is," said Jimmy. "That *makes* it dangerous."

"I know the rule, milord." Leo looked at the Weird Thing with what appeared to be some kind of strange, Virginian-made spyglass. "But really, how often is the rule relevant?"

"It's always relevant," said Jimmy. He started walking towards the Weird Thing. "It's just not always *true*."

#

Up close, the Weird Thing looked even weirder. It was supposed to be some kind of framework, Jimmy decided; at least, there were eight spheres and twelve sticks, all arranged to theoretically form a cube. The only thing was, one end of one of the sticks on the bottom of the cube had been knocked loose from a sphere. Jimmy wasn't sure, but he thought this broken bit might be where the spike of magical energy was coming from.

"You got any idea what this is?" Jimmy yelled back to Leo (*he* didn't mind doing that). "Because I think it's leaking magic."

"What? Why aren't you running away?"

"I don't think it's leaking *bad* magic," explained Jimmy. "I'm not feeling funny or sick. It's not raw mana or anything like that."

"Is there a spell attached?" Leo was starting to sound more interested than worried, as Jimmy kept standing there and not, say, exploding or mutating. "If there is an active enchantment being stymied, that could be causing the increased magic levels."

"Oh, yeah! Good point." Jimmy squinted at the artifact. "Yeah, there's a spell here. Smells like... oh, crap."

"What is it? A trap?"

"No, worse. It's a warding spell." Jimmy spat. "This thing is a cage. A broken one."

It took Leo a moment to figure it out. And when he did, he didn't sound happy about it. "There's nothing inside."

"Exactly," said Jimmy. He motioned everybody else closer. "Where's the nearest town to here?"

#

The huddle of Quawk — the Universal Dominion didn't have 'towns,' really — looked like the rest of the liberated territories always did: too poor to afford the luxury of trash. Jimmy hated going into Dominion huddles, and always felt guilty for it. There was a *reason* why the very shacks and lean-tos themselves seemed to be half-cringing against a kick that could come at any second, and it was known locally as 'long experience.' This part of the former Dominion was probably going to end up getting grabbed by the Kentucky Free State once the war was over (*and wasn't **that** a strange thought to have?* he mused), but Jimmy wasn't quite sure whether he wanted the Free State to have it.

Then again, all the other real estate now up for grabs labored under the same problem.

Quawk being slightly on fire was a bit out of the ordinary, though. It *had* been a while since the huddle had been liberated. And it wasn't all on fire, either; it looked like somebody had come in from the fields and started moving to the garrison, burning everything in its way. *Magic*, thought Jimmy, and he called out, "SECURE GUNS!"

RSA was a successful and professional organization; Jimmy made damned sure his crews could neutralize their firearms on a moment's notice. They all quickly and steadily detached magazines and cylinders from their rifles and revolvers, dropping both in the special magic-proofed, sealed bags each Adventurer carried, then adding their extra ammunition. The firearms themselves went back into holsters, after first double-checking to make sure there wasn't a bullet in the chamber.

A skilled Adventurer could go through the whole process while concentrating on something else, and RSA both hired and trained at that level. Within half a minute the crew was reasonably safe from any random gunpowder-exploding spell, although there was always the chance of somebody forgetting a loose bullet somewhere. But one exploding bullet couldn't wipe out the whole crew. Not having guns still cut RSA's effective firepower in half, which was never fun when you were running into a literal firefight. Like most Adventurers, Jimmy thought of fair fights as being lovely things, for other people.

Jimmy rode his horse as close to the outskirts of the huddle as was practical, then dismounted. His other riders did the same, then handed off reins to the wagon driver and the two non-combat specialists. He had eight fighter-types to work with, including himself and Leo; which just have to do.

(A while later, somebody asked Jimmy why he had run in. There was a garrison in the huddle, wasn't there? What was he expecting to accomplish? Jimmy had looked at the questioner in a way which wasn't even mad, just — puzzled. *There was something burning houses and people*, he said. *You just let that go by with-*

*out finding out why, you're **always** gonna regret it later.)*

The good news was, the garrison was still in one piece. The bad news was, it was facing a fire elemental. Jimmy told himself the elemental was small, at least, which was maybe true in relative terms but didn't really make him feel any better. There's not much difference between a six-foot tall living flame and a nine-foot tall one.

#

Adventurers knew how to do assaults. Bandit camps, underground dungeons, the occasional smuggler's lair (but only the *bad* smugglers, naturally): these were all solved problems. But Dominion huddles took getting used to.

The problem was, they weren't really towns or villages; they were holding pens that had been allowed to develop randomly. There weren't any streets or blocks, just a set of winding paths between wooden shanties in various states of repair. One set of paths led to the fields which fed the former slaves; another set led to the river where they got their water. Aside from that, the buildings simply clumped where they clumped. It made it easy for Jimmy's team to go through safe, but almost impossible to go through quick.

Quawk never had a garrison when the Dominion was in charge, mostly because its former masters only cared about it and similar huddles whenever they wanted another batch of human slaves for 'processing.' The Alliance had different opinions, especially since the Dominion had been pushed back all the way to the Mississippi river. Engineers had cut a road through from the mage-road to the huddle, and widened the path to the river; they had also put together a few paddocks for actual animals, and tried their best to make some usable streets. Probably at some point people would just give up and clear enough land for a new town, but that hadn't happened yet.

Alliance artificers had also thrown up quick bastions all along the river, with plenty of space rough-cleared around the perimeter. This one was new enough that the stumps were still there, which would make difficult running anywhere besides the official path. Otherwise, the fortification here looked as stolid and sturdy as the rest: the classic star fort style, six-sided to prevent the Dominion from turning the whole thing into a giant pentagram.

It was also made out of concrete, which was why the elemental couldn't just burn it down. It couldn't fly over the twelve-foot walls, either; it wasn't one of the ones with wings. In its current form, it looked vaguely humanoid, with oversized hands and skin that reminded Jimmy of half-cooled lava. The 'face' was featureless and kept cracking and crackling; the elemental didn't have a head so much as it had a lump at the top of its 'body.'

Faceless or not, the elemental could aim fireballs just fine: Jimmy winced as he saw one ignite some poor bastard of a Quawk peasant who decided to run out of a smoldering shack at the exact wrong second. The peasant wasn't even trying to run towards the garrison, either.

"Crap," Jimmy said. "This thing is one of the mean ones." Beside him, Leo nodded reluctantly.

"That happens," he said. "Fire elementals don't like cages. Back home we always have to let them travel in the open when they go anywhere."

Jimmy stared at him. "Virginia lets elementals wander around unsupervised?" he asked, incredulous.

Leo shrugged. "Until one shows it can't be trusted, milord. Fire elementals aren't even the ones you have to worry about most. They know enough to be careful."

"Right." Jimmy decided to let it be. Virginians were simply weird that way. Everybody knew it. "So this one was going to be crazy anyway, you think?"

"Oh, of a surety, milord. And being trapped in a Dominion cage? It is undoubtedly quite mad by now." Leo shook his head. "I hope you were not planning to try to save it from itself."

"Ah, no," said Jimmy. "Can't say it was my first priority. What with the garrison, and everything," he added quickly.

"I understand," said Leo mournfully. "It looks very stupid, too. Maddened beasts must be put down, alas. Even if they are magical beasts."

"Thoughts on how?" asked Jimmy.

"You've already spread out the crew," Leo said. "Their weapons will work on elementals, thank Awen. But they must not attack hand-to-hand!"

"Gee, you think?" Jimmy looked at the elemental again. It was now lobbing fireballs at the fort itself, more or less at random. "This would be a really great time to have some fire protection amulets or ice potions, you know."

"I agree, milord, but you know how it is. Every competent enchanter and alchemist on the continent knows the Grand Alliance will pay top coin for their wares, especially now that they're about to push across the Mississippi. The troops on the front lines need every scrap of magical power they can get."

Jimmy snorted. "In case you haven't noticed, Leo: we're on the front lines right now." He paused. "And yeah, you're right. We *do* need every scrap we can get."

#

When asked, *How do you fight a fire elemental? Carefully?* Jimmy would always laugh. *'Carefully.' That's what amateurs would say*, he'd reply, then go on, *Actually, they wouldn't say anything, because they'd be too busy screaming to death.* Then he'd take another drink of beer. *Nah*, he'd say, *you can't fight **carefully** something with infinite fireballs. So you don't even God-damned well **try**.*

But you could still fight *smart.*

Nobody else in the damned huddle seemed to have a crossbow, a problem which kept cropping up in the liberated lands. Something about how the Dominion used to turn any of their slaves caught carrying arms into bears, half-starve them, and then release them in their home huddles. For some reason, Dominion mages thought that was a *hysterical* joke, because it was always bears. It took a while for the former slaves to understand how the rules were different now. (It had also taken a few hangings to make certain soldiers understand how the *Alliance* rules were still the same, but Jimmy didn't dwell on that.) Clearly this particular huddle still had a wait-and-see attitude on the new dispensation.

On the bright side, at least that meant everybody firing a missile weapon in this fight would be one of *his* people. *Or the garrison, if they figure out how to pull their thumbs out of their adels,* Jimmy thought. An unfair thought, he knew. Who'd think the Dominion would waste a fire elemental on *this* place?

Worry about that later, Jimmy reminded himself. *Fighting now.* And he was going to have to play it pretty smart to keep from losing people, too.

Adventurer crews didn't go much into over-complicated plans; they trained on knowing what the other people in their crew could *do*, and they worked out *intentions* ahead of time, but when it came time to the actual fighting, things got chaotic and stayed there. Take the momentum early, keep it, and improvise like mad. And don't split up! At least, not too far. Make sure that everybody on your side knows where — or, if you're a sneaky type, *generally where* — you're going to be skulking.

Against a trained military force — Second Republic Marines, say, or Imperial Orcish Legionnaires — this strategy would be pure suicide. But when fighting a single monster, or even a mere band of them, things could generally be finessed properly. Although a fire elemental really *was* going to be a problem.

Then again... Jimmy raised his crossbow and activated the little magical doohickey that let his crew 'hear' his commands. He couldn't talk, just pick one of five different tones, but hell: how many did you need in a battle, really? As long as one of them was "fire," right?

And fire they did. At his command, ten crossbows (including his and Leo's) thudded, all aiming for the elemental's center of mass. No head-shot nonsense *here*, because, again: a fire elemental was a *problem*. And Adventurers traditionally solved *problems* by shooting them full of holes.

It didn't like the crossbows, and it didn't like the staggering volleys that the two squads proceeded to toss into it, either. Fire and air elementals weren't always the brightest spirits out there, and it took another two crossbow volleys before the elemental focused enough to toss back fireballs with something approaching actual aim. But by then the crew was ducking out of sight, into cover — and far, far away from any barrels. When wood explodes from being fireballed, it explodes nasty.

Jimmy and Leo hadn't fired after the first volley; in fact, the volleys were to keep the fire elemental distracted while they moved. Not that Jimmy minded softening up the damned thing first. He even allowed himself the ridiculous hope a stray bolt might hit the restraining charm keeping this elemental captive and mad on this plane of existence, although the odds of *that* were roughly equivalent to picking all six numbers in the next Greater Hershey Stupidity Tax. But even if Jimmy didn't hit the lottery today, the two were still getting closer to the place where they could do something useful with their time.

"You have a strategy, milord?" Leo said as they ducked through an alleyway barely large enough to get dirty and edged their way to the corner. "Though I'll understand if you're still coming up with one." From anybody else, that would have come across as heavily sarcastic, but Leo honestly seemed merely curious.

"More or less, Leo," Jimmy admitted. "We close with this bastard and hope the fire resistance spell I just threw up keeps us from melting. If it does, we stab the elemental until it's gone. That work for you?"

Leo contemplated the question for a moment. "Yes," he said. "I think so, milord. It's at least dead simple."

"I'd prefer *live* simple, thanks," drawled Jimmy.

#

The fire resistance spell held. Enough, at least. Nobody's hair actually caught on fire.

Close up, fire elementals are terrifying (as were all elementals, really). It's not just the "being made of fire" situation: it's that elementals are not native to this plane of existence, and it shows. There's a shimmy on the line between where the elemental ends and the regular universe itself begins, representing the sheer revulsion space-time itself has for the interloper. And if you can *see* the shimmy, you're probably far too close to the elemental.

Then again, if you're so close to a fire elemental, it can only fireball you by accident; it takes a moment for the balls to actually ignite. One actually bounced off of Jimmy's shield, arced in the air, and only *then* burst into flames. The sudden flash illuminated both Adventurers as they closed the distance to the fire elemental, then struck.

The elemental really didn't like being attacked, and while the Adventurers' flesh didn't quite catch fire from the creature's punches, those clumsy blows still hurt. Unfortunately (or possibly fortunately) for the fire elemental, Adventurers are used to fighting while in pain. Indeed, they considered mild agony to be an effective positive reinforcement, of sorts. A way to encourage you to do what's needed to make the pain *stop*.

In this case, both Leo and Jimmy were aiming for the same thing: a tangled charm of clay and wire and glowing letters that writhed unpleasantly, half-embedded in its body. Jimmy saw it first, and turned his sword-slash into a sudden chop which hacked at the place where the charm and the elemental's fiery flesh met. Leo shifted to the left, trying to keep the elemental off-balance.

That helped, Jimmy saw as he pulled back his blade for another chop, but not enough. The fire elemental was probably being compelled to protect the charm, whether it wanted to or not; if a single cut wasn't enough to sever it from the creature's body, it would force the 'wound' closed. The healing would weaken the elemental, some — but Jimmy didn't want to do this all day. And wasn't even sure if he could.

No help for it. He activated the doohickey again. For a moment nothing happened, which made Jimmy almost happy, but then eight crossbow bolts fired. Possibly the volleys were a little ragged, but he understood why. It's kind of hard to calmly fire into a melee your boss is in, even if he did just tell you to.

RSA hired only professionals, though, and they all knew how to shoot. Five of the bolts thudded into the elemental — one in a headshot, which was either recklessness or luck — and if the other three missed both the elemental, they also missed Jimmy and Leo, which was nice. Still very good shooting for this kind of fight; more importantly, it completely distracted the fire elemental, and its ability to force-heal its wounds. *This* time, Jimmy's sword-chop ripped the charm free of the creature.

It immediately dropped back, and half-dropped, half-slumped to its knees. The two Adventurers stepped away, swords raised and teeth gritted from the pain, but the creature took no heed of them as it started to lose cohesion. The flames now bursting through the crust of its flesh began to spiral outward and upward, individual tendrils of fire licking around each other as the fire elemental's *true* form appeared: a series of interlocking circles of incandescent plasma, growing ever brighter as they turned.

Or so Jimmy assumed; he was too busy ducking for cover to really pay attention. Long experience had taught him: when something like *this* started a transformation like *that*, a wise Adventurer immediately looked for some way to break line of sight, before something exploded.

Jimmy grinned as he heard a soft *whump* and felt the sudden breeze. *Or implosion,* he thought. *Sometimes they implode instead.*

#

Major Judith Pine was pretty obviously from the Dwarven-wood; Jimmy wasn't sure where she stood in the dwarves/dwarfs half-feud the 'Wood was known for. Probably it wouldn't matter. The Grand Alliance military was a real skunkbear for making its troops forget about all that stuff from home when they put on Alliance green. And, besides, she was busy trying to keep the rest of the huddle from burning down.

She still remembered her manners, though. "Thanks for coming to our rescue," she said readily enough. Hell, Judith even gave Jimmy a sidelong look he thought he recognized; he just didn't know yet whether she was assessing Jimmy the elf, or Jimmy the business owner in a profession which routinely hired war veterans. Jimmy figured he had no objections, either way.

Just not both at once, you odil idjit, he reminded himself. *You don't diddle the staff. You get them a good job with a decent crew, stop signing their paychecks, and* **then** *you diddle them.* This rule had served Jimmy well for years, and he intended to have it keep doing so for more years to come.

So instead Jimmy flashed a friendly but not over-friendly smile and said, "Happy to help, Major. We found traces of the creature on the mage-road, and we figured it needed putting down. Sorry we couldn't get here earlier."

Leo spoke up. "Excuse me, Major?" At her nod, he went on. "Was there any sign the fire elemental was compelled to come here? Did it seem like it had a purpose?"

The questions got a scowl from the major. "Yeah. It was coming for us. Not a beeline, but it didn't care about any of those poor bastards out there unless they got in the way. It wanted us."

"You, the soldiers?' asked Jimmy. "Or you, the fort?"

"Us, the soldiers. We always have a patrol out, keeping an eye on things. That monster went for the patrol first, took them apart, and then attacked the fort." The scowl got deeper. "I had a trooper volunteer to go get help, but the second she was over the wall the monster went after her and burned her down. Then it came back here. I was getting ready to just rush the damned thing before it whittled us down any more when you lot showed up. Were you tracking it?"

"Yeah," said Jimmy. "We found a broken cage on the mage-road. So we just followed the burning fields until we got here." He swigged some coffee (drink ale when you're back at the inn and the money's deposited in the bank). "The rest you know."

Major Pine's eyes narrowed. "Hold on," she said. "Somebody's using the mage-road to transport dangerous monsters?"

Leo and Jimmy looked at each other, startled. After a moment, Jimmy spoke. "Well, shit. When you put it *that* way..."

#

Maps eventually were pulled out; even a garrison as small as this had a solid set of Alliance-made regional maps, on the principle that you never knew. Major Pine examined the one which showed the border forts from Quawk up to Newbahn. "Where did you find the broken cage?" she asked.

Jimmy pointed on the map a little south of Quawk. "About five out from the end of the Peoria-Gladstone mage-road," he said. "There's patrols on that road and they sweep pretty often, and nobody's said anything about Alliance soldiers going missing."

"Any signs of a caravan or even wagon?" asked the major, and Jimmy got the feeling she already knew the answer.

"No, ma'am. Not a bit. It was just lying there, right out in the middle of the road, and I don't know how it got there."

"I do," said Major Pine. "It fell out of the sky."

Jimmy froze for a second, and then shook his head ruefully. "Of course it did," he said. "Whoever was moving it took to the air and used the mage-roads to navigate. The Dominion still knows where the towers are, even if all of 'em on this side of Mississippi are in our hands now."

"Yeah," said Pine. "And we still don't have enough air units to keep the Dominion from sneaking over the river and scouting with their own flyers, as long as they don't give themselves away."

"I imagine secrecy must be hard for some of them," said Leo with a harsh chuckle.

Pine grinned quickly, but then shook her head. "Not as much as you'd think, Mr. di Lubsang. They're learning. Or at least the ones who *can't* learn are all dead by now." She tapped the map again. "It looks like this was the closest garrison to where you were — no, wait, there have to be troops at Gladstone. Why didn't the elemental go there?"

"That's a damned good question," said Jimmy. He brought out the pieces of the charm from the fire elemental; they were still a little magically 'hot,' but that's what the silk wrappings were for. Pine prodded at them with a stick.

"Okay," she finally said. "It's a local made charm from the Peoria Sefirot arsenal. Not from the core Dominion lands."

"Are your dwarven senses tingling?" asked Jimmy.

"Yeah," she said, which meant among other things Jimmy had pegged which Dwarvenwood faction she was from. "That and the armory markings. It's definitely from Peoria."

"I suppose we haven't found all of the Dominion's secret military caches." Leo did not really make it a question, and Major Pine didn't take it as one.

"Depends on who you ask," she said. "We got most of them, sure. Probably. Fifty-fifty odds, at least. But we didn't get all of them. We overran this Sefirot too fast for the Dominion to expend their stocks, you see. And they were real paranoid about who knew about what, so none of our prisoners knows where *everything* is. So there's probably enough leftover military magic out there to start something. The question is, *what?*"

"Well, trouble," Jimmy said. "And I think that it's aimed at y'all. Whoever bound the elemental wanted it to go after Alliance troops. Specific kinds of troops."

"Like those in the river garrisons?" said the major. "That'd explain why it didn't make a beeline for Gladstone. The big garrisons are strongholds. We're more like a tripwire here."

"Doesn't this bother you, Major?" asked Leo.

Major Pine shrugged. "Somebody has to be. And we look more vulnerable than we are. The Dominion comes over the river, we'll know early enough to get reinforced. We've got troops in reserve we could call up if we needed them, too — they can get to anywhere on this side of the river pretty quick, and then the fun starts. Oh, it'd be hot work at the battlements for a bit, but the enemy would break a few teeth on us, too." She smiled. "And when we punched back, we'd break more than teeth."

"You're supposed to get reinforcements?" said Jimmy. "Why aren't there any now?"

"Well, Mr. Waterblossom, there you got me. The elemen-

tal came out of nowhere, so the reaction force wasn't ready—
SHIT!" The major straightened, said, "Excuse me, gentlemen,"
and ran out the door, calling for an orderly.

Leo looked at Jimmy. "What just happened?"

"The major realized something about the same time I did,"
Jimmy replied. "Everybody's figures the Dominion's going to
counter-attack before long. They have to, because when we get
enough forces together to get over the Mississippi, it's the end.
It's the God-damned end to the War, right there."

"So the Alliance is watching for signs that the Dominion is
coming." Leo nodded, slowly. "But they are looking outward,
across the river, are they not? They are not looking behind
them."

"Right," agreed Jimmy. "So some clever stay-behind bastard
sussed it all out, and he also knows where the Dominion hid
some of their toys. He must have a network or something.
They're going to hit all the garrisons on the river at once, blind
us as much as possible, and then the Dominion can roll up and
raid on *this* side of the river."

"It will not knock you out of the War," pointed out Leo.

Jimmy snorted. "Hardly. Even if they pushed us back, there's
still Deseret and the Imperium. But the Mormons are on the
edge of their supply lines by now and the Dominion is sending
all of their best troops south to hold back the orcs. So scrambling *us* up maybe buys them a year — but it's a year more than
they have now, hey?"

Leo sighed. "I wish they would just surrender to you. I wish
they *could* just surrender to you. And I suppose I should wish for
a new pony, as well." He paused. "You intend to pursue this further, yes?"

"I do," agreed Jimmy. "That bother you, Leo? I know the Virginians are neutral in all of this." *And damned if I know why,* he
thought. *Y'all hate the Dominion even worse than we do, and you've
done everything **except** declare war.*

"Only if you let RSA be formally drafted," replied Leo. "It
would be helpful if we were instead hired as independent con-

tractors to carry out whatever mad scheme the major will undoubtedly recruit us for." They both smiled: 'mad scheme' was an Adventurer's bread and butter.

#

"I have changed my mind, milord," Leo said a day later as he speared another giant leech. "RSA should have let itself be drafted. And then appealed our case."

"What, you don't like taking a stroll by the river?" Jimmy said, then fired his crossbow; twenty feet away, a screeching monstrosity of nature fell, writhing, from a copse of steaming trees and into the mud. "Watch your six, Pat," Jimmy called ahead to the first line. "That goes for the rest of you, too. This is Bat Country."

Only without actual bats, he thought. 'Bat Country' was an old Adventuring term for 'a place so screwed up you hope it's just a hallucination,' and it definitely suited the Big River Menagerie. 'Menageries' were where the Dominion kept their little monsters until they needed to warp them into big monsters, and 'little' to a Dominion flesh-mage meant 'man-sized or below.' RSA had been on jobs like this in the past, and they weren't ever fun.

But this was one job they had to do. Pine had gotten the word out about twenty minutes before the attacks had started; it hadn't been enough to stop some of the assaults, or even a couple of massacres, but regular Alliance forces were able to reinforce, relieve, or retake the river bastions from Daven to Burly. Quawk's own garrison had been hit by another two elementals and a scissor-bug, but the battle had ended quickly. Failed ambushes usually did.

So everything was under control — except in the depths of the Menagerie. The three heavily-fortified posts watching over it had failed to report in at all; from what Jimmy overheard, they had missed a communications check yesterday. It happened often enough on the border that it normally took two missed checks in a row before people started worrying, but somebody should have really noticed three going dark at once.

But recriminations could wait. In the meantime, the closest

fort needed to be checked out, and since RSA was on the clock now for the Grand Alliance, why not use them? This was, after all, their sort of thing.

"And dammit, it is," Jimmy said as he reloaded his crossbow and started looking for another — bat? Octopus? Mini-dragon? Those things were seriously messed-up looking — to shoot. Leo looked sideways at him while twisting his spear free.

"I was not arguing with you about 'Bat Country,' milord," he said. "Or were you talking with yourself again? Twenty feet ahead and left, ten feet up."

"Spotted." *TWANG!* "Thanks. Good eye. Yeah, I was just thinking about why we're always out here doing nasty shit like this. Right foot."

SPLASH! "Ah, but the answer is obvious, milord." Leo lifted his spear, the giant leech impaled on it still feebly wiggling, and wrist-flicked the leech off in a practiced motion which ended with the creature splattered against a tree. "We are here because we enjoy it, and it pays most exceedingly well."

#

The Dominion might not have cared about overgrowth and keeping clear fields of fire along the river, but the Alliance did; fortunately, nobody had come along yet to clean out this particular tangle of wood and muck. It made a decent observation site. Well, after the pack of feral Spite Beavers had been dispatched, but that was practically routine for an Adventurer.

Leo peered through his spyglass, since it was late enough in the morning that the risk of a flash of light was diminished. "Well, milord," he finally said. "That is, as we say in my realm, diagnostic."

Jimmy nodded, unhappily. The closest Alliance river bastion had been swarmed, it looked like. Literally swarmed: there were still heaped piles of what looked like Dire Hornet corpses. There were, unfortunately, also heaped piles of Alliance corpses. They had been stripped of their gear, but not clothing, and it looked like the Dominion was planning to burn the bodies to deny them to the enemy.

"How many people does the Alliance stick into these things, Leo?" Jimmy was looking through his own multiply-repaired, almost-guaranteed Old American heirloom binoculars. Eight hundred years of magical repairs had turned them into linked, smoothly oval tubes, but they worked, which was the important thing.

"Usually about a company, milord. Here that means one hundred and fifty soldiers."

"Looks about right." The sight of rather more dead Dominion slave-soldiers didn't cheer Jimmy up, although the four stripped corpses *did*; the Dominion only reliably looted mages. "They must have used all of their stay-behind forces to get this many fighters." Which would be a good thing for the region, at least. If not for these dead soldiers.

Jimmy took another look at the corpse piles. "Oh, for a certified corpsefixer right now," he murmured. "I'm willing to bet all those boys and girls wouldn't object to some old-fashioned, post-mortem payback."

"You don't know any necromancy at all, milord?"

"Ehh. Just enough to talk to a spirit," Jimmy admitted. "No way I can bind even *one* back into its own body, never mind twenty. I should have made the major give me a healer."

"You tried."

"Not enough, Leo. Always bring everything you can to a job. You're always gonna need it in the end." Jimmy put away the binoculars and weaved his way to another vantage point among the woven beaver-hedges. He sturdily ignored the occasional mouse skull crunching under his foot, although that one spot where six of them had been neatly lined up had been highly unpleasant, for several reasons. "They got seriously ripped up taking the place, at least. I count twenty, maybe thirty Dominion soldiers. Half patrolling the walls, half hauling bodies, and they keep switching off. Six mages. You?"

"About the same, milord. Plus three Dire Hornets well enough to fly, and a flash of some kind of strange beast I've never seen before. Like a monkey shoved on top of a tripod."

"How many eyes?"

"Three, I think. Why, does it make a difference? I would have thought my description was specific enough."

"Not when it's the Dominion. They just love to mess around with monsters, *and* they just love scaring their peasants with local nightmares. If it has three eyes, it's a Renfield. If only two, it's a Cohol."

"And the Renfield is more dangerous, naturally," said Leo.

"Yup," agreed Jimmy. "How did you know?"

"Our luck has been consistent that way. Do you have a plan?"

"I'm trying *not* to have a plan," said Jimmy. "What I want to do is figure out what these Dominion forces are planning. Once we know their intentions, all we have to do is mess them up. Things are already going bad for them."

"They could still try to force a river crossing here," Leo pointed out. "I am surprised they haven't."

Jimmy shook his head. "The Dominion's not going to throw away any more armies, more's the pity. If the river border forts aren't knocked out, then they aren't; the enemy doesn't lose any of their own resources and at least their stay-behind troops roiled the Alliance lines. The Alliance won't get the invasion they're waiting for unless the enemy thinks there's still something in it for them."

"This is starting to sound like a plan, milord."

"Oh?" Jimmy considered it. "Okay, but getting the Dominion to think we're really in disarray over on this side of the river just won't work. They have to know the ambush didn't come off properly." He paused. "Or do they?" Jimmy went on, his voice speculative.

"Maybe not, milord," Leo replied. "After all, the ones over here must be the stay-behind troops. In their regular forces, the ratio of slave-soldier to mage is usually one to one hundred. So why haven't they retreated back across the river?"

"Ask me an easy one, Leo." Jimmy looked through the binoculars again - but past the fort, to the water beyond it. It was strange, seeing a river this big that was also this empty. The woods were so thick they looked like you'd need to clear them with a forest fire, and there was obviously no traffic on the water. Legend said that the Mississippi was once a center of civilization; history said that the Universal Dominion had spent centuries grinding that civilization's bones into powder. *I hate these people*, Jimmy thought. *I well and truly do.*

Aloud, he went on, "They were supposed to bring off a *successful* ambush. Since they didn't do that, the next best thing would be for them to die gloriously for the Universal Dominion. And if they didn't want to do *that*, the Dominion would go ahead and use them as target practice. And since the Alliance has finally figured out how to block Dominion divination spells, the enemy can't see what's really happening on their own. These guys would have to get a signal out, only they can't. At least not until they can work out how to spin it as 'we won'."

"And thus we see the benefit of scouts," murmured Leo. "Ones who *aren't* also ravening nightmares out of legend, as ready to flense as they are to observe and report back."

"Well, it worked for them for centuries," Jimmy said as he stashed his binoculars. "I guess even Dominion mages get lazy. So: we know what they're planning. They're planning on waiting for a miracle. So how do we screw up their plans?"

"By giving them a miracle, milord," said Leo promptly. "We disguise ourselves as an ambush party, just in from one of the other sites. We tell them success has been achieved, they open the gates, we fall upon the mages, and then we go up to their tower and send word to the Dominion that the attack can go in. *Then* we run away and let the Alliance military handle the problem."

Jimmy stared at Leo in mingled respect and horror. "Is this how Virginians usually plan things out?" he finally said.

Leo looked pained. "Well, no. I regret to say I decided to simplify my idea quite a bit. You see, normally we would have to assume that one of the slave-soldiers would be the long-lost relative of one of our crew, meaning we would need to rescue him or her while we took the fort. But we just do not have the time to check! This situation is unstable, and must be exploited, no matter the personal cost." Leo sighed. "War is, indeed, Hell."

#

First things first: reporting back, on the principle of *Let the next guy know what killed you* and *Always get paid for the job*. One thing that the major *had* given them was a message raccoon. It couldn't fly, but it was smart enough to get back to the garrison and not get eaten in the process. A communications spell would have been faster, but Jimmy was absolutely sure the mages were looking for those.

Second? Well, they ended up sort of using Leo's plan, but Jimmy simplified it further. After all, as he pointed out to Leo, they didn't need the mages to actually *open* the main gate; they needed them looking at the gate for just long enough to let a few folks from the RSA crew climb up over the back wall and cause some mayhem. Suitably led, naturally.

Am I getting too old for this shit? Jimmy thought to himself as he and his people climbed the back wall, keeping to the lengthening shadows of afternoon whenever possible. *God, I hope not.* But it was a good question. Maybe not today, maybe not tomorrow, probably not even next year — but even elves got on in years, and Jimmy wasn't exactly in the safest business. There'd be a day when he'd have to tell somebody else to pull crazy-ass stunts like this.

But today it has to be me, Jimmy thought as he reached the parapet and felt the unmistakable sensation of a spell being permanently maintained. Like he'd thought, the Dominion mages had warded the top of the walls. Also like he'd thought, they had then promptly stopped worrying about the walls; they hadn't even put a slave-soldier up there to guard it.

And like Jimmy had hoped but not dared rely on, the ward spell had been hastily made and applied. Better yet, the idiots hadn't shielded the ward itself from arcane analysis. Jimmy grinned as he quickly muttered an information spell simple enough for him to use, but complex enough to be worth casting. Regular Dominion troops wouldn't have made that mistake, but these were stay-behinds. They were probably fanatical, but not real bright — or at least supremely arrogant, which was the same thing.

Getting past the ward wouldn't be hard, now that Jimmy could see the pattern. Getting his *people* past it the same way would be harder, and they were rushed for time, so he settled for short-circuiting the ward in a way which would keep it from sounding the alarm for about five minutes. Which would be enough time for his group to get over the side, he thought. He hoped. Either way, it was happening so it was time to start moving.

There were stairs for the parapet at regular intervals, and Jimmy's team ignored them as naturally as they breathed. Ropes were almost as fast, free from traps, and it was just a good habit to get into. Likewise, the team didn't stay on the ground, either. Rooftops were always preferable, and nobody ever looked up.

The inside of the bastion looked like any other Alliance military fort: a central keep, several small buildings used as barracks, storage, and stables, and a clear space for drills and mustering. It smelled considerably worse than usual, though: spoiling blood mixed with the acidic stench you learned real quick to associate with Dominion monsters. Which reminded Jimmy: he sent three of his men to carefully plant a half-dozen small satchels on the roof of the building reeking the most of Dire Hornets. That was clearly where the Dominion forces were trying to force-grow new ones.

Afterward, it was all about getting themselves in position before the ward on the bastion's walls finally shorted itself out and went boom. Jimmy made it with a good minute to spare. Hell, from the way Leo was expounding over at the open gate, the strike team could have taken their time and used up another half-hour, easy. The Virginian was really selling 'half-crazed but manic mage,' even from this far away; it was going to be the rest of his group that would give the whole thing away. Some people just can't act.

But they managed it for long enough. Jimmy didn't wait until one of the mages started to scratch his head before pushing the go-button on his doohickey. If you wait until they start to figure things out, you've waited too long.

#

How do you kill a mage with a gun? Well, as the saying goes: very, very carefully.

Three of the RSA had mage-poppers: single-use firearms with reinforced barrels that would *not* turn into shrapnel when the bullet inside of it suddenly exploded. They were accurate enough, but too expensive for even a successful Adventurers' group like RSA to afford as anything except an emergency weapon. And since Jimmy figured this was an emergency, he made sure the three best shots had come along on this ambush.

They didn't kill all three mages in the first and only volley. They did kill two, and put the third on the ground, writhing from a gut wound. Jimmy felt some small, detached sympathy, but not enough to put a crossbow bolt through the mage's head. There were still more mages to fight, and the easy part of the ambush had just happened.

Well, almost. Dominion mages in the field had long since unlearned the reflexive habit of tossing off area effect gunpowder-explosion spells, but this lot were stay-behinds. They had probably never encountered the War until it had finally rolled over them, so they instinctively cast their anti-gun spells. All *that* did was thoroughly explode the satchels of gunpowder and steel balls planted on the building presumably holding the half-grown Dire Hornet hive. The screams from inside were distressingly aware, but Jimmy also pushed that thought down deep in his head as he head-shotted one of the three suddenly-enraged Dire Hornets with his crossbow as it charged from the wreckage.

Because *now* the easy part of the ambush was over. The ward had chosen that exact moment to finally go off, which meant that the surviving mages instinctively looked up. Worse: so did the monsters.

Two of Jimmy's squad managed to take out the same Dire Hornet, which was just the way things went sometimes but still left one of the damned things streaking towards them. It barreled through one of Jimmy's crew in a flash of yellow and crimson spray, barely slowing down; as the Adventurer went sprawling off the roof, Jimmy had already jumped forward, pulling out his sword as he leapt... and jammed it into a convenient chimney.

An unenchanted weapon would have broken, or at least let Jimmy lose his grip on the hilt. But this item was good Virginian steel, triple-forged to take enchantments; so instead he used the check on his momentum to lift himself up and *kick* the remaining Dire Hornet in the face, well away from the buzzsaw stinger that would have done for him the way it did for his crew-member. The monster's momentum was thrown off, too... right into the roof. It was still feebly trying to lift up when Jimmy's boot came down to crush its head in.

That took care of *his* immediate problems, at least. Jimmy stuck his head over the lip of the roof, to see how Leo was doing. Not badly, all things considered. The Virginian had picked his own target carefully; when things went down, Leo had daggered the mage controlling the Renfield, right in the eye. Seen one way, this was insane, since the Renfield immediately went nuts; seen another... it was *useful* insanity, because the two remaining mages had sensibly ran back inside rather than face their own monster.

The fight was already going badly for the Renfield. Leo was bleeding in several places, and one of the crew with him was being dragged to safety by two others. But the other two were getting good crossbow shots in from their cover, and Leo was... well. Jimmy had once seen him dice a hardboiled egg with his twin swords. He wasn't so much attacking the Renfield as *whittling* it. By the time Jimmy had his crossbow reloaded, Leo had spun, made two precise cuts, and let the Renfield's own momentum finish slicing it in two. And then Leo made a frankly impressive backflip, in order to avoid the fireball thrown at him.

So: two mages and twenty-three enslaved soldiers against eight Adventurers. It was *almost* a fair fight, even then. And if there's anything Adventurers hate, it's a fair fight. So Jimmy needed to uneven the odds still further.

Fortunately, one of the two mages was an easily panicked idiot; he wasted time throwing fireballs at Leo and the RSA crew through the partly-opened gate, instead of concentrating on the ones inside who could conceivably hit back. The other one was marginally more sensible, working to take control of the slave-soldiers suddenly bereft of mage 'leadership' before they went as berserk as the Renfield. Jimmy wondered briefly why the enemy hadn't just picked one mage to be the controller, but he wasn't being paid to analyze Dominion battle practices. The important thing was to kill the bastards.

Deciding which bastard to kill first was tricky, but Adventurers are trained to make decisions quick, and hopefully not entirely stupidly. The panicking mage wasn't specifically dangerous right now, while the one gathering up soldiers would be, very soon. She'd have to be put down, and fast.

His crew was keeping enough of an eye on Jimmy to see his signal for 'distraction,' and they certainly managed to make one via shooting at the panicky mage. Which meant they also attracted his attention, but he hadn't settled down enough yet to actually *aim.* They'd be fine enough for government work; Jimmy had his own job.

It helped if you thought of mind-controlled soldiers as something like less smelly, but better-armed skeletons. Adventurers knew how to fight people, sure. They could even learn how to do it without getting broken inside. But it's just easier to get in the right mindset when fighting monsters, because then you don't have to feel bad when you kill them. Besides, in this case Jimmy didn't even *want* to kill them; he was after the mage.

Looked at one way, it was him and three other guys against twenty-four. Looked at another, it was four against one, with the one having twenty-four bodies to sort out on the fly. And in yet a third way, it was him against the mage, only the mage was distracted by the way Jimmy's three companions kept switching attacks and pushing her slave-soldiers around. It wouldn't work for long, but Jimmy didn't care about 'for long.' He cared about getting within sword range of the mage controlling the fighters.

And he did. There's a theatrical quality to a lot of Adventurer-style fighting. It's for practical reasons. The best combats are the ones you don't have to have, because people are so intimidated by you ahead of time that they're ready to be reasonable — and one of the rules of Adventuring is, *Be reasonable*. If you can make a deal, make the deal, and don't get caught up over who killed who.

But, yeah, that didn't come into play when it was a Dominion mage. Them you just killed, preferably from behind; and you didn't worry too much about making it clean. Quick would do well enough — and that was only to make sure there'd be no death curses uttered.

Afterward, he whirled the mage's blood off of his blade and shook his head at the waste. The slave-soldiers had been set to frenzy after being too long without a controller, as usual; they were mostly going wild on each other. Not completely — one more of his crew was down, and it took a few moments of brutal sword-work to keep the now-feral soldiers from ripping out the throat of a second — but it was more butchery than fighting. Jimmy always hated these scenes, hated feeling like he was a murderer. But what could he do? The Dominion refused to give up cruelty, even in its death throes.

But the enemy was beaten, at the cost of 'only' two of his troops dead, and another too wounded for full duty. That was a really good score for a military operation against Dominion mages, as far as Jimmy was aware, but Adventurers operated under less forgiving rules. Leo at least looked all right, with only two of his team heavily wounded, and no deaths.

"Did any of the mages survive, milord?" Leo asked.

Jimmy shook his head. "No. The dumbass throwing the fireballs tried to escape, but he dropped the last one on his foot.

These weren't their best people."

"Damnation," said Leo. "This plan would work better if we had someone to give us the code words."

"Probably," agreed Jimmy as the now-smaller RSA crew fanned through the keep, looking for whatever the Dominion used as a communications room. "But we don't need to be on for long. Get on, babble something about how they have to go ahead with the plan *now*, then cut the connection. They're gonna *want* to hear how everything worked, right?"

Leo's voice was as cynical as a Virginian's ever got. "That would be the *hope*, milord. It will be up to us to make that hope live."

#

The diehards had set up communications in the highest room in the bastion, probably out of habit; their rig consisted of... a crystal ball. Which was almost a little *too* stereotypical. "They don't even have any filing cabinets," Jimmy muttered.

"Or typewriters," agreed Leo. He smiled at Jimmy's reaction. "What, milord? Did you think Virginians write out all our documents with quill pens?"

"...Yes?"

"Well, that would be very tedious. And silly." The Virginian looked over the crystal ball. "There are no obvious warding spells etched on the ball. I think you'll be able to use it properly."

"I'm not seeing any, either," said Jimmy. "Although I don't have your familiarity with magic."

"And I do not have your access to magical power. There is enough of a trickle coming through that I can feel it. You do know how to activate it, milord?"

"Enough for what we need to do." Jimmy mentally reviewed the simple — very simple — message he would project into the ball, slapped both hands on the base, and... nothing happened. He tried again. "It's not working," he said.

"Curses," Leo said mildly.

"No, I'm not feeling any kind of attack," Jimmy said.

"That's not what I meant... ah, never mind." Leo frowned. "Does it feel like it cannot work, or is it that you cannot *make* it work?"

Jimmy concentrated. "The second one," he said after a moment. "I can feel the communications link, but it won't let me reach through."

"It is a security measure, then," said Leo. "You do not meet its criteria, so it will not let you connect."

"Crap," said Jimmy. "Crap, crap, crap. You think it's because I'm not a Dominion mage?"

"Possibly? Is it waiting for some kind of password?"

Jimmy closed his eyes and touched the ball again. "No," he said after a moment. "More like there's something about *me* preventing the transmission."

"Perhaps it is... ah. How obnoxious," said Leo. "It can tell you are not a human."

That stopped Jimmy cold. "Since when the hell do they care about *that*?" he said, indignantly. "Being elves never stopped them from trying to enslave us!"

Leo shrugged. "Perhaps the Dominion has finally conceded they are not going to reign over the Earth entire, and thus are not even pretending that there is a place for non-human mages under their rule. Or perhaps they are losing so badly that they cannot afford to feed their delusions of omnipotence."

Right then, *something* warned Jimmy about the ball; he was never sure whether it was magical senses or Adventurer's instincts, but he jerked his hands away just before the ball started to glow with a green, crackling light. The two jumped back as the ball dropped onto the table. Which promptly started to smoke, a little.

"More security measures," Jimmy snarled. "Time to run."

"Thirty Seconds, milord," said Leo. That was an Adventurer's thing, enough to stop Jimmy in his tracks. Leo said, quickly but clearly. "I know how to get around the blockage; I think I can send the message myself. Is sending it worth it to the War?"

You have to think fast during a Thirty Seconds. "Yes," said

Jimmy, "but it's high risk." Dominion counter-intrusion measures were often vicious; they had gambled the diehards hadn't
put them in place for this mission, and lost. The smart thing
now was to run away, a *lot*.

"Less risk for the crew if I do this," said Leo. "Trust me, milord."

"Do it, then," said Jimmy. "Do I stay?"

"Oh, HELL no!" shouted Leo as he turned to the crystal ball.
"Get outside as quickly as you can!"

#

Jimmy did not get outside the walls, although he could have
— and he certainly used his doohickey to give his crew the
Boom Coming Down warning. There was a reasonably sturdy-
looking chimney to hide behind, and you never knew when
somebody doing a damfool thing might need backup. Besides, if
the Dominion could blow up entire forts with something that
small, this War would have been going on for even longer than it
had.

The blast, when it came, wasn't even too bad. Somewhere
between a concussion trap and a fireball cast in room smaller
than its radius, in Jimmy's professional opinion. It knocked him
down, sure, and when he got up again he was pretty sure this
floor was now no longer safe for human occupancy, but it meant
Leo needed medical help, *now*.

Only, he didn't. Leo needed a healer, and there wasn't one
within running distance. The ball had detonated, and ripped up
his gut in the process, but the real damage was from him being
smashed against the far wall. Even one glance was enough to tell
Jimmy the only thing he could do was to make Leo comfortable.

Leo looked up as Jimmy ran in. "The message went through,
milord," he said wanly, and far too wetly.

"Fuck the message," Jimmy said as he tossed off a couple of
pain-killing spells. They wouldn't do anything to actually heal,
but that wasn't the point. "You said the risk would be less," he
went on. "That's supposed to mean less risk to *you*."

"Naturally you would think so, milord. You are party

leader." Leo sounded stronger, but it was an illusion. He was still going to die, and soon. "But it worked. It worked better because of the explosion, I think. It gave the whole affair a matter of greater urgency. 'Launch the attack *now*, before it is too late!' Quite believable, I thought."

Jimmy knelt over Leo, in the quickly dashed hope that maybe there was something which could be done. "Anything you need?" he said, gruffly. "Water? Something stronger?"

"A whiskey would be nice," admitted Leo. After he drank from Jimmy's flask, he even smiled. "There. Now I am ready to 'walk it off'."

Jimmy was trying not to berate a dying man, but he had to say something. "Dammit, Leo, we would have both been fine if we had just run!"

"Indeed, milord. But if the attack happens, it will shorten the War by months. What would you have done, in my place?"

"The same thing," Jimmy admitted. "But I would have worn belly armor, too."

"Spoken as a true Adventurer, milord," said Leo, with admiration. "Always look for the loophole, hey? But I knew sending the message would kill me, somehow. That is how it works. There are no loopholes for this level of interference." Jimmy frowned in confusion, but before he could say anything, Leo said, "It was worth it, though. Damn the Universal Dominion, and all of its works."

And died.

After a time, Jimmy stood up. *What did he mean by 'interference,' there?* he thought, with sad puzzlement. *Is it a Virginian thing? Poor bastard.*

And then Jimmy went back to the job. The keep had to be sorted out, secured, and carefully cleaned out of the stuff that could be gleaned; and the bodies had to be taken care of. Because this was part of the Adventuring life. People died. You powered through.

And, Jimmy considered as he looked back at Leo's smiling corpse, *at least Leo just might have taken a lot of Dominion mages out along with him.*

There were worse ways to go.

People's Glorious Union of
Haida Sovereign Councils
Free Canada

Pacific Trade
Confederation
(Deseret)

Cold-Lands

Dwarvenwood

Deseret

Universal Dominion

Universal Dominion (occupied)

République Impériale
de Canada

Second Republic

Greater Hershey

Virginia

Halfling
Protectorate

Kentucky Free State

New California

Estado Libre y
Soberano de Sonora

Imperium Orci

Elf-Lands

Newhome

Imperium Orci Client-states and minor alles

Grand Panama

NORTH AMERICA
3054 AD

Legend

- - - National Border

- - - Sub-national
Border

1000 Kilometers

600 Miles

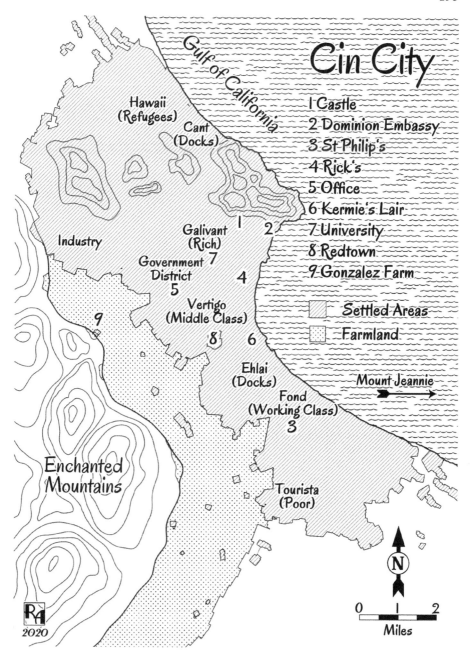

Cin City

1 Castle
2 Dominion Embassy
3 St Philip's
4 Rick's
5 Office
6 Kermie's Lair
7 University
8 Redtown
9 Gonzalez Farm

Settled Areas
Farmland

Gulf of California

Hawaii
(Refugees)

Cant
(Docks)

Industry

Galivant
(Rich)

Government
District

Vertigo
(Middle Class)

Ehlai
(Docks)

Fond
(Working Class)

Mount Jeannie

Tourista
(Poor)

Enchanted
Mountains

N

0   1   2
Miles

RH
2020

ACKNOWLEDGEMENTS

We'll start with my editor: Beth McCoy, who remains invariably helpful when it comes to reminding me that action-adventure stories need to have things like action and adventure in them. The beta readers / long-time supporters were a huge help: Anda Olson, Michael LaReaux, Michael M, Mija Cat, Robert Nealis, and Sheryl Sahr. And my wife and family were great, as usual.

I would also like to thank the following people for their Kickstarter support: A David Merritt, Allen Hueffmeier, Amber McKee, Christopher Goetting, Christopher Guilfoyle, Craig Cicero, Dan, Dan Bennett, Dr Ace, Fred Barnhill, James King, jbsaff, Jeff Niles, Jeff Weimer, Jimmie Bise, Jr, Joey Blabaum, John P, Adams, Katie Kenney, Lady Alicia of Cambion, Laura Wilkinson, Mark Blair, Mark Erikson, Mark Garbowski, MaryAnn Fedor, Matt Armstrong, Matt Blackwell, Matt Trepal, Michael Cleveland, Michael Ganschow-Green, Michael Meneguzzo, Miriam Blume, Moria Trent, Nicholas Sylvain, Nick Robbins, Oyster, Phil Smith, Robert Nealis, Sonya Gross, Symoller, Thomas Abella, Tim Deckert, Torrain, Travis Foster, Walter Milliken, and WuseMajor.

BOOKS BY THIS AUTHOR

Frozen Dreams

The best post-apocalyptic high urban fantasy pulp detective novel you will read today!

Anagnorisis

Four tales of transformation. 32,000 words, horror/spooky, with illustrations.

Revisionary

Four tales of the Cthulhu Mythos. 32,000 words, with illustrations.

Made in the USA
Middletown, DE
04 February 2022

59382921R00166